Positive

The Tannellith Trilogy: Book 1

R. G. Brown

-To all those who ever felt hopeless-

CONTENTS

charC

"For in this hope we were saved. Now hope that is seen is not hope. For who hopes for what he sees? But if we hope for what we do not see, we wait for it with patience."

Romans 8:24-25

1
ELEANORA: CAPTURE

A vivid array of pictures sprawls the wall in front of me, a mere specter of a past life, resurrecting distant memories of times before the Maraloxis Virus broke out. Each image captures the bliss of an instant, a fragile moment, only to soon dissolve from the powerful chemical of reality. It was just a year ago when my brother and I would race out to the yard of our colonial-style house after school, carefree as we spent hours imagining beyond the limits of this world until our mother would call us inside just as the sun drifted behind the trees, causing rays of sunlight to paint images on the grass. Happy memories, yet they still incite heartache. Outside, daybreak bleeds into the sky and paints pinks and reds on the horizon in a brilliant display of morning.

A soft pattering on the hallway's hardwoods alerts me to the presence of a rat cowering outside the door frame of my bedroom. It analyzes the surroundings, and I watch until I remember it's a potentially rabid creature traipsing through my house and slam the door shut. I'm not thinking clearly, but I've been deprived of much human contact for such a long time, the occasional reminder that I'm not the only living being is comforting. I hear the rodent scurry away behind the door, the soft sound of its footfalls echoing throughout the empty, bereft home. At first, the invasion of creatures and insects bothered me, but I've gotten somewhat used to the disturbing prospect that mice occasionally steal portions of my meals and ants frequent the kitchen. Animals are flourishing in the remnants of the Virus, and they aren't the cute kind. Rats, mice, and carrion birds haunt the province of Senneforte. Rodents easily slink into my countryside house, especially with the broken window in the living room, which I was going to tape up, but I'm afraid it could give away my secrecy.

My gaze falters on a single photo, the most recent one on my wall. I rise from my bed, tracing the seasonal frame with my hand. *The ink seems dull, or maybe my memory just paints it much more lucidly.* My mother and father stand behind us, with my brother, Isaiah, and me in front. The leaves on the trees had changed to perfect, picturesque reds and yellows and had begun to fall. Isaiah and I chased each other around the beautiful park on the bank of Lake Superior while our parents just let us be kids. At twelve and thirteen, our minds were free in the make-believe, childish world that would soon be forever distorted by the changing reality.

Although it was only a year ago, it seems like a whole different lifetime. Pictures and bittersweet memories are all I have left of my family, for now, at least.

Bang.

Submerged in my mind, the pounding on the front door doesn't register soon enough. The sound echoes through the house like a blaring alarm, instigating an immediate adrenaline rush. Even though I've prepared for this for months and been through the experience once already, my mind goes horribly blank. Hurriedly, I rip the pictures down, shove them in my backpack then crawl under my bed and tuck myself as close to the wall as possible. I hug the backpack to my chest, the hardwood floor cool against my skin, trying to detect what's happening outside my room.

The crash of breaking glass resounds, interrupted by a thud and creaking; one of them opens the door. Thundering footsteps follow as two or maybe three people storm into the house, searching for anyone who remains, or pillaging the homes of those who have been found. They're looking for me.

It's the Mordolus, an army-like group of volunteers devoted to our Queen, Morzanna. The Mordolus formed after the Virus erupted in an attempt to order the madness that ensued. I want something to occupy my mind and give me some purpose during this time as well, but my morals would never allow me to align with the Queen.

I shouldn't have wasted time taking down my pictures—I could have gotten to a more sufficient hiding spot. Then again, their presence might very well have given away mine.

I hold my breath as one of them treads into my room, reading the vibrations of the floor until they stop inches away. Time ceases to advance as I stare at the rim of black boots, scrutinizing the red insignia of a cursive *M* that I've come to despise. A snowstorm of icy fear brews in my heart, leaving me frozen and rigid. It seems like years go by before he stoops down. I squeeze my eyes shut, and the next few seconds are a blur. I'm ripped from the safety under my bed and abruptly lifted to my feet by a strong gloved grip.

"Found someone else!" he calls to the other members, who rush into my bedroom. They're all clothed in mainly black uniforms, stitched with deep red designs and fringed with silver accents. Behind their elaborate leather face masks, all I can see are their eyes—every one of them wears a blank, cold stare. I clench my fists to hopefully prevent them from shaking.

"Why are you hiding?" my captor asks fiercely, holding onto my arm in a firm grasp. I take a deep breath, trying to calm myself. After failing to yank myself away, I settle with an intense glare.

"I don't know," I reply, fighting to keep my voice level. "I'd rather *not* be abducted."

"We're trying to help you," I'm informed, though his tone warns me otherwise.

"News to me," I say acidicly, shrugging despite the tension in my shoulders.

"You take her back, I'll check the other houses," he says to the other member, trading me off.

I'm shoved out of my room, into the living area, and dragged toward the front door. I dig my heels into the ground like a stubborn steed and grasp my backpack tightly. A van is parked along the road outside, bearing the Queen's symbol, the same one that's embroidered onto the Mordolus uniforms. After forcing me into the backseat, the kidnapper I was left with gets in the front and locks the doors. The cold leather makes me uncomfortable, and bars between the driver and me give the illusion that I'm headed to jail for a crime. The driver tosses me a simple fabric face mask and orders me to put it on. I obey, but I'm hyperventilating so much that I instantly feel like I'm suffocating and rip it off the second he's not paying attention. A frenzy of wild emotion swarms inside me, and I slowly twirl a strand of my blond hair, holding onto my backpack and sinking into the back seat.

The same thing happened to my brother. I wasn't in the house at the time but saw it happen, nonetheless. During the past few months, Isaiah and I would always hide when we heard the Mordolus approaching. Anticipating that soon we may be in danger of abduction, our parents took extreme measures to try and secure our fading safety. We were forbidden from leaving the house to protect ourselves from contracting the Virus and to keep us safe from the Mordolus. Few days elapsed that my brother and I didn't spend hidden in the attic or a closet as our rural neighborhood was left virtually vacant. Our mother is a pharmacist and continued working even after the lockdown, and our father helped her despite the regulations. People still needed medications, especially to try to treat the new disease, but the day came that our parents didn't return home. It was only weeks later that Isaiah was seized as well. There's no doubt where this Mordolus member is taking me.

When the outbreak first began, we were told to take minor precautions, since most cases proved harmless. But soon it came out that the Virus was extremely fatal and highly contagious, with little justification for their error other than the disease's longer prognosis and subtler symptoms. This lethal and elusive illness is called the Maraloxis Virus, and almost everyone in our province of Senneforte has been infected within a short time. No one knows the origin of the Virus, and the government authorities don't appear to be looking into it. Queen Morzanna told us there is no discovered remedy, and she's searched extensively for one, but nothing was found. This news brought country-wide pandemonium. Morzanna, to help the crisis, made a few controversial decisions, one of them being the formation of the out-of-control Mordolus in lieu of our military.

A few years ago, the Queen was put in power over our country, Willowmire, after the death of her father. In that short time, the government has undergone drastic changes. Morzanna has almost half the vote in everything, and the rest is divided among the delegates from Willowmire's five provinces. Unless all the delegates agree, nothing can transpire federally without Morzanna's consent. The Queen hasn't done anything blatantly wrong, but that could reflect a separate issue since we haven't heard much from her concerning the Virus in a long time. Although, I'm unsure if without a cure anything can be done. Not much was or is known about the new Queen, especially since the Virus has captured everyone's attention indefinitely.

I gaze out the window at the hundreds of newly dug graves—graveyards that were once parks and fields—casualties of the Virus. Senneforte has been practically destroyed, and it's sobering to recall what it used to look like merely months ago.

Along the rural road, pine boughs sway gingerly in the weak August wind; white pines were once the state tree of Michigan, that is, when it was a state. Nearly forty years ago, there was unrest due to the individual states not agreeing with the federal law on civil issues and religious rights, and it resulted in a total division of the United States. After ten years of political turmoil and fights, the country was finally divided over the issue. It was a civil war, although it consisted primarily of constant, intense political debates. Most of the states split into individual countries, and some, like Alaska, joined existing ones. Wisconsin and Virginia are complete anarchies, and most people have fled those broken places. Ever since the Separative War, all the states became independent and were put under new governments and names. Michigan was split into two separate countries: Willowmire and Erigate. Willowmire used to be known as the upper peninsula and still is in casual settings. Erigate was once the lower peninsula of Michigan. Our province of Senneforte, the second largest of the five provinces, aside from Ellismark, is roughly from old Alger to Iron.

Despite my prayers that we will never arrive, we turn down the dreaded road, only three miles from my home. They're taking me to be tested for the Maraloxis Virus. My family have all contracted the illness—well, I assume that's the case since they never returned, leaving me on my own in this tragic new life.

My childhood friend, Graydon, and I have been trying to develop a cure, however impossible that may be. Once our parents were gone, it was evident there were few civilians left healthy, so Isaiah and I made the decision to leave the safety of our house and help

Graydon, whose parents were captured as well, and attempt to find an antidote. I have to believe one exists and hope that I'm negative because Graydon and I need to keep working. We haven't gotten very far, but over the past few weeks, we've at least made progress. I hope it's not too late for us.

Anyone who tests positive will be kept in the Infirmary, where all patients stay for a few weeks or a few months until they eventually die, to stop the spread and to supposedly treat them as best they can. It's only been four months since the first cases in Senneforte, and Graydon is the only person I know who hasn't been captured and taken to be evaluated. In the beginning, people willingly went to be tested, but after we realized we'd be locked away, everyone hid and the Mordolus began forcefully extracting people.

But perhaps a cure does exist.

I'm broken from my thoughts as we pull into the dreary parking lot outside the Infirmary where testing takes place. Peering through the window, I scowl at the infamous building. There's a large gate as we drive in and the entirety is fenced.

The driver gets out and opens the door. I contemplate running, but I quickly smother the thought; it would be nearly impossible with all the people around. For me, attempting escape will be inevitable, but I'm not stupid enough to try anything yet.

The Infirmary is a huge, two-story building. It seems to go on for miles and reminds me of an abandoned warehouse from the outside, causing my heart to drop knowing it is filled with the dying. I stare at the line of people waiting outside and pull my shirt over my face, regretting leaving my mask behind. Afflicted with chills, overt paleness, and lethargic behavior, these people are clearly sick. Some of them even rub their hands together; a way to temporarily abate the paresthesic pains caused by the Virus in its latter stages. Even if I'm fortunate enough to be negative, I'll certainly contract it from being around these people. The driver walks me to the end of the line of about twenty people. My suspicions grow. *So, the Mordolus constantly come in contact with the infected, and none of them have contracted the illness? I don't believe it. Even though they wear protective outfits and gloves, they still run a huge risk of infection. Many of them must be sick, and what does the Queen do with them? Why would they all sacrifice their health and possibly lives for whatever the Queen offers them? Or maybe they actually think the Infirmary is humane. It might be if it wasn't so strict and tyrannical.*

My family may have already been lost to the Virus. *With the deaths rising each day, and zero contact with them, how do I know how they're doing?* The life expectancy of this disease is up to four months, and they've been gone for two, so I still hope.

The line shrinks as person after person is dragged inside the Infirmary doors. The testing takes a while, twenty minutes per person, and I watch hopefully for the well to be released, but it seems the Virus is even more prevalent than I had thought.

Digging through my backpack, I take out my phone and check again to see if, by any chance, someone other than Graydon found a way to contact me. Perhaps a friend or family member who could come to Senneforte's aid?

I'm shocked and slightly overwhelmed to see there's a text.

It's from Isaiah.

2
GRAYDON: THE MARALOXIS VIRUS

I grab my backpack off the kitchen counter and sling it onto my shoulders. I open the back door. From the step, I take in a deep breath of cool summer-morning air. I lock the door and shove the key in my pocket, hopping down from the stoop. The gravelly ground revolts against my attempt to be quiet. Pausing, I check the surroundings of the ghosted neighborhood. Overgrown grass and shrubs surround the yard and block most of my view. A docile breeze rolls through a row of tall pine trees on my right. I head down the street toward the laboratory.

The trip is short from my new house. After my parents were captured, our home was destroyed. Burned. Another of the Mordolus's endeavors to eradicate the Virus. So, I chose somewhere closer to the lab.

I take a shortcut through the forest. It's best to stay off the roads. Pine needles and dry oak leaves crackle beneath my feet. Brambles claw at my clothing and leave my skin looking like I was in a fight with a feral cat and lost. I pay close attention to where I step so I don't end up walking through stinging nettles again. That's not something I want a rerun of. I spend way too long concentrating on the ground and walk into an occupied spider web. *Nice.*

Eleanora and I have been trying to complete a cure using the information given by my dad. He's a biotechnician and worked at a laboratory with a few other scientists to find a remedy for the Maraloxis Virus. They were only a few steps from finishing what could have potentially been an antidote when one of the scientists tested positive.

They worked closely with and received projects and funds from our government. Despite trying to keep the outbreak a secret, the Queen found out. Due to their 'safety', and even after a lot of persuasion, Queen Morzanna refused to let them continue. I had to help my dad break into his own lab and extract the medicine. It made everything real. Shortages in preventatives and disease protection caused issues. People were out of work, schools closed, and eventually everything—literally everything—shut down. Hospitals closed and patients had to be transferred somewhere else by family fast or they'd be kicked out, people who needed medicine couldn't get it, and food was in critical shortage. Senneforte was getting sick and there was nothing to do but run to Morzanna for help. She disbanded our small military and replaced it with the Mordolus. Because of Willowmire's loose ties with the other surrounding countries, help didn't show up soon enough. Or ever. We're on the brink of war with Erigate, the lower peninsula, over mainly government, property rights, and old wounds from the division. We used to be one state, and now we can't cross each other's borders. Some people tried to leave Willowmire for Erigate, but I don't think they welcomed our possibly infected refugees. That left only Infrethia, the dangerous, abandoned anarchy of Wisconsin. It's rumored all the convicts that were released in the wake of the Separative War lurk in Infrethia to escape their punishment.

After the attacks on September 11, 2001, fear, division, conflict, and panic were violently stirred up. The government fell apart. States fought against each other, blamed each other, and preexisting disagreements arose. Eventually, the safest decision was to separate. The United States were no longer united; they were enemies. No one would have guessed that the actions of a few people could ruin one of the markedly strongest countries in history. To this day some of the states and cities still have hate, like Willowmire and Erigate. That's what fear does. That's what hopelessness does. It destroys. It divides. It corrupts. And that's what happened in the Separative War. Forty years have passed, and our world's still broken. Morzanna instilled a few debatable peace-related laws including regulated borders, the full ban and confiscation of firearms, and plans to deal with Infrethia. Then she unleashed the Mordolus.

After the laboratory locked down, I helped my dad. I learned a lot in those few days leading up to my dad's forced test. Mom was taken around the same time. My best friend Isaiah wasn't there to help me for long. After Isaiah's capture, his sister Eleanora and I were left to complete the antidote. She's fourteen, and I'm fifteen. With just a confusing combination of chemicals and some notes, we haven't gotten very far. I don't think we'll finish it. We don't even know if it would work. No one would have blamed us if we never even attempted to keep searching. Few have hope for a solution.

I trudge up to the makeshift lab, less than a mile away in the same suburban neighborhood. A big red 'X' marks the doorframe of each house that's been emptied. Usually, either windows are shattered, or the door is broken in. I climb up the front steps. The storm door here was smashed but the wooden one's intact. When I try the handle, it's still locked. I apprehensively take out my key and open it. As I step inside, I don't like the silence.

Eleanora should be here by now. I tiptoe through the wrecked living room and open the garage door. The tables are still set up with all our supplies. Nothing *looks* wrong.

"Ele?" I call out suspiciously. Instantly, I have the strange intuition that something's up. Something bad.

After I get no response, I check all the other rooms. Empty. I run a westward block to Ele's house. Sticking near the trees to keep hidden, I follow the familiar road. I'm not as cautious as I should be.

Hilly fields and forests reach out until they touch the mountains in the distance. I run down the road, Gilded Way, and approach the familiar colonial home. I trip over the out-of-control rose briars, stumble up the back steps, and wrench open the sliding-glass door.

I can see straight through the house. The front door is wide open.

"Ele?" I say. "Eleanora?"

The house gives off a sinister feeling. The wind whimpers through the busted window, crying the story of whatever occurred here to cause the emptiness. I try to convince myself that the muddy footprints that dance around the hardwood floors don't necessarily mean what I think they mean. I don't really believe my rationalization.

I text Ele. Thankfully, I still can; communication with anyone outside the province is blocked. Every time I've tried to contact a relative or friend outside Senneforte, it says undelivered. There's a cell tower somewhere that works since the Mordolus need a way to communicate as well, and we're lucky for that.

Anger ignites inside me. I hate the Mordolus. But…maybe we should have been more careful. Maybe I could have found Ele somewhere safer to stay. Maybe I've been too careless. *Maybe this is my fault.*

I close the front door and sit inside on the bottom stair, ready to give up. But I have to keep trying. For my parents. For Isaiah. For everyone. I wish there was something to hope in other than myself.

I ban myself from using the word "maybe". It's a dumb term anyway. I decide to head back to the lab and try to get some work done. At least going to the lab will distract me.

The Mordolus is split into three main groups; the guards, the nurses and doctors, and the Hunters. The Hunters are especially savage and search the province for any untested civilians, then bring them to the Infirmary. Afterward, they raid houses and buildings.

They'll be back to clear the house eventually. But I can at least prevent that. I search Ele's room until I find her paint box, retrieving some red. I take a paintbrush and boldly mark the front door. Unless the Mordolus go on an arson spree, the house should be safe.

I step outside and survey the dead street. This is how it is now. Constant kenopsia and loneliness.

I pass an open field on my way back. Trees line the right side and dead grass mingles with the red clay. It gives me a good view of the towering wall in the distance, a constant reminder that one cannot escape the province. The fence is a recent addition. I don't know what it's for, but there's no getting beyond it, especially since it's guarded—maybe from both sides.

On the other side of the wall is Ellismark. That's where Solstice Keep, the Queen's fortress, is located. It used to belong to King Cyrus Nixon. He was a good king but died from a sudden heart attack a few years ago. Later at his funeral, his adopted daughter Morzanna claimed the rule.

Just as I arrive at the lab, I get a text from Ele. I was right. She has been captured. If she's positive, they'll keep her forever, just like my parents. The reality sinks in that now with Ele gone, I'm on my own.

I have to finish the cure. If not, both our families will die.

3
ELEANORA: POSITIVE

After glancing over my shoulder, I click on the message from my brother, excitement trickling down to my quivering hands. I haven't heard anything from my family in a long time, and it seems unreal. This message could entail such a great number of things that my emotions are already going haywire.

Hey Ele! How's it going? I stole my phone back today. We're okay, just hurry w the cure. Are you okay? Love u, gtg. Text back.

I type a quick response to make my brother aware of my situation. My family is okay for now, which gives me just enough hope that I begin thinking.

I have to escape now before they lock me up. I'll try anything because, really, what's the worst that could happen? The wire gate isn't going to work since it's currently locked and guarded by two probably armed Mordolus soldiers. The fence is most likely my only option, and I bite my lip, searching for apertures I could escape through.

The chain link barrier stands seven feet high, at least, steadily enclosing the entire parking lot and a portion of grassy field. On the other side is the graveyard, which is obviously pretty empty of any life right now. *The fence looks very secure, but maybe I can climb it.* Surveying the area, I note that none of the Mordolus seem to be watching me at the moment.

Then I run. The sharp, uncut grass stings my legs, leaving behind tiny lacerations as I hurtle toward the fence. Everyone watches me, and I force myself not to look back again so I can focus on sprinting. If I can get over the fence, I can head toward the woods and find my way home from there.

Reaching the barrier, I hurriedly place my foot on a rock and hop to grasp the top of the enclosure. Raw fence wire rips into my hands, but I try to ignore it and risk a glance behind me. The guards totally noticed and are heading toward me; they already know the ending to this story, but I'm still aiming to rewrite it. My shoes keep sliding off the chain fencing, and my thin arms can't pull me up fast enough. A wave of defeat subdues me as two hands clamp around my waist and haul me down. I scream, emotion boiling in my stomach, and the guard, who I recognize from the house earlier, yells at me for my attempt. He drags me back, and I, chagrined at my failure, violently kick.

Everyone stares and murmurs as I saunter back into line, arms crossed and glaring. My chest stirs with disappointment, regret, and the realization of my stupidity. My wrists throb from getting yanked from the fence so abruptly.

Eventually everyone forgets about the event, except me. I'm upset and a tiny bit embarrassed because I probably looked like a little kid throwing a tantrum. Tired of standing so long, I plop down on the ground, holding my backpack in my lap. I pull out my phone, and two text notifications light up the screen. One is from Isaiah, and the other is from Graydon, which I read first.

Where are you? I went to your house. You okay?

I ridicule myself for not texting Graydon earlier and quickly respond.

I'm okay. They stormed the house. I'm waiting to get tested. It may be a while, and if you don't hear from me, then keep working on the project and assume they've taken me in. I'm sorry.

Isaiah's message is less encouraging than his first but gives me more insight on what might be occurring.

If you get out, keep working on finding a cure. We're losing time. I know you and Graydon can figure it out just hurry. I'll try to find you.

Maybe Queen Morzanna is right and being honest about this disease. I hope we're not wasting time trying to complete the remedy. The last thing I want to do is squander my family's final days away from them on some lunatic mission. But if it could save their lives, it's worth the weighty risk.

Two small children chase each other around the parking lot, giggling carelessly, unaware of the danger that could soon destroy every grain of their happiness. Their mother holds another younger child, watching from her place in line right behind me, pain and sorrow etched deeply in her grave expression.

My cheeks are flushed as the sun's blistering rays beat down upon me. It feels like hardly any time has passed yet at the same time I've waited so long. Either way, I'm next in line. The gravity of the situation weighs heavy, and my rib cage feels full of rocks. A table cluttered with paperwork and trays containing hundreds of fresh syringes and other testing instruments is covered by a wooden overhanging beside the Infirmary entrance. I find myself standing in front of the table with the woman asking for my name. Lightheaded, I place a hand on the table to steady myself.

"Eleanora Brooks," I say, standing up straighter. The middle-aged woman does everything in a numb manner as if she isn't about to tell someone whether or not they'll live, and I grit my teeth. I give her my age and answer a few more questions about my exposure to the Virus. She writes some of it on her paper and eventually beckons me closer, reaching for one of the needles.

She seizes my wrist and jabs it into my forearm, sending a shock of pain spreading all the way down to my fingertips. The nurse draws my blood, taking far more than seems necessary. Relieved when it's over, I watch her immediately empty the syringe into a small jar. Another of the staff members brings something that looks akin to one of those devices they prick your finger with and places it on my bare shoulder. It's pretty painless, leaving a blue-hued pinprick on my aching arm; a way to tell whether someone's been tested or not. The color depends on which month you are tested. At first, they were red; then in June, green; then purple; and August is apparently a stark shade of royal blue. If we ever survive this, there are going to be thousands of people with small permanent marks inked on their shoulders.

The nurse mixes my blood with some bronzy solution, replaces the lid on the small, clear container, and shakes it up. She tells me it will take a few minutes for the results of my Maraloxis Virus test, the thing that will determine the course of my life—or end it. I tuck a lock of blond hair behind my ear as my eyes drift over the hundreds of completed tests lying in a discard box beyond the table—very few negative blood-red ones mingled among the positives that are a sickly green. I try to count them but eventually tear my gaze away, hating the overwhelming superiority of the green-tinted ones. I turn back to the woman, harrowing anxiety settling over my restless insides. Hysteria builds like a vicious tempest within me, and I freeze as my eyes fall on the viridescent liquid in her hand.

Positive.

4
ISAIAH: THE INFIRMARY

I walk down the white hallway. Turning the corner, I head toward the door. The narrow halls and glossy floors are like an ordinary hospital. Everything here in the Infirmary is white, bright, but gloomy at the same time. It's way crowded too. When I reach the door, the sign posted on it reads, "Do not enter". Signs like that only make me more likely *to* enter. It's not just insurrection. Well, not *all* the time. It's mostly curiosity and necessity. I take a deep breath and reach for the handle. Glancing around the hall, I push open the door. Light floods in, chasing away the darkness inside the room. The smell of alcohol and latex hits me immediately. Multiple filing cabinets line the walls. Lists of names and ID papers tower on a desk in the corner of the small, square office-like room. I turn on the light and quietly pull the door shut. A door to my left is labeled "Storage". In the back of the room is another. I leaf through some of the papers scattered on the desk in front of me. I open the top drawer. Pages are haphazardly thrown in and sprawled with black ink. I rummage through them until something catches my eye. A note, handwritten in red. I pull out the piece of paper and read the sloppy writing. *Pass- 4138.*

I instinctively slam the drawer shut. Voices echo outside the door. I rush to turn the light off. I stuff the paper in my pocket and crawl under the tall wooden desk.

The door in the back opens. I hold my breath. *Please don't let anyone find me,* I pray. A man dressed in white ambles in. I resist the urge to inch closer to the wall and don't move. Briefly, the man stops to sort through some papers and puts on a face mask and gloves. Then he walks out the other door to the hallway.

After a few uneasy minutes, I leave my hiding spot. I walk to the back door. It's solid and metal. Digging a small, rusted key from my pocket, I unlock the door.

Endless rows of cardboard boxes line the spacious, bland room. They're filled with people's confiscated belongings: phones, bags, books, pictures, and more. Thankfully, it's alphabetically organized. I immediately head to the B section. After a while of searching through the mess, I find my phone near the bottom of the eighth box. I grab a random phone charger from one of the other bins. I plug it into an outlet across the storeroom.

I wait nervously. Someone could come anytime now. Eventually the device turns on. Fifty-three unread messages. I scroll through them. They're almost all from Ele.

Isaiah?

Are you okay?

I miss you

How are mom and dad?

I love you.

I check the dates I got them. The most recent is August second. That was just two days ago. There are also a few texts from Graydon.

I've been here a good ten minutes and started to get antsy. I pocket the charger and take my phone, leaving the stolen key on the floor in the walkway so it looks like someone dropped it. I jog back through the first room and into the hallway. I wind my way through the corridors of the Infirmary. My room is on the second story, so I open the door to the stairwell and climb the wide, long staircase.

I shouldn't be able to sneak around this easily. I've done it enough though that I've gotten good. It's simple to get lost in the crowd. There are so many captives here. Section One houses five thousand. There are three of these. I've never even been to the others since they're blocked off and separate. If someone gets transferred to another section, you can bet you'll never see them again.

I arrive at my room. It's pretty empty but so small it's crowded. The furniture has almost all been taken from residential homes. Of the two beds in the room, mine is cheap, sturdy, and metal, while the other is a rickety old wooden-framed twin. There's a single chair in the corner, and one small window near the ceiling. You can see the field-turned-cemetery next to the Infirmary from there. We're lucky to have a window at all, but I try not to look out of it often.

"What's that?" Reece asks. He's my roommate. Reece is younger than me by more than a year, but honestly, it's not noticeable because he's nearly the same height as me. He's tall for his age, and I'm barely average for mine. Reece puts down his pen and jumps up from the lonely chair.

"I found it," I answer. He snatches my phone and inspects it.

"Yeah, you just found it," Reece says. His pale green eyes flash with suspicion as he hands back the phone. He goes back to writing on the wall nearest the door. Reece does that a lot. I'm not sure if it's to be rebellious, or because he likes to. Either way, he's covered almost a whole wall with a variety of short stories, poems, and other ramblings. It definitely annoys the Infirmary staff, but they don't do anything. They don't have time to. The writings really aren't hurting anything.

"Don't think I didn't notice you leave earlier looking especially up-to-something-you-shouldn't-be," Reece comments. For twelve, Reece is unusually observant. Sometimes annoyingly observant. "So, where'd you 'find' it?"

"Somewhere I shouldn't have been," I admit.

"You snuck into the Belongings Place?" Reece asks immediately. "And didn't tell me?"

I nod, rubbing my forehead. I'd never even had a headache until the Infirmary. I get them all the time now. That's my only major symptom so far.

Reece raises an eyebrow and goes back to writing. "I bet you didn't even check for cameras. Or sensors. Wait, what'd you do with the key? Where'd you get the key anyway?" he asks. "Did you steal it? When are you going to teach me pickpocketing?"

I taught myself how to steal things when I was younger. I practiced on my sister and classmates. I usually returned what I took, but I still got a lot of *thou shall not steal* lectures. Reece has been begging me to teach him.

"Probably never," I say. "It's not a good habit. Maybe I won't have to take things here soon anyway."

"Because we'll be dead?" Reece asks blankly. I look at him, concerned. "I'm joking," he adds.

"No, because we're going to figure something out. Ele will finish the cure," I respond.

"I hope so," Reece says.

The screen of my phone flashes, alerting me to a text from Ele.

After reading it, I'm super happy she's okay. A desire to leave the Infirmary burns inside me. I sigh and take out the paper I found earlier. I turn it over and then put it inside my phone case. We aren't really allowed to have paper, so they might wonder if they find it lying around. It's a passcode to something. Maybe it's important.

I glance at the time on my phone. It's almost two. I hide my phone behind my pillow and start toward the door.

"Where are you going *now*?" Reece asks, jumping up.

"To meet my parents," I reply.

"Let me come with you!" Reece begs. "I'm dying of boredom."

"It's not safe," I point out. Reece shrinks. He fidgets and stares at the floor.

"I know. It's not far though," he says slowly.

"Okay, if you want to. I have to tell them about the text from Ele," I say.

"You got a text from Ele?" Reece asks, surprised. He knows a lot about her because we've talked to only each other for weeks.

"Yeah. She's getting tested. So, she might be here soon I guess," I say with a shrug. "You coming?"

Reece shifts a little. "Maybe not. It is dangerous. Tell them I said hi. Oh, and hurry back or you'll miss recreational activities," he adds with an eyeroll.

"Oh no," I say sarcastically. "Thanks for reminding me, bro. See ya in a few years."

"Um, no. I'm staying, but you are not going adventuring again and leaving me to suffer through recreational activities alone," Reece says, crossing his lanky arms.

We have recreational activities every Thursday morning and occasional afternoons. Reece and I literally dread them. We decided they misinterpreted the phrase because they most definitely are not enjoyable. Hardly bearable is more like it. Usually, we have to help clean the check-in area or do the laundry or something else horrible. I'm thirteen. My mom still has to rearrange the dishwasher after me. There's no greater form of torture than chores. We've decided this might be a violation of our child labor laws. It wouldn't be the only law broken here in the Infirmary.

"I'll be back soon," I say seriously and open the door.

After jogging downstairs, I walk until I reach a corridor lined with thick metal doors. They're like prison cells. The cold air and dim lights, along with securely locked doors leave me reminiscing. Faint cries, screams, and sobs echo down the hall. Eventually they'll stop and be released from their temporary cages. Sometimes if they don't they get taken to the Double Guard—a high security unit where you aren't even allowed out of your room. When I came, I was locked up for three hours. Each little room is dark and cold. I would have done anything to get out of that place. After several hours they released me. They do it to break you of the hope of getting out of the Infirmary. They use loneliness to brainwash you. I call those the Hopeful Rooms. Only the ones who have hope for survival and escape end up there. Sometimes I'm disappointed that I gave up trying to find a way out. Many others have too. I've chosen to focus my energy on helping the other patients. I know there's still a chance for us. We just can't give in and lose faith.

I arrive at the check-in area. I shove past several people, eyeing the guards at the desk. Finally, I spot my mom and dad. Mom stands next to the dark pillar in the middle of the hall reading the list posted on it. The list of the dead. She's wearing a mandatory face mask. We're all supposed to wear our masks. Most people don't. Like what are we gonna do? Get someone sick who's *already* sick? The Mordolus wear thick gloves and black leather face masks already. Masks are the one rule they don't really enforce because here it's pretty useless. But my mom's a rule-abider.

Dad stands nearby, watching as the nurses check in people, listen to questions, and take daily medication requests. The guards watch me. I pretend to read the list next to Mom. I act like I don't recognize her.

"Hey," I whisper, scanning the paper. "How're you?"

"I'm alright," she responds quietly. Mom's worse off than either of us admit. She's too pale and clearly isn't eating enough.

"Mom, I got a text from Ele."

"What?" she asks, a little too loud. We both glance over our shoulders. Thankfully, the guards all seem fixated on handling the other patients.

"How did you get your phone back?" she demands quietly, playing with a blond piece of hair. It's a nervous habit that belongs to both her and Ele.

I don't respond and step closer to scan the list. None of the names are familiar. But each of them represents an individual taken by the Virus.

"I told you not to!" Mom whispers harshly. "Really Isaiah, you're going to get caught!" She sighs and stands up straighter. "What did she tell you?"

"Sorry," I say, then relay Ele's message. Mom stays silent, so I whisper a goodbye. I wait for a second after she leaves before walking over to Dad.

"Hey," I say quietly. The staff already eye us. "I got a text from Ele."

He doesn't have the same reaction as Mom. We're careful not to make eye contact, but a hint of excitement grows in his blue eyes. "What'd she say?"

I quickly recite the text. Before he responds, one of the guards tells us we've been here too long and need to leave. I don't argue. None of our undercover meetings are lengthy.

As I walk back, my mind wanders. The Queen lets thousands of people stay here, just until they die, without doing anything. Yeah, we're supposedly cared for here, but it's too strict. I could never force so many families to separate. She has to be doing something. But I don't know what. Maybe it's just Senneforte, and we're being quarantined to protect the other provinces. But shouldn't we keep looking for a cure? This whole thing seems wrong. Maybe it's my upbringing, or personality. No, it's my faith. I just won't give in when things seem impossible.

5

ELEANORA: TRAPPED AND CONFUSED

Powerful thoughts control the moments after receiving the news that I've contracted the Maraloxis Virus: *I can't let them lock me up because I've got to get out of here. I need to save my family, and I can't do that very well if I'm stuck inside the Infirmary, can I?*

Emergency alarms blare inside my head as the guard shoves a paper into my hand and points toward the Infirmary's open door. An ominous hallway greets me, but I take a deep breath, hook my thumbs under the straps of my backpack, and step inside. The door slams shut, and the golden daylight vanishes instantly.

I loiter there, everything distorted by the dark lens of surreality. A young woman with two braids of straight black hair and dressed in a gray suit comes over, taking the paper from my hand before guiding me down the hallway. My legs are weak, but I follow her closely. There is a loud hall lined with steel doors up ahead, and the woman opens one of them and orders me to go inside. I hesitate, staring into the dark room, but knowing I have no other option, I step into the cell. Metal clicks as the door locks. As my eyes adjust from the bright hall, I survey the small room. A tarnished, metal bed occupies the back wall, but besides that the room is empty. Each sound echoes off the walls and bounces around like a thousand pebbles crashing to the ground. The tile floor is clean but cracked, and fissures spider out across every square. The only light present streams in through a blurry, scratched-up, glass pane in the door.

I sit down on the dirty bed, trying to touch it as little as possible. Opening my backpack, I take out my phone and text Graydon to tell him the results. *Who knows how long until they confiscate my things.* I barely send the text when the screen flashes and then goes black. I sigh and toss it back in my backpack. *I'll never have the opportunity to charge it, so I guess that's it for communicating.* There's no electricity anywhere except the Infirmary that I know of, and I've been having to charge my phone manually. I lean against the wall and stare at the ceiling, flawless in contrast to the abused walls. My heart races the more I think, but from nowhere, words overwhelm my mind.

Have peace.

Anxiety still haunts my mind, but tendrils of serenity pick their way through and eventually overtake the shadows. *I'm going to be okay.* A crisp chill bores into me and chisels thousands of goosebumps across my skin. The bed is a hard, uneven place to sit, nevertheless, not long passes before sleepiness rolls in and conquers my discomfort like a foamy wave washing over a sandcastle.

Distressed voices permeate the air from the other cells when I wake. I stand up and stretch, pangs of hunger gently nudging my insides. Walking over to the door, I try my best to see out the small window. The tinted glass gives everything a honey-colored haze, and from what I can tell, there isn't anyone around.

I'm trying to take note of everything so that later I can use the information to my advantage. *If I can find my family, perhaps we can escape together using what I learn.* I once again walk over to the door, but the hall is empty, leaving me feeling terribly lonely. I pound on the door, distraught and angry, hoping to get someone's attention so I can ask how long I'm going to be stuck in here. It's like I'm imprisoned in some dark dungeon, and even though it's only been a few hours, I just long to talk to someone. I gaze out the window and notice someone coming down the hall. I'm overwhelmed by shock and complete disbelief.

It's my brother.

I bang harder, only adding to the depressions on the metal door, calling out to him. But I'm drowned out by the noise of the other prisoners. Pain shoots up my leg as I kick the door in defeat and watch Isaiah disappear.

The Virus has taken a toll on him as well, which I deduce from the odd paleness and dim look in his eyes. A fresh urgency to escape this place awakens in me.

I open my backpack and leaf through my photos, blindly selecting one. It's a blurry picture from years ago, and I was no older than eight. The image captures a little blond girl with one arm around her best friend and nearly strangling her brother with the other; the even younger blond boy with crazy hair glares at his sister; and the oldest, a brown-haired boy, just smiles. I feel like I don't know those people. Isaiah, Graydon, and I have changed so much. Graydon and I were close as kids, but after about twelve we didn't really hang out with each other as much since we were older and had other friends.

My daydreams are shattered by the door slamming open. I turn to find a man clothed in white standing in the doorway. He's older, wearing pensive rectangular glasses, and with gloved hands, he pats me down. I notice the guard from earlier standing outside the door and grit my teeth. I'm not exactly pleased to see either of them, but zeal to be free from this room springs to life in my soul. The man snatches the photo from my hand and grabs my backpack.

"Hey! That's mine!" I seethe, but he slams the door closed behind him. I grab the handle and try to turn it, but the door doesn't budge—I let out an angry scream. *All my pictures are gone.* The two are talking outside so I put my ear to the door.

"When will a room be ready for her?" the man in white asks. "The penalty for attempting escape is the Double Guard."

"In a few hours. We'll put her where that other girl was."

"Make sure she doesn't escape," the first adds.

"Of course," the guard responds mockingly. "No one ever does."

"Thanks, Ash."

Disdain once again builds up. *I hate them all, and I hate him most of all. Ash took me from home and probably helped take my family.* Fierce frustration spills over and out of me in the form of a furious sigh as I sink to the floor, defeated.

When the door opens again, hours have passed. A new woman comes in and takes me by the wrist and I flinch, the bruises from my fence-escape catastrophe aching under her grip. She walks me down the widest hallway, and we pass the door I came in. I instinctively prepare to run. *Maybe I can escape now since there's only one person.*

"Don't try," she says, reading me. "Or they'll put you back in confinement."

I roll my eyes and let her drag me down the hall.

We come to an area that's blocked by a red barricade, and the woman carefully moves it aside and guides me past. Only a few halls away, we come to a big set of doors, also marked in red drooling paint, reading '*Double Guard*'. The lady takes out a set of keys and unlocks the door, and once we're inside, she releases my arm. I should feel freer now, but for some reason, it seems to signal even more severe imprisonment.

It seems like we walk for ages before stopping in front of Room 138.

"What's your name?" she asks.

"Eleanora Brooks," I reply. She takes out a pen and scribbles my name on the paper hanging beside the door, and I roll my eyes. She wrote E-L-L-A *space* Nora. It's hit-or-miss whether people will spell my name correctly and think of it as Eleanor-a, not Ella-Nora. The woman opens the door and lets me inside the room, and after she shuts it, keys jingle, so I know she's locked me inside the room.

Two identical brass-framed twin beds are lined up across the wall adjacent to the door, and there's a little plastic table missing a leg standing limply in the corner. A window sits above the middle bed, but all I can see is the sky. Despite the number of beds, I appear to be the only one here, and everything is filthy.

I flump down on the bed that appears the cleanest and wearily contemplate everything. *How did I get here when this morning I was in my own room?* Every once in a while, there are oddly random sounds then strange knocking, which makes me slightly apprehensive since they don't appear to have any particular origin.

Suddenly, there's a slam as the closet door opens abruptly. A girl tumbles out onto the floor. She's a little younger than me and wears an oversized T-shirt, black shorts, and a worn pair of sunshine-yellow high-tops.

"Sorry, sometimes the door sticks. Clearly not that time!" she says with a laugh. I just stare at her. She props her head on a hand and smiles at me, then jumps up and walks over, full of energy.

"Hi, I'm Marie!" she says, pushing her dark, curly hair out of her face and throwing out a hand. "Who are you?"

"I'm Eleanora," I say, rather startled, and give her a sorry handshake.

"You're my new roommate, right?" she asks, her animated brown eyes flashing with excitement. "Or did you just sneak in here?" she stage-whispers, looking around mischievously.

"No, I assume I'm your roommate," I reply.

"GREAT!" Marie says, bouncing up and down. "I've been so dang bored lately! I got another friend now! I'm SO excited!"

"What were you doing in there?" I ask, gesturing to the closet.

"Well," Marie says, then pauses. "Oh! I'll show you!"

Grabbing my hand, Marie pulls me inside the closet. She yanks the door shut, and the only thing I can see is the thrilled glint in her eyes as she clicks on a flashlight. The closet is filled with sheets, clothes, and a variety of other random things—an ordinary closet—but a bit of adventure glitters through the air.

"You promise not to tell?" Marie whispers excitedly, and I nod.

She reaches into the corner and pulls out a bunch of papers. The handwriting is so bad I can hardly read it, but I make out some numbers and words. Abstract images paint the pages and lines, arrows, and various other symbols swirl around the letters in a tangle of ink. Marie hands some to me, and slowly, I bring them close enough to read, shocked at what I see.

6
GRAYDON: INTRUDERS AND BROKEN GLASS

I grab a cage off the wooden shelf to my left. Within the plastic walls, a mouse dives beneath its bedding. Its tawny fur is flecked with white, and the hay quivers as the creature draws fearful, labored breaths. Two black frightened eyes stare at me from beneath the mountain of straw.

I figured out how to infect rodents with Maraloxis using syringes of blood from other contaminated creatures. My dad showed me once and I remembered enough to spread the illness from the last rat he left behind. They show symptoms within a few days. I make injections containing the partial remedy that's been constructed so far then add a new trial ingredient. I use them on the mice, wait a day, then test again. The testing materials were left by my dad. He got them bootleg from another scientist who stole them from the government. I simply take a blood sample, mix it with the testing liquid, and wait for the result. So far I've gotten no negatives. Viruses aren't supposed to have a cure. You can't cure a virus. But maybe some medication gives people a chance to fight it. What we have currently is a combination of chloroquine, oseltamivir, and a few basic ingredients, which my dad had already come up with. That's just a base that allows the antiviral ingredient to work. And that's the part I don't know. I got a text from Isaiah that zinc and magnesium help, but they only seem to reduce symptoms.

I fill another needle with liquid. I'm trying a rimantadine mixture this time. I haven't moved outside testing medicines yet. I'm thinking what's going to finish this cure will be some kind of antiviral med. Throwing on some gloves, I carefully lift the trembling, squeaking, creature from the cage and inject the test substance. I quickly return the mouse to its cage, replace the lid, and set it on the shelf among several others.

Taking a beaker of liquid magnesium hydroxide, I pour in fifteen milliliters of heated alkaline water from an Erlenmeyer flask. As I mix it, a magnesium precipitate begins to form. Slowly, I strain the liquid from it. I place the white, amorphous reduction on a tray and set it on the shelf to dry completely. I still have hope that magnesium will be part of the solution.

I walk over to the table and pull out some books from the shelf above the table and sort through them. Under the old microscope, I watch how each of the chemicals react to the Virus. I have no idea what to look for, but I keep my eyes peeled. Dad taught me a lot about science, chemicals, and medications over the years, especially recently.

I'm just hoping when I finish this cure, Morzanna will finally step up and help us distribute it. Maybe the Infirmary will turn into a healing center. The Mordolus will become a rebuilding group. Maybe Willowmire will be restored at last.

I've read entirely through my dad's typed notes and handwritten annotations twice. I've studied so many books on science, medicine, and basically anything that might help. The Virus is different—it's not just a virion. Some new material transforms it into something else. My dad said the Maraloxis Virus is like a viral combination of influenza and malaria, which makes sense because most of the base ingredients are treatments for those specific diseases. This new element, a metal called lenvernium, mutates the virus into a lethal disease. I haven't found anything in any book about viruses and metals combined. I've done research on vaccines too. The Maraloxis Virus as a mutation with the lenvernium kills cells. When a virus infects the host cell, sometimes the cell is injured or eventually dies, but with Maraloxis, once the cells are attacked, they *always* die, but only after replicating the DNA of the Virus, causing it to spread and become fatal. It specifically targets the nervous system and brain, which is why common symptoms are numbness, paresthesia, loss of consciousness, and seizures. I wonder if the Virus without the lenvernium mutation is as destructive. Or if that version even exists.

In the nineteen forties, the first vaccine was developed for influenza. Over ninety years have passed since then, and knowledge of medicine has increased significantly. Designed experiments are generally performed on animals first, to ensure the correct effect and safety, I read from a textbook.

I haven't made it past the animal testing phase. I've only managed to accidentally kill three or four mice, but other than that my remaining test subjects have been unaffected. Animals can contract the Maraloxis Virus, but the effects are different. None of mine have died from the Virus' progression. Though, I haven't really kept them long enough to find out. But I figured if animals were dying too then I'd see more dead creatures outside. Maybe the Maraloxis Virus can be reversed with normal remedies in early phases like the incubation period or prodromal stage.

I study until I can't focus. Getting up, I start to collect my things. I've spent so many days in this empty, ill-lit garage. Too many things captivate my mind. Fear. Death. Solitude. Panic. Thirst. Clean water is scarce. I have a water filter device for camping, but it's a lot of work. Hunger. I'm *so* hungry. People have turned themselves in and prayed they were positive because they were starving. The rest of us, if there is an 'us', have to make do with what we have. It's starvation or isolated captivity. Both are prisons. Both will kill you. For now, I'm fighting the temptation and staying out here. If I look hard enough, I can find something to eat. Sometimes it's in the wreckage, or sometimes I just look harder than the Mordolus do. I'll find something to keep myself alive. I just *can't* be caged.

I organize the vials on their racks beside the door. One section is for the base mixture itself and another is for the ingredients to make it. The very top shelf holds new chemical substances I haven't tried yet. I close up Dad's notebook.

Suddenly, there's a strange clattering sound outside. I freeze, the binder of notes tucked under my arm. I shut off the garage light and drag a chair over to the garage door window so I can see out. I watch the street outside, the creak of a vehicle meeting me the second I stop and listen. I dash out of the garage to make sure the door is locked and take a new viewpoint from the living room.

Across the road, a girl peeks out from behind the row of buildings. She looks back and forth, fear and dread stark in her expression. After trying a few of the doors and finding them locked, she darts between houses like a scared squirrel as the Mordolus vehicle nears. All the doors on this street have been crossed out in red and locked tight after the Mordolus searched them. This house is the one unknown exception. That's because I broke a window and found the key in a drawer. I have to do something to help that girl.

She sprints to my side of the street, hiding behind a cluster of rose bushes. I hurry to the back door and slowly push it open. Crouching, I make my way over to a fence right next to the rose bushes. It's so hot out here. The girl scans the road, waiting for the Mordolus to appear.

"Hey," I whisper. "Hey."

The girl jumps and scrambles back a few paces. The sun streams onto her face, revealing the sullen shadows in her complexion. Her wavy hair is the russet red of autumn leaves. That's not the first thing I notice though—it's her eyes. Wide with shock, her vibrant blue eyes glow like drops of seawater on her pale skin. She pushes up the sleeves of her significantly oversized shirt and crosses her arms. I bet she has the Virus. It makes me uneasy, but I've already been exposed to my family so I think it's too late for me anyway. She might be sick, but I still have to help her. I'll try to be careful.

"Come with me, fast," I say, crawling closer to her. "Hurry!"

She shakes her head until the Mordolus truck appears in the distance then she finally nods hesitantly. The two of us race to the back door. I hear the vehicle nearing, but I think we managed to evade them. Once we're inside, I lock the door. By the time I turn around, she's already run into the other room.

"Wait!" I call, chasing her into the living room. She stops, turns, and stares at me with those striking blue eyes, keeping her distance. I walk toward her, reading her fear. She takes a few steps back toward the corner, tripping. She lands in the shattered glass, a grim look of inspiration growing across her round face. Quickly, she picks up a large fragment.

"Don't come any closer, Mordolus boy!" she demands, threateningly. "Or I swear, this razor-sharp piece of glass will be embedded in your face."

I was going to be all nice and explain that I'm not in fact part of the Mordolus, but I don't like her attitude. *I* saved *her.* So I take a large step forward out of spite.

The girl holds to her promise and launches the glass right at me. I duck, having prepared, but apparently so did she. The glass hits me right on the cheek. It's not as 'razor sharp' as she said and glances off, but it still hurts.

"You're a stupid Mordolus boy!" she says, taking up another piece of glass.

"Stop! I helped you, *girl!* I'm not part of the Mordolus!" I say, cradling my injured cheek. "I'm going to assume you aren't either? Even though you just assaulted me?"

She shakes her head but doesn't put down the glass. "Who are you then?"

"Graydon. Who are you?" I ask.

"Bexley. What were you doing?" she replies, dropping her inventive weapon.

"I live here," I say, which is partially true. I borrowed the space from whoever used to live here.

"You scared me to death," Bexley says, laying a hand over her heart and standing. She glances out the window. I think the Mordolus are gone now. "I didn't think anyone was still out here. Much less that I'd run into someone."

"I haven't seen strangers in a long time. But it's not like people are out in the open either. There could be others, but who knows," I say.

"Well, evidently there are at least two of us," Bexley says, tossing her auburn-red hair. She annoyedly dusts the small glass fragments off her hands. I think she's younger than me, but I'm not sure.

"Are you okay?" I say. "Did you get cut?"

Bexley shakes her head. "No."

"Well I did," I retort, removing my hand and showing her the bleeding slice from her attack.

"Oh, sorry," she says. "It doesn't look too bad. I did warn you."

"Whatever. So where did you come from? What were *you* doing?" I gaze at her tattered clothing, noting her scraped and bruised arms and legs. Her clothes are bizarre: obnoxious, faded colors, and not the correct size.

"Oh, I was bored, so I was exploring." She plays with a small silver charm bracelet on her wrist, swirling it in circles. "Because there's nothing else to do."

"Yeah right," I say. "And what happened there?" I point at her injuries. "That's some dangerous exploring. Really shouldn't do that anymore."

Bexley gives me a sideways glance. "Fine. Tell me what you were really doing because I know you're at least partially lying, and I want to know what's in that fancy book. Then I'll give you my real story."

I look down and realize the notebook with my dad's name on it is still under my arm. "Okay, fine. Come on," I decide, leading her back to the garage. We step down the stairs.

"So why do you have all this strange, sciencey stuff?" Bexley asks, picking up one of the vials containing dexamethasone and looking it over.

"I'll explain," I say, gently taking the vial from her and setting it back down.

"Something important, I guess. So, do tell." She stares at me curiously, a subtle smile lighting up her expression.

"I've been working on something," I state.

"Okay, and what is it?" she presses.

I stare at her for a second. "An antidote for the Maraloxis Virus."

I show her a vial containing the cure base and open the notebook. Her eyes widen. "My dad was creating it. He worked with some other techs and pharmacists, but after that got shut down, I helped him. He was taken to the Infirmary last month, and we were left to finish it."

"That's awesome! A medicine really exists after all? A friend in the Infirmary told me that people were secretly working on a cure. I honestly didn't have much faith in it. Do you think it'll work?" Bexley asks excitedly. "And who's 'we'?"

"Eleanora. She's my friend. They took her today to get tested," I explain. "And I don't know if the medicine will be successful, I mean, I hope. But I won't really be sure until it's finished."

"Now tell me what happened to you." I insist, pulling a chair from the table and sitting.

Bexley takes a chair too and begins, "My parents and I were taken to get tested together, and we were all positive. I was kept in the Infirmary, of course. This was in, like, June, so several months ago. I sort of lost track of time. I tried to escape but got caught, so they put me in the Double Guard."

"What's that?" I ask.

"It's like super guarded. In the rest of the Infirmary, they have certain perimeters you have to stay in, but the Double Guard is for people who cause trouble. You're constantly locked in a room. You can't go anywhere," Bexley says.

"That sounds terrible," I say, and she nods.

"I was trapped for over a month. I got sicker and realized I needed to get out and find some solution. At least see my family again. My parents and I were separated, and I was never able to find them. I think they may have been put in one of the other Sections. My sisters, Hadley and Hallston, are both older, and I don't know what happened to them. When I had a chance, I tried again and finally got out. I fell from the fence when I was climbing it, and there were brambles at the bottom. I've been staying in abandoned homes for two days. The Mordolus were chasing me again, and all the houses I tried were locked, breaking a window would be too loud, and I can't hide very well in all this getup," she says, motioning to her bright clothing: a highlighter-yellow T-shirt, neon orange pair of shorts, and ragged teal flip-flops. "So I panicked. That's how I ended up in that bush."

"That's crazy! I didn't think anyone could escape the Infirmary," I say. *Maybe there is hope for Eleanora, Isaiah, and my family.*

"Well they're certainly not going to announce it to everyone. If people knew they could escape, they would try," she comments, kicking at the floor. "There really is little hope at the Infirmary anyway, since no one knows there could be a cure."

She's right. We may not find the last ingredients for the Maraloxis remedy.

"Hey, random question, but why'd you choose a garage? It's so drafty and dusty in here," Bexley asks.

"Honestly, it was big, secure, and the least likely to catch on fire room I could find. Also, when you're working with chemicals, you need it to be drafty so you don't asphyxiate," I say. Another upside I don't mention is that I can catch mice in here super easily.

"Oh, okay. So how long will it take to finish the cure?" Bexley asks.

"I don't know. It could take months or even years. You never know." I shrug. I want to add 'if at all' but decide it's unnecessary.

"I hope you can finish it," she comments. I give her an optimistic smile.

Bexley suddenly gets a strange look. "You don't mind that I'm sick, do you?"

I shake my head. "No. I mean, it's probably too late to worry. I've been around my family and Ele, so I don't really care."

"I can wear a mask at least," she offers.

"It's fine, but do whatever you want," I say. "I don't care."

"Oh, are you sure?" Bexley asks, and I nod, but she still takes out a black face mask from the pocket of her shorts. "I'm gonna wear one."

"So, what's in the cure so far?" she asks. I start listing off the long list of chemicals.

Bexley and I talk for hours. Bexley has to be starving after two days, so I share with her everything I have in the lab. Soon the bright sunshine is drowned by dusk. We're both tired, so I leave Bexley there at the lab for the night where she'll be safe. I reset the mouse traps outside, the simple metal cage type, then start off for home. *I'll come back first thing in the morning.*

Sneaking through the forest, I make it to my house and unlock the back door. Striding upstairs, I toss my backpack on the floor and take out my phone. There's a text from Ele.

Hey, I'm in the infirmary. Guess I got the virus after all. I might not be able to text bc I think they're gonna take my phone soon. Don't worry about me, I'm okay.

My mind whirls. *Ele's trapped.* Now with the new knowledge that escape from the Infirmary is possible, a slight bit of hope rekindles in me. Maybe my parents aren't doomed after all.

7

ELEANORA: ESCAPE AND CAPTIVITY

I inspect the papers under the flashlight's bright glow. The scribbles form overhead maps of the Infirmary, and each page portrays an intricate idea; they're plans to flee the Infirmary. I gape at my new roommate, Marie.

"How many times did you try to get out?" I ask.

Marie shrugs. "Eh, maybe twenty," she replies.

"Twenty?!" I say.

Marie nods with a proud grin, her tight, bronze-brown curls bouncing. "I keep getting caught. But I think I'm getting close to my plan actually working!" she says.

No wonder she's in the Double Guard. I'm a little stunned by her brazen attempts to break out. Leafing through the stack of papers, I discover some involve disguise, deception, taking down the guards, and thievery.

She snatches the papers, stashes them back in the depths of the closet, and opens the door. I step out, blinded by the sudden light change as I contemplate that odd and abrupt introduction.

"I must tell you something," I say. Marie listens with thrill and numerous questions as I explain everything about the Maraloxis Virus medication I've been helping to formulate.

"Whoa, you're a legit celebrity!" Marie says. "You guys are like heroes!"

"Well, not exactly," I say with a blush. "But it will be something if the cure is completed."

"So now we gotta get out of here ASAP," Marie says with glee.

"Has anyone ever actually succeeded?" I ask.

"Well, no. The Mordolus do a great job preventing it. Because you know, 'it's better for us here', and 'it will help to stop the Virus from spreading'. Like come on, we all have it. And no one should be able to lock up other people, no matter what kind of disease there is. But I'm gonna escape. I can be the first one." Marie smiles determinedly. "Or maybe *we* can?"

I beam, relieved that I'll have someone else, especially someone with more knowledge about the Infirmary than me, to assist in my endeavor to escape.

"Great! I'm so excited! I've been alone for a long time! I need someone to help me with the maps. I'm not very good at the writing part. I get mixed up. Bella always does it for me. So now you can—"

I cut her off. "Wait, who's Bella?"

"Oh, she was my roommate and best friend. But she died."

I remember the conversation I heard from Ash and the other Mordolus member.

"I'm sorry," I say, rapidly changing the subject. "I'd be happy to help. I already tried to escape in the parking lot, but obviously, it didn't work. That's how I ended up here."

"Well, it'll be harder here. Since we're in the Double Guard," she says, thinking.

"Hey, have you seen a boy, thirteen, his name is Isaiah?" I interrupt. "He's my brother."

"Nope," Marie replies. "I haven't really seen anyone since I've been here though."

I sit down on the bed across from her. *I was so close. Isaiah nearly saw me too.* However, there's no use being upset about it; I'll have another chance.

"What happened to your family?" I dare to ask.

"They're here too. My brother's five, so he's somewhere in the children's section. I got put in Double Guard after trying to get in there. I haven't seen my parents since I got here last month. Neither of them was doing great, especially my dad. I asked the nurses about them, and they said they didn't know. So, I've given my time to planning," she explains.

"What can we do now?" I ask, eager to move on as fresh inklings of worry for my parents find their way into my head.

"We can work on new plans. We have to be careful though because they have cameras in here," Marie says, pointing to the corner. "If they see us doing anything suspicious, they'll send someone to check the room. That's why I only work in the closet. Someone will come and bring us food and stuff later."

"How come they don't worry about you vanishing when you're in the closet?" I ask.

"Sensors. Have them on the doors and things to keep track. It also tells them if I try to leave," Marie explains, bouncing.

"Why did you stay in the closet for nearly twenty minutes after you heard the nurse bring me in?" I ask.

"I wanted to make an entrance. I also didn't know you were coming and couldn't decide whether to stay in there or just pretend it was normal to be hanging out in a closet and walk out. Then I got too excited and couldn't wait any longer!" Marie says with a laugh.

I gently kick the side of the metal bed frame, thinking. My emotions have given up their battle for now, and I glance out the window at the golden-pink sky, exhausted.

"I'm so tired," I admit with a yawn.

"Okay. I guess you can rest," Marie says. "Just make it fast 'cause I'm bored. They'll come to check on us this evening. I'll wake you up then."

I'm thankful that at least the sheets are fairly clean on my chosen bed. I embrace the welcoming call of sleep surprisingly quickly, drifting into a dream world where no virus exists, and life is still careless.

I awake abruptly, finding the door open and Marie standing over me with an enthusiastic grin. An older woman walks in, wearing average gray scrubs, and her short, peppered hair and demure brown eyes make me feel less threatened than I have by any of the Mordolus I've encountered yet.

I sorely roll over, suffering pain from the bruises acquired earlier, realizing how hard and painful it is to move my hand. I glance over to Marie, who has returned to her bed to sit and wait, clearly bored. The woman, a nurse I think, hands Marie and me each a plate of food and some water. Starving, I devour the food that normally I would complain about. I guess what my mom said was true: if you're hungry enough, you'll eat anything. The water, served in a faded plastic cup, tastes terrible and strongly metallic, though I am a water snob. When I'm finished, the nurse still stands there.

"Come with me," the woman says, gesturing to me. I stand, surprised when the woman pulls out a pair of handcuff-like devices. She tries to put them on me, but I step back. Marie shoots me a look that adds to my conflictions, so I reluctantly step forward and allow her to bind me. I flinch, my wrists in pain from my previous handling at the fence. She leads me out the door and into the hallway.

"You've caused some issues and tried to run away," she says, and I don't respond. "That's why I was instructed to bring these."

She takes large, determined strides, and I struggle to keep up as we make our way through the Infirmary. We turn at the end of a long hallway and eventually pass by the entryway to the Double Guard. The nurse leads me to a quieter corridor and guides me into one of the vacant rooms. She has me sit down in a chair in the small, bland office and performs a check-up similar to an annual doctor's appointment. She inquires about whether I think I need any form of medication, and

I decline. I feel fine, other than my throbbing wrists, which I mention in avid detail. The nurse fetches a roll of bandages and binds my wrists after applying a pain-relieving salve. She surprises me with her clemency, and I decide maybe not all the Mordolus are as savage as the Hunters. Afterward, she replaces the binding cuffs to my arms, right above my bandages, and we leave.

I check the door handle when I arrive back in our room to see if, by a stroke of luck, the woman forgot to lock it, but unfortunately, she didn't. Marie is already fast asleep, and the lights are all extinguished except the dim shine of the bathroom's single bulb. Outside, the sky is the dark, lovely black of twilight, and the stars whisper melodies of hope. When my mind calms, I lay down, certain tomorrow will be better.

8

GRAYDON: RATS, MOLES, AND REMEDIES

I wake up to a dreary, gray sky, listening to the sound of rain softly plinking on the roof. Trees rock gently in the gale and tap playfully against the windows. I rise from the creaky bed and collect some scraps of food, saving half for Bexley. I'm still hungry after eating as usual.

Glancing out the second story window, I survey the street. Everything looks sad. I close the blinds after I hear the rumble of a vehicle nearby. A picture of Michigan apple blossoms hangs beside the door to the closet. It's been thirty years since Senneforte was even part of Michigan. I stop by the bathroom mirror. There's a thin cut and light blue bruise across my right cheekbone from the glass yesterday.

Tiny pools form from water blown in the chipped glass windows in the dining room. I hop downstairs, grab my backpack and hoodie, and throw on my shoes. Rain splatters onto the sidewalk and pours from the gutters, trickling down to form streams that meld into muddy puddles. Burnt buildings are just shadowy skeletons of the past. As soon as I step out the door, I'm soaked. The cool wind makes it way worse. Summer will be over in a month. I walk down the street, carefully checking each time I turn a corner. Recently, the Mordolus have been way too close.

I follow the same road until I reach the quiet cul-de-sac. I climb the lab's brick steps. Pushing open the door, I walk in, rainwater pooling at my feet. Bexley must still be asleep because she's not in the garage. I check the bedroom she's in, just to make sure she didn't get, like, kidnapped or something. I don't stay long because staring at someone while they're sleeping is super creepy.

I trudge back to the garage and walk over to the table. I take a deep breath before delving into the pages of a chemistry book. I've got to figure out how to get these two chemicals to mix. I don't know how to increase the solubility without affecting the volume and concentration. For almost an hour, I prepare new combinations to try and dabble with random concoctions of medicinal chemicals. I peer over again at the notes my father collected during his research. It's a lot of scientific jargon I don't get. It seems like a somewhat simple recipe. But there are way too many assumptions like that I would know what extrapolation means or how to precipitate magnesium. This disease has a variety of random symptoms, and people are often asymptomatic for weeks. That part I can't figure. That and the metal/virus connection.

Sunlight creeps in through the small windows in the rain's wake. I boredly play with the strings of my hoodie. There are no more chemicals left to try.

I decide to go out and search for fresh materials. I cross the concrete floor and turn off the light, accidentally sticking my hand in a spider web. I climb the stairs, step back into the house, then head outside.

The hospitals, apartment complexes, larger warehouses, and stores are covered by extensive security systems. My options are limited, and they all require breaking in. I tried the landfill once, but it's nearly seven miles away and I hardly found anything. Following the winding street, I creep until I find an obsolete, abandoned house crossed with red. The less rich the house looks, the better chance the Mordolus did a less thorough clearing. Sneaking to the back of the house, I throw a rock through the glass section of the door and let myself in.

I walk into the ghostly house. I've discovered some bad things. Tragic letters. Pets locked up, dead. Once, I found a corpse. I stand in the foyer beneath a crystalline chandelier, examining the shadowy gray walls. Everything inside looks intact. Before the Virus, no one would note anything strange other than the absence of the owners. But I've learned the signs: the all too familiar boot prints, the chair slightly out of place, the cabinets still open; it tells a story.

A family—parents and two children: a boy and a girl, if the pictures on the wall are correct. The children were rushed to hide in the cabinet, the parents probably fought but were still taken. The children were found as well. The Queen has no right to allow people to be taken from their homes and tested for a virus that she cares nothing about, leaving Senneforte all ruined and empty.

I wander into the kitchen, trying the faucet to see if it works, which unfortunately only produces a few rust-colored water drops.

Continuing my search down the hall, I find some medicines in the back of the cabinet. I gladly place these supplies inside my backpack. Half the houses are burned, and the ones that aren't are locked, raided of food except perishables that are long past usable without electricity. There's plenty of normal useless stuff left. I start back to the lab with one thought on my mind: *the longer it takes to finish an antidote, the more people die.*

When I return, Bexley's awake, watching the mice scamper around their cages with disgusted interest. Without a word, I hurry back to work, flipping through a few of the books. Bexley gets up and ambles over to me.

"What are you doing?" she asks, combing through her hair with her hand.

"I'm trying to make an antidote," I say.

"Oh, obviously," Bexley says, picking up an old work titled *Molecular Chemistry Formulas and Stoichiometry.* I've been collecting as many books on science and chemistry as I can for research. Bexley sets the volume down. "I meant specifically. Is it something I can help with? Please. I really want to if I can."

"Honestly, I'd love help. I don't have any idea what I'm doing, and all I have are books and these notes from my dad," I say, standing. I open the metal chest in the back of the garage, revealing all my dad's old supplies and tools.

"Oh, wow," Bexley says. "What are all those things?"

I move aside some bubble wrap, revealing all manner of glass containers. "The wide cylindrical ones are beakers, and the tapered one is an Erlenmeyer flask."

"What about the round one?" she asks.

"That's a distillation flask. You heat stuff up in it," I explain. "This is an alcohol burner. It works like an oil lamp, but with isopropyl alcohol."

"Oh cool!" Bexley says, then picks up a tall glass tube with measurements on it. "Oh! I know what this is! It's a graduated cylinder. We used them in science class."

"Yep," I say, taking a few clean vials out. "I have something you can do."

Bexley leafs through a smaller tub of pH sheets, tweezers, eye droppers, and mixing utensils.

"Great!" she says as I close the chest.

"I like your eagerness but don't get overexcited. Trying to save the world isn't that thrilling sometimes. Here," I say, handing her three full vials from the metal holder on the shelf and replacing them with the empty ones. "Take these, make the solution, and then fill the syringes."

I show her the proper amount of sterile water to use and how to counter it with half of each vial's contents. She picks up super-fast on all my instructions.

"This is chloroquine, right?" Bexley asks, inspecting the bronze-brown bottle.

"Yeah, how'd you know that?" I ask.

"In the Infirmary, the Mordolus limits the amounts of drugs people get, and some people are neglected from what they need. My friend and I would research and steal medications for the Maraloxis Virus, ones that actually worked, and we would give them to people. He's also the one who told me a cure might exist," Bexley says.

When I was eleven, I taught Eleanora and Isaiah science with all kinds of projects and experiments. Isaiah and I loved to explode potassium in water and burn any flammable substance we could find. We had access to a lot of chemicals from my dad's work. I used to be science-obsessed. My parents jokingly said I was 'nerdifying' Ele and Isaiah. They weren't wrong. I always wanted my dad to teach me more. Science has always been a way to distract myself. Little did we know how useful it would be.

I stare at the formulas covering the page in my chemistry book. Bexley flips another open to the periodic table.

"It says for the base we need to make a solution of twenty-five moles of chloroquine and fifty grams of sodium with a volume of fifteen milliliters," Bexley reads from my dad's notebook. "So we just mix it up, right?"

"I wish. We have to calculate the molarity, and then we have to heat it up to increase the solubility and a whole lot of other stuff that's not really fun," I say.

Bexley frowns. "Oh great." She flips through the next few pages of the book, wide-eyed. "How many steps are there for making the base?"

"Forty-three or something," I say, taking out a few sheets of scrap paper. I write down the molar masses and start adding them up with a calculator.

Bexley takes a pencil from the table. "Can't we just look up the answers?"

"Sure, go ahead," I say.

Bexley glances around the table. "Wait, how?"

"That would be the problem," I say.

Bexley sighs. "Ugh, I wish we could use the internet. But of course, that would be way too helpful."

"It's okay, I've already done this once before," I say.

"I wish there was more information in here," Bexley says, turning through the book.

I lay a hand on the extensive, annotated notes left behind for me. "My dad left all this. I'm thankful for that. And anyway, this wasn't written for a teen to follow. There are obviously gonna be some obstacles."

"I don't know how you do this," Bexley says, daunted. "I would have given up a while ago."

I shrug and stare back at my calculations. I've wanted to give up. A lot.

Bexley tops off the alcohol in the burner and takes out a lighter. She tries it once and fails to get a flame. "Do you actually like this stuff? You seem to know what you're doing."

"Yeah, I guess. Not all of it, definitely. Honestly, I used to like science a lot more until now," I say. Dad's a scientist and Mom's a math tutor, so I've been surrounded by academics my entire life. Bexley clicks the lighter again.

"Well, I kind of hate this. But it is more fun when it's not a homework assignment. And you have someone to do it with," Bexley says, trying and failing with the lighter.

"Need help?" I ask, dropping my pencil on the table.

She rolls her eyes and tosses me the lighter. "Something's wrong with it. I swear I know how to use a lighter."

I successfully light the alcohol burner on my first attempt. "Yeah, some faulty lighter."

Bexley glowers. "Whatever."

I finish the molarity conversion and find a stirring rod. I hand it to Bexley and go to the vial rack to find the ingredients we need.

"Who thought it was a good idea to make a glass stick and expect it not to get broken?" Bexley asks, holding the long, fragile stirring rod carefully. "It just wants to get dropped."

"Certain chemicals will affect metal and wood's too porous, so it has to be glass," I say. "I've already broken two, though."

I take out a beaker and measure the specific amount of water, salt, and zinc in a volumetric flask. Bexley fills an Erlenmeyer flask with three milliliters of dexamethasone. Suddenly, an idea pops into my head.

"Bexley, who was your friend? What was his name?" I ask.

She tilts her head. "His name is Isaiah."

9
ISAIAH: HOPE, HELP, AND FEAR

I wander down the cold, straight hallway. The Infirmary is a prison. The world inside is a mental cage. The other patients are either terrible or trying to commit as much good works in their final days as possible. Some people are crying all the time. Some are mean. There are also smokers, addicts, and alcoholics. They're experiencing cold-turkey withdrawal. Dad shares a room with a chain-smoker. He said that the first weeks were really bad. I guess maybe the fact that those people don't have access to their vices is good long-term. I heard there's a psychiatric unit in the Double Guard, too. It makes sense given the Mordolus targeted all medical facilities first. Including institutions. The prisoners? They ended up here too. Sometimes it's not just the Mordolus I fear. It's the other patients. I've come up with a collection of truths to remind myself. It helps me not lose faith. *God is good. He saved me. This is His will. Christ is my hope. I will make it to where He wants me.*

I get to my room. Reece is waiting for me.

"How'd it go?" he asks.

"Fine," I answer. Reece doesn't have any siblings. He grew up with a lot of pets. Apparently, his mom had a thing for animals with disabilities. We had a dog, an old beagle. A few days after my parents were gone, he ran away chasing a truck and never came back. He was a pretty stupid dog, but he still warned us every time the Hunters were out. It's weird, but Reece sort of has the mannerisms of a dog. It's the way he stares at people and follows me around. Like one of those gangly street dogs. Head always low, taking in everything.

"How are we splitting it up?" I ask, walking over to my bed and reaching under it.

"I don't want to go to the children's section. It's kind of spooky there. And dangerous." Reece says.

"Okay," I agree, pulling out our secret supply. "I'm not afraid, I'll go. You take the unrestricted section."

"How many are left?" he asks.

I drop the tiny cardboard box of medications on the table and open it. Only a few doses and syringes are left. After work, research, and carefully stealing supplies, Bexley and I collected a lot of medicine. We read medical articles we stole from the office. Observation helped too. We made mixtures of some of them. Mom helped with instruction since she's a pharmacist. We couldn't meet her often. Mom disapproves of breaking the rules. She doesn't like that I consistently pilfer the medical supply room. Me and Bexley have a secret plotting area behind some storage shelves in the unrestricted areas. We haven't been able to grab any more medicines. Our supplies are low.

"Not enough," I report.

I'm glad to have Reece here. He's like a brother. Being completely alone would suck. Sometimes I don't realize how much has changed or how much I miss my family. But I have hope for something to get better. This can't be the end for us.

The medicines that they give here don't really help much. All they offer are insufficient doses of over-the-counter medicines like pain relievers, decongestants, and fever reducers. The Virus needs something more. If I noticed, you'd think the Mordolus would, too. I'm a bright kid, but still. I thought it would be good to try chloroquine and oseltamivir. Those are some of the ingredients from the antidote I remembered. Using those with a combination of magnesium, zinc, and diphenhydramine, we made something that seems to help. I give half of the remaining medications to Reece. Sometimes I forget how risky it is to do things like this, but I won't stop.

I head down the hallway until I get to Room 12, resisting the urge to deliver what is left to my parents. I gotta focus on the worst off. I open the door slowly, scanning for anyone coming. Inside, I see the dark-haired boy lying there, unconscious. He's about thirteen, maybe older. I don't know his name.

I shut the door quietly behind me and walk to the bed. Every time I come, he's got more needles in his arms. The air is still and silent. It's eerie. I get out one of the syringes. It's the same concoction we give everyone else, but he's in no state to be taking a pill. Nothing in his pale, freckled face suggests he even knows I'm here. He's not the only one like this. There were two others in this room, but they've been gone for a week. I guess they were taken to hospice. Unconsciousness is the end stage. It can last weeks depending on the person's immunity. Sometimes people just shut down to fight the Virus.

I hate this part. It makes me so nervous. Reece refuses to use needles. I won't let him either. Reece is young. So am I, but I'm more mature.

I remove the cap and plunge it into his shoulder. At first, he would whimper or stir when I stabbed him with an injection. Now, I get nothing. He's so emotionless. I turn and leave as soon as I can. I'd never seen someone almost dead until I came to the Infirmary. I constantly remind myself to be thankful I'm the one giving out medicine, not receiving it. This boy could die any day. I'm surprised he's still alive. I doubt it has anything to do with the medications anyone gives. I think it's merely providence.

I sneak down the hallway. After two more stops, I head down to the children's section. It's hard to get in there since it's super guarded. Parents and family members attempt to break in and see the children all the time. I stop a few turns from the entrance. I need a plan. Should have thought this through earlier. I'm out in the open, so I quickly step into a trashed storage closet. I need time to think.

Surrounded by random cleaning supplies—which they need to use more often—I get an idea. It's better than nothing. I quickly stash the medications behind a shelf and exit the closet. I run back to the unrestricted area and toward the place I stole my phone earlier. I call it the Belongings Place. I head to the left. The hall opens into a wide room. The space has a few chairs and a desk. At the desk is a Mordolus member, adorned in a classic, black uniform. She takes the next patient in the short line. I quickly take my place behind her.

In front of me, a woman has a very heated argument with the guard.

"We've checked, and it's been deemed dangerous," the guard says.

"Dangerous? How could my glasses be dangerous?! I can barely see!" the woman fumes. After she starts throwing around names for the Mordolus, one of the guards escorts her back to her room.

"Name?" the person at the desk asks.

I step forward. "Brooks," I say.

"And what do you want back?"

"I want my rings. There should be two. Silver."

"Rings," the guard repeats gruffly. "I'll check."

I watch the guard walk through the door. There are two doors to the room where they keep belongings: that one and the one I discovered earlier. The only camera is at the nearest door, so here I'm safe. Hesitantly, I walk to the other side of the desk. I need the keys. Chances are that the guard will have one for the children's section. If I can find them.

The guard will return at any moment. I find nothing. *She must be carrying them.* I lean on the wooden desk and wait until the door opens again. I note her returning a set of keys to her left pocket. Perfect.

"There are no rings," the guard says. Anger burns inside me. I remind myself that isn't the reason I came, just a distraction. But my parents' wedding rings are gone. They gave them to me before they got captured so they wouldn't be lost. I still had them when I got caught. Since they had some value, they ended up stolen and are now Morzanna's. A lady I talked to here once told me Morzanna sells all the valuables she's stolen from homes and people secretly to other countries.

"Okay," I say, lingering for a second. "Can you take me back to my room? I don't remember the way."

The guard considers me for a second. "Alright."

Confidence surges inside me. I know I can get the keys now. Unfortunately, I quickly lose the feeling. She calls someone else to take me. Of course, the guard can't just leave. But now I have no idea who will come or where they'll have their keys. I'm still thinking it over when a guard arrives.

"Do you know your room number?" the guard asks blankly. I nod and tell her.

"Okay, come on," I'm told.

She starts to lead me back. I intentionally walk close to her. This is my only chance, but uneasiness nags me. I stray slightly behind. I make a quick analysis. I have an idea of where the keys would be, but there's room for error. I take a breath to calm my nerves. *Please, God, let me get these keys.* As we turn the corner, I take action.

I plunge my hand into her pocket. My fingers graze cool metal. I quickly draw the keys from her pocket. She doesn't seem to notice. I was right. I figured that since the guard opened the door with the right hand, she must be a righty. So, the key would probably be in a right pocket. She seems protective of her jacket by the way she always straightens it. I also noticed she kept a notebook in the topmost pocket, so the keys must be in the right bottom. I waited until she brushed by the wall so she would be less likely to notice.

Instantly, I hide the keys in my fist, feeling the cold bite of the metal. I slip them into my pocket.

When we get back to my room, I thank the guard honestly. As soon as she leaves, I check to make sure one of the keys is for the children's section. It is.

I make my way back to the children's section. I retrieve the medications from the closet, hiding them in my shirt, pockets, and shoes.

I head toward the door and unlock it. It's exciting. I live for adventures.

I'm immediately met with children's cries. Every inch of me wants to turn and leave. Instead, I stealthily tread down the hall. My heart races. I reach the room I'm looking for and listen to make sure no guards or nurses are inside before stepping in. The room is relatively small, but several children share it. It's bland. There's really nothing to occupy them. A few even share tiny beds. I get the attention of one of the children.

The five-year-old boy gallops over to me. "Isaiah!"

"Hey, Axly!" I say quietly, picking him up.

He smiles at me, and I set him down on one of the beds. His eyes are tired. He's gotten worse lately. All the medications I've tried so far haven't seemed to improve anything. I'm praying this one will.

"I'm sorry I haven't visited in a while. It's been dangerous," I explain. Axly looks at me with as much understanding as a five-year-old can give.

"No needles?" he asks hopefully. He stares up at me through his dark mop of curls. His sorrel eyes are wide.

"No needles. I told you those are never for you," I assure, handing him two tablets. It's an ibuprofen and molnupiravir combination that Bexley and I put together. I try to memorize the names of the medications. My mom would be proud.

I'm careful to be quiet. And aware. Every second is a risk. A couple of the other kids crowd around me.

"Are you leaving?" a girl Axly's age asks.

"Don't go, Isaiah!" Axly pleads innocently. "The other kids are sick too, and all the adult people are mean. I don't like it here."

"I'm sorry. I can only stay for a minute," I say, conflicted. I recognize the calling to help. At the same time though, I really don't want to get caught.

"I miss my parents. And my sister," Axly says quietly, clinging to my hand. "I don't know when they'll find me. My sister is the best. I hope she's looking for me."

"I'm sure she is, and I bet she misses you just as much. They'll find you. And you'll get better," I say. Axly presses his face against my arm. His feverish cheek is hot on my skin. *God, please don't let Axly die.*

"I'm scared," Axly says. "The other kids too. They don't have anyone. I want my mom and dad." His lip quivers and tears spring into his eyes. I sit down and pull him onto my lap. I hold him tight. Axly's right. These kids. All of them. They're breaking. Sometimes I tell them about Christ. They're young, but they need hope just as much.

"I've gotta go. But I'll come back soon," I say a minute later, addressing each of the children. "Remember, this visit is our secret. If the nurses find out I can't come back."

I get up to leave. I hate it. Axly begs me to stay, and I wish I could. I wish I could help him get better, along with all the other children.

I carefully leave the room, slipping into the hallway. I follow it a few feet before an abrupt turn, leading into a wider hall. I quietly jog down the dingy, tile floor to the door. I frantically start to unlock it. I hear footsteps behind me as I throw open the metal door and run. I pass numerous rooms, as well as a few locked storage rooms, the closet I hid in, and the hall that leads to the Emergency Care. Once I'm back in the unrestricted areas, I see the smaller hallway that leads to the entryway and the Hopeful Rooms. It's so loud. My head starts to ache, which happens a lot now with the Virus. I pass signs for the Double Guard, thinking of Bexley. I've never tried to sneak in. The Double Guard might be my limit. It has ominous, thick metal doors. After Bexley was put in the Double Guard, I never saw her. But we left notes for each other. We slid them under the Double Guard door at exactly ten when Bexley got taken to her daily medical check-ins. I guess that should have warned me how sick she was. One day, she just disappeared. I used to pray every day for her. I unintentionally gave up and stopped. *God, don't let me keep giving up. Help me to have faith.*

I pause by the general medical center and secretly drop the used needles in the biohazard box. Then I head back.

Along the way to my room, I drop the stolen keys. The guard will suspect me if the keys aren't found. If that happens, I'm going to be in major trouble. It would be so helpful to have a set of keys, but it's not worth going to the Double Guard for.

The room is only a short distance further. Reece is back. I stop abruptly in the doorway. Reece sits on his bed with a horrified look.

"Reece?" I ask, running over to him. "What happened?" I say, more urgently. My mind already dives into awful scenarios.

Reece looks up at me, panicked. "It's your mom."

10
REECE: DISCOVERIES IN DARKNESS

I waited half an hour for Isaiah to come back. "I knew you didn't want me to take medicine to your parents since they're not too sick, but I got worried about them the more I thought, so I went anyway. But your mom is gone," I explain. "I don't know what happened."

Isaiah looks at me, his eyebrows knitted with concern.

"What? She just wasn't there?" he asks, wavering. "She had no appointments. She's been off the recreational activities schedule for weeks. Mom doesn't just leave her room."

I nod, having already thought through all the possibilities about a hundred times. "I asked everyone if they'd seen her, and they hadn't. Your dad's in recreational activities so I couldn't ask. Her roommate said she was acting weird, but she fell asleep. When she woke up, your mom was gone. I searched the check-in area too," I say.

Isaiah paces the room a few times. He runs his hand through his wild, blond hair.

"You know what that means, Isaiah," I finally say.

He shakes his head. "No, not always." A few strides later he bitterly kicks the bed frame. "How did this happen? A few hours ago, she was fine!"

I choose silence, observing the situation.

"We have to go find her," Isaiah announces a minute and several fiercely deep breaths later. I stand up, my face growing hot with nervousness. *How are we going to find her?* It's probably going to be dangerous. I'm not going to say anything and for once going to take a risk and try to be brave for Mrs. Brooks.

I know Isaiah and I are thinking the same thing: she could be dead. That's what happens when someone disappears in the Infirmary. There's always a chance though. At least, that's what Isaiah tells me. He's always more hopeful, valiant, and logical than me. When I think about it a lot, I'm envious. I'm just the kid who's afraid of everything.

With a deep breath, I follow Isaiah out the door and toward Mrs. Brooks' room. Isaiah seems not to care at all about caution right now, and it scares me almost as badly as his mom going missing.

We're going to get caught. We're going to die. The annoying thoughts assault my mind, bringing a chilling breeze of unease.

Three corridors and five turns down the hallway, we make it to Mrs. Brooks' room. Isaiah's brief investigation confirms my story. She still isn't here, and there are no clues to where she is. Isaiah begs his mom's roommate, the one who gave me the information earlier, for answers.

"I don't know. I suspect she left on her own because I would have awakened during a removal. It was all so sudden. Leona seemed to be in fair health earlier," the woman says. She's older than Mrs. Brooks, or maybe it just seems like it because she's gray-haired and sort of wrinkly. "If you continue searching for her, be careful, or you'll both end up in the Double Guard, and that would be worse for your mother than whatever's happened," she warns.

"What now?" I ask quietly as we step outside the room.

Isaiah scans the hallway before answering. "That wasn't exactly helpful. We just have to start looking. She could be anywhere. We need to check the ICU and Emergency Care."

"What are you two doing over here?" a voice behind us demands. I quickly turn around. One of the nurses approaches. We can't feign much since the rooms are roughly arranged by age, and even Isaiah wouldn't dare try to get away with telling them we're forty-five. Patients are expected to stay in their rooms after 8:00 p.m.

"We were hungry," Isaiah says coolly. He's good—my plan was to bolt and find somewhere we could hide for the rest of eternity.

"Starving," I add, nodding quickly. The nurse promptly checks his watch.

"You should have gotten dinner an hour ago," the nurse says suspiciously.

"We're growing kids," Isaiah replies innocently.

"You can't be roaming around here unless you're accompanied. No lingering near the other rooms. If you need something, go to the check-in area. The kitchen is closed now, so you'll have to wait until morning. Come on, I'll take you back. What's your room number?" he asks.

We let him take us back to Room 69. On the way, we're lectured about the rules of leaving our room. We're only allowed in the check-in area or Belongings Place, unless escorted by a nurse or guard. Even in the unrestricted area, there's no visiting other rooms. Restricted areas are always off limits unless our room is located there, and if it is we shouldn't have left our room anyway because they're locked. I'm pretty sure he won't shut up until we get to our room. Too much noise drives me crazy.

"Stay in your room," the nurse says seriously, dropping us off. After he leaves, there's a pause, click, and crinkling sound. I think he's writing something. That can't be good.

"We should wait to make sure he's gone," I say when Isaiah immediately heads for the door again. He sighs and flops on his bed.

About four seconds pass before Isaiah's peeking out the door. "He's gone. Let's go."

"No! He'll still be around," I say. The longer we wait, the drowsier I'm getting. Because of the illness, it's exhausting to do anything now. I'm scared I'll fall asleep any second, and we keep arguing about when it's safe to leave. Isaiah thinks he's significantly wiser and more mature than me, which isn't completely wrong, but he's so reckless sometimes.

"Come on, Reece. It's been ten minutes. We'll be fine. Stay if you want, I'm going to find Mom," Isaiah says.

I shake my head to clear the jadedness. "Whatever. I'll come."

We head out the door and sneak toward the intensive care unit.

"What if she's not there either?" I ask abruptly. Isaiah stops and looks at me for a second with an unreadable expression. He never answers. It was a stupid question with really only one awful answer.

We carefully make our way through the Infirmary, passing by the children's section and heading toward the entryway. I grow more nervous the closer we get.

Isaiah takes me down past the restricted areas. I've only been beyond the permitted barriers twice—both times with Isaiah, who ducks under the roped-off section undeterred. Luckily, it's late so there aren't as many guards or nurses out managing and monitoring patients, and none performing any appointments.

Eventually, the hallway opens up into an airy walkway with two large doors in the middle. We reach the door, behind which nurses scramble around and voices murmur. The intensive care unit.

"How are we going to get in there without getting caught?" I ask, staring through the small, rectangular window on the door.

"I don't know. Look for a safe way in," Isaiah says, gazing around the hall. I peer through the glass a bit longer. Across the spacious room inside, there's a door. One of the nurses walks out of it, and I discover the room is for storing extra medical equipment, bedding, and medication. I look back at the beds and cringe at the sight. Nurses attend to the coughing, motionless, seizing, and deteriorating people.

There are a few dividers that cut the room into four different sections. The nurses move around blankly, and I wonder how they can possibly be so dead to all the, well, death. Actually, it makes sense that they'd be numb after exposure to those horrible things.

I observe that there aren't many nurses for the number of patients—they're probably overwhelmed right now.

"I have an idea," I say, pulling Isaiah through the doors as the nurse walks past. We duck into the dark corner beside the door. "It's pretty stupid though."

"Those ones usually work," Isaiah whispers, looking a little shocked that I dragged him inside. Honestly, so am I.

"We need to get to that door," I say, pointing. "We make our way to the back, and we can hide behind those barriers. The first chance we get, run into that room. It's just storage."

"That could work," Isaiah says.

Our entire conversation is muffled by constant noise. We stand there in the shadowy corner until a few of the nurses walk into the storage room again, leaving only three nurses in the entire unit. The closest section is clear.

We creep across the room, scanning each bed for Mrs. Brooks and ducking behind them whenever a nurse is nearby. This is the most terrifying thing I've ever done.

Suddenly, something crashes. Instantly, Isaiah pulls me beside one of the beds. A nurse walks by, chattering on her phone and dragging along a cart of supplies. I lean closer to the side of the bed. The occupant coughs violently.

"I didn't see her," I whisper, glancing around the room. "What are we going to do?"

"Since she's not here, we need to get out and check the Emergency Care," Isaiah murmurs.

I nod and look beyond the bed.

"Come on, let's go," he says, crawling out from our hiding spot. We barely get it to the storage room before a nurse enters from the main door. My legs are so wobbly.

Isaiah opens the door and I follow him inside, glancing around the room. There are no nurses in here. A bunch of boxes and cabinets reach to the top of the low ceiling, cluttering the entire space.

"We almost didn't make it," I comment, shaken up.

"Yeah, just wait til they check the camera footage," Isaiah says. I think he meant it as a joke, but I don't find it funny at all.

There is another door in the back, and I go over and slowly open it. It leads into a clear, empty corridor I don't recognize. Strange hallways are better than getting caught. I open the door wider and let Isaiah have a look.

"Cool," he says. "Let's try it out and hope it gets us to Emergency Care."

It's like all other halls here: white, cold, and foreboding. Eventually, the hallway splits with one way leading to the left and the other to the right.

"Which way?" I ask, a sense of dread growing. Isaiah examines both routes.

"This way," he says confidently, gesturing to the left.

A few minutes later, we stop at a corner. Voices come from far behind us, meaning we need to hurry, and closer ones echo down the hall to our right. Isaiah notices too and runs back a few paces to find the source, while I peek ahead.

The hallway opens out into a large room that appears to connect many other halls. A few Mordolus members talk around a desk in the left-center of the area. It sort of reminds me of the check-in area, but different, almost like a Mordolus meeting room.

A television stands on the desk. Senneforte's delegate, Devyn Hettler, is portrayed on the screen, speaking. Morzanna was at least smart enough to leave each of Willowmire's five delegates alone, even Delegate Hettler, who manages the most affected province. The scene appears to be new. Hettler is in some dark, clean room. Her long, black hair is slicked into a perfect ponytail, and her dark eyebrows give her a fierce look, reflecting her tone.

"Morzanna should not be able to do this to Senneforte! She's destroying the province and hurting innocent people! I can say with pride that it was NOT my vote that gave her the right to launch the Mordolus! Whoever did should be locked up, alongside the Queen!" Hettler speaks so furiously, it almost startles me. The weird part is that all the delegates are so young. None of them are over thirty after a mass assassination during one of their meetings five years ago and all the delegates had to be replaced. Being a Willowmire delegate is a lifelong position unless one is removed by simple majority, in which the monarch and delegates have equal voting weight. Delegates start young. I always thought it was strange, but it's so that elections occur less often. We use federalism, so ruling works differently for province-specific issues. Each delegate has a group of ten elected associates with equal votes that decide on the delegate's proposed decisions for their province. Since Willowmire has such a short past, I heard a lot about the new government formation in history class. Honestly, history is the most interesting subject.

One of the nurses promptly turns off the screen and Delegate Hettler disappears. The delegates can't do anything on their own, but it's comforting to know Hettler still protests against Morzanna.

Isaiah jogs back and asks, "What do you see?"

"There's an open room and more hallways. A few guards and nurses are talking around a desk," I answer.

"So…we can wait and hope that they leave, or we could run," Isaiah whispers flatly. I nod. Tempestuous fear whirls inside me, but I know we have to find his mom. She's like my mom, too.

When I came here, my mom was dying. We were separated immediately like it is for all children since they categorize by age. I didn't hear anything from or about her for two weeks. But then I did— I found her name on the burial list. It was…intense. A couple of days later I met Isaiah and the Brookses. Isaiah tries everything possible to see his parents, and when they found out about me and what happened, they included me in their family meetings. If I couldn't or wouldn't come, they would write me notes when they could get paper or send messages with Isaiah. Over time, the Brookses sort of temporarily adopted me.

"Let's run," I say. It's the best plan—also my least favorite. "I think they saw us back there in the ICU anyway. We'll go down that hall." I point to the third hall to the left.

I don't really comprehend what I just agreed to do until Isaiah gets ready to run. Then, we sprint.

We could just pretend we're headed somewhere we are allowed to go, like the check-in area, but I've never been here before and I'm pretty sure this is in the restricted areas. We certainly can't stop and ask.

I fix my eyes ahead. Instantaneously, footsteps resound behind us, but I don't dare look. We reach the hallway, and it splits. I try to make out what the signs read. One is labeled *Rooms 250-280*, and the other is marked *Emergency Care*.

"Left," Isaiah says, and we turn down another unfamiliar hall.

It's darker and sort of eerie, but I don't have time to do a thorough inspection. They're right behind us. My legs burn from all the running, and I just want to collapse. This is so nerve-racking, I might pass out. I need to spot somewhere to hide.

As we turn the corner, there's a set of open doors, leading to another hallway. If my directional sense is right, it probably goes back toward the unrestricted areas. My head screams, *Run away, find somewhere to hide! Ms. Leona's already dead, and you're going to get caught! ESCAPE.* It's the usual cowardly thoughts that plague me.

Beside the door, there's a dark, narrow space between the doorway, some shelves, and the wall. It's barely visible, and there is just enough room for us to hide. I dash down the hall and pull Isaiah with me into the small hiding spot.

An outline is cut into the wall a few feet back, hidden by the doorway and partially blocked by shelves. Could it be a door? No handle. I put both hands on it and push gently. It swings open freely. We dash inside, closing the door behind us.

It leads to a strangely quiet hall. The lights are all super dimmed and warm-colored, and a few of them even flicker. The ceilings are normal height now. A silent golden murkiness cloaks everything. I don't like this.

"Abandoned passageway," I mumble. The whole empty hall is lined with doors. Isaiah and I hide in the cave of the doorway.

Footsteps and voices echo from the hall, but soon the only sound is us panting. My legs are so tired I collapse onto the floor. Isaiah does the same.

He catches his breath. "Good idea, I didn't even see this place." I nod, still out of breath. I carefully listen one more time, making sure they're gone.

"Let's go, we've got to find your mom," I finally say and stand up. "Besides, this place is sort of creepy."

"Yeah." Isaiah stands too, looking around with a peculiar spark. I really don't like that look. "But I'm kind of curious about this. Why is there a hidden, abandoned hallway? Let's just go a little further and see what we find," he says.

Isaiah always reminds me of a sailor; sturdy, tanned, confident, a bit prideful, audacious, and very adventurous. But now is not the time to get distracted.

"It could be dangerous. I don't think it's a good idea. We need to find your mom," I say, glancing around suspiciously.

Isaiah gives me a pleading look, begging me to give into his daring impulse. We haven't had any *good* excitement in a long time. I scowl.

"Okay, fine. But we have to hurry," I say, following Isaiah further into the darkness.

11

ISAIAH: TUNNELS AND TURMOIL

Lights are out further down the shadowy passage. Cobwebs drape between every corner. Shadows twist into shapes and feed my imagination in good and bad ways. It's thrilling.

"You go first. If there's a murderer, let me know, and I'll be going," Reece whispers.

Doors line the hallway. A few stand half-open. The rooms are trashed. Cabinets are open and papers are strewn across the overturned tables. The floor is littered with broken scientific tools and shattered glass.

"Whoa, what happened in here?" Reece asks, stepping inside one.

"No idea," I say. We wander through the room. "There are lots of footprints."

"Murderer footprints," Reece comments. I roll my eyes.

"Well, at least it looks like it's been a while since anyone's been here," I say, noting the dust on the windowsill and the empty feeling.

Reece traipses over to one of the cabinets standing ajar in the corner. He opens it. It's bare. Except shards of dark metal corroding the bottom. Rust grows over the edges and taints the shiny metal.

"Maybe this was just a storage room," I say, picking up some of the shiny metal. It smells strongly of iron. "With strange metal stuff."

"Yeah, but what about the footprints? They're muddy. Why is everything so dirty?"

I look around, noticing Reece is right. The floor is covered in dirt and rubble and even the handles to the doors are mud-covered.

"We should keep looking," I say, massaging my forehead. I forgot to take any ibuprofen.

We leave the room and continue our exploration. More mud paints the floor, glittered with metal from the cabinet.

Reece looks in the next room. He cautiously takes a step back. "Okay, that's creepy."

"What is it?"

The floor of the next room is splattered with something that looks suspiciously bloodlike.

"Is that blood?" Reece asks uneasily.

"I really hope not," I respond, closing the door and backing away. I feel sick just thinking about it. We decide against looking in too many more rooms.

"Maybe we should leave," Reece says, rocking. "It's really sketchy in here. I just know there's going to be a murderer somewhere."

He could be right, but it just feels so abandoned. I don't easily back down from an adventure. We should keep exploring and see where this leads. We could have uncovered a new mystery in the Infirmary. The key to figuring out what's going on. I gesture for Reece to follow me.

Taking the straight hallway, we come to a few flights of stairs leading downward. I can't see the end of it. It's like the mouth of a monster. Dark. Humid. Evil. *So adventurey.* Excitement kills any fear like sand on fire. Water drips somewhere hidden among the shadows. Every step we take, it gets hotter.

"Why would they abandon this part?" Reece asks quietly. "They're always complaining about not having enough space."

"Maybe they don't know about it. It was hidden," I say, barely seeing the ground in front of me. A few steps further, I notice something strange: the ground isn't hard marble anymore but softer and gravelly. It's also leveled out. I bend down. It's like dirt. I look at Reece, who stands a few feet behind me. I can barely see his silhouette.

"What is it?" he asks.

"Come here," I call. I run my hand along the wall. It's dirt too.

"That's so weird. It's like a tunnel," Reece says. "This is just strange."

"Does explain the mud. This has to be why it isn't used," I say.

"Yeah, but why would this be here to begin with?" Reece points out. "And where does it lead?"

It's cold again in the tunnel. The ground slopes further down. A draft from below blows through my blond hair. It's pitch black.

"Let's go back now," I say. Fear rips through me. Something's suddenly off.

"Yeah. We shouldn't be down here," Reece agrees. He feels the change too.

Something sounds like footsteps. Reece's murderer theories might not be so far off.

"You hear that?" I ask, but Reece has already headed for the stairs. We silently climb the staircase. Soon, we duck out of the hidden door.

"So, I guess it's this way," I say, pointing to the left once we are back in the hallway outside our new discovery. Worry starts to seep back into my brain.

"Yeah," Reece responds. "We should hurry."

I hope Mom's there. *Please, please let her be okay.* Our exploration served as a good distraction. I'm not sure how I got so caught up, though. In the bland, quiet hall again, all I can think about is my family. Reece sinks into a thoughtful silence. Meanwhile, I turn to my only means of peace: prayer. *Please don't let Mom be dead. Just…let everything be okay.*

We have to hope. It's the only thing keeping us alive. The hopeful are the ones who will escape, the ones who will find a cure. The ones who have a chance of survival. I just pray my confidence isn't deceptive.

Following the long hallway, I glance up and see another sign pointing to Emergency Care. We're back in the unrestricted areas, but we sure aren't supposed to be around here this late. I remember our warning from the nurse earlier about the rules.

The lights above us dim. The signal that it's midnight. I'm surprised I'm not tired. Reece doesn't look good, though. He might fall asleep standing any second.

Five minutes later, we finally arrive at Emergency Care. This is one place I've never been before. I see two doors. Distressed voices and clattering create familiar background noise. I look through the window on the door. I don't see my mother from there. I really don't want to search through a unit again.

"Isaiah," Reece whispers, pointing to a paper listed on the wall. I walk over. It's a list of all the patients in Emergency Care. I hurriedly scan the list. There's a chance she could be somewhere else. I don't see anyone with the last name, "Brooks". She's not there. Neither is anyone else in my immediate family.

She's not in her room, not in the intensive care unit, not in the Emergency Care, and she doesn't leave her room unescorted except to meet me. That only leaves one option.

"What does this mean?" Reece says quietly.

"I-I don't know," I say, trying to calm myself. *Think logically.* There has to be another explanation. "I hope it means she's somewhere else, safe, or something. Just not…gone."

He knows what I mean. "Isaiah, what if she is?"

I take a deep breath. I pride myself on always being in control. Well, I sorta pride myself in everything, and it's a little bit of a problem. I always like to fix things. But right now, there's nothing I can do. I can't fix this. I'm not in control. It's really testing my faith. "I don't want that to happen. But it will be okay."

"Okay?" Reece asks, horrified. "If she's dead?"

"I have hope," I say. "If she's dead, it'll be okay. I'm trusting in God. Death isn't the end. Mom knows that. I know she'll be okay, even if…that happens. God doesn't promise ease in life, but He does give us hope in death."

Reece stares at me, wide-eyed. "I'm sure she's alive. We'll find her."

"Let's check her room just one more time?" I ask. Reece nods. Each step is agonizing. This is the last place we can check. But weirdly, there's a calmness about it.

I recognize the halls now, so we're in a safer place. Normally, we would see other patients or some nurses. At night it's quiet. We aren't the only ones who break the rules to visit family. As long as they don't catch you, you can do it. Mom and Dad meet up daily since their rooms are close. They've never been spotted.

We reach my mom's room. I take a deep breath before reaching for the handle. Pushing on the door, I close my eyes. I'm afraid to open them, but finally I do.

I sigh. Mom's back! She's pale and tired but alive. I watch her sleep and see her breathing, even though it's shallow. I want to hug her, and I don't usually because *eww*. I don't wanna wake her, though. She needs as much rest as possible. My mom's strong. I mean, she has to be to keep a daughter like Ele in line. Seeing her here so weak—it's wrong. I just wish she could tell me it'll be okay—to remind me again, no matter what, God's in control.

"They brought her back half an hour ago," the roommate says quietly. She sits up from her bed. "I've been waiting for you to come back. I knew you would. I asked, and the nurse told me they found her in the hallway having a seizure. They took her to check up on everything and gave her some new medication. It was probably caused by the Maraloxis Virus, but they told me your mom's okay for now."

I nod, feeling a mix of emotions. "Thank you."

I quietly shut the door and smile at Reece, letting him know she's fine.

"Hey, what are you doing?" a voice, again, says behind us. It's the same place, but a different person this time. It's one of the night guards. The night guards wear dark uniforms like the other guards. They have 'NIGHT GUARD' sewn in red on the back. I have suspicions that they carry weapons somewhere.

I quickly step away from the door, hoping that she didn't see me go inside.

"What are you two doing over here?" the guard repeats impatiently.

"We got lost," Reece says in a strange tone, and I wonder what charade we're going for this time.

"What are your names?" she asks. After we tell her, she checks her paper.

"Your night check-in says you were missing. So, you've been out here for over two hours?" she asks. I nod.

"Yeah. We got lost," I say again.

"Why were you out here?" the guard presses.

"We were hoping to hide. We have recreational activities tomorrow," Reece admits with feigned dismay. The Mordolus knows everyone hates recreational activities.

"You better get back to your rooms now, or I'll schedule you two extra sessions," she says with a scowl. Reece and I both nod.

"Yeah, sorry," I say.

We sprint back to our room. We've gotten stopped twice today. We'll probably get marks for the Double Guard. Six marks for misdemeanors, and we go to the Double Guard.

The trip back drags on. It's almost one in the morning. I'm actually thankful for the Mordolus. They saved my mom's life. If she hadn't been taken to the Infirmary, she might be dead. Confliction visits me about what I've always believed about the Mordolus. *Are they really all bad?*

When we get to our room, the adrenaline wears off. Reece drops into bed and doesn't move again. I fall asleep nearly immediately too. Tomorrow, I'm sure we'll have some other exciting adventure. We always do. But we always manage. Hope really can change things. And real hope only comes from God. He protected Reece, my mom, and me today. God's always in control, no matter how chaotic things seem.

I awake to a loud knock on the door. Sun pours in the lonely window. It must be late. I'm still drained from last night. I pretend I don't hear it. The knocking continues.

"Recreational activities!" someone calls. "We meet at the check-in area in five minutes!"

"Shut up!" Reece groans, rolling out of bed. Tiredness leaves dark marks beneath his eyes. He sleeps a lot of the day and still always seems drowsy. He coughs a lot at night, too.

"It's Tuesday. I thought you made that up yesterday," I say, dragging myself to my feet.

"So did I," Reece says.

The Infirmary has many issues. Recreational activities are one of the major ones, but there are others. Deodorant is not something they have an abundant supply of here. And you can usually only get a shower once a week. It's a bad combination. Food is limited. You get two meals brought per day. If you're well enough, you can go to the kitchen and get a third. It's not really anyone's fault, I guess. There are a ton of people here the Mordolus have to support.

Recreational activities are the last reason I want to get up. Sometimes I guiltily hope I qualify as too sick to participate. We step out the door.

"Do you think they'd notice if we skipped?" Reece asks as we follow the nurse who called us and several other daunted patients to the check-in area. "We could ditch after they write down our names and hide in that one hallway nearby," he suggests.

"I don't think that'd work," I say. "Do you know what it is today?"

"I think it's floors," one annoyed boy, several years older than us, says. He'd clearly been listening to our whole conversation very closely. I hadn't noticed he'd been there. "And if anyone's planning on skipping, I wanna join."

When we arrive at the check-in, we're met with a menagerie of brooms, mops, and other cleaning supplies. He was right.

Unfortunately.

I shake my head, fighting off a migraine. I haven't had anything to eat or drink or had time to ask for headache medicine today. I'm in pain and exhausted. I pick up a broom and think to myself, the *faster we finish, the faster we get to go back to bed.*

"That was the worst session ever," I say when Reece and I return to our room two hours later. I collapse onto my bed. I feel better in our cool, quiet bedroom.

"Agreed. And with whatever-his-name-was, it seemed to last a week!" Reece says with a contemptuous look. "Seriously, no personal space."

"He was nice. It might help if your personal space wasn't a twenty-foot requirement for a stranger," I joke.

Reece rolls his eyes. "Hey, anyone could be a murderer. Strangers are worse, but people in general just get too close." I give him a whatever look, to which he replies, "Well, I'm going back to bed before we face another crazy day."

He's right. We never know what excitement the next day will hold. I'm really hoping tomorrow doesn't involve dirty floors.

12
ELEANORA: THE PLANS

"Get up!" an urgent voice says, and someone excitedly shakes me awake. "Elllllleanora!"

"What?" I mumble, opening my eyes to find a grinning Marie only inches away from my face. I instinctively push her away as bright light from the mid-morning sun cascades from the window and illuminates the room. *It must not be very early.*

"Come on, Eleanora, get up! We've got to work on the plans!" she whispers in my ear. I shield my eyes from the ocular homicidal beams and drag myself up.

"Fine," I groan, much less enthusiastic than earlier to start scheming, exhaustion still tugging at my consciousness. "What time is it?"

"I think it's almost ten," Marie says with a bounce. "I literally almost died waiting for you. I've been up since like five. I've been SOOO bored."

Standing, I plod over to the small mirror on the wall, and I'm startled at my own reflection. My hair is in knots, my clothing is dirty and wrinkled, and my wrists are still wrapped from the day before. As a person who cares something about their appearance, I am troubled that this is the effect of only a few days away from home. It doesn't help that half the mirror is shattered. *What happened to me? I look like a freak.*

"They brought you some clothes and food," Marie states as I inspect my current attire. She points to the table in the corner, jumping up and down. "Make it fast, I can't wait any longer to do something. I'll be doing laps to get some energy out!"

"Okay," I say, walking over and staring at the dry toast on my plate. There's also a cup of something else unidentifiable. I'd rather not find out what it is, so, instead, I pick up the clothes and step inside our tiny bathroom, which has no mirror or bath.

The top provided is a little tight and an unflattering shade of green, and the black pants are several sizes too large. I keep on my ankle boots and discard the flip-flops that are clearly way too small. I do my best with my hair and put back on my sapphire blue headband. *At least it's better than before. Although, I wish I could have a shower. Wait, do we even get showers here?* It's a valid concern.

"Hey, do you have a nickname or something? Eleanora is a looong name. I can make one up if you want because long names confuse me. Like Bella's real name wasn't actually Bella. I gave her that name because her's was too long," Marie says, wildly sprinting back and forth across the small span of the room.

"Ele," I reply, walking out of the bathroom. "Not many people actually call me Eleanora—just Ele."

"Oh great!" she says, flopping onto the spare bed, out of breath.

"So, where do we start?" I ask, nibbling on my toast. Marie jumps up with so much energy, I'm surprised she doesn't hit the ceiling. Grabbing my hand, she pulls me once again into the dark closet. Marie dives into the back of the closet, retrieves her papers, and obtains a flashlight from inside one of the cases of a spare pillow on the floor.

"I've already started it," she says, plopping down onto the aforementioned pillow and pointing to one wrinkled paper. The two of us huddle over the pages, Marie opens a homemade folder crafted from thread and two flimsy trays like the ones we received our dinner on last night. She frantically flips through it before adding an extension to the other paper. "It's my best idea yet," she announces.

Except, it's a lot more mumbled because she has the flashlight in her mouth. I consider asking if I can hold it for her, but then decide it is too late—and far too gross.

The path of escape is mapped out, twisting through hallways, each room marked and labeled. I finally have a better idea about the size of the Infirmary; it's absolutely huge. I learn that it is divided into three sections, each functioning on its own with little relation to each other due to the sheer number of people there are to accommodate for. I assume the blank areas identify places Marie has not yet explored, but the map still takes up the whole paper that's at least three times as big as a normal sheet. The drawing is surprisingly detailed; however, that doesn't make the confusing arrows and scribbles any more legible.

"These," Marie points to the maps, "are VERY important. Bella had to steal a lot of information, and there's no way I can remember all of it, so we can't lose these." She squints and points to a section on the map. "What does this say?"

"*Unrestricted areas—secret hallway,*" I read. "So, we get out of our room, then travel down this hallway," I point to the place where the arrows signal a change of direction. "Then we turn here at the check-in area, and head further beyond those first rooms," I say, tracing the rest of the directions. "Marie, why is there a question mark at the end of this path?"

"I've been down here before, but I don't know where it goes." Marie says.

"How do you know there's an exit?" I ask.

"Because I was walking this way to this door while I was down there. There were no guards around or anything. But it was all locked up," she says, gesturing to an invisible barrier.

"But that means that there isn't a place," I say obviously.

"No. The only other door is on this side of the Infirmary. I've seen them taking people past my old room before, a long time ago. They took them to go get signed in. So, they must've come in a different door," Marie explains and points to the question mark. "This one. It makes sense."

"So we don't really know what's there, but we know, allegedly, there's some way to get out," I say, trying not to get lost in the mire of information.

Marie nods.

"That's good, but I have another question: how do we get out of our room and actually make it there?" I ask, my optimism growing.

"I don't know yet, but you can help me!" Marie pipes, setting the book down. She shoves a paper and a pen at me, and I begin to write out what we already have, with Marie clarifying details. I thoughtfully tap the pen against the paper.

"So we're locked in here, and there are cameras. So, if we do get out, we only have several minutes at most until they notice," I guess.

"Yeah," Marie confirms. "Maybe we could get a key. Or we could always knock down a wall or something."

I nod slowly, lost in my thoughts. *Definitely not the wall thing, but a key would work.*

"So who has a key?" I wonder.

"For our room? Only that woman who came last night and the nurses that replace her, and they keep one in their office for emergencies I guess," she replies.

"How do you know that?" I ask.

"Bella told me. She saw a room where they had a bunch of keys with room numbers. I assume they have one for our room too," Marie explains.

"That makes sense, and—" I start, but I'm promptly interrupted. There's a loud commotion outside the room, and Marie instantly signals for me to be quiet.

The door to our room opens abruptly. There's a new vivid fear in Marie's chestnut eyes while she hides the papers under an unfolded sheet and turns off the light.

Is that one of the nurses or guards? Imagine them finding Marie and me in this closet composing blatant plots of insubordination. I'd hate to discover what grave punishment that might illicit! I back further toward the wall and out of the closet's doorway, tugging on a lock of fine hair. Holding my breath, I hear a door shut outside. It's disturbingly quiet, aside from slow dainty footsteps pacing the room then there's a long silent pause.

The closet door opens.

It's not one of the Mordolus standing wide-eyed in the doorway. It's a boy. He seems about Marie's age, which is twelve, and takes a step back almost instantly.

"What are you doing here?" Marie asks. I suspiciously scan the boy's terrified expression.

"What are *you* doing in *here?*" he counters, referring to the fact that we're in a closet.

After Marie crosses her arms in silence, the boy shakes his head and answers. "I'm trying not to get caught," he says, glancing around the room, pale-faced.

"Well, you better hide!" Marie says, pointing at the camera perched above the door before pulling him inside the closet with us. She turns the light back on and slams the door shut.

With three people inside the closet, it's quite crowded, and Marie stands in front of me on one side of the narrow closet, with the taken-aback boy shrinking away on the other.

Marie, poised to lead the interrogation, points the flashlight at him. "So, what were you doing before you came in here? Also, how'd you get the door open?" Marie asks excitedly. The boy nervously crosses his lanky arms.

"I was looking for someone. Then I saw one of the nurses coming so I ran in here," he tells us, fidgeting. "And the door was unlocked from the outside."

"Wait, so is the door unlocked now?" I ask, and he shrugs. I throw open the closet, dash out, and try the door to our room. *Please let it be unlocked.* Despite my hopes, it doesn't open.

"So how am I supposed to get out!?" the boy asks frantically.

"I don't know. I guess they'll see you on the cameras and come get you," Marie says. The boy throws his hands over his face.

"I'm going to get in so much trouble. I shouldn't have come here! Why is everything so dangerous? I don't like dangerous things," he mumbles to himself, hyperventilating.

Marie raises an eyebrow as the boy wrings his hands. "I really need to go. I bet this is going to get me major marks for the Double Guard. This was stupid. Isaiah never gets caught, and the one time I do—"

"Isaiah?!" I interrupt, feeling like my heart nearly leaps out of my chest. "What's his last name?"

"Brooks. Wait, you know Isaiah?" the boy asks, confused.

"He's my brother! Hold on, how do you know him?"

The boy tilts his head. "He's my roommate."

13
REECE: SISTERS AND SOAP

"So you're Ele?" I ask. Isaiah always calls his sister Ele, so for a long time, I didn't even know her name was actually Eleanora. Apparently, she really hates it when people call her Ellie or Ella.

She nods, her long hair dancing. It's several shades darker than Isaiah's but still blond. While Isaiah's are brown and hers are blue, they both have wide, round eyes. They have the same nose too, just Ele's is larger. Because I've seen their parents, I notice the similarities between them. Isaiah looks like their dad and Ele looks like their mom.

"Yes!" Eleanora says. She's tall and willowy; Isaiah's on the short side.

"Where's Isaiah?" she asks.

"I think he went to the children's section," I reply. The other girl perks up.

"The children's section? What's he doing there? How did he get in?" she demands, waving the flashlight at me.

"Isaiah has a talent for going in places without getting caught," I answer with a shrug. I like to rehearse my conversations before I have them, so this experience has not been awesome. "Who are you?"

"I'm Marie. I'm just a random kid," she tells me, shaking her dark curls out of her face. "Who are you?"

"Reece," I say.

"I seriously need to meet Isaiah," Marie says, looking like she's already formulating a plan. Marie's over-the-top excited the whole time and it sort of stresses me out. She gives me, 'I'll be your friend, but I'm unreliable' vibes. Marie's really short, but I think she could take on anyone under fourteen and win. She's one of those small scary people and clearly has little personal space awareness.

"Why were you in the Double Guard to begin with?" Ele asks.

"I'm looking for my dad," I say. That's the only reason I'd ever enter the Double Guard, and honestly it was the most daring thing I've ever done. I'm majorly regretting the decision now and don't know what I was thinking. I didn't find him anyway. I've learned from being friends with Isaiah that bravery and stupidity go hand in hand, and the worst part is they're both contagious. But even Isaiah's never ventured in here. I must be going insane.

"So, do you just hang out in the closet? Because that's abnormal," I say, staying in the depths of the left-side of the closet.

I knew when I walked in someone had to be here; the beds were unmade, and someone had left food on the table. I also noticed that the paper outside said no one was checked out, so the closet was the only logical option.

Eleanora and Marie look at each other for an unusually long second. I start getting real weirded out. Marie leans closer to me.

"You have to promise not to ruin it," she says quietly.

"Okay, sure," I say, backing away from her as far as I can.

"We're planning to escape," she announces brightly.

I almost laugh at her. No one escapes here, and I think it's a dumb idea. "Are you serious?" I ask.

"Umm, dead serious," Marie says, crossing her arms.

"No one's ever gotten out," I say doubtfully. "And there are thousands of people. *And* you're locked in the Double Guard."

"So?" Marie says defensively. "We're still working on it, *obviously*. Ele needs to keep working on a cure. I'm not spending my last days in this stupid place." She throws her arms in the air, gesturing to the whole Infirmary. She grabs some crumpled papers and shoves them at me. "Take a look."

"Where did you get paper from?" I ask. "And the flashlight?"

Marie giggles. "I tore the paper off the back of the mirror. Also, my roommate Bella smuggled some in when she got moved. I found the flashlight in this closet," she tells me while I unfold the pages and stare at the map. Isaiah and I don't even have a closet in our room.

"That's our plan so far," Ele says. "We really are going to try to escape."

Even though I think these two are crazy, the maps and plans ignite something strange inside me. I fold the pages and hand them back to Marie.

"Great, I hope you succeed," I say. "But I really need to leave."

"Okay, so here's my best idea for you," Marie informs me. "Look down so they can't see your face on the cameras, then when they come get you, make a break for it. Don't stop until you get out of the Double Guard."

"Alright," I say, grasping the handle of the closet door shakily.

"Wait!" Ele says, jumping up. "I want to see Isaiah!"

"I'll bring him here soon," I say before thinking over my statement. The thought of coming back to the Double Guard already daunts me, and I wish I could unsay that promise. But I feel bad for Ele and Isaiah; if I had a sibling, I'd probably do anything to find them. "I promise I will," I reiterate despite myself.

The three of us step outside the closet. We wait in silence, and I'm careful to stare at the floor the whole time. *I'll be in trouble for sure.* The more I think about it, the more the floor seems to be whirling, and the less stable my legs feel. My instinct is to hide in the girls' closet for the rest of my life, but despite my fear, I resolve to leave.

A woman opens the door. She has jet-black hair and despite her mask, I can tell she's seriously not happy. I hesitate for less than a second, terror numbing my senses. Then I duck past the angry nurse and sprint as fast as I can.

"Tell my brother I love him!" Ele yells after me. I don't think, I don't breathe; I just run. I panic and, as usual, immediately scout out a hiding place. Marie told me not to stop, but like any sane person, I take the first door I see that has potential.

Soon, I find myself hiding inside a cramped cabinet, surrounded by soap, in the men's shower room.

"I'm going to die, I'm going to die, I'm going to die," I mumble, rocking back and forth.

Outside, I hear running water and the screech of shower curtains, but I think I lost the nurse. I'm freaking out. A fire burns in my cheeks like it always does when I'm scared. I already feel like I'm gonna asphyxiate from the mint-scented soap. Or maybe that's just because of how fast I'm breathing. Like a coward, I stay hidden in the narrow cabinet for nearly an hour. My fears take the reins. I woke up this morning with a sore throat, which means I'm getting worse. I don't want to die here. Finally, the dread that someone's gonna need more soap pushes me to crawl out of my hiding spot. I step out the door and back into the hall.

I instantly wish I was back in the cabinet. The nurse is right in front of me, glowering. She walks over to me and grabs me roughly by the arm. I should have listened to Marie.

As she drags me down the hall, I start to worry that they might not let me go back to my room, among other things. Maybe I'll be stuck in the Hopeful Rooms, or even moved to the Double Guard.

"What were you doing?" the nurse asks. "How did you get in that room?"

I wait silently for a second, trying to formulate the best words to keep me from trouble. I think the truth might be best. "I was looking for my family. I heard someone coming, and then I got locked in. When you came, I got scared and ran into the shower room."

"Don't *ever* do that again, or you'll really get in trouble," she says, glancing around before releasing my arm.

The nurse walks me back to my room. She brings me a different way than I usually go; by the main check-in area then through the hall adjacent to it. The nurse takes me up to the front desk and gets out my paperwork. She writes something on it then turns the page around to show me. There are two more big Xs right under 'Double Guard'. I've got four of them now. It was Isaiah's influence that earned me the first two. Two more marks and I get sent to the Double Guard forever, without Isaiah. Though, he's likely to get sent before me.

The nurse returns my papers, and I glance around the foyer. In the middle of the hall, standing a couple hundred feet inside the main entryway, I see it: a dark colored pillar with a piece of paper pinned up. The paper's edges are torn, and random objects decorate the floor below it, among some fake, faded flowers.

I'll never forget that place. Every day they pin up the names of the dead in their sad attempt at an obituary. The paper only lists the person's name in sorry handwriting. It's the Queen's only recognition for those that are lost.

It's one of the only places we're allowed to go unattended. When I first came to the Infirmary about two months ago, the only thing I really did was check that list. I would visit multiple times a day, every time anxious that I might find a name I recognized. Senneforte's population is small, so I found the names of some people I sort of knew, but never anything more.

I'll never forget the day I saw the worst words I could have ever read.

Alaina Ashford

My mother's dead. It was the worst day of my life. I didn't know where my father was, still don't, and he might even be dead too. It was horrible, and I was sure that soon my name would be on the list, too.

Only several days after that discovery, I got transferred to a different room. They were low on space, so I'd be sharing from then on. I wasn't exactly excited about having to socialize with another human. But then I met Isaiah, and Isaiah had hope. And that changed everything.

I'm very glad when we get to my room and the nurse opens the door. She gives me one last warning look before walking away.

"Reece? Where have you been? It's been three hours!"

I collect myself and turn to Isaiah, smiling.

"You won't believe it," I say, walking over to where he stands. For a second, I consider not telling because I know if I do, I'll have to keep my promise to Ele. And that means going back to the Double Guard. But I can't imagine not telling, living with lying, and the thought that Isaiah and Ele won't ever get to see each other because of me.

"What?" Isaiah asks. "You just got brought back by a nurse. That's never good."

"It is for you. I told you I was looking for dad, so…I went to the Double Guard."

"What? You, *you,* went to the Double Guard?!" Isaiah says. "I honestly don't believe you. And you're acting happy after a nurse returned you. Have you gone insane, Reece?"

"I'm serious, I did go," I say with a shudder. "We'll talk about it later, okay? I have something to tell you."

"Fine," Isaiah says, still shocked. "Go on."

"Someone saw me, and I had to find somewhere to hide, so I ran into one of the rooms because apparently they're unlocked from the outside. When I got there, I didn't see anyone. Then I heard something in the closet," I explain,

"And?" he asks, probably wondering what I'm even talking about and thinking I've finally lost it like some of the other patients. I wait a second for suspense.

"So, I opened the door," I say. "And it was your sister."

He steps back in shock. "What? Ele was there? *Here?* In the Infirmary? In the Double Guard? Are you sure? I didn't even know she was here! Wait, why was she in the closet? It *was* Ele? Are you lying?"

"I don't lie to you," I reply. Isaiah paces our little room, thrilled.

"You saw Ele. She's here," Isaiah says, trying to rationalize. "She's okay?! This is crazy! You can take me to see her?"

"Yeah. She was fine," I answer.

Isaiah sits down on his bed, wide-eyed, with a blank grin. "I'm so happy you found her! Thank you!"

14
GRAYDON: THE MORDOLUS

"Really? Isaiah Brooks?" I ask, shocked to find out Bexley met him at the Infirmary.

Bexley nods. "Yes, how do you know him?"

"He's my best friend," I say. I've known Isaiah and Ele since I was five.

"Oh, that's so cool! What a weird coincidence," Bexley says.

"How'd you meet Isaiah?" I ask, setting aside the chemical mixture I was stirring together.

"One day about four weeks ago I was hunting for supplies. It seems so crazy it was only a month ago. As I said, the Mordolus limit the things they give you, and so I would steal things to give people to make them more comfortable like extra medications, rations, and things to keep them occupied. My roommate at the time had a terrible cough and they were overly restricting her medications. I'd gotten into one of the storage rooms to try and find her more. When I was about to leave with my stolen supplies, Isaiah came in. We were really surprised to see someone else there. When we realized that we were both stealing things to help people, we decided to work together. Then we created an underground group for it," Bexley explains.

"That's really cool. Was it just you two?" I ask, watching out the garage window as the sun crests the rooftops.

"There was another boy, Isaiah's friend, who helped occasionally," she answers. "I wasn't really the one delivering the supplies or anything, I mostly just worked on the medicines and stuff on my own. I'm not really good at sneaking around anyway," Bexley explains.

"Then how'd you manage to escape?"

Bexley shakes her head wistfully. "That's a great question. I honestly don't really know. Oh, I suppose I was lucky. Isaiah always said that if you have hope, your chances of survival will be better. I guess he was right. I just wish I had told him I was planning to leave. I'm scared he thinks I'm dead."

"Because you just disappeared?" I guess.

"Yeah." She taps the stirring rod gently against the beaker, thinking. "I don't know if I regret it. I mean, of course, I wish we could have both escaped, but it never would have worked."

"Yeah, I get it," I say. Ideas start popping into my head at an alarming rate. "I'm surprised you escaped at all. Maybe if you could, Isaiah can too. Maybe we could find a way to rescue him and Ele. Maybe—"

"It's not so simple," Bexley interrupts. "We can't just get back in there and break people out easily."

"But it is possible," I point out.

"I suppose," Bexley replies. "But there's a very good chance it won't end well."

"That's probably true, but I'm going to figure it out."

Really, I'm hoping to convince myself that it could work, too. I hate to admit it, but I've mostly given up on ever seeing any of them again. The only reason I'm still working on the cure is because, somehow, I know there's still a chance. I guess I haven't really given up on *them*. They're in an impossible situation. They can't escape. I think I've just given up on my ability to save them.

"Hey, weird question, but do you have any hand sanitizer?" Bexley asks.

"Maybe in my backpack," I say. After searching, I find a small bottle among all the papers and books. "Here."

"Thanks," Bexley says, putting a liberal amount on her hands. "I'm a hand sanitizer fanatic. Do you mind if I keep this?"

"No, go ahead," I say. "We should probably get to work now."

Bexley tips a flask into the beaker over the alcohol burner. "Am I doing this right?"

"Yeah," I say, watching her pour the favipiravir into the mixture we made yesterday. She starts adding drops of acetic acid to the mixture. "Just go easy on the vinegar. Don't add too much. And watch the temperature. Don't let it boil."

"Got it," she says, adding a few more drops and picking up the stirring rod. I flip through another book, *Guide to Increasing Reaction Rate,* trying to figure out what catalyst will speed up the reaction for copper sulfate for the testing solution, since right now it takes three days to complete, when Bexley asks, "Have you always lived in Senneforte?"

I nod. "Yeah. Have you?"

"No, we lived in Kelsmore until I was nine."

"Where's that?" I ask.

"It used to be Tennessee," Bexley says. "My parents didn't like the government it took up. It's a catholic theocracy. The one thing my family loved about the United States before was freedom of religion. We would have left no matter what religion they forced, and we aren't catholic anyway. My family considered moving to a different continent that's less wrecked. But we moved to Willowmire. My parents liked the idea of the delegates and all. I guess that didn't work out as well as they'd hoped."

I never paid a whole lot of attention in geography class because things got confusing fast. After the division of the United States, the map's a mess. The worst part of the disunity is the social and political separation. That's probably why no one's done anything about the Maraloxis Virus outside Willowmire. They don't know and some places wouldn't care. Hardly anyone has lived in these new countries long. After each state became a country and determined its own government, they were all so different, and people moved to the places that shared their values.

"Bexley, are you watching the temp on that?" The liquid is bubbly and grows.

"Huh?" Bexley says, tucking a strand of red hair behind her ear. "Oh!" She looks down at the thermometer. "What's it supposed to be at?"

"No more than a hundred eighty," I reply, staring at the notes.

"Oh, that's not good," Bexley says, eyeing the rising chemicals.

"What's it at?" I ask. In the time it takes Bexley to turn off the burner, the mixture overflows all over the table. It sizzles in contact with the hot stand, leaving the room smoky.

"It was at two-twelve," Bexley says with a sigh.

"It's okay," I say. "I'll do it next time."

Later, Bexley and I decide to search for more supplies. We head outside and into the bright afternoon sunlight. A mockingbird chirps from a nearby fir tree, and the wind blows green leaves that were lost in the storm across the street. Even if we don't find anything, at least we can finally get outside.

"So, where do we go?" Bexley asks.

"We need to find a house that hasn't been raided yet," I say, glancing around to make sure it's safe. "Or at least looks like something might be left. They do less thorough removals of the poorer houses. They usually just burn them." With so many people gone and children separated from their parents, abandoned homes are easy sources of supplies.

I play with the strings of my hoodie, contemplating taking it off. It got super-hot out, but there are also bugs, and I don't want to get bitten. That's my least favorite part of summer in Willowmire. Because of the Great Lakes and all the water, it's humid and buggy.

Bexley and I carefully make our way through the abandoned streets. We try to stay at least partially hidden. We don't talk much, and I check each street corner, walkway, and road, glancing behind me every few feet. Bexley walks gracefully like she belongs in a field of flowers with girly music playing in the background. I look like a homeless street kid.

"It stresses me out always having to worry about the Mordolus," Bexley says, peering out from behind the broken window.

"Honestly, you get used to it," I say, stepping out from the abandoned thrift store after I check for Hunters. Glass fragments from the display window and useless broken merchandise cover the floor.

We trek down the road to where another street splits off then cross the road to a drugstore on the corner.

I freeze. There are voices nearby.

"What's tha—" Bexley starts, but I drag her over to the store and pull her behind a grove of bushes. Unsatisfied with our hiding place, I look out from between the branches. Four or five members of the Mordolus march down the street. They are clothed in dark suits adorned with the Queen's insignia and are carrying weapons. These are some of the Hunters.

"What are we going to do?" Bexley whispers from beside me. I don't take my eyes off the group and watch for any sign that they saw us. They're too far away to distinguish what they're saying, but a younger girl carrying an impressive silver bow points in our direction.

"Are you insane? What are you doing?!" Bexley whispers as I step out from behind our cover.

"They saw us," I say, motioning for her to join me.

"Yeah, but we don't need to basically turn ourselves in! You're crazy!" she says, crossing her arms.

"If you stay hidden behind this bush, I can't help you," I say. She mutters and begrudgingly follows me.

"You are insane," Bexley reiterates.

"I know what I'm doing. Try not to act suspicious. Just be quiet and let me deal with it. Trust me," I say, trying to formulate a plan. Bexley glares and twirls her charm bracelet.

The Hunter girl is probably seventeen or eighteen. She has at least two daggers strapped to her cargo pants. The girl's black bomber jacket has the Mordolus symbol embroidered on the shoulders. The other four have similar outfits. They all wear thick black face masks and thin leather gloves to protect themselves from the Virus while they patrol the streets. Their leather combat boots portray a blood-red 'M' stitched into the rim. Sometimes I feel like that leather—like Morzanna and the Mordolus has been sewn into everything. The blood red represents the death they bring. Even if the stitches are removed, tiny holes will always be there. A permanent reminder. Nothing's ever going to be okay again.

"What are you doing out here?" asks a middle-aged Hunter woman with crooked teeth as they approach us in the parking lot. She stands in front of us with superiority.

"Nothing," I say. She tilts her head and looks at us as if we're little kids.

"You shouldn't be out here," she says. "We've got to take you to get tested."

She makes a subtle gesture, and the other four of them surround us. I try to act as if I don't notice, or even better, don't care.

"We already have been," I say.

"You're lying," the younger girl sneers.

"No," I say, a little nervous but refusing to show it. "I'm not. Go on, show them." Bexley looks apprehensive but slowly nods. The woman indignantly examines the pinprick, purple-hinted scar on Bexley's shoulder.

"It's purple," one of the others, a gray-eyed scowling man, says. "We get to retest after six weeks."

Bexley looks defeated, and it frustrates me.

"It's been four weeks," I say. "We got tested mid-July."

"Can you prove that?" the first woman asks.

"Can you disprove it?" I shoot back.

She rolls her eyes. "In theory, yes, but I'm not going to take the time to go through all our records."

"Fantastic, so, we'll be going. See you in two weeks," I say, knowing full well we will not willingly go back to get tested. Bexley and I turn to leave.

"Wait," the glaring man says, grabbing my arm. "She might be okay, but what about you?"

"Good question. Show us," the woman says. I grimace, and Bexley looks at me hopefully. "Come on, we're trying to help. Wouldn't want to give any diseases to your friend."

"Nothing to show," I respond plainly.

The girl with the bow giggles. She reminds me of some kind of annoying, gross bird. Like a crow or seagull or something.

"Right," the woman says with a tense, smug expression. "Let's go then."

I allow the scowling man to take both my arms. Anger flares in my stomach.

"What?" Bexley says in disbelief. "Oh, no, don't take him!"

"Bexley," I say quietly. "I'll be fine. Go now before they decide to take you too."

She hesitates, but finally Bexley nods, gives the still-smiling girl a nasty look, and walks back toward the drugstore.

As we leave the street, rage burns inside me, only put out by a wave of fear. This wasn't supposed to happen. *If we'd just stayed at the lab today…*

The Hunters are quiet as we head off in the opposite direction I was taking Bexley. We make it to a wood-lined street when there's suddenly a shrill scream.

The crooked teeth lady who was leading spins around. "What—"

The scowling man loosens my arms a little, and I strain and look. There stands Bexley on the pavement seven feet away, poised with the Hunter girl's silver bow. The Hunter girl scornfully glares at her while rubbing her head, and Bexley aims the silver bow at the member holding me. I don't know how she managed to get that bow, but I'm relieved—and terrified when I realize that if she isn't a really good aim, I might be in trouble. How is that crazy girl gonna stand up to five armed adults?

"What's going on, Shirla?" the woman says, her voice thick with annoyance.

"Give it back!" the girl screams at Bexley.

"Not until you let him go!" Bexley demands, keeping her aim even though her voice falters when we make eye contact. The man holds my arms tighter.

"You can't take us all down. Even if you do hit anyone, there are still four of us left," the woman says unamusedly. The others mutter in agreement.

So Bexley directs the arrow at Shirla instead.

"You couldn't!" Shirla shrieks. "Someone do something about her! Help me! *Help me*!" None of the four Hunters move.

"I will do it!" Bexley says, pulling the string more taught, her hands are trembling. She's dead serious.

"You wouldn't be able to shoot me," Shirla says. "Probably," she adds, uncertain.

"I don't know, that rock hit you square on the head. I'm not afraid. And listen, I don't have to be good to hit you four feet away," Bexley confidently points out.

Shirla grits her teeth. The first woman laughs from behind me, and all but Shirla join in. The second man looks at the fifth member, a woman who looks a lot like him, with a sardonic eyeroll. He leaps toward Bexley and snatches the bow in one swift movement, tossing the weapon to Shirla and grabbing Bexley harshly by the arms.

Shirla grins once the silver bow is back in her hand and leans toward Bexley. "I really hate you."

"That was idiotic, you know," the lead woman says to Bexley, who stares wide-eyed.

"Well, at least I tried," Bexley says timidly. Shirla still seethes.

"Ya know what?" the first woman says with a chuckle. "Let them go."

Bexley gapes in shock, and I stare at her in dumb disbelief. "What?"

"But why?" Shirla asks, horrified.

"They'll die out here anyway," the woman says. "If they want to be stubborn and refuse our help, let them die painfully. Let them die from the Virus. Let them die from starvation. Let them die *alone*."

Shirla gives an evil smile and giggles a little. "Let them be a paradigm of what happens when you won't rely on the Queen. When they see the video of us dragging your rotting corpses to the graveyard, the citizens of Senneforte will think again before refusing Morzanna."

Bexley looks unconvinced until the scowling man lets me go and she's released. With one last confused look, we silently turn and slink away. Even after the Hunters are out of sight, I keep checking to make sure we haven't been fooled.

"That was so insane, Bexley," I finally say, then sigh with a relieved laugh. "But I'm really glad you did it."

"Thanks. I didn't know what to do, so I followed you guys," Bexley replies. "Please tell me that doesn't happen often."

"First time I've really been caught, actually," I say.

"Lucky you had me there, huh? Of course, I could have just shut up and let you deal with it," Bexley deadpans.

"Thank you for saving me," I say with a laugh. "Do you actually do archery?"

"Yeah, some," Bexley replies. "My dad is a redneck and got three daughters. He taught us all kinds of things. I'm not fantastic, but I can hit something if I need to."

"That's cool," I say and glance up at the sky. "We should get going. We still need to find supplies."

We walk a couple of easy miles, still talking over our close escape and following the roads quietly. After an hour, we stop and sit under some shady willow trees outside one of the province's only colleges, Senneforte Community College.

"We used to drive past this place every day," Bexley says wistfully. "I went to school down there." She points to the left, where the road disappears into a wooded path. A green road sign aims in that direction, reading *South Delta Middle/High.*

"So did I," I reply.

"We went to the same school?" Bexley asks. "And we never saw each other?"

I shrug. "We could have. I don't remember everyone I've seen at school. There were a lot of people, and we were in different grades."

"Still. We went to the same place every day and never knew each other. It's weird," Bexley says. "Wait, how old are you?"

"Fifteen," I say. "But I only finished eighth grade and three-quarters of ninth before school closed. My birthday's right after the cut-off date, and I got held back a year."

"Why?" Bexley asks. "You're not dumb. You're way smarter than I am."

"Because." I shrug. "How old are you?"

"Thirteen, but I'll be fourteen in December," she says.

I'll be sixteen in a month, but I don't like to think about being that old. I glance down the street. My church is also on that road. The Brookses went to Senneforte Baptist, too. That's how we met them.

Bexley sighs. "I never expected this to happen. When I first heard about the Virus, I didn't think anything of it. It's been less than a year, and the province is ruined. Half of us are dead and everyone else is dying. It's apocalyptic."

"I know. My dad told us about the outbreak in Ellismark right after it happened since it was part of his project at work. It was interesting and all, but I never thought it would affect me. I was too busy thinking about school and other unimportant stuff to care. I mean, things like this have happened before, and it wasn't a big deal or whatever. But then it spread here, and people started talking about it. People were sick, and we had no idea what was happening. And then everyone freaked out. School was canceled, people left work, and within a week they started getting tested and being taken to the old medical warehouse converted into the Infirmary. Pretty soon, we had to steal what was concocted of the cure so my dad could try and finish it after their lab was shut down. Sometimes I wonder if he knew I'd be stuck finishing it when he roped me into helping with the cure all the time. I'm glad I did though. Then people disappeared. My friends disappeared. Eventually, my parents disappeared. And here we are, seven months after the first case, still without a cure and half the population of Senneforte is dead. And all Morzanna can tell us is it came from a distant country," I say.

Bexley sighs and stares at the grass. Her thick, chestnut red hair dances in the breeze. "When I heard about the Virus, it was from my sister Hadley. She was taking classes in Ellismark to become a teacher, and her school was going to close because several people there had contracted 'the mystery illness'. I honestly thought it was dramatic since we had hardly any cases in Senneforte. I only really cared that my sister was home again after being gone to school for a year. Oh, then everything went downhill," she says, picking blades of grass and watching them float off in the wind.

"My mom's parents live in Haarlem. She lived in the Netherlands until she was twenty-five and came to the United States when she married my dad. His parents lived just southwest of Amsterdam until nineteen ninety-five," I say. "Most of my family lives in the Netherlands. They probably have no idea what's going on here."

"Do you think somehow Morzanna is keeping everything a secret and trying to hide what's happening?" Bexley asks. "No one's come to help us, and no one's allowed to leave. She lied and said the Maraloxis Virus was harmless. I bet she's trying to hide it."

"No one would be proud if this is what happened to the country they were supposed to be ruling. She's probably scared," I say.

Bexley nods. "If we could get a message out, do you think someone would help Willowmire?"

"Definitely. I promise, Bexley, I'm going to fix this," I say. The Hunter's words haunt me. Bexley and I could really die out here any day. Pressure grows the longer I think about everything. I've got to finish the cure. Hopefully then Morzanna will step in and help us treat everyone. Then we'll be free.

Bexley glances at me with a smile. "And I'm going to help you."

The two of us head off again. We walk until we finally get to a street with pretty untouched houses. Almost every third house on the way here had been burned down. The air is stagnant with the smell of smoke.

"Sunlit Street," Bexley reads from the road sign. "Never heard of it."

"Neither. Fitting name though," I say, watching the setting sun stream from the cloudless sky onto the pavement. "Looks alright."

We've been extra careful. I bear the weight of responsibility for what happened earlier. This street must've been abandoned a long time ago before disguising became a thing. Even Ele and I took time to make our houses look raided or vacant so the Mordolus wouldn't find us. It's not a hundred percent effective, but it helps.

"So, what now?" Bexley asks with a sudden rush of enthusiasm.

"Let's start with that first house on the other side. We might have to stay here tonight, unless you wanna walk back in the dark," I say, looking up at the sky. I don't want to admit it, but frankly, I don't know if I could find the way back in the dark. I'm not great with memory. The sun falls behind the tops of the evergreen trees that churn in the Michigan wind. It's probably around seven. We lost an hour with the Hunter incident, and I misjudged our time.

Bexley agrees, and we walk toward the first house. The two-story building sits sadly in the middle of the small yard. An ocean blue Honda Odyssey with a small splotch of red on the bumper is parked in the driveway. Vines grow up everywhere, devouring anything they touch. It's like time froze, and the street was trapped in the moment, even though the world continued to corrupt around it.

I stride up to the door, listening to be sure it's completely vacant. The painted door is ajar—they must've left in a hurry.

"This is so creepy. Oh, what if someone's here?" Bexley asks, glancing around.

"Does it look like anyone's here?" I reply, loudly opening the door and stepping into the house. Everything is still, leaving a ghost of what once was. Spider webs dangle from the mantle. No one's been here in months.

"What if there's like a bear in here or something?" Bexley whispers, cautiously stepping inside.

"There's not," I say, rolling my eyes. "We don't even have bears in Senneforte." At least I don't think so. I shut the door.

"Isn't this technically stealing?" Bexley asks, sadly surveying a picture on the wall of the family that used to live here.

"I don't know. Yeah. The sad reality is that most of them won't ever return. And I'm sure they won't care, especially since we are trying to make a cure," I say. "You look downstairs, and I'll check upstairs, okay?"

"Sure," she replies.

I walk up the creaky staircase. The steps open into a big room. A desk and some chairs are overturned on the floor. I enter the first room to the left of the staircase. It's a large bedroom with a dresser, another desk, and a bookshelf. An unmade bed sits in the center of the room. There's a fish tank, green with algae, on the nightstand. Clothes and books are scattered around the floor. The walls are painted sky blue. I walk over to the dresser and open a drawer. Girl's clothes. I check the desk drawer, and find new notebooks and pens, but nothing significant.

I'm about to begin the next upstairs bedroom when there's a shatter accompanied by a piercing scream downstairs.

"Bexley?" I bound down the stairs and into the kitchen. Bexley stands with broken glass covering the ground around her.

"What happened?" I ask, looking around frantically. She runs over to me.

"There was a rat or something in that cabinet! I almost touched it too!" she says, burying her face in her hands.

"That's it? I thought you were hurt or something!" I say.

Bexley nods. "Clearly, you don't understand how horrible that is! I could catch a disease or get bitten!" She shivers, genuinely concerned.

"Calm down. It's gone, whatever it was. Maybe we should just look together," I suggest.

"Okay," she says, still glancing around nervously as she takes out her hand sanitizer.

"Did you find anything?" I ask.

"No. I guess the Mordolus collected everything, and the rats ate the leftovers," she says, pointing a shaky hand toward the empty cabinets.

"That's alright," I say. We walk upstairs to finish the second floor.

"There are some clothes in that first room," I suggest.

Bexley glances down at her worn outfit. "Oh, perfect!" she says and goes to get some clothes.

We don't find anything else upstairs, so we return to the first floor.

"How long ago do you think they left?" Bexley asks.

I step into the laundry room and pluck a few items from the cabinet over the dryer, stashing them into my backpack. We always need more alcohol for the burner and turns out they had some kind of small mammal in addition to the fish because there's some food I can give the mice in the lab.

"A few months probably. You can usually figure it out. Like look, here's a calendar. It's still in May," I answer. Bexley ambles over and opens the closet door.

"Oh, it's so sad. Someone *lived* here," Bexley says. She's right. Everyone either fled, ended up in the Infirmary, died, or, maybe, still lives out here like us.

"Yeah," I say.

Bexley searches through some bottles on a nearby counter, squeaking every time a beetle crawls out from its hiding spot.

When we exit the house, I shut the door back. It's dusky enough I have to get the flashlight out of my backpack.

We search the next few houses, and soon it's totally dark. The only light is from the moon that's high in the twilight atmosphere, full and glowing like a beacon. We walk through the tall grassy backyards.

"I'm really tired," Bexley says after yawning. "It's spooky out here, but the sky is gorgeous with the moon so big and bright. I keep thinking there could be kidnappers, or worse, diseased animals," she whispers.

I scoff. "Terrifying. And there are kidnappers—the Mordolus are everywhere."

"I'm not dumb, I know that," Bexley says. "But really, Graydon, I'm so exhausted."

"Just one more house then we'll break. We can walk back tomorrow," I say, marching up to the last house on this side of the street.

"Fine," she says.

We step inside the small old home. It is only one story, and the outside is painted a dusty yellow. Overgrown bushes with small, pink flowers line the front yard.

"You wanna wait here?" I say, gazing at Bexley. "I'll look."

She looks relieved and nods. I take the flashlight she holds and head off into the darkness. I walk into a kitchen decorated with flowery wallpaper. Down the hallway, I enter a bedroom. I stop just inside the doorway. Unlike all the other houses I've been in, this room is cluttered with tons of things. Sheets and blankets cover the windows, creating a somber feeling. Clothes lay neatly across the floor and bed. Ants crawl in and out of an open jar of honey on the windowsill. Someone must have lived here after the Virus. It's evident they don't anymore. In the cabinet in the corner of the room, more sheets like the ones dressing the windows are crammed inside. Thinking, I take out a few of the sheets and shake them out. As I hoped, things fall out onto the ground. I shove the cloth back into the cabinet. On the floor, I find two half-full jars of rice, a small amount of flour, and a tiny blue bag. I quickly add them to my backpack but stop to inspect the contents of the bag. Inside, I discover a small silver necklace and a glass vial. The vial contains a peculiar, rose-colored sand. The strangest part is a small curly "M" engraved near the top of the glass. The Mordolus symbol. Unsure about the last two items, I walk back to where Bexley is waiting. She sits on the wooden floor next to the door with a sickly expression that worries me.

"Okay, let's go. We need to find a place to rest."

Bexley nods, and I hold out a hand and help her up. It's probably around midnight. I can barely see anything, and I don't want to turn on the flashlight outside and attract the Hunters again. I bound down the steps and turn to find Bexley still standing on the porch. Her face is pale, and her blue gaze is distant. She stares into nothingness and wavers.

"You okay?" I ask.

Then, Bexley collapses onto the cold ground.

15
ELEANORA: PEACE

"Marie, we have to finalize the escape plan now," I announce the instant Reece leaves, chased by the nurse. "Isaiah will come soon, given Reece outruns that nurse, and we need to be prepared. That way we all escape together and have a reasonable chance at it."

I truly miss my brother, and our recent encounter with his roommate excites me. Isaiah is crazy, but he's my brother, my only sibling, and I've started to miss even his annoying behavior.

"Yeah! All four of us can escape," Marie says. "And we can find my brother too."

"Definitely," I say, my soul dancing with excitement. "I just hope they return soon."

"What if Reece never comes back?" Marie asks.

"He better." I stare at the beat-up vinyl floor, thinking. "I need to talk with Isaiah. Maybe we could even take my parents if Isaiah can lead us to them."

The likelihood of that is frustrating, but I can't just abandon my parents. My heart wants it to be possible, to believe we can save everyone, even, but a fine line is appearing between realistic aspirations and wistful dreams.

Marie hops onto her bed. "We can't rescue everyone. We've gotta think about the big picture. We escape, you finish the cure, we save everyone who's left, and the Mordolus free them. If we stay here until we can get everyone out, if that's even possible, we'll all be dead. It won't happen. Time's running out. I know we can't bring my brother with us now, Ele, so forget about it. I was just dreaming. We need to focus on the cure *then* our fam," Marie says like she knew I was wrestling with the problem myself.

I know Marie's right, and I hate to believe it. *Right now, the best way to save everyone is to escape and help Graydon.* Even if we never free our families, as horrible as it is, finding the remedy is more important. It may be the only way to save the world.

"You're right," I admit. "I just hope we aren't too late." I twist a piece of my hair. *Right now, all those people are dying. What's happening to them, after they die? How are they being buried?* Reality breaks in like a peace-robbing thief. *I could die! What will happen after death?* Uncertainty ravages my conscience, leading me to question the foundation of my beliefs. *Where do I commit my eternity? Do I really believe and have faith in God that's good enough? Why is this all happening?*

"It's all Morzanna's fault! She's letting everyone die! How can she do that? Why isn't she helping?" I rant. A grenade of disappointment explodes in my head, and lava-like rage devours any patience I have left.

"She's probably glad people are dying. I don't know how she's still Queen. If I had anything to do with it, she'd be in jail, at least," Marie vents.

"Maybe we should just send her here to this horrid prison. We have to wait and watch everyone die, and there's nothing we can do!" I put my head in my hands. "I don't want to see myself, or you, slowly succumb."

"Yeah, first they get all lethargic and cough a lot—act kinda blehhh—and then they start talking crazy and get all shaky. Then they just fall asleep and don't wake up again," Marie says, and I grimace. "Too much info?"

"A bit," I say.

"I hate thinking about all the little kids without their parents. My brother's only five. I'm afraid about him seeing all this. I really miss him. And my parents. And Bella," Marie says and stares at the floor.

I kneel beside her and put my hands on her shoulders, giving them a reassuring squeeze. "We're gonna find your brother too. We'll get him out of here—I promise." *Marie has no idea if her parents or brother are even alive, and here I am complaining when I'm certain mine are.*

"Thanks, Ele," she says, a smile slowly returning to her expression as she gazes at her bright shoes.

"Of course." I look around the room, my determination growing. "We need to solidify the plan."

"Let's just talk about it. I don't want to risk losing the plans. If they notice us in the closet too much, they might search our room. Or check the sound on the cameras. That'd be bad," Marie says. I nod and sit on the bed across from her.

"Now that we know the doors are unlocked on the outside, we can use it to our advantage," I say. "If we could get Isaiah and Reece to let us out, then we've solved Problem One."

"Yeah. That'll work. The challenge will be them getting into the Double Guard. It's crazy to get in, and I'm shocked Reece did. But I bet they can figure it out again. We could try at night. Then we might have a better chance. It could be more dangerous though. The guards at night are armed. I learned that from experience."

I look at her as shock's force breaks through my confidence. "They tried to hurt you?"

"Well, no. I was trying to escape again. It wasn't a very good idea. I tried to escape through the main entrance. I saw someone else doing the same thing. Maybe he would cause a distraction for me. Well, they saw him, and it got crazy. Alarms. The night guards even had guns! It was scary. He didn't get hurt, but I never tried to escape at night again."

"So either we get caught, and maybe get put in a harder place to escape from, or we almost get killed?" I ask.

"I guess," Marie says, playing with the laces of her yellow high-tops. "This is going to be tougher than I thought. You sorta make me think then everything gets complicated."

"We'll figure it out when we get there, then. We'll trust Isaiah to choose the time of day, since we can't contact him anyway," I say. "We might not have another chance since I don't think Isaiah and Reece will keep coming to the Double Guard. I just hope you are right about there being a way out. If not, I don't know what we'll do."

"Same. But I've thought about this. If anything goes wrong, we'll figure it out. We can do this," Marie says. "I just won't give up trying until I'm dead."

Hours pass before someone comes to our room and brings us dinner. It's the same woman that took Reece, and she looks suspiciously at Marie and me, but remains silent. I want to ask if she caught Reece but decide against it.

A seedling of hope grows inside me, pushing through the darkness that threatens to trap me. There's nothing more we can plan. I just wish we could get a message to Isaiah and warn him about our scheme.

As night falls, my mind turns to tomorrow—maybe I'll see my brother. My hope every day is to just see Isaiah and my parents; it's what keeps me going. That, and fear. When I think I'll never find rest, powerful words appear in my mind from deep memory. They bring a rush of security.

For I consider that the sufferings of this present time are not worth comparing with the glory that is to be revealed to us (Romans 8:18).

Maybe I can have peace.

16
ISAIAH: WILL I FINALLY SEE HER?

Reece explains more. I'm so excited. I can't believe he found my sister! Accidentally. And in the Double Guard. It's so crazy! He explains that he hid on one of the layered carts they transport the dead with. Death is inevitable but slow, so it's uncommon. Reece got lucky that he happened to find a cart going to the Double Guard parked outside the doors.

"Can you take me to see her tomorrow?" I ask.

"Maybe. We can't get caught again or we'll really be in trouble, and so will the girls. Six marks, remember? We've each got a few already, and that nurse gave me two today." He wrings his hands before sarcastically adding, "And anyways, they'll be too busy with their escape plan."

"For real? I'm not surprised Ele's trying to get out," I say to myself. "I need to talk to her." I gave up on escaping weeks ago. I've just been betting on the cure. Actually, I'm pretty confident that I can escape if I really need to. How? I don't know, but I'm smart enough to figure it out. Probably. But my parents are here, and there are people to help. Ele's different. She has drive to be free. A desire reawakens. I wanna be free too.

Reece rolls his eyes. "You too? How do you think a few kids can escape this place? Hundreds of people have tried, and it's never worked. You guys just need to accept that we're going to die. If you really want to live longer, stop wasting all your energy," he lays down on his bed and stares at the ceiling.

"Why do you have to be like that? There is a chance. There's only one Mordolus member to every ten patients. How do you know that no one's gotten out? We don't know for sure. We've never even explored the whole Infirmary to see the possibilities. We haven't really tried. We have to hope that we can survive this. I know we can," I say.

People are slowly getting worse, losing their consciousness, and dying. Even Reece's mom died. The list of the dead seems longer every day. Reece thinks it's hopeless.

But I know that there's something to strive for. There are lives to save. Souls being lost. I have a permanent mission. An inability to give in. I know Someone's in control and there's a plan for this all. Christ gave me a reason to live long before the virus.

"Reece, we have to at least try. I'm not going to wait around until we die. We can escape and survive. If not, at least I never gave up," I say. "There's more to life than death. There's an eternity to fight for."

"I guess," Reece says, sitting up. "But how can you really believe that we'll survive? We have no chance."

"When I see all these people, it gives me strength to try and save them. I would do anything for them. God commanded me to fight for truth and have faith," I say. "There's a way out. We just have to find it. We make it around locked doors and cameras. I've stolen keys before."

"If you're so adamant about what God says, then why are you fine with stealing from the Mordolus?" Reece asks incredulously. "Isn't stealing bad?"

"Well, I think it's still sorta wrong, but I can't just do nothing and let this go on. I honestly don't know. It's the lesser evil," I reply. "I'm not perfect."

Reece looks unsure but nods. He coughs a couple of times. "My lungs feel weird. You don't think it's, ya know, the Virus, and I'll die?"

My brain says "Probably," but "No," comes out instead. Reece already has ninety-nine voices in his mind telling him he's gonna die. I wanna be the one that doesn't. "Tell them though. They might give you something for it," I say. That's why Reece has been especially on edge. He's freaking out.

Reece takes a deep breath. "I'll try to take you to see Ele tomorrow."

Most of the evening I spend pacing our room. I'm so excited-nervous about tomorrow. I fixate on it.

Reece is in a pretty bad mood all night. I'm not sure if it's related to our conversation or what. His wall writings today have some very strong words.

Later, a nurse comes to check on us. Reece scowls at whatever he's writing, refusing to acknowledge her.

"Do you have to destroy everything in here?" the nurse says, annoyed. She stares at all the writing on the walls.

"You could give me some paper. That would help," Reece says, bitterly. "You won't do anything about it anyway. You don't have time. And, if you take away the only thing I have to do, you'll find out how much trouble an unoccupied twelve-year-old could cause."

"Maybe we'll transfer you to the children's section. I could convince them to let you in since you're only two years older than the age range," the nurse says. "I think less freedom is necessary for you."

"Oh yeah, let's see what more I could do there," Reece says. "I could teach them all to draw on the walls."

"The Double Guard is always open," the nurse offers with a sneer. "Currently, you're not too far away from ending up there."

Reece stays silent after that. The nurse performs her quick, required check-up. Mostly, she asks a few questions to make sure we don't need extra care. I put in my daily request for headache medication. They only let us have a certain amount of medications a day, especially as kids. The best time of my day is four to six hours on a painkiller.

Before she leaves, the nurse takes Reece's pen from where he left it on the table, turns off the lights, and slams the door.

Reece pretends to be upset until she's gone. Then he gets another pen from under his bed and sloppily scribbles very large on the wall above the window. I can clearly read 'I HATE THIS PLACE'. Reece's eyes flash vehemently around the room before he climbs into bed.

I wake up real early the next morning. I watch the sun rise from our small window. I'm miserable until morning finally dawns. Climbing out of bed, I'm eager to see Ele. I wait impatiently for Reece to wake up. He sleeps so long. He's tired all the time because of the Virus. I pace the room. There's enough time to discover how many vinyl tiles make up the floor.

People are outside in the halls. It's completely light outside. Our room is too.

"Come on. We've got to go see Ele," I say, gingerly shaking Reece.

"What?" he asks.

"Ele."

He sighs and drowsily crawls out of bed. "Fine. If we get caught, it's your fault. Not that it matters because I doubt we can really escape, but whatever," he says walking to the door with a yawn. I roll my eyes and follow.

We step out into the hallway. A few guards and some nurses patrol and prepare for the day, but not many people are out this early. I follow Reece toward the Double Guard. In the unrestricted areas, no one pays much attention to us. If they did, we could tell them we are going to check the list or get breakfast early. We're safe here.

We get to the stairwell. Reece opens the door. We head downstairs.

I realize why people don't try to escape anymore. They've been told that there's no cure or medicine to save them. For them, it's hopeless. Life is hopeless. The Mordolus forbid us from meeting with family or talking much with other residents. I have hope for a cure. And my family is alive. Many don't have that. Some don't have hope in death either.

We walk past Emergency Care, toward the entryway. There are more people here. We'll blend in. I see the doors I entered weeks ago when I was separated from Ele.

Reece leads me down the hall. He looks cautiously ahead before letting me go first past the barrier to the restricted areas. Amused, I read the signs listed about not entering and punishments.

"We don't have a way to get in," Reece says, visibly nervous. This is only the second time he's been to the Double Guard, and last time he got caught. I'm anxious too. I've never been.

"We'll figure something out," I say, thinking.

Reece gets a strange look. "I have an idea. It's crazy though. We could steal a key. I've seen where they keep them."

"Whoa. You're seriously suggesting something that dangerous?"

"Shut up before I change my mind," he says, blushing. "Are you agreeing?"

"Yeah," I say. "There's no other way."

"You sure it's over here?" I ask, staring out from behind a cabinet. "This is in the unrestricted areas. Why would they keep the keys here?"

"They have them in the closet at the check-in area. I assume it's because it's sort of the main place. When they check people in, they assign a key to the nurse. It's practical," Reece says. From where we are, I can see the check-in desk, the entry area, and the hallway adjacent to the death pillar's location. It's busy here since it's the only place anyone is allowed to go other than our rooms. However, people always get in trouble for loitering. Currently, a group of patients participate in recreational activities. It's laundry day. They'll collect all the dirty clothes in here then haul them off to the big laundry room to be cleaned then randomly redistributed. You never get the same clothes back.

"Look," Reece says. "Over there, behind the desk. See the door?"

At the desk, two nurses and a guard are talking. Behind them, there's a door about forty-five degrees to the right, facing toward the outside. That has to be the key room.

"Yeah. How do you know that's where they keep the keys? How are we going to get there? And how are we even going to find the right one?"

Reece gives me a borderline annoyed look. "First of all, I've watched. They bring someone in, write their name down, go into the room, and return with a key. It's simple. I assume they have them labeled, or how else would they find what they need," Reece says. Of course, he noticed all that, and I didn't.

"How come you never told me about this before?" I ask. "Easy access to a key would've been super useful."

"Because. I knew you'd want to steal one," he says. "I didn't want you to do anything stupid and dangerous."

"Why are you telling me now then?" I ask. "That's literally what you suggested."

"Because I know how much you want to see your sister," he says. "If I told you before, you'd probably be caught by now and wouldn't ever see her."

That's surprisingly thoughtful. "So how do we get the key?" I ask.

"I figured out everything else. You have to do something." Reece shrugs. "Come up with an amazing plan for us."

"Okay, let me think." I lean against the cabinet. Really, we don't have to be hidden here. But it would be suspicious if we were just staring, and they might send us away.

"Reece?" someone calls, jogging around the cabinet. Reece spins around and suppresses a groan. "You remember me, right? River?"

"Yeah, hi River," Reece says as we exit our planning center.

"What are you guys doing?" It's the boy we met at recreational activities. His hair is black, but the ends are bleached and dyed a faded red. River's a full-grown, easygoing boy. "Why are you hiding behind here? Planning something cool?" he whispers, stepping closer. Reece looks at me helplessly.

"Um, no," I say. "We were just…Actually, yeah, kind of."

"We are?" Reece asks quietly.

"Cool," River says, stepping way too close. He doesn't notice how Reece and I back up toward the wall.

"Yeah. We're going to complain. Going to the desk to complain about everything. About the rooms, the food, the rules, how mean everyone is," I say, standing. "We're getting tired of it, ya know?"

"Cool. Can I come? I have a few dislikes too," River says. I nod.

Reece gives me a strange look. I shrug. The three of us walk up to the desk. This is definitely gonna go so wrong.

"Can I help you?" one of the nurses says. She stares at us blankly.

"Yeah, we have a few concerns," I start. Reece shrinks.

"Names first," she interrupts, and types each one into her computer.

"Concerns about what?" she asks, but I can tell she really couldn't care less.

"Oh, where do we start?" River says. "How about the showers? Like seriously, we only get one once a week. And recreational activities? What even are those? I think there's a better way to execute chores."

River drones on for a while. The nurse just grows steadily angrier. Eventually, another nurse and a guard join her to listen.

I whisper to Reece, "While they're not watching, one of us needs to try and get into the key room. Wait—is there a key for the key room?"

"I hope not," Reece says.

"We need to get the key now," I say.

"Okay," Reece nods, thinking. "I'll help River. You try to get into the key room."

"You know what else? Do you guys always have to act like you hate us? Like seriously, we're stuck here, and you're all rude!" River goes on, leaning over the desk. A few of the other patients watch us.

"And it's also *so* boring. We have literally nothing to do. Is this really how you're going to treat dying people?" Reece says loudly. I'm surprised because Reece never, NEVER, talks like that, but somehow he pulls it off. I wander toward the righthand hallway and casually duck out of sight.

All three of the Mordolus listen, and tension grows. I crawl to the edge of the desk and glance at the door to the key room. My heart races.

River and Reece are still arguing with the nurses and guard. In a split second, I slink to the door and open it as little as possible. I close the door behind me.

I stand up, breathing heavily. I made it. The walls are lined with hundreds of hooks and fifty bazillion keys. Each one has a number on it, corresponding to a room. I frantically gaze up and down the walls. *Double Guard, Double Guard, Double Guard…*

I fumble with a few of the keys, scanning the paper tag labels on each ring. There are so many. I'm overwhelmed. I keep searching.

There are a few hooks with more than one copy of a key, which must mean significant places. Forever later, I finally find the Double Guard key. I grab it off the hook and shakily pocket it. Without thinking, I open the door to the key room.

I quickly duck down and dive to the other side of the desk.

"When are you going to let us see our family? We're dying! I have six younger siblings, and I don't get to see any of them," River rants.

I lean against the desk, panting. I glance up at Reece. He catches my eye, and I nod.

"I think you two need a lesson in gratitude. Do you not realize how privileged you are to be here? Queen Morzanna provides abundantly and deals mercifully with you. How dare you complain?" The nurse admonishes.

"She's a despicable woman!" River interjects.

The nurse leans closer, seething. "Your lives are being protected by the Queen! You are selfish, insubordinate children who clearly don't realize how hard we have to work here. We all must learn to submit fully to Morzanna for there to be any peace. Morzanna is the protector of Senneforte, and the rules she has put in place here are good, kind, and true."

River starts to retort, but Reece turns bright red and starts apologizing. "We're really sorry. We were wrong. Morzanna is, uh, kind and all."

I jump in. "The Virus is affecting his brain. He's my roommate and says all kinds of crazy things. I didn't mean for it to go that far, I simply wanted to request more care for him."

"Poor excuse," the guard cuts in. "If there is a problem then we can search for availability in the Double Guard."

"No!" River says. Reece is on the verge of having a heart attack.

I hold my composure. "There's no problem. They just need rest."

The three Mordolus staff members don't look convinced but make no effort to prevent us from leaving. We quickly get out of there.

"One mark for the Double Guard each!" the nurse calls after us. That was a weighty sacrifice. For me, it's worth it. But I feel bad for River. It's our fault he got the mark.

"I'm really sorry, River," I say.

"Hey, it's fine. I knew the risk," he says with a shrug. "I gotta go. See you guys later."

River strides off in the direction of the stairwell. When we're alone in the hallway, Reece takes a deep breath. "That was absolutely terrifying."

"But we have the key," I say.

"We'll have to take the other way to the Double Guard," Reece says as we come up to the restricted areas on the other side of Section One.

We approach the door to the Double Guard when no one's around. It's a darker color than any of the others. Bold red letters read

'Double Guard' above the doors. The drippy paint resembles blood. Fitting.

I glance around and unlock the door with the stolen key. It clicks and opens.

I'm thankful that no one's on the other side. Several hallways split off from the main foyer. Reece pauses for a second, breathing heavily. He looks unsteady.

"I think it's safe now," Reece whispers, leading me down the leftmost hallway. We slowly find our way to the room. Every sound is nerve-racking. We go down the wider hall and turn left. There's a smaller one for a while. Eventually, Reece stops outside Room 138.

"Is this it?" I ask. Reece nods. He reaches to open the door but stops.

"We have to stay out here. They have cameras," he says. I nod impatiently. Reece opens the door.

I can't believe it. I'm finally seeing my sister.

17
GRAYDON: WORSE THAN IT SEEMS

"Bexley!" I call, sprinting up the sidewalk to where she collapsed on the steps. "Are you okay? Bexley?!"

She lays unconscious on the concrete stairs. The wind carries a strange, exposed feeling through the dark street. I end up half-dragging Bexley inside the house.

"Bexley," I say again, ripping off her mask. She eventually opens her eyes with a start.

"Are you okay?" I ask, relieved. She nods, but I don't think she is. "What happened?"

"I don't know, but I think I'm alright." The waver in her voice is unconvincing. Bexley sits up shakily.

"Stay here," I say, standing. "I'll be back."

I need to get her some water. I brought some, but we drank it all already. Since it rained this morning, I find some water pooled in a cleanish-looking birdbath and fill up the water bottle. I return to the sunshine-colored house. When I open the door, I'm shocked. Bexley's gone.

"Bexley?" I ask in a half-whisper. The house is empty. I can't see a thing in the endless darkness outside. There's no time to try and remember where I left the light.

I call Bexley's name again. I run into the street, scanning the two rows of houses. Each is a duplicate of the one next to it, creating a confusing visual at night. A few of the streetlights still work and leave flickering spotlights on the pavement. A cool wind wisps around, and a perfect silence hangs in the air.

I spin around when an eldritch scream rings out from one of the houses. I run as fast as I can toward the noise. Throwing open the heavy wooden door, I dash inside. My footsteps echo off the walls, and it's so quiet I can hear the creak of the floorboards. I don't see anyone.

"Bexley?" I whisper. Leaving the foyer, I step into the empty dining room to my right. The sounds came from here. There's a giant picture hanging on the empty wall. It's Morzanna, taken at the coronation I believe. Her hazel eyes seem innocent and kind. A thin, coppery gold crown sits atop her waist length, black hair. She wears a royal blue satin dress, decorated with white lace and bronze embroidery.

I follow the hallway across from the door. I walk into one of the rooms further down the hall as quietly as possible. There's a familiar red-headed heap in the corner of the completely empty room.

"Bexley!" I say. She sits with her legs to her chest. "What's going on?"

Bexley looks up at me, scared. "I don't know. It was dark, but someone dragged me here! He told me to be quiet, or I'd get caught. I didn't know what to do, so I listened to him. Then, he disappeared."

"Who was it? Someone working for the Queen? Is he still here?" I ask, glancing around and pushing the door shut. Bexley shrugs.

"I don't know," Bexley shakes her head. "I don't know what happened. It was weird. I think I passed out," she says before getting interrupted by a fit of coughs. She's obviously still out of it.

Anger and fear boil inside me, but I try to suppress it. "Did you try to fight him?"

"Oh, of course not! I'm thirteen! And a girl!" Bexley replies. "I'm scared."

I slam my palm against the wall. "Uhhh! I don't know what to do!"

"I told you there might be someone around," she whispers.

"I'm sorry. But we need to get out of here to somewhere safe. Come on," I urge.

Bexley nods, and I help her stand. I walk Bexley out of the house, contemplating what to do next. There's no way we could make it back to the lab with her like this, especially at night, but whoever that was could still be around.

I decide we should go back to one of the houses. I have a feeling that whoever took Bexley is nearby. For him to know that she was alone, he must have been watching us. *Who did he mean would catch us?*

All these questions swirl in my mind. But, most importantly, I need to figure out what's wrong with Bexley. I have a fair idea.

"Here," I say, handing her the water I had first gone to find after adding iodine and letting it sit. She takes and drinks it. Bexley sets the bottle down on the kitchen counter and sits at the table.

"I'm sorry," Bexley whispers.

I shake my head and sit across from her. "No, it's my fault. I should have let you rest before. And I shouldn't have left you."

Bexley gets some color back and wakes up more over the next few minutes.

"We should go before he comes back," she says, standing up weakly. "Come on," she calls and steps toward the door.

"Wait! We can't go back. It's too late and not safe."

She looks at me, annoyed. "It's not safe *here*. Now come on," Bexley says, stumbling out the door. I quickly grab her arm and pull her back inside.

"No. You can hardly walk, and you know there are people out there who will take us, and then we'll never finish the cure. It's too dangerous at night with the Hunters out. If he does come back, I don't know what we'll do, but he hasn't hurt us yet. Maybe he's gone." I shut the door, locking it as if that'll help.

"Ugh. Fine," she says reluctantly. Bexley plops down on the chair next to the door and puts her mask back on. "I don't like it here."

I sit on the floor and shove my hands into the pockets of my hoodie. "We'll go back early tomorrow."

If we make it until tomorrow. Tired, I lay down on the rug, ignoring the uncomfortable chill. I can hardly sleep though. I'm worrying about a lot of things. It's the usual: the cure, my family, Isaiah, Ele, and now Bexley. But I pretend to be asleep so Bexley won't detect my nervousness.

I know it's the Virus ailing her. I'm filled with a familiar loneliness and longing to have my parents back safe. I'd be more worried if I hadn't been exposed to my family already. I think I'm getting sick, too. Still, I want to be cautious around Bexley. She wears a mask almost all the time, and I try to keep my distance. I want to get back to the lab as soon as possible, but it isn't logical to go now.

I'm half asleep for a while, but the smokey haze of worry engulfs me.

"What was that?" Bexley whispers, bolting upright. She stares toward the kitchen. I locked the doors, so if anyone enters, we'll at least hear them break in. It helps a little knowing that, even though there's nothing we could do. "Graydon!" She kicks my arm.

I sit up. "Chill out. I didn't hear anything. There are still animals around."

"With diseases?" Bexley asks, looking around in the dark. She takes out her hand sanitizer.

I shrug. "I guess."

"Oh, great," she says sarcastically, leaning back in the chair.

Every sound jars me. I keep watching. I'm paranoid. Convincing myself that the noises are just the wind is hard. I spend most of the night sitting and watching the doors. I wonder what Isaiah's doing. I hope he can find Ele, and they can both get out. I don't even want to think about my parents right now.

Eventually, I'm sure it's approaching morning. Then I fall asleep. However, it isn't long before I'm awakened by a hand over my mouth.

18
ELEANORA: ALONE

Morning dawns around seven, but I've already been awake for an hour. Against my own judgment, I wait anxiously for Isaiah to come all morning, and each minute drags on like a weight has been tied around the hands of today's clock. The bedding here is infested with lice and bed bugs, and it's been a challenging trial to get used to. Every few seconds I find myself glancing at the door, overcome with boredom, anticipation, and excitement. I'm also finally experiencing symptoms of the Virus, and I've had a headache all morning. Last night, I had such intense chills, Marie felt the need to ask if I was demon-possessed.

I attempted to bathe in the sink today, which took an uncanny amount of time since the water pressure is so weak it took ten minutes to fill the sink halfway. Laying on my back in my bed, I sigh, thinking. Marie just finished giving me a lively gymnastics demonstration, which resulted in the *other* half of the mirror getting smashed during a misjudged back-handspring.

"I wonder when Isaiah will arrive," I say, twisting a strand of hair. Marie sits breathlessly on her bed across from me and kicks her sunshine yellow high-tops against the wall.

"Dunno," she says. "It probably isn't safe him to come yet."

I rub the spot on my wrist where I recently removed my bandages.

"I'm sure he'll come eventually," Marie says.

"I hope," I say. "I'm sorry I'm being so whiny. I know I'm lucky to know my family's even alive. We should go over the plan again, so when they come, we'll be ready."

Marie gives me a smile. "Don't worry. It'll work. I know it will."

I pace the room while Marie hops between the twin beds, each creaking loudly, but I don't have the brain space to be bothered by it.

Suddenly, loud knocking startles me and the door to our room is thrown open. I jolt up, and Marie jumps down from whichever of the beds she's on. Standing in the doorway is the nurse who took Reece, accompanied by two guards. I quickly recognize, with disgust, the one who brought me here, Ash. I glare at him, containing my anger only because I know I can't do anything. *Someday,* I promise myself, *I will get revenge on Ash.*

"Come out here," the nurse orders, gesturing to the two of us. For a moment, I'm paralyzed. "Hurry up!"

Reluctant, I follow Marie outside our room and into the hallway. The nurse harshly grabs our arms and drags us with her down the hall toward the entrance to the Double Guard. I glance over my shoulder, and the guards march inside our room.

"What are they doing?" Marie asks as I struggle against the nurse's grip.

"They're searching your room. After yesterday, I suggested it," the nurse says. I take a sharp breath with realization. *If they find our plans, they'll not only confiscate them, but most likely take us to a different room—and make sure that our plan fails. That will leave us with no way to escape and no way for Isaiah to find us.* Fearfully, I look at Marie, but she doesn't seem too concerned. *Maybe she doesn't want to act suspicious, or maybe I put too much faith in her; after all, she has no reason to care about whether Isaiah can find us. I barely know her.*

The nurse takes us through the entrance to the Double Guard. It's ominous with its huge doors and blood-red lettering, and even the entry hall is painted deep crimson. It makes me think about all the people who have lost hope coming through these doors and how I'm not going to be one of them. The nurse brings Marie and me to one of the rooms I was put in when I first arrived. *This is the last place I saw my brother. I can't let the nurse lock me away; if they find the plans, Isaiah will never find me. I must stop this.*

The ground before me suddenly contorts as panic-induced dizziness comes over me.

"Ele," Marie whispers in a warning tone as she obeys the nurse and steps inside the little room. "Chill."

She tries to take my hand, but I shake her off. Marie makes no effort to escape, and it annoys me. I struggle so much, my headband falls off and bounces across the floor. Eventually, the nurse wrangles and throws me in the room as well. I yell as she pulls the door shut and the lock clicks. The dingy room casts a hopeless vibe, feeding my hungry anger.

"Ele, stop it!" Marie says. I ignore her and kick the door, screaming. "Shut up!" Marie demands, pulling me away; I'm still fuming, but I allow her.

I bit my lip, and my own screams ring in my ears. "I'm gonna kill them!"

"No, you won't!" Marie says, pulling my arm. She gestures for me to sit on the bed—or what's left of the rusty dilapidated frame— and I do. Marie reaches into the pocket of her beat-up jean shorts and pulls out a few crumpled pieces of paper.

"How did you—" I ask, once again shocked. Taking them from her, I look over the plans to make sure they're real.

"I was worried last night this might happen, so I took them. Guess I was right," Marie says with a giggle.

"We won't die after all!" I sigh. "Marie, you're brilliant. Hey, but what about the other ones, the old ones?"

"I'll make up an excuse. Besides, I've tried most of them, so they probably won't care," she responds, placing the paper carefully back in her pocket.

"So you don't think they'll make us switch rooms?" I ask.

"No. Anyway, they're low on space. But listen, I have an idea," she says, lowering her voice to a whisper, not that anyone could hear us over the noise of the other rooms. "Since we're out of our room and beyond the Double Guard's barriers, if only one nurse comes to get us, I think we might have a chance to go and check if our plan will work."

I raise an eyebrow. "Really? How?"

Marie looks at me with a spark of anticipation, thinking. "We just have to wait for the right chance then we run. Before they find us, we'll already be back in our room. We'll give a reasonable explanation, and they won't punish us."

"I don't know," I say, shaking my head. *It's a risk, but I can make sure I won't be leading my brother into something significantly unsafe.* "Only if the moment seems perfectly safe. We'll check it quickly then get back fast?"

"Yep," Marie says confidently. "You worry too much. I've been here a while now, and I know how to be careful." I look at her questioningly.

"But haven't you gotten caught like a bunch of times?" I tease, but it is a merited question. "I mean, isn't that how you ended up in the Double Guard to begin with?"

Marie waves her hand. "Well yeah, but I've learned. Each time I've gotten better."

She wouldn't intentionally get us caught, but Marie's rather reckless, and I don't know if it's a good idea. But, she has been here longer than me, and I suppose we do need to know if our plan will succeed. Maybe it will give me a chance to explore more of the Infirmary too.

Ever since I came here, I've been caged—and who knows, maybe I'll see Isaiah or my parents. I nod, agreeing to Marie's plan.

Perfectly timed, the door opens, and the nurse waits outside. She summons us from the cell, still glaring beneath her mask, after which I see Marie is right; she once again came alone. Marie gives me a secret thumbs up, but I still find myself wringing a piece of hair.

By a stroke of luck, we arrive in a quiet hallway. I can't hear anyone nearby, and it seems like our best chance. Marie meets my gaze then there's the slightest hesitation in her step.

Marie kicks the nurse hard in the leg. The nurse loosens her grip just enough for Marie to yank herself free. Marie gallops down the hall in the direction we just came from. I try to run too, but the nurse has recovered enough that she holds my arm even tighter. So, I punch her in the stomach with my free hand before sprinting off after Marie. *I can't believe we just did that!*

I'm completely unaware of where we are, and behind us the nurse calls for help on her phone. I run even faster knowing soon her request will be answered, and Marie and I will be in danger.

My feet begin to hurt from pounding against the solid floor, and our loud footsteps echo off the empty walls, filling the lonely silence. Marie takes out the map and quickly reads it, stopping every once in a while to briefly scan the paper up close.

"Sorry, I'm pretty blind," Marie comments, mid-run. "It takes me a second to read your teeny handwriting."

"Marie, where are we going?" I ask, still running and breathless.

"Just a little farther! Then we'll be there!" she replies, glancing up from the map and turning the corner before bursting through a smaller door. Beyond it, there's a dark hallway. I know this isn't somewhere we should be, especially after I notice warning signs posted all over the walls. We come to fork in the hallway, and I'm convinced there are faint voices coming from behind us. Signs hang from the ceiling pointing to the intensive care unit one way, and a scribbled one to the left I can't read. Marie turns down the dark, unfamiliar hallway and I hesitantly follow her.

"Are you sure this is it?" I say, aware of the approaching voices. She nods, slowing down, and the further we walk the more unsure I become. Warning signs about radiation and dangerous chemicals are illuminated by the dim eerie light, and strange markings and words are scribbled out on the walls. Marie keeps glancing at the plans with a weird look and it concerns me.

"This is it!" she suddenly announces, regaining her confidence and skipping down the hall again. I follow her, and in front of us appears a metal door with a window. Marie stops and looks at it excitedly.

"Are you sure?" I ask, my heart racing. Marie nods.

"Of course! Well, I don't know *know*. We won't find out if we wait around forever! Now help me!" she says, taking hold of the rusted door handle. Sunlight pours in from the fogged-over glass and glints off the metal of the door's lock. Hope grows inside my soul, like a deprived plant exposed to sunlight.

"This *is* the exit, Ele!" Marie says. She laughs and struggles with the handle. "This door leads right outside!"

"Wait, we know it's here, so come on, we have to get back before they find us!" I say turning to leave.

"I want to be sure! Let's see if we can break this lock or something. Otherwise, we'll need to get a key. Come on Ele, you want to make sure for your brother, right? Please help me," Marie insists, pulling on the door. I grab hold of the handle as well. After a while, the rusted lock begins to fracture.

"It's working!" Marie exclaims. I grit my teeth and focus all my energy, hearing footsteps approaching. With one last pull, there's an audible crack before the somewhat weak lock falls to the floor in several pieces, and the door swings open.

Beams of light sting my eyes as I'm met with the warm morning air, and I stumble back, panting. Beyond the doorway is a small field of overgrown weeds; a fence surrounds half of it, but there's a road not far off. There are a few buildings in the distance. It's been so long since I've been outside, and Marie runs out the door, staring up at the sky.

"Look, we did it! We're free!" she says, twirling around. I watch her from the doorway. I want to join her—everything in me wants to run away and to leave this awful place—but I know we need to get back.

"I know, but, Marie, I hear them coming," I say, gesturing back the way we came. Her smile vanishes, and she looks to the ground.

"Come on," I say eagerly, taking a step down the hall.

Marie shakes her head, and a strange look falls across her dark eyes. "Listen Ele, it's been so long since I've been out, and I don't know if we'll get this chance again."

I stare at her, confused, but I know better than to say anything yet.

"I know I promised to go back, and I can hear them coming too. But we might never have this chance again. We either leave now or maybe never. I don't want either of us to be trapped again. Come with me," Marie pleads. "We can be free! If we get a chance, we'll come back for our families. But we have a shot to live again!"

"What? No, I-I can't! I have to find my brother and my parents. I can't just leave yet!" I exclaim, hurt. She looks at me with a sad expression. "And what about your brother? Your parents? You're going to abandon them too and never come back?" I go on, breathlessly.

"I'm sorry, Ele. I'll try to come back for them, but it's better one of us gets out, right?" Marie says. "If you can't come with me, then…" she looks off in the distance. "Then, goodbye."

Marie shoots me a guilty smile then turns and runs off, and I watch her disappear into the unknown buildings beyond. I can't believe what just happened, and time seems to stand still as I stare at the swaying, overgrown grass.

I'm drawn back to reality by noise behind me. I block out what just happened and try to focus on my current problem.

Quickly, I shut the door and replace the broken lock as best I can to make it look untouched. Only then does the thought cross my mind that I could have gone with Marie. My actions and choices, and everything that results from them, are my responsibility. I have to think through what I'm doing and what might happen as a result. And if I don't, I have to deal rightly and justly with the fallout, especially if my decisions affect other people. I would never abandon Isaiah, and if I can't bring my parents this time, my number one goal will be to return for them.

Running through the labyrinth of doors, I try to remember the way back, vacillating between feeling betrayed and terrified, wondering what I am going to do on my own. I turn down a hallway, certain it's correct, but a few minutes later I'm doubting it. *Am I going the right way? Is this the hall we took earlier, or was it the other one? What if I get caught before I can get back?*

Pausing and looking around, I try to get my bearings of this unknown place. My heart races with doubt, but I push on.

I turn around to go back, knowing I must have gone the wrong way. Not paying attention, I run right into someone. I stumble with a rush of frozen fear, then, surprised, I look up.

"Ele?"

19
ISAIAH: ELE?

I'm in disbelief. We find Ele's room empty. Both beds are vacant. The closet door is open. They aren't here.

"Are you sure this was it?" I ask Reece. He nods quickly.

"Yeah, of course!" he replies, equally confused. He scans the room. "They're not here, but someone else has been in this room recently."

I glance at him. "Someone, as in…?"

"Yeah," he says. "The Mordolus." He points to a paper on the wall. "This is their room, and they've both been checked out."

I try to step inside their little room. Reece stops me. "Cameras."

I pace the hall in front of the door. I absentmindedly count each of the deep scratches in the glassy floor.

"What are we gonna do?" Reece asks.

"We'll have to leave. Maybe we can check again later," I say.

Reece nods. He isn't confident in that idea. Honestly, neither am I. I didn't plan how to get in here again or even how to get out now. The plan was to see my sister.

I close the door. I detect a distant third set of footsteps. Someone's coming. We run back to the entrance to the Double Guard.

"We've still got the key," I say, taking it from my pocket. I quickly unlock the door.

We bolt back to the unrestricted areas. I try not to show it, but I'm super worried about Ele. *God, let her be okay.*

"Isaiah?" Reece says. "What if we don't find your sister? Maybe—maybe this is all wrong. Should we just, I don't know, listen to the Mordolus? What if they're right? Maybe it is all useless."

I shrug. I should probably say something encouraging. I'm so tired of having to be the one who convinces everyone else that there's hope. Especially when I feel there isn't much.

"I don't know. We'll have to figure something else out then," I say. Reece nods.

"But, like what? Are we going to try and escape?" Reece asks quietly. "Give up?"

"I don't know," I snap. Annoyance nags inside my head. "Just stop asking about it."

Awaiting your own death is something children should not have to deal with. You accept it eventually. Certain people you always see just disappear. They're gone. You learn what's important, but in the process you realize you're losing those exact things. It's hard. But if you want to survive, you have to fight. To be strong. You can't give in to hopeless circumstances. No matter how dark they are. I just have to pray that Ele remembers that.

We walk in silence for a while before I finally say something as we pass the Hopeful Rooms. *God is good. He saved me. This is His will. Christ is my hope. I will make it to where He wants me.*

"Reece, I'm sorry. It's just that I really don't know, and it's bothering me," I admit.

"It's okay," he says. "We'll find your sister, don't worry."

"Wait," I say, freezing. On the floor in the corner, there's a teal satin object. I run and pick it up.

"What's that?" Reece asks, crossing his arms.

I examine the headband. "This is Ele's."

"How do you know?" he asks. "It could be anyone's."

"She's been wearing the same headband everyday for the past three years—*I know*. That means she was here. Recently too," I say, thinking. We've got to find her. Tomorrow, maybe.

We're about to turn the last corner before getting to our room. Suddenly, someone slams into me. They thud to the floor. I look down, surprised. I'm not prepared for the force of the shock that collides with my whole reality.

"Ele?" I gasp. She looks up. Her wide eyes sparkle. Her locks of blond hair are longer and a little unruly right now. She seems older. And disheveled. It is Ele.

"Isaiah!" she screams, attacking me with a tight hug.

"Are you okay?" I ask, taking a deep breath.

"I'm fine!" Ele says, beaming.

"We tried to find you, but you weren't in your room!" I tell her. "What are you doing, anyway?"

"They were searching our room, and Marie and I decided to see if our escape idea would be successful. We ran away, and honestly I don't know what I was thinking, Isaiah. Now I'm going back before they find me," Ele explains.

"Wait, where's Marie?" Reece asks anxiously.

She hesitates. "She didn't want to risk not being able to escape later on, so she left when we found a way," Ele says. "But I know how to get out!"

She turns back toward me. "I can't believe I found you!"

"I know. Here's your headband," I say, handing it to her. Loud voices ring from the hallway behind us. "What's that?"

"Oh no, I'm sorry, Isaiah, but I have to leave now!" Ele says. She starts to walk away.

"Wait!" I say. "When will I see you?"

"Those voices are getting closer. We're going to get caught!" Reece mumbles, mostly to himself.

"Come tomorrow!" Ele says and turns away. "I love you!" she adds and dashes off.

"Okay, come on Reece," I announce.

A second later, the guards chasing my sister run by. They don't pay attention to us. With a renewed hope and a prayer for Ele, Reece and I head down the hall.

20
GRAYDON: KIDNAPPED

Adrenaline courses through me. Bexley's still curled up in the chair across the room as I'm dragged to my feet by two strong arms. I try fighting, but I don't think I can free myself. His hand is still over my mouth, so I can't scream because I can hardly breathe. Anyway, Bexley couldn't help me.

The back door slams shut, and I stumble as I'm forced down the steps to the deck. He takes me to the same house where I found Bexley. After tossing me into an empty bedroom, he exits and shuts the door. My mind races. I try the door, and it doesn't budge. A dark cloud of emotion settles in my brain. My heart pounds so hard, it's like my blood's trying to escape my veins. I throw myself against the door and yell for him to let me out.

It opens. "Be quiet!"

I take a better look at my kidnapper. I'm not sure how old he is, but I guess early twenties. His eyes are a mysterious hazel gray. He's a tall, hefty dude, with a short, neat beard. Dressed in mainly dark attire, he looks like a Mordolus member.

I can't think straight. Coherent versions of ideas meld with illogical ones. Maybe it's because of the hot vexation burning in the pit of my stomach. *I'm going to have to fight.* I glance around for anything I can use as a weapon, but the room is virtually empty.

"Please calm down," my abductor says, stepping inside the room and shutting the door.

I roll my eyes. *I just got kidnapped, I'm locked in a room, and I have no idea what's going on with Bexley. I'm not going to calm down—I'm getting out of here.*

"NO!" I shout, trying to get to the exit.

"Just listen. I want to talk to you," he says, standing in my way.

"I'm not going to just talk to someone who's trying to murder me!" I say, diving for the door with a fresh rush of reckless rage. The kidnapper blocks me, so I yank off my shoe. I'm super thankful it was raining today so I wore trench boots. I throw it. He isn't expecting it, and the shoe hits him right on the shoulder. Didn't help. I get another idea, glancing at the window right behind me. I rush for the boot again and throw it toward the glass as hard as I can, aiming for the weak bottom section of the single pane. Thankfully, it shatters. I scramble for a broken fragment, taking Bexley's idea from our first meeting. It worked decently for her—I think I'll have a permanent scar on my face. I don't have as great of aim as Bexley, but it's better than me standing here wielding a shoe.

My attacker approaches me, and I back into the wall, out of ideas. Coming toward me, he pauses before grabbing me by the shoulders. He spins me around and puts an arm across my neck. He's choking me. I drop the glass instinctively and try to escape his grip. Lightheadedness rushes through me. My vision obscures, and my head feels so wrong. Suddenly, there are three doors instead of one. I claw at his arms. *Don't pass out, please don't pass out,* I beg myself. But I can't breathe. I can't hear anything, and my legs give out. Everything disappears.

I awake a second later, at least I think, tied to a chair with my mouth gagged, alone. The memories flood back. My throat hurts and I groan, a headache growing. The only thing in the dark, musty room is my chair. It's a different room than before, which freaks me out. The door is shut. I struggle with the ropes, but they're too tight to move and cut into my wrists. Another rope is tied around my middle. I try to chew through the fabric in my mouth. After only a few minutes, I taste blood and have made zero progress.

I wait forever before footsteps approach behind the door. There's a familiar jingling. Bexley's charm bracelet.

The door opens. Bexley strides in, followed by my kidnapper. He shuts the door, and they both stay silent. Bexley glances around like the anxious tension is so severe she can see it.

I probably look insane. I only have one shoe, and I notice the other is beside the door. I can feel blood dripping out of my mouth. Bexley's expression only confirms my state.

"Have you calmed yourself?" the guy asks. I glare at him. He sighs, watching me strain against the cords. "Will you be quiet and civil?" I slowly nod.

Bexley unties me at his prompting. I stand up, knocking the chair over in the process. I stumble over to him.

"Who are you?" I ask, straightening.

"Atticus, and I'm *trying* to help you," the stranger says.

I scoff. "Yeah, for sure. You nearly killed me! I bet you're part of the Mordolus and think helping us means shipping us off to the Infirmary!"

"I'm not," Atticus assures.

"Why do you dress like that then?" Bexley asks.

"I don't want to get caught either," he says. "It helps me blend in. You two were going to get yourselves caught. You didn't listen the first time, and I'm surprised you haven't been discovered yet. I knew the second you arrived," he says.

"There's no one else out here but us," I say, confused and concerned that he was watching us.

"Actually, that's not true. Obviously, you don't know there's a base barely a mile away that Morzanna uses as a bunkhouse for the Mordolus. They constantly use these streets and send out frequent patrols," he explains.

I cross my arms. "Then why are you here?"

He avoids eye contact. "I've been watching them, trying to learn more about Morzanna's plan."

"Morzanna's plan?" Bexley questions, equally confused.

"You haven't noticed? She's planned something. I know it."

"I know *something* is going on. She has to have something to do with the Maraloxis Virus. But it seems pretty stupid to use a virus that you don't even have a cure for," I say.

Atticus examines me cautiously. "She isn't using it, she created it."

Bexley's eyes widen. She takes a few steps back as if punched by an unseen force.

"WHAT?" I ask.

"Morzanna created the Maraloxis virus," he repeats.

I finally put things together in my mind. I shake my head to clear the shock. "Why?"

"I don't know yet. That's what I'm trying to figure out," Atticus says.

"How could she do this?" Bexley says quietly.

An inferno of anger and disbelief overwhelms me. I'm completely mind blown. It makes sense, even though I don't want to believe it. I step back, needing to think, but I still don't trust Atticus. "What if Erigate is in on this too? What if Morzanna is working for them, or maybe she's a fake and never was Cyrus's daughter? She could be using the Maraloxis Virus to destroy us," I ramble, slamming a fist against the wall. "They've been wanting war for a while." Atticus simply shakes his head. I rub my sore neck.

"You okay?" Bexley asks.

"Yeah," I say. "I'm fine."

"I'm sorry. You wouldn't listen to me. The Mordolus were going to hear, so I had to do something," Atticus apologizes. I nod, but I don't know if I forgive him yet.

I still can't comprehend that Morzanna created the Maraloxis Virus.

"We need to go," Bexley says.

"You're right, we have to leave," I say. "We're working on a cure for the Maraloxis Virus right now. We needed supplies for it."

Atticus looks at me carefully. For some reason, he doesn't act surprised. "Come on then. Quietly," he says, opening the door.

"Wait, Bexley's sick. She won't be able to walk all the way back now. It's several miles," I say.

"Yeah, and let's not forget you were just knocked out!" Bexley adds.

Atticus looks at me, then Bexley, and walks out the bedroom door. I glance at Bexley, and she shrugs. I stop to put on my shoe, and we follow him down the steep carpeted staircase. It kind of weirds me out because I definitely don't remember coming up any stairs. I still feel disoriented. He takes us through the house and out the back door. The yard is a mass of maple trees and overgrown grass. The wind is strong, and it's still pretty dark out. A tattered, moss and algae-covered fence looks like it grew around the house straight from the ground.

"Wait here," Atticus says, before disappearing. He walks out of sight behind another one of the houses in the suburb street. A few seconds later he returns to the driveway with a car. I haven't seen any cars in use for a long time except the ones manufactured for the

Mordolus. No one would risk getting caught, not to mention there isn't really anyone left outside of the Infirmary. I see cars *parked* all the time, though. The Mordolus haven't picked every one up yet.

Atticus gets out and walks over to us. The vehicle has the Queen's insignia printed on the side. It's the same as all the other Mordolus vehicles: black, van-like, and dirty.

"Where did you get that?" I ask.

"I have ways," Atticus says with a shrug. "It's stolen," he adds, noticing my skeptical look.

He hands me the keys and Bexley our bag of supplies. I wonder where he got my backpack. Now that I think of it, I don't know how he got Bexley to come with him earlier. I look down at the keys.

"Wait, I don't know how to drive!" I say. He looks at Bexley, who holds her hands up to say she doesn't either.

He tilts his head. "How old are you?"

"Fifteen," I say.

"You're old enough. It's simple. Work together, and figure it out," he says. "None of the Mordolus drive well. Just don't crash and you'll be good. Don't ever return here. Stay away from the base. Good luck with the cure."

Atticus heads inside the house. Bexley looks at me before hopping down the steps to the car. I follow her, and she makes it evident she will not be the one driving. Reluctantly, I climb into the driver's side. I try to get my bearings. Bexley gets in, waiting for me to start. I put the keys in the ignition and step on the brake. Not only do I not know how to drive, I haven't even been in a car in months. The

Mordolus sold all the gasoline to other countries, too. I saw them loading it on trucks a couple months ago. I wonder how Atticus filled the tank, but he seems to have some kind of resources. I really hope he hasn't duped us.

I take a deep breath. Honestly, I'm scared. Bexley looks at me.

"Are you gonna go?" she asks. I glare at her.

"Care to drive instead?" I offer.

She shakes her head. "I believe in you," Bexley says. "You've got this."

I finally harness enough courage to put the vehicle in drive and take my foot off the brake. Instantly, we start rolling down the hill. I pretend not to be afraid for our lives.

It's starting to get brighter, which is good because I have no idea how to turn on the lights. I come to the first turn, which I take way too fast. Bexley starts laughing at me. So far I haven't killed us yet, so I guess that's good.

"Shut up," I say. She continues to giggle. I will myself not to show my humiliation when it happens again at the next corner.

I improve. At least enough that Bexley isn't stifling laughter every three seconds.

"So, what do you think about what Atticus told us?" Bexley finally asks.

"I don't know. It's so wrong. If he was telling the truth then the Queen isn't very smart. Morzanna has all the Mordolus out and exposes them, and herself, to the Virus. And I can't even imagine why she would create the Maraloxis Virus to begin with. That's absolutely evil," I say.

"Well she must have a reason. Some very, very, twisted motive. It doesn't make sense though. If everyone dies, maybe even herself, then why would she do it? No one will be there to help her or anything. Atticus told me, after he took you and came back, that he had been looking into Morzanna's backstory before the outbreak. She's been very secretive about what might give us clues to her purpose. It's all confusing," Bexley says frustratedly, but starts tittering again when I accidentally hit the brakes instead of the acceleration.

The sun crests the distant mountains. For once in a long time, it's not raining, and the sun shines over the treetops. Despite the disturbing news, a strange peace settles over us.

"What was that?" Bexley hisses, glancing over her shoulder.

"What?" I ask.

"I swear I saw something in the back," she says uneasily. "I heard something too."

I shrug and look in the mirror. "I didn't. It's probably nothing."

Bexley bites her lip. "What if there's a rat? Or a snake? Or maybe a—"

"Stowaway?" I interrupt. I laugh when she gasps. "Seriously, it's probably nothing. Enough with the 'what ifs'."

Suddenly, Bexley squeals again. I slam the brakes.

"I know you heard that," she says, covering her face. Soft shuffling comes from the back.

"You need to calm down," I say, glancing toward the noise. "I almost killed us because of your freak-out."

"I will, but just figure out what it is," she demands, sinking into the seat.

I consider telling her to do it herself if it's that big of a deal. Or just keep driving. But Bexley's stubborn and I'm nice. "Fine," I relent, opening the door.

"You gonna put it in park?" Bexley asks. I sigh. *How'd I forget that?*

After making sure I'm not going to send Bexley and the car careening into a tree, I get out and open the back door.

"Do you see anything?" Bexley asks from behind her hands.

"Not yet," I respond, searching the floor. My heart sorta races. I bend down to look under some empty crates. A blueish gray streak blurs out from underneath. Bexley shrieks. I laugh as I stare at the sky-colored, feathered creature that sits on the dashboard.

"What is it?" Bexley cries, her eyes still covered by her hands.

"I think the terrifying little birdie is gonna attack you!" I tease. She uncovers her face. Bexley sighs and rolls her eyes, but her cheeks grow red with embarrassment.

"Just get rid of it so we can go," she mumbles. I laugh again and scoop up the bird. I'm about to release it outside, but I notice the bird has a little metal ring around its right leg. It's been banded. I should have realized immediately from its vibrant blue feathers. A lot of people just released their pets at some point so they had a chance if the owners were admitted into the Infirmary. I don't know how a domestic bird survived this long. I glance at the sky.

"What are you doing, Graydon?" Bexley asks, dumping a ton of hand sanitizer on her hands. She carries that bottle everywhere, and it's already almost empty. I turn over a plastic container on the floor of the trunk, covering the bird and fastening it with some string from my backpack as a makeshift enclosure.

"We can't leave it outside," I admit, climbing back into the front.

"It probably has diseases!" Bexley whines.

"Probably," I say.

"Great, now you have a pet," she says sarcastically.

"Come on, Bexley," I say.

After a few more minutes of complaining, Bexley swallows her pride. She starts planning on where we'll keep the bird, what we'll feed it, and brainstorming names.

I can't wait to get to the lab and stop embarrassing myself. By the time we get there, I've accidentally run into two medians and nearly crashed into a stop sign. Somehow the windshield wipers got turned on, and I can't figure out how to turn them off. Bexley laughs so hard she can't even speak. I park the car behind the lab so no one will see it, nearly colliding with the back steps. I deem that sufficiently hidden.

As we enter the lab, my thoughts are back on the cure. I hope the ingredients we found will finally give us our breakthrough.

21
ELEANORA: DECISIONS

Leaving my brother and Reece behind, I speed down the hall toward the Double Guard. *I can't believe I saw Isaiah!* Everything in me except my logic wants to turn around right now and drag him with me back to where Marie escaped.

I try to recall the way back through the labyrinth of hallways, but I don't have the map nor do I think this is the way we came. Bright lights shine from the ceiling and reflect on the floor, and the air is electric with excitement.

I have to tackle getting back to my room before the Mordolus find me, which is proving harder than anticipated, since every hall here is identical to the next, and I have no idea where I am.

I race around the corner and, for the second time today, slam into someone. *I really need to be more careful.* Unfortunately, this time it isn't Isaiah or my parents or some long-lost friend.

No, it's the same nurse who we escaped from earlier. Immediately grabbing my wrist with a scoff, the nurse drags me back toward my room, her face set in a fierce scowl.

"Where's the other one?" she sneers, and I shrug.

"I don't know," I say quietly, and I'm not lying; I don't know where Marie is for sure, just that she is not in the Infirmary anymore.

Luckily, the nurse doesn't question me anymore and proceeds to bring me back to the Double Guard. I'm fortunate she found me because I never would have made it back alone. I willingly enter my room, and she locks the door. I'd never thought I would be happy to be back, but I am.

I glance at the two beds, feeling lonely thinking about the loss of my exuberant roommate. The silence is a cold reminder I'm on my own now to figure out how to escape, but at least I have my brother back. *Listen Ele, you've got to get it together. You've spent long enough worrying and thinking things over, now's the time to get it together. Now is the time to take action.*

The continuous mystery of how anyone could follow the Queen overwhelms my mind; I just don't understand it. Maybe it's true that some of the Mordolus really do care more than they show. Perhaps Morzanna's interaction restrictions lead them to seem fouler than they are. Everything is unclear as if there's some great secret hiding within these walls, waiting for someone to discover it. *Will I ever figure out the truth or will it stay shrouded behind lies and mysteries? I can only hope one day this will all make sense.*

22

GRAYDON: AMARYLLIS

In the garage-turned-lab, it's utterly hot from the August heat. Still, I'm glad to be back.

"We need a cage," Bexley says, hopping down the concrete steps and eyeing the cardboard box in her hands. The bird chirps and thrashes wildly inside.

I locate the one I found a few weeks ago in the hallway closet. I only kept it to catch invading rats, but I don't mention that to Bexley. The square cage is rusted and intended for a different animal, but it'll work. Bexley retrieves some cuttings from a crepe myrtle tree in the backyard and adds them to the enclosure. She puts the bird inside, and it flits around for a minute before perching on a branch.

"So, let's get started," Bexley says, taking out each of the scavenged items we collected and setting them on the table neatly.

"I'll get the base supplies," I say, heading over to the storage shelf.

Bexley rearranges vials and tools on the table. "I think what we need to do is get more organized. Have you documented what chemicals haven't been successful and which ones you're trying?"

"Well, no, but I have all the leftovers labeled and stored in that box over there," I say.

Bexley drags out the large plastic tub of vials and bottles from under the table. "Oh, this is a cluttered mess! You're never going to remember what you've done. I'm reorganizing. It will also prevent duplicates. No use wasting time on something we've already tried," Bexley says. "I need a notebook ASAP."

I toss her one from a small stack on the wooden wall shelf directly above me.

"You get everything prepped while I fix this," Bexley says. She sits down at the other end of the table and starts documenting each of the pill containers and medicine bottles.

"Be sure to put the chemical title, not the generic name," I say. "When you're done, we can start testing the new ones."

I check up on the mice to make sure none of them have died. I shut the last cage and head over to get out the base mixture from the vials on the rack.

"Oh, I've got it!" Bexley exclaims.

"What?"

"We're naming him Stormy," she announces.

"The bird?" I ask.

"Yes," she responds. Stormy hops around inside his cage and chirps. Teal blue feathers contrast his ash gray pinions. His black eyes are like two tiny, dark pearls. "Also, I've finished." She holds up the notebook, and each chemical is listed with an X beside most of them. "I haven't marked the chemicals we got today since we haven't tested them, but if they don't work, we can put an 'X' next to them too."

Hours later and way past nightfall, I can barely stay awake. Other than ruling out ivermectin, remdesivir, and amantadine, which I've been wanting to try for a while and just recently found, we made no progress. I think we need to move outside common viral treatments and try something new like possibly a mineral or vitamin. We also get some mice prepared for testing.

I stop and watch little moths dance around the lights. Sometimes I feel like those moths; I'm always chasing after something I'm never going to get. The only sound is the quiet scratching on paper as Bexley scribbles down what chemicals we just discovered aren't successful. Bexley finishes writing and sighs tiredly.

"I guess it's time to take a break," she says, standing up and coughing roughly a few times. Bexley says goodnight, grabs Stormy, and goes off to her room. I check that all the mice cages are secure and turn off the light. I step out of the garage, lock all the doors, and climb the stairs to one of the bedrooms. It isn't destroyed, which is good because I think the Mordolus like to ruin the houses as much as possible. Almost always windows are broken, it's a mess, etc. This room is fairly untouched. It's too late to go home now. This room is a guest room, I think. Bexley's is the master. I like the guest rooms best because I don't have to think about how this is possibly a dead person's room. I especially hate the empty children's rooms.

I drag a blanket and pillow off the bed then curl up on the ground. The floor is more welcoming than the bed. I used to sleep on the ground when I was uneasy.

Something clanks against the wooden floor. It's the bottle I discovered earlier at the house. I take it from my pocket and put it aside. The Queen's insignia is its only form of identification, which is the only reason I kept the bottle. I'm intrigued by it. Eventually, it dawns on me that the sand inside seems to be glowing, which is weird. Unsettling. I haven't slept much in two days, so pretty soon I fall asleep.

The next morning, I wake up late to the sound of soft rain on the roof. It's the peaceful kind that reminds me of when Isaiah and I would put on our rainboots and play in the water and mud. Unfortunately, the memory is interrupted by pain in my back. I guess that's what I get for sleeping on the floor all night.

I finally get up when the sky grows from dark gray to white, and the storm slows. I take the mysterious bottle with me. I head downstairs to the garage. The light's on, and Bexley has Stormy out and plays with him. She's finally changed out of the ripped, dirty clothes she was wearing and greets me before putting on her mask. Bexley's good about wearing it, and we always sit at opposite ends of the table. I've been taking some vitamins I found to try and keep myself well. Also, I gave Bexley some leftover cough medicine last night I had from a failed concoction, and it's helping her symptoms some.

I share my new ideas, and soon I find myself taking notes while Bexley studies virus-to-mineral reactions under the microscope. She describes some vague shape or composition change, and I find it in one of the books. On a shelf above the table, the obnoxious bird chirps its annoying song. Every time I start to concentrate, Stormy squawks and feathers rain down onto the table. I suggest putting him away in one of the other rooms, but Bexley insists that he would be lonely. I just roll my eyes.

"I need to find some food for him," Bexley finally decides, getting up and coughing several times. "Maybe it will quiet him for a while." I nod in agreement.

"Here," I say, searching through a few things in the corner, before handing her a quarter bag of bird seed that had been left behind in the garage from its previous owners. Again, I used it—not inside, of course—to lure mice into the traps for testing. Bexley sprinkles some inside the cage and it seems to satisfy Stormy.

The rain has started up again, joined by lightning and dark storm clouds. Bexley has another coughing fit. She's been having them all day and leaves the garage so I don't catch anything. It might be too late. I've been feeling off already, which I've allotted to subtle beginning symptoms. I'm often visited by hatred. I hate trying to find a cure. I hate the thought that I'm dying and have to spend all my time trying to come up with a cure. But I have people counting on me. That makes it bearable.

I pick up my father's full, frayed notebook. I've nearly memorized these pages. The same words bounce around my head, but

I still don't understand them. It's like another language. It took me a long time to collect the chemicals I needed to make the base and something's still missing to finally overpower the Virus. And I have no idea what it is—if it even exists, and it seems an ever-increasing possibility that it does not.

I take the glass bottle out of my pocket. I run my fingers across the engraved M.

"What's that?" Bexley asks.

"Don't know. I found it at that last house," I reply. She takes it from me.

"Cool," she says. Bexley unscrews the lid and pours a small amount out onto the table. "Pink sand. In a bottle. With the Mordolus symbol."

"Yeah," I say.

"It smells so odd. Something like cinnamon and chlorine," Bexley says. "Here."

I take the bottle. "Yeah, it does. Maybe it's poison."

"Well I'm not going to test it out," Bexley says, then adds wistfully, "Or maybe it's fairy dust."

"Fairy dust?" I scoff.

"Oh, I'm joking, of course," Bexley responds. "It is sparkly though."

"And it glows," I comment.

"Oh really!" Bexley says. She takes the vial, caps it, and looks at it in her hands. "It does!"

As she goes to put the bottle back, it slips out of her hand. The thin glass shatters when it hits the edge of the metal dish she had been working with. Suddenly everything is coated in pink, sandy powder. A rose-colored fog hovers over the table. Bexley looks frustrated.

"I broke the fairy dust!" she sighs and coughs. "Ugh, I think I inhaled some!"

When the dust settles, everything on the table is a mess. Glistening glass pieces are scattered all over. Tiny grains of sand land on Bexley's face and fiery hair making her look sparkly like red tourmaline. She takes off her mask and shakes it out.

"It's fine, it wasn't that important anyway—" I start.

"I got some in this!" Bexley says irritatedly, gesturing to the base mixture sitting in front of her in a clear round dish.

"It's fine, okay? Just throw it out, we have plenty," I say, which isn't entirely true, but we have to limit the experimental variables and can't risk using contaminated ingredients.

"Okay," Bexley says, dusting off the table. She sweeps up all the glass pieces with two pieces of paper, muttering ridicules to herself as she dumps them in the trash. "Goodbye, lovely glowing fairy dust."

I turn back to my concoction and fill a needle. I'm using hydroxychloroquine. It's probably too similar to chloroquine that's already in the cure, but we have to try everything. I go over to the wooden shelving and take down one of the plastic containers. Throwing on some gloves, I open the cage.

"Ugh," Bexley says, backing away. "Diseases."

"Yeah, Bexley, that's the point," I say and inject the silver-furred rodent.

"Poor victimized creatures," she says sadly.

"We have no choice," I say, replacing the lid of the cage. The truth is, I always release the ones that survive and never reuse them. I'm not cruel. I take out a marker and label the cage 'twenty-nine: hydroxychloroquine'.

"Oh, we should give them names!" Bexley says. "I'm not going to just call it twenty-nine. That's so boring."

I shrug. "If you want to." I'm definitely not going to admit that I like to call the two in the corner Fox and Fawn. And the really orange one is Sage.

I walk over to the cages and look for a new mouse. Bexley makes sure the lid is on tightly before picking up the first enclosure.

"This one's name is Emmaline," she says. I find an unused mouse and take it over to the table. I remove the lid and carefully reach for the rodent. Bexley looks that one over. "And this is Amaryllis."

"Yeah? Well, Amaryllis just bit me," I say frustratedly as I finally wrangle the wild creature. Gloves are mandatory for working with mice. I've gotten bitten way too many times. Like right now. Thankfully, its sharp teeth don't go through the gloves. That's happened before. I made sure to clean those wounds so I didn't get an infection or something.

Bexley finishes combining the mixture she was making in a tall glass graduated cylinder.

"You better do it," she says and hands me the prepared needle. "I just can't stab Amaryllis. Also, diseases."

"Okay," I agree. Bexley has animal issues. And disease issues.

"So, how do we know if the cure is successful?" Bexley asks.

"After about twenty-four hours we can test the blood with the solution. If the mixture fades to red, we know it's negative. The testing solution is dark green, so the indicator won't shift unless the virus isn't present," I explain. "If the test turns any other color than red, the mouse is still infected."

"Oh, that makes sense," Bexley replies.

Afterward, we don't have anything else to test, or any more mice, so I just scan some science books for the rest of the afternoon. It's really hard because the font is so tiny I can hardly see it, and I can't stay focused long enough to finish one paragraph. Bexley tries reading out loud, but that doesn't work either because she mispronounces every other word, and we keep laughing. After giving Bexley some more important details on the process of finding an antidote, it's about eight. We cook up some rice on the alcohol burner and have some mint tea. I've learned adding things to the water treated with iodine tastes a lot better than having it plain. Afterward, I head home for the night.

The next morning, we have something to do at least: test yesterday's mice. I don some gloves while Bexley gathers the cages. I get out the Maraloxis tests and place them on the table, along with empty syringes. I draw the blood and hand it to Bexley to mix with the testing solution.

"What are we going to do today?" Bexley asks, setting out each of the little jars and filling them with a tablespoon of the testing solution.

"We could go out and search for more ingredients for the base or new chemicals. We're running super low on dexamethasone. Or we could catch more mice," I say.

"Oh, how fun," Bexley says sarcastically. She shakes up a test in a small round container then sets it with the rest to process. "Any other options?"

"No. We are almost out of rations and water though. I think we have like maybe two days left of meals," I say, drawing the final needle full of blood. The mouse jumps out of my hand and luckily back into its cage. "Unless you have an idea."

Suddenly, Bexley shrieks. She jumps up so fast, one of the cages tumbles off the table.

"What is it?" I ask quickly. None of the mice have escaped their cages, even the one that fell. She squeals and mumbles incoherently.

"Just look!" she says frantically, holding something out to me.

I take the jar from her. It contains a strong red liquid. I quickly glance at the other four tests, all still dark green. But this one's red.

Negative.

I jump up too, shocked and overwhelmed with disbelief. "What? Negative?! Which one is it, Bexley?"

"Thirty!" she says excitedly. "I mean, Amaryllis!"

"You did that one! What'd you put in it?!" I ask hurriedly, confirming with my memory that that cage had tested positive to begin with.

"Rimantadine," she tells me.

"What? I've done that before! Are you sure?" I ask.

Bexley instantly checks the label on one of the cages and nods vigorously. "Maybe I missed that one while documenting?"

"Do we have any of it left? Did you save any?" I urge. She starts hunting through the vials on the table. Several of them roll off, but neither of us pays much attention. Bexley picks up one, light pink in color.

"This is it," she says.

"That doesn't look like the one I made with rimantadine before," I say, looking it over, reading the label, and thinking.

"I don't know, but that's what I put in it!"

I remove the lid. It smells like spices and bleach. "Bexley, did you ever throw out that first part? The one that got the sand stuff spilled in it?"

She shakes her head. "I didn't want to waste it."

I laugh. "Bexley! That's what it is!"

"The fairy dust!?" she asks excitedly.

I nod. "The fairy dust. That's the final ingredient."

Bexley snatches the vial of pinkish liquid. "So this is the cure?"

"I guess!" I say, thrilled. "We actually completed an antidote for the Maraloxis Virus!"

Bexley jumps up and down and squeals, laughing with the unrestrained glee of a child. She throws her arms around me. "Oh, I can't believe it, Graydon!"

"I know," I say, my heart pounding. "Everyone's going to be okay."

Bexley steps back. "We should try it to make sure it works. I volunteer."

"Are you sure?" I ask. "Testing it on a mouse is one thing, trying it on a person is another. We haven't even done a second trial. It's super risky."

Bexley nods and holds up the vial. "We can't use all of what we have on tests and never find out if it truly works!" She pours out half of the rose liquid—about twenty milliliters—into a random beaker from the table.

"I'm serious, Bexley," I reiterate. "We have no idea what was put in that vial. We've only tested it once."

She sets down the beaker. "I'm getting sicker. If it doesn't work and I get poisoned, I'm going to die anyway."

"Okay, that's a little rash," I say.

"I'm just so excited, and I want to try it now! Unless there's something special about Amaryllis, that fairy dust cured her. Someone's going to have to sacrifice and try it, and I'm the only sick one here," she convinces, picking up the beaker once more. Good points. I don't argue anymore but prepare myself for something to go wrong.

"What do I do?" she asks.

"Drink it," I respond. "I could never get the mice to even taste anything I tried, so I had to resort to injections."

After taking off her mask, Bexley slowly raises the beaker to her mouth. She hesitates for a second before downing it. "That tastes so strange. How long will it take to know?"

"It probably won't work immediately," I say. "That's given you got the dosage right too."

"I feel so impatient," Bexley says eagerly.

"Here's what we'll do: you go rest, I'll clean up in here, and after we're pretty sure you haven't been poisoned, I'll go home. I'll come back in a few hours and see how you're doing," I say.

"Sounds good," she says.

Bexley heads to her room. I sweep up the broken vials, tidy the table, and return the cages. I put the mystery medication into a new bottle and set it in a wooden box on the table. Bexley must have been super excited: she even forgot to take Stormy. It's been about an hour, so I take the bird to Bexley's room.

"It's working already!" she promises me. "Just wait, by tomorrow, I'm going to be all better."

"We'll see," I say, trying to suppress the explosion of excitement going on in my head right now. If she's measurably improved when I return, I'll let myself believe it.

Cleansing relief washes over me as I walk home. Excitement bubbles inside me. The realization hits. My parents can be saved, my friends can survive, and a remedy does exist.

I go home, change, and take a minute to breathe. Two hours later, I'm back at the lab. Bexley meets me in the living room.

"Graydon, I'm okay! The cure is working!" she says. "I have so much more energy, I haven't coughed in thirty minutes, and I can just tell. We have to go find more of that powder now." She grabs Stormy's cage and sprints for the door. It's working so quickly and well. Bexley's right. I really think she's getting better. I've been in shock for the past three hours.

"Do we really need to bring the bird?" I ask, breaking out of my unbelieving daze.

"Of course!" Bexley yells back, and I smile. I leave the cure in its box and don't take any for myself. A feeling nags that we might not find any more of that fairy dust—I mean powder—and I'm saving the cure for my parents, and if there's enough, Isaiah and Ele.

I follow Bexley, watching as she runs down the stairs with exhilaration and trips over the third step. We laugh, not really because it's funny, but because suddenly we aren't dying.

"You should break things more often," I joke.

"So what's the plan?" Bexley says, crossing her arms as we follow the sidewalk. A pair of mourning doves flies to a new tree, calling to each other.

"I don't know. Maybe find Atticus and ask him? He knows more about Mordolus things than we do," I propose.

"Great idea!"

She dashes to the car we've borrowed, still hidden in the backyard. I stare at the hated symbol, the Queen's insignia. The red-colored sign bears a sharp 'M' in the middle, the same that was on the bottle. Sometimes I wonder if it is for Morzanna or Mordolus. Either way, I think it would be better to stand for Murderer. It's revolting. Bexley tells me to hurry up.

"You're driving this time though!" I call, running after her.

Big mistake. I might be a slightly reckless driver, but Bexley drives like she's a hundred-fifty years old. I'm lucky if she reaches thirty miles-per-hour.

"Bexley, there's literally no one else on the roads. You don't have to stop at every single stop sign," I comment after I'm pretty sure we've been on the road for forty-five minutes to get five easy miles.

Bexley sighs. "Graydon, I'm abiding by the laws of our province. That means I stop at the stop signs. Since the traffic lights don't work, you treat it as a four-way stop."

"The Mordolus aren't going to. If they see someone stopping at intersections, they might wonder, take a second look, and realize there's a thirteen-year-old driving," I point out. "Then that's it for us."

"Okay, Graydon. Fine. *Fine*," Bexley says, clearly annoyed. She goes right through the next stop sign.

"Good," I say. "See? No one's going to pull you over."

"Oh, whatever," she replies.

"You could go a little faster too," I suggest.

"Well, I was trying not to give us whiplash like last time we were in the car," she says properly. I look out the window and ignore her comment. She picks up the speed though.

We finally stop outside Atticus's house. We step out of the car and walk up to the door. I convince Bexley to leave Stormy in the car. I look around the street, eager to get out of the open.

"So do we just go in?" Bexley says, stepping up behind me on the tiny cement back porch.

The door then opens. Atticus stands in front of us.

"What are you doing here? I told you not to come back," he says, peering out over my shoulder. Even though he helped us, I'm still intimidated. I mean, last time Atticus assisted us, I ended up incapacitated. It was probably for the best.

Atticus sighs. "Give me the keys. You can't leave the car out there. Come inside and wait for me."

Bexley hands him the keys and he leaves. When he returns shortly after, Atticus shuts and locks the door before leading us to the second room inside.

"We need to talk with you. We found this bottle with the Mordolus symbol, and it's a long story, but it's the ingredient we needed to complete a cure," I explain.

"You finished it? It works?" he asks suspiciously from me to Bexley. I nod.

"Look at Bexley," I say. She doesn't seem as pale. Atticus stares at Bexley for a minute, and she straightens energetically. "She took it and has quickly improved."

"We'll see," he says unconvinced. "So, what did you find?"

"It was a bottle, I would have brought it, but it got broken. It had some pink powder in it," I explain.

"Fairy dust," Bexley intervenes. I ignore her.

"I found it in a house that someone had been hiding in during the shutdown. We accidentally broke it and realized it was the final ingredient we needed for the cure. The test on a mouse was negative. Bexley tried it, and I think it's working."

"It is!" Bexley adds.

Atticus nods slowly but doesn't respond yet.

"And now we need to know what it is so we can get more," Bexley interjects into the silence.

"You can't blame me for thinking it's hard to believe. A couple of kids created an antidote for a disease that scientists couldn't? The one that was said to be impossible?" Atticus stares at us. Doubt begins to sneak in, but I overcome it.

"Well, yeah? But actually we just *finished* it. My dad's a biotech and was working with a group of other scientists. They made most of it. We only had to find the last ingredient. And you told us the Queen is using the Virus, so maybe those scientists were lying," I say. "When my dad and the other scientists were gone, I had to complete it. Thankfully, I had help," I say, and Bexley smiles at me. I miss my parents so much. I'll do anything to get them back. *Anything.* "Please, Atticus, help us."

23
BEXLEY: GONE IN A BLAZE

"Who is your father?" Atticus asks.

"Madison Pierce, a biotech at Willowmire Epidemiology and Drug Development. Please help us," Graydon entreats.

Atticus receives the plea with a moment of silent consideration. "Before the complete lockdown, I was also investigating an antidote. There's always been some way to stop epidemics in the past. Yellow fever, influenza, polio, ebola…there's been some remedy, some treatment. Maybe it's a vaccine, but there was always some way to fight it. I didn't think it'd be a cure since traditional viruses can't be 'cured'. But there's also never been a virus with 100% fatality. Maybe it's true you have developed—or finished—some treatment. I've watched the Mordolus, but I don't have any idea of what the bottle was or why it was there," Atticus tells us. "It's curious that it bore that symbol. I need time to think on it. I can't help you now."

Graydon glances at me, reflecting my own disheartened feelings.

"Oh," I say. "Well, thank you anyway."

"Do you have the Virus?" Graydon suddenly asks Atticus, looking up from the floor.

"We probably all do," Atticus says. "We've all been exposed at least."

Chances are without our remedy, it's over for all of us. We've got to find more fairy dust and figure out what it is.

"How far do you think it's spread?" I ask.

"It started in Ellismark, where they have something there like the Infirmary. It's called the Sanatorium, I think. People said something about an outbreak in Valerrow, and a few cases in Lossaree. But I can't be sure since communication is gone," Atticus says.

"So you do believe us, though, about the cure?" Graydon asks.

"If I do, it explains some things—and confuses others," Atticus says. I was hoping his reaction would be something like 'A cure Fantastic! Let me help you save everyone!'. The disappointment draws me from my joy of the antidote's discovery and leads me to wonder.

"Is there anything else? Any more information that we could use to find it?" Graydon asks.

Atticus shakes his head. "Sorry, but if I find anything out, I'll tell you. I'll look for more or find the source in the meantime. I'll check out that house where you discovered it too. Here are the keys. The car is parked in the back."

I want to ask how he will find us to tell us, but I realize that since he found us before, he probably can again. It's a slightly unsettling thought, considering the Mordolus might have the same ease.

"Thank you," I say.

We leave the house, crestfallen.

"That wasn't very helpful," Graydon says, leaping down the brick stairs, after glancing around the road and listening, of course.

"I'm so confused right now. Why would the Queen have the fairy dust? It really could be anything. What if it's something typical we have on hand, and we just have no idea?" I say, brainstorming. "How are we going to find more of it?"

"And if we do, how do we get the cure to everyone? The Queen's not gonna just let us into the Infirmary with the cure—the one she said was impossible, for the Virus she probably created. No one would ever trust her again," Graydon adds.

"You really think if we told her we had a cure, she would care that much about her queenship to not give it to everyone?" I ask.

"Who knows? Especially if she did create the Virus to begin with," Graydon replies.

"Well, maybe if we can just figure out what the sandy powder stuff is, we can tackle the main problem right now, AKA making the cure," I say.

"Maybe from what we have left, we could run some tests and find out what it is," Graydon suggests.

"You know how to do that?" I ask, surprised.

"No," he admits, shrugging. "But it's worth experimenting."

I stare up at the hazy, gray sky, which signals that at any moment we might be caught in the violent storm that's brewing. I hear a crack of thunder close by.

"We need to get back to the lab," Graydon says, glancing at the darkening sky. "Definitely don't want to be caught in that." Cool raindrops splatter on the pavement around me, and an icy chill cuts through the warm August air.

The instant we leave, heavy streams of rain come down, making it hard to see. Graydon looks nervous, and I'm especially glad I don't have to drive. It's not until we get closer to the lab that I detect thick plumes of smoke rising from nearby.

"The Mordolus must be burning houses again," Graydon says grimly.

That's what they do to help get rid of the Virus: burning the homes of the sick. I notice a cold, worried look on Graydon's face.

Right after we turn down the road to the lab, Graydon pulls over. Hungry red flames lick the tops of the buildings through the thick smoke like the claws of a ravenous monster ready to devour its prey. I jump out of the car as soon as I can get the door open and run toward the lab. Graydon grabs my arm to stop me. I suddenly detect voices nearby. The Mordolus. The two of us crouch behind a fence until I hear the hum of a vehicle and the voices vanish.

We sprint to the lab, but we never make it there because it's gone. A wave of heat meets us, and embers dance through the air, landing on my skin just as they cool and turn black. The flames sizzle as raindrops meet the wild blaze. The lab, as well as several other buildings caught in the inferno, is destroyed. All that work, and the cure, even all the notes collected, are devoured by the fire. Everything we have worked for, our only hope for survival, is gone. I doubt we can salvage anything. I stare in blank disbelief.

Graydon dashes towards the open front door, which reveals lapping blue and white flames consuming the lab from inside out.

"No!" I say, jumping in front of him. "It's too late."

He watches the fire, panting, fists clenched.

"It's all gone," I whisper to myself as I sink into the wet ground. Everyone will die now. We aren't safe anymore. Every time I think things are going to get better, the Mordolus intervene. I don't even know what to feel through the shock.

We're still kids, not unrealistically smart or insanely lucky. We were fortunate enough to finish the cure to begin with. Without time, the notes, and aid, there's no way we can figure out the recipe again and obtain the supplies we need.

I have a sickening realization. I'm the only one who's ingested the cure. What if everyone else dies? What if I end up being the only survivor—the only person left in the whole world? Oh, that would be a nightmare, so I try really hard not to think about it.

Graydon stands nearby, staring into the flaming abyss. Eyebrows low, he kicks the empty oil can they must have started the fire with hard across the ashy grass. He rakes his hand through his dark hair, his brown eyes flickering golden-red, reflecting the flames. He doesn't say anything as he rigidly glares at the flames. I can't imagine how Graydon feels; I didn't even know a remedy could exist until a few days ago, but he's been working on this for months. Now, it's all ashes.

I sit on the ground silently until all that remains are smoking ashes and charred wood. The rain has stopped now, and the sun has returned from behind the clouds. My clothes and skin are covered with wet ashes and mud. Graydon walks over to me. I can't believe the cure and the lab are destroyed.

"Are you okay?" I finally murmur, watching raindrops fall onto the singed ground.

"Not really," Graydon says, helping me up. "But come on, we can't stay here forever."

"What are we going to do?" I ask.

"I don't know, but there's no use staying here and worrying about what's gone," he replies. His expression falters. "We'll figure it out. Trust me. We shouldn't be here so out in the open with the Mordolus nearby. Let's walk to my house and think about what to do."

I get Stormy from the car. We decide to abandon the vehicle since the Mordolus could be near and we don't want to draw attention. Leaving the car, the lab, and our hope behind, we start off. I glance back one last time at the smoldering remains, knowing the cure is gone for good.

24

ISAIAH: SUSPICIONS

We turn back toward our room. Reece gives me a smile. The footsteps of the guards chasing Ele faded long ago, but voices converse from the direction we are headed. We follow the familiar path back to our room. We're safe here in the unrestricted areas.

I wonder what the staff are talking about. Their tone's suspicious. They grow closer. I can't stand unsolved mysteries. Curiosity begs me to listen and wins again.

Impulsively, I pull Reece with me into the shadows of one of the hallways. I give in to the silent call of interest. We hide behind a laundry drop-off bin. I peek over the top.

"What are you doing?" Reece asks, confused. I hold a finger to my lips and point to the hallway. The two people I heard talking approach. Reece looks too. Both men are armed guards. As they come into view, I unravel their conversation.

"Any word on how much longer?" one of them with a strained voice says. He coughs.

"Soon, she says, but there's no exact time yet," the other replies, monotone. "It's getting difficult, but we will endure until the time the Queen orders."

"Of course," the first agrees, coughing again. He keeps rubbing his hands together. That happens when someone has paresthesia. A symptom of the Virus. I glance at Reece, still listening. *So some of them are getting sick.*

"You need to go. I'll cover for you," the second says quietly. The conversation is weirdly stilted. He says something else, but I miss it. The first one nods.

"I will. I haven't had time," he says. "Hail Morzanna!" He turns and marches down the hallway where Reece and I just came from. The second mutters something in agreement before leaving down the opposite corridor.

I duck back behind the big bin. I wait impatiently for the footsteps to pass. Reece watches over the top of the desk. A second later, I spring from behind the counter. Both guards are gone, but I know the sick one just turned the corner.

"What was that about?" Reece asks, standing up.

"Not sure, but I feel like we should follow him," I say, deep in thought. Reece gives me the *Are you insane?* look. I reply with a pleading expression.

"It's dangerous, and if we get caught, it's your fault," Reece says, following me with clear reluctance. "I'm still confused as to what is so intriguing that we need to risk our lives."

"Just come on," I whisper, walking before our suspect gets too far away. "That guard is sick, and I want to see where he goes."

We cautiously follow the guard into a part of the Infirmary I've never been to before. Reece and I trail him through numerous twisted white halls. We pass like hundreds of rooms.

I've put together a mental map of the Infirmary. But I've never been here before. We had to come through this weird door and up a flight of stairs. An inordinate number of warnings are posted on the walls. Reece threatens to go back. I convince him we can do it. The sign basically says if we get caught here, it's straight to the Double Guard. And that we might suffer severe unlisted punishment, but I cover up that part before Reece reads it.

I haven't seen anyone else for at least ten minutes. The walls are painted with strange shapes and words I can't read. The guard keeps looking to make sure no one's around. Reece and I must hide quickly. Scratches and dirt cover the floor. A metallic smell hangs in the air. The guard is out of sight. I peek around the corner. He comes to a stop in front of a large, secure door. I knew something was coming after all those warnings.

"A door," Reece says quietly from behind me, glancing at the biohazard signs on the wall.

"We'll probably need a key or passcode to get in," I say.

"How about we don't try to get in, and we leave now?" Reece says, nervously swaying.

There's a panel on the wall. The man types some numbers in it, and the door slides open. It closes once he's through. I didn't see what he punched in. It has some sort of special privacy screen. At least we won't need a key, but there are infinite combinations.

"Come on," I whisper after the man's gone. I sneak over to the machine. The screen glows and has numbers on it. We need a passcode. It doesn't even tell how many characters I need. I'm afraid to try the wrong thing. It could set off an alarm or something.

"Isaiah, this is so dangerous! We shouldn't be here!" Reece says.

"I know, but—" I pause, thinking. "There has to be a reason."

"A reason for what?" Reece asks impatiently.

"For everything. But mainly, why they have all this security right here. I want to know what they do with sick staff."

"What do you think is in there?" Reece asks, vexed. He tries the door just to make sure it's secured.

"I have a few suspicions," I stare back at the screen before he can ask what they are.

"Any ideas?" I ask Reece. He shakes his head.

A few jump out in my mind. Most of them are dumb. I take out my phone to see what numbers correspond with letters. I think about words related to Morzanna. All I come up with are my own opinions about her.

"Let me see," Reece says, snatching my phone. Defeated, I nervously pace the hall. My mind blanks. Reece stares at my phone. I start to doubt us ever figuring it out. I just have to see what's on the other side of this door. It's driving me crazy.

Reece goes through my entire phone. I'm too busy trying to think to care.

"What's this?" Reece asks, holding something up. It's the paper I found in the room when I got my phone. I'd left it inside my phone case and forgotten about it. *Pass - 4138*

"I found that earlier," I say, taking it.

"Oh, when you *found* your phone without me?" Reece says in an accusatory tone. I nod. He looks at me expectantly. "It's promising. Are you going to try it?"

I hadn't thought of that. This could potentially be it. Though, it could be the passcode for anything. I hurriedly type in the numbers. Reece and I prepare to run if we have to, anticipating an alarm to be set off. With a mechanical sound, the door slides open. Inside is a long, straight hallway.

"Yes!" I say, excitedly. "Let's hurry! We gotta catch up with him!"

"I still don't understand why we're here!" Reece comments, but I know even he has no intention of turning back now.

We inch down the narrow corridor. The lighting here has a blue glow. There are few doors and no other hallways. He must have entered one of the rooms. We walk to the end of the hall. I don't detect anyone inside any of the rooms. They all have blurry windows. I can see inside, but the images are too abstract to identify.

"So what do we do?" Reece asks. I shrug.

"Let's try some doors," I say. I reach for one of the handles to the left. It opens to a small, vacant, storage room. Only a few empty boxes occupy the space and an unlit lamp sits in the corner. Reece walks inside and looks around.

"Nothing exciting here," he says, coming back toward me. Suddenly, one of the doors opens a few feet away. I quickly dash inside the storage room, shutting the door softly. I listen through the door. Footfalls, and they sound like they're walking away. Must not have seen me. For half an hour, doors open and footsteps wander. Meanwhile, Reece and I wait in the closet. I silently pray no one comes in here.

Several sets of steps come from the door that leads to this hall. I know because I hear the mechanical sound.

"There you are! Hurry up," says the new person. An older-sounding woman. "Someone's missing."

"What? Who is it?" the man we've been following asks.

"Marie Hale, Double Guard. We don't know how it happened. We need to get out there and start looking," the new woman says.

"But it's the end of my shift. I need to rest in the barracks until the raxoxin kicks in," he says.

"You haven't taken it yet?" she asks.

"I haven't had time. She's had me working eighteen-hour shifts. Besides, I've only had symptoms for a few days," the man says.

"You must help us now. A missing person is a massive issue. I'll talk with Manager Ward about your hours—only if we find the girl," the woman proposes.

The two people march through the passcode door.

Ideas dangerously prick my brain. I look at Reece. My heart races as unrestrained excitement springs to life. I love adventures.

I open the door. "We need to search that room."

25
REECE: HOW?

Isaiah and I exit our hiding spot. The blue glowing hall is empty as we walk over to the door the man emerged from earlier. I cautiously pull open the door. Cabinets line all the walls, and a low luminous ceiling reveals a ton of tables. We step inside the room. Papers, folders, and empty vials are thrown across all surfaces.

"What do you think this place is?" I ask quietly, slinking over to one of the closest cabinets while Isaiah picks up some of the sheets of paper.

"I don't know, but I hope something will give us clues," Isaiah says. He picks up the vials one by one, examining them, then sets each down. Isaiah's like a raccoon; he's curious and has to touch everything. I'm opposite, especially when it comes to people because I can't stand anyone touching me. I glance over the tables since I'd rather just observe everything from a safe distance.

"What do you mean 'clues'? We really shouldn't be here," I say, but Isaiah doesn't seem to hear. I hate being confused, and it only really happens when Isaiah gets some irrational hope.

I'm so tired. Also, my sore throat is killing me. I like to pretend I'm not sick, mostly because the thought freaks me out, but I shouldn't be this tired all the time. Isaiah likes to play the game too, but some days he has such bad headaches that he can't do anything, and I don't think that's normal.

I open the big metal cabinet. Cold air flows out, not like a freezer, but noticeably cooler than outside. Inside are clean, organized shelves filled with cases of vials, the same as the ones on the table, but these are filled with a sort of rose-colored substance.

"What is this?" I whisper to myself. I inspect the closet, and all I find are a whole lot of those vials and a few sheets of paper tacked to the back of the door.

"Did you find anything?" I ask Isaiah, leaving the cabinet and walking back over to him.

"I don't think so. I don't know what any of this means," he says, throwing some of the pages on the floor after scanning them. I help Isaiah by starting on my own stack of papers. A lot of what I'm reading is all medical terms. Fear grows more the longer we stay. If I'm risking my life, it better be for something important. Isaiah knows more than he's telling me, intensifying my curiosity.

I pick up a stack of papers neatly piled in the corner, hidden behind some books, and begin reading them. My dad is a doctor, so I recognize some vocabulary and concepts, even though most of it doesn't click. This paper's a list of symptoms and measurements with some random notes. It's all about the Maraloxis Virus. The heading reads 'Sulfavirdoton'. I scan through the catalog of ingredients, instructions, and rules, and my gaze wanders to the red symbol of Morzanna at the bottom. As I continue to read, my cloud of confusion and misunderstanding lifts, and fragments of ideas fit together like perfect puzzle pieces. Everything that's happened starts to gain meaning. I realize what Isaiah's been thinking the whole time. I mean, I've seen the signs: the suspicious staff, the unrealisticness of the Mordolus' sacrifice. I just can't believe it. The three simple words in bold at the bottom of the paper mean so much. *Maraloxis Virus Treatment.*

I freeze with the paper and vial in hand. The shock has shot my ability to move or speak or breathe. I finally find the courage and words to say, "It's an antidote."

"What?" Isaiah asks, looking up. I bound over to him and shove the paper into his hands.

"The man, the vials, and all the security! They've developed a cure!" I say, gesturing to the open cabinet filled with light pink vials. Isaiah drops the paper and stares. Like a storm-worn owl coming in for a slow, cautious landing after a heavy rain, Isaiah takes a long breath and blinks repeatedly before the truth finally sinks into his consciousness.

"No way," he says, a smile forming and dropping just as fast when a mixture of emotion confuses his expression. He puts a hand on the table and breathes deeply. "Reece, the cure?!"

I hold out one of the four-inch vials for Isaiah.

He gazes at it intently and takes it from me with wonder. "Why didn't we know? Why are they hiding it? We have to take it and give it to people!" Isaiah says quickly, crossing the room and picking up another vial from the cabinet.

"I know! But if they kept it hidden, we can't just take it!" I remind him. "There must be a reason they have been hiding it."

"Yeah, because Morzanna is a murderer!" Isaiah says before solemnly whispering. "How could she do this…"

"Maybe the cure is new, or maybe they're still testing it…or something!" I say, but I think Isaiah is correct. Burning fury ignites in my chest.

"I can't figure out why with all these people dying, they'd have it locked away in here. You're probably right," I say, holding up a pink vial.

This little vial would have saved my mother, and Morzanna hid it from us. Confused and angry, I don't know what to do, but I want to cry. *Morzanna murdered my mother.* The shock feels like a punch in the throat. I also feel like tearing down the whole Infirmary and taking this cure to the people who actually deserve it.

The wall of horror silently shatters when voices approach from outside.

"We'll figure it out later!" Isaiah says urgently, taking out more of the vials from the cabinet. I nod, stashing the precious cure in my pockets. They're getting closer, and I slam shut the door to the cabinet.

I glance up, and a bowling ball of panic plummets from my brain into the pit of my stomach.

"Isaiah," I mumble. He looks at me, and I point to the corner of the room.

"Cameras," he realizes, dragging a hand across his eyes.

"We've got to get out of here!" I say. "They check all recordings at least once a day. And it's super protected here, so they probably do it more frequently. They're going to know!"

We sprint out of the room to the blue-lit hallway. Thankfully, the Mordolus members must have entered one of the other rooms, giving us the chance to escape. We stop outside the big door, and there's another of those passcode things, so Isaiah quickly types in the same number we used before. The door opens for us with a loud clink.

"We've got to find Ele and get out of here!" Isaiah says as we run down the hall. "We can use her escape plan. We just need to get out now!"

For once, I don't argue. When they check the cameras and find some vials of the cure missing, we're going to be in serious trouble.

When we get back to a familiar place, we slow to a walk. I try to act normal, even though I'm listening to the vials clinking together inside my pockets.

After we descend the staircase, someone watches us. The woman nurse from before eyes us from across the hallway. I kick Isaiah and nod toward her, and we come to a silent agreement that if she makes a move toward us, we'll have to run. But she doesn't say anything and walks away. I take a deep breath and focus on the floor.

"Reece," Isaiah whispers and stops, wide-eyed. Our room is only a hundred feet away. I immediately freeze. I take in a huge breath, unable to swallow as a cloud of terror settles in my throat.

One of the worst Mordolus members, Ash Henderson, waits outside our door. Ash has an infamous reputation, mainly for being the leader of the Hunters. He sees us and waits expectantly.

"What do we do?" I ask hurriedly, very aware that Ash still watches. "We can't run—this has never happened!"

"There's nothing we can do. Try not to act suspicious. Come on," Isaiah says, coldly. After everything: sneaking into that room, finding the cure, and escaping—this happens. There must be some way out.

Ash crosses his arms as we approach, his olive-brown eyes closely inspecting us. We're in trouble. Mordolus authorities should not be waiting outside our room. Maybe they found out about where we've been. Maybe that sketchy nurse ratted on us. I stare at the floor. Ash's boots are dirty, and I wonder if they've been out catching civilians again. I bet the silence is for effect, and it's definitely working.

"Can we help you?" Isaiah finally asks, playing innocent, which I've seen him do before. Isaiah clenches and unclenches his fists, and I know he's scared. I force myself to look up at Ash and receive his boreal, dark stare. He's got to be at least 6'14", and I guess you need muscles like that when you hunt people all day.

"Yes," he says plainly. Ash takes two pieces of paper from a folder and hands one to each of us. A rush of heat tingles my face as I look down at the sheet.

This can't be happening. At the top of the paper is my name, and underneath it is several other forms of identification, the date I came here, and my age. The worst part is scrawled at the bottom.

'Double Guard: X X X X X X'

Everybody has this list to keep track of misdemeanors and rule breaking. You might get a mark on your paper, and if you get enough, they send you to the Double Guard.

I never thought I would get all six marks though.

I drop the paper like it's on fire and glance at Isaiah, and he looks just as shaken.

"Also, we found a clip on the cameras of you in the key room," Ash sneers to Isaiah. "Where's the key you took?"

Shaky, Isaiah looks at the floor and digs the Double Guard key out of his back pocket. Ash takes it, scowling.

"Come on. Now," Ash says, and I wouldn't dare argue. *This is it. They're going to find the cure and we'll be locked away forever. We'll never escape.*

"Can we do anything?" I whisper to Isaiah while Ash leads us toward the Double Guard. I gaze at the people we pass, each room, the kitchen, and the entry room just in case I never see it again. Isaiah looks downcast.

"No," he says rigidly. "We can't do anything."

We pass the entryway, and I catch a glimpse of the familiar, dark, death pillar. The glass vials of the cure clink in my pockets. The cure that could have saved my mother and everyone else who's died— and can still save everyone who remains. If I could survive finding the cure to begin with, maybe we can get out of this.

"Yes we can," I reply quickly as we reach the doors to the Double Guard.

Ash leads the two of us inside, using the key Isaiah returned to open the doors. They slam shut behind us, and the walls seem even tighter than they were before. Ash doesn't even force us, we follow him, and I find it dumb. Why are we following him when we know he's gonna lock us up?

"Isaiah," I whisper, glancing up to make sure Ash isn't listening. He's talking with someone called Manager Ward on the phone. I examine the hallway, an unfamiliar feeling of a reckless plan brewing inside me. "We have to run," I say quietly.

Inside the Double Guard, it's super loud. This makes sense because everyone here is bent on escaping or breaking rules.

"Reece, no, we'll get caught," Isaiah says seriously.

"So? Even if we do, what are they going to do about it? We've always feared ending up in the Double Guard, and here we are. There's nothing stopping us now," I say. It's a strange new freedom, but it sort of excites me.

"Reece—" Isaiah pleads.

"No. I have a plan, and it's absolutely crazy. We have to get rid of Ash though," I say.

"Reece, it's not going to work!" Isaiah whispers, the waver of a hopeless captive in his voice. "We can't get rid of Ash."

Isaiah is really afraid of Ash. Ash was the Hunter who captured him to begin with, and it left Isaiah scarred. Isaiah's scared of Ash and worried to attempt something.

"We have to at least try," I say.

"You realize they're going to separate us, right?" Isaiah asks suddenly.

Actually, I hadn't realized that. I don't want to be alone again.

"That's why we have to go! We have—*ya know*—and we have to find Ele!" I whisper, collecting my scattered courage. I don't find much, but it's enough. "Get it together and help me figure out how to get rid of Ash!"

Up ahead, Ash hangs up his phone and calls over another guard.

"I need you to take this one to the new room," Ash says, and the other guard glances at Isaiah and agrees.

The guard tries to grab Isaiah's wrist, but, surprising everyone including me, Isaiah ducks and dashes off back the way we came. The guard jets after him, and Ash takes my arm and follows. Isaiah's faster, especially since Ash has to pull me along, and I drag my feet and clutch the wall to stall.

We get all the way back to the Double Guard's entry area, and that's where it gets bad. Two other nurses stand before us with two other patients they were leading. Now, there are four we have to lose. That familiar nurse with the black braided hair peers at me. She's practically everywhere. Both patients are younger. One, a girl, looks to be around sixteen. The other is a boy, about the same age, and I quickly realize it's River. Guess he got into the Double Guard too. I wonder what he did in a couple hours to get in.

Suddenly, an idea launches into my mind from the part of my brain I usually try to shut down. I gesture for Isaiah to stop, and he halts right in the middle of the hallway. Ash shoves me to the other guard and snatches Isaiah's arm. River stares at me intensely and obviously recognizes us.

Isaiah looks at me, trembling, while Ash yells at him. With my free hand, I reach into my pocket and clutch one of the glass vials. I take a deep breath and hold it up.

"Hey everybody! They have the cure! They've been lying to us the whole time!" I scream as loud as possible, waving the vial around in the air. The nurse gasps; the guard drops my arm, trying to snatch the vial; and I run. I jump out of the way, holding my pockets closed so none of the vials fall out.

River surveys me quizzically. I send him and the girl a look, pleading for help. River tries to wrench his arm free from the nurse, and the girl falls to the ground and thrashes. I look at the vial in my hand.

Ash gives me a deathly scowl, Isaiah frantically tries to escape, and the other guard approaches me. I should run, but instead, I hurl the vial.

It smashes against the wall right behind Ash in an explosion of glass and pink liquid. It splashes into his face, and Ash wipes at his blurry eyes. Isaiah writhes to escape his one-armed grip. I claw at Ash's arm and kick at his legs, and Isaiah wrestles himself free. Reeling, Ash shoves me to the ground hard. He turns and chases down the girl whose nurse dashes off toward the wide doors to get other staff involved. The girl shrieks as Ash catches her by the waist. Someone grabs my hand and helps me off the ground.

"I have a lot of questions, but I'll ask them later," River says quickly. "I'll keep them occupied. Now go!"

"Thank you, River," Isaiah says sincerely, scrambling away from the scene. Then, the two of us run as fast as we can for Ele's room without looking back.

The guard and Ash are arguing, shocked and furious that we have the cure. The nurse wrangles the other two patients with their help. Maybe that will slow them down.

Panting, we stop right in front of Room 138. I can't believe we made it. I watch the corner of the hall as the footsteps draw closer.

"Hurry!" I whisper. Grasping the handle, Isaiah goes to open the door but freezes.

It's locked.

"What are we going to do?" I ask frantically. He starts knocking on the door. I don't know how this is helping but whatever. Isaiah won't leave Ele. And Ele has the escape plan.

"Ele!" Isaiah calls. There's a crash inside the room. Footsteps.

"Isaiah! What's wrong?" Ele says, muffled, from the other side of the metal door.

"It's locked, Ele. We found something, and we need to get out now," Isaiah says quickly. Suddenly, the moment I'm dreading—it happens. I throw my hands across my face and rock on my feet.

The nurse, the one who always ruins everything, comes running toward us.

"Her again? Why can't *anything* work out?" I mutter to myself. Before I complete my thoughts, she runs to us and yanks Isaiah away from the door. She pulls out a key and unlocks the door.

"What are you doing?" I say, dumbfounded. She throws the door open, sweeping her dark hair out of her face.

"Why are you doing that?" Isaiah asks. Ele steps out the door and runs to her brother, gaping at the nurse.

"I'm Jess. I'm undercover. I've been helping people here to escape," the nurse whispers. Her posture and expression lose their rigidity and her tone gains emotion. "I have to be careful, or I'll get caught. That's why I've been so harsh. You need to hurry! Those guards are coming!" Jess warns. "Now get out before it's too late! Clearly, you know about the antidote?"

"Antidote?" Ele asks, looking from Isaiah to Jess to me. Isaiah nods to Jess.

"Yeah, we do," he says, a tone of adventure playing in his voice again.

Jess looks at me. "I told them I'd catch you while they went to go figure out why you had the antidote and cage the two kids, but they'll be back; they called for help. You need to hurry! This hall loops around to the entrance. Take it so you don't run into them. Now go!"

Isaiah hesitates for a moment, confused. "Wait so you—"

Jess interrupts with a swift nod, gesturing for us to leave. "Go!"

Then, I sprint down the hall with Isaiah and Ele, a storm brewing behind us, but the promise of hope growing brighter in the distance.

26
ELEANORA: ARE WE FINALLY FREE?

My thoughts are a blur of confusion and excitement as heavy footsteps sound in the hallway behind Isaiah, Reece, and me as we run toward the door to the Double Guard. *We might actually escape from the Infirmary!*

"What do you mean antidote?" I ask again, gasping for air.

"Tell you later!" Isaiah responds.

We approach the entrance to the Double Guard, and before we can even face the issue of being locked in, Jess races down the opposite hallway. Her keys jingle as she unlocks the door, missing the keyhole twice. I don't have time to worry if the two guards who come sprinting down the hallway just as the door shut saw Jess assisting us. The four of us, including the undercover nurse, run as fast as we can.

Wait, Marie had the plans! That means I have to remember how to get to the door through all those winding hallways and flights of stairs!

I do my best to remember the way to the exit at the far east side of the Infirmary, despite the constant stream of doubts flowing into my mind. We sprint down a flight of stairs and fly through a long, doorless hall.

"It's this way," I say, trying to conceal my hesitation as I lead Jess, Isaiah, and Reece down the hall, through the unrestricted areas— I know because we pass what Isaiah announces are the Hopeful Rooms—and toward the west side of the Infirmary.

"Are you taking us to the back entrance?" Jess asks, surprised.

"Perhaps," I respond, and Jess, noting my doubt, takes the lead.

A shower of relief washes away my doubt as the familiar doorway comes into view, leading into the dim, gloomy hall. I throw open the swinging French doors, stepping inside as the chaos draws closer.

"Hurry!" I say as Jess pulls the door closed behind us. Some of the strange symbols on the wall look vaguely like the Queen's twisted red insignia.

We don't hesitate to run, making our way through the maze of corridors. I stop for a second to try to orient myself when I notice a light streaming from one of the halls. It's bright, white light, not an eerie, bronzy lamplight; it's daylight.

Finally, back in the dead-ended hallway, I stand in front of the door. A wave of disappointment overwhelms me.

The door is barred up. Wood is nailed over it, and a shiny lock replaces the old, rusty one that lays in pieces on the floor. They must have discovered Marie escaped here. I pull on the handle just to make sure, but to no avail. *There's no way we can get out here; it would take hours to work through, and we don't have the time.*

"How do we get out now?" Reece whispers, rocking and glancing around. His eyes are the color of trees when they first leaf out in spring; a pale, hazel green. I always feel like I'm being analyzed, but at the same time, the constant fear present in his eyes reminds me of a deer, which always watches for a reason to run.

"I don't know. This is the only exit I know of. Jess, do you know somewhere we can go?" I say, turning around to find only the two boys. "Wait, where is Jess?"

"You don't think she went to help them catch us? Or got captured?" Reece asks. I shake my head, and Isaiah paces the hall.

"I don't know, but either way, we have to go. We can't worry about Jess. We still have to find a way out," Isaiah says.

"I know, but she could help us—and what if she's discovered?" I ask, as we step back into the main hallway and begin walking in the direction away from the door.

Isaiah doesn't respond; we're both watching Reece, who glances around at the walls strangely. He places a hand on the blemished paint before wandering down the opposing hall.

"Reece?" Isaiah asks. Reece gestures for us to follow him, so we do.

The chill of emptiness overwhelms this passage, and it reminds me of many of the abandoned buildings I've been in since the Virus. Cobwebs and dust blanket every surface, the few lights flicker, and an unnerving silence dares us to continue. Reece follows the wall for a minute, looking deep in thought, before turning down one of the hallways. Reece stops in front of a dim double doorway.

"Isaiah, don't you see where this is?" Reece asks. Isaiah looks confused and shakes his head, and my brother and I await an explanation. Reece points to a sign above the door, *Emergency Care.*

"Remember the tunnels we found?" Reece asks.

"Yeah," Isaiah says.

"They're right over here, and I have an idea." Reece hops off down the hall, and I look at Isaiah. He shrugs, and the two of us follow. At the end of the hallway, Reece disappears inside a little space, barely visible, made by the wall and doorway. Isaiah crouches down, gestures for me to join, and steps in after Reece.

I quickly glance behind me, twirling a piece of hair. Then I crawl into the space. Instead of a wall behind the shadows, there's a small door hidden in the darkness, and I have to duck to fit inside. Isaiah and Reece wait for me on the other side of the doorway.

"What is this place?" I ask, amazed as it opens into a hallway, similar to the one we were in previously. It looks much older, and the air is musty, making me want to cough.

"We don't know," Isaiah says with a spark of adventure.

Taking the hallway past several rooms, Reece leads us down a tile staircase. It's almost completely dark, and the warm air melts away my goosebumps almost instantly.

"So, where are we going?" I ask.

"Yeah Reece, what's your idea?" Isaiah adds.

"Isaiah and I explored down here before. We'll get to the tunnels soon. I bet they go on for a long time. I'm hoping that, maybe, they lead out," Reece explains, a hint of a waver in his voice.

"Okay," I say.

"But they might not, and then we'll be trapped down here forever. And then we might get lost," Reece mumbles, suddenly taking a sharp breath. He glances up at Isaiah and me. "At least we can hide here until we think of something else? Because no one seems to know about the tunnels."

"Good idea, Reece. Come on, Ele," Isaiah says, walking further into the darkness. I hesitate, but I decide to trust Isaiah since he's explored this place before, and I can't think of anything else to do.

I follow Isaiah and Reece, inspecting the old hall in the light from my brother's phone and a flashlight Reece found in the hallway. Ahead, the cracked tile floor turns into a dirt path and the walls into smoothed natural clay. Here Isaiah explains, "The plan for not getting lost is we're going to stay on this main path", which seems overly simple and full of liability. Nevertheless, neither Reece nor I present an argument. As we enter the tunnels, I hear the entire story of how they found the cure, and I'm left taken aback by shock. We descend into the vast tunnels below, and a curious feeling tumbles into the pit of my stomach.

"We actually have a cure?" I ask in unbelief. "Wow."

"Yep. Right here," Reece says, removing a vial to show me. The dim phone light reflects off the glass vial and the engraved 'M' at the top.

The realization finally sinks in like a stone slowly descending in tar. *We have the cure. We're going to be okay.*

"Isn't that amazing, Ele?" Isaiah asks, and I nod.

"Yes! I just can't believe it," I say with a joyful laugh.

The tunnels are about as big as the hallways in the Infirmary, although the size varies. Every few feet, another path splits off from this one, but they're smaller, and the main corridor is identifiable with little effort. Some of them lead upwards and some down, twisting and turning like the insides of an ant hill.

The main tunnel we're following leads further down, seemingly away from our goal. Although, I wouldn't advise leaving the main trail for fear of losing our way. The voices following us faded long ago, leaving me wondering: *what happened to Jess? Did she get caught or is she safe? We should have made sure she was okay, seeing as she helped us and I assume many others by risking her own safety. I can't believe she's not with the Queen, but it explains her actions. Jess knew about the cure and most likely received some herself, so I wonder if she has been able to get it to anyone. I wish we knew more about her now.*

The ground continues to slope downward, and a blanket of exhaustion hangs over my shoulders as the excitement of escaping dissipates and the common fatigue of the Maraloxis Virus returns. A horrified, sick sensation settles over me. *Morzanna has had an antidote the entire time while all the people are dying or have died.*

"What do you think these tunnels are for?" I ask to get my mind off troubling subjects. "Why would there be tunnels inside the Infirmary, and why does no one seem to know about them?"

"I don't know," Isaiah says. "I've been wondering the same thing."

"Maybe someone dug them to escape, and they'll lead out. Or maybe they were here before this was the Infirmary, and we just discovered them," Reece suggests, shining the flashlight around uneasily.

"Maybe, but how would they not notice them? I assume that since the Mordolus are the only ones allowed in the restricted areas, the other patients wouldn't know, but the staff would," I comment. Reece only shrugs and runs up ahead, leaving only a small trail of light to assure us he's not too far away.

"Isaiah, something about this doesn't feel safe," I say once we're alone.

"No, duh," he says. "We just broke out of the Infirmary chased by the Mordolus."

"What do we do if we can't find a way out?"

"Don't worry about it, Ele. We'll figure it out," Isaiah replies.

"I know we had no other option, I'm just worried." I stare at the gravelly ground until the courage to finally voice my question surfaces. "How are Mom and Dad, really?"

"Honestly, not good. It's hard to gauge how long we have left by symptoms. But we have to get them out and give them the cure. Soon," Isaiah responds then goes quiet, which I don't like.

"And what about the patients in general?" I ask, just as scared of the answer.

"I just don't know. That's the problem. Especially with the younger ones. The symptoms are subtle then it's too late. By the time I try to help, it's not long until they're gone. We need to get more of the cure and give it out. Fast."

He nervously runs a hand through his hair. It's imperative we find a way to deliver the antidote to the people of Senneforte. If we can find Graydon, we can try to replicate this cure.

"What's Reece doing?" I ask.

Isaiah shrugs. "He's not usually like this. I think he's on a high for figuring out how to escape. He doesn't really like strangers, either. He's probably avoiding you."

"I wish he'd bring back the light," I say.

"Ele, I don't understand. Some of the Mordolus were good people before the Virus. But they keep the cure secret. Why would they let everyone die? They joined to help, so why don't they do something about it? Maybe there are some other people like Jess, but either way, someone would tell," Isaiah says after a lull in time.

I think for a second, considering his every word and wondering the same thing myself. It doesn't make any sense.

Suddenly, Reece urgently calls from up ahead. "Isaiah, come here!"

Isaiah disappears down the tunnel in an instant. There's hardly any light left since he has the phone, and I roll my eyes. *Really? Isaiah just left me in the dark? Ugh, he's an idiot sometimes. I better hurry and catch up before they get any further away, and I really can't see.*

A quiet, unusual sound echoes through the tunnel walls, interrupting my footsteps. I stop and spin around, adrenaline exploding inside me. I can't place what the sound was—something akin to breathing and footsteps. I play with a piece of hair, glancing around the smaller tunnels. The light I was following fades as the boys get further away and I try to convince myself it was nothing, but my feet refuse to move until I'm certain.

Lurking in the shadows of one of the tunnels to my left, a muddled silhouette appears. *It's so dark I'm seeing things. I should find Isaiah and Reece before my imagination gets the best of me.* Then, the shadows shift enough for me to be certain something's there. A dim light flickers on, revealing my worst fear; someone is there. The light grows, revealing the face and figure of a young man. He stares at me with a disconcerting expression from behind tousled, brown hair. The light glints off what I conclude are scars covering almost all his exposed skin. He's young, but still many years older than me. Between his sickly, emaciated look and extreme injuries, he has a cadaverous appearance. He silently gazes at me, and a scream catches in my throat and my legs grow unsteady. My mind yells; *Danger! Danger! Danger!,* but I finally understand what it means to be frozen with fear as a wintery wave of terror crashes inside me, leaving me in shock from its ice-cold waters. He takes a few steps forward.

"Ele?" Isaiah calls, not far away. The person looks in that direction before darting off down the opposite tunnel. My heart tries to leap out of my chest and hide. I let out the breath I was holding in the form of a scream, and I run down the tunnel, panicked.

"Ele? What's wrong?" Isaiah asks worriedly. I wildly throw my arms around him, burying my face in his shoulder.

"There was someone back there," I say between short breaths, pointing. Reece covers his face and looks around the tunnel through his hands, slowly inching up the path.

"What do you mean?" Isaiah asks. "Was it the Mordolus? Did they follow us?"

"No. Well possibly, but he didn't have the Queen's symbol, not that I could see, anyway," I say, catching my breath and dragging Isaiah by the hand further down the path, away from the frightening person.

"He had scars everywhere," I explain, running. "We need to get away, now."

I notice the light coming from the tunnel ahead when Reece points it out, "Look, light! It must be the way out!"

I force my legs to run faster, and soon the tunnel becomes steep. I climb up, stumbling and leaving the clueless boys following. The loose ground causes me to fall a few times, but I manage to clamber to the top.

Eventually, I find myself standing above ground, the cool, night air biting back my lingering sweat, and the sweet smell of earth drawing me back to reality. The moonlight illuminates a circular field, surrounded by trees in all but one small opening. The boys emerge from the dark tunnels behind me, gasping.

"It did lead out!" Isaiah exclaims, giving Reece a high five and drawing a deep breath of fresh air. "Ele, we made it out!"

He drops on the ground, touching the grass and dirt in awe and staring up at the setting sun. *We've escaped the Infirmary and we have the cure! Whoever that was is gone now.* The boys excitedly chatter, and I remember that they haven't been outside in months. I feel like it's been forever since I've breathed the fresh outdoor air despite only having been locked away for a week.

"I can't believe we actually escaped!" Reece says, jumping. Isaiah agrees, sweeping his blond hair out of his eyes and grinning. All of us take a moment to comprehend our accomplishment.

Isaiah eventually looks at me. "We should go. We have to find Graydon tonight."

I nod and look around, but I don't recognize anything. There is a road in the distance beyond the field and the line of trees.

"We need to stay hidden or else we could get caught again, right after we just got out," Reece says, glancing around and stepping behind some trees.

"You're right, that would be bad," I say, scanning the black night and stepping behind the cover as well.

"Where are we going to go?" Reece asks, a slight nervous quiver in his voice.

"We can't be too far away from the Infirmary," Isaiah says and looks around, uncertain. "I hope. The road seems like a good idea."

The three of us walk to the road, guided by the dimmed phone flashlight. Once we're standing on the dark pavement, there's a street lined with houses across from us.

Something small moves in the darkness to my right and races across the sidewalk. In seconds the little creature halts in the grass at my feet. A needle-sharp pain follows as I kick the squeaking, furry creature away.

"What was that?" Isaiah asks, glancing around in the darkness with his phone. "Was that a rat? Are you okay, Ele?"

"I think so," I say, rubbing the little slice on my ankle. "It bit me."

"Leave my sister alone, stupid rat," Isaiah says, frustratedly. "They think they run Senneforte now. Watch where you step. Let me see, Ele."

Isaiah shines the light on the bite, but we conclude it's nothing serious and keep moving. Reece nervously watches the ground around us.

We walk for a while, cautiously staying in the shadows and keeping quiet. Once we make it past that street, we come to a small two-lane road that leads us to a cluster of destroyed businesses. After a short discussion, we decide to try the road to our left, Hollyvale Lane, which sounds better than Graveyard Avenue, the alternative.

We're never going to get there, and I'm exhausted. Reece keeps asking how long we're going to be lost, and Isaiah keeps telling him we aren't lost. I'm pretty sure we're lost.

"Wait guys, I think I know where we are," I say as something tingles with recognition as I stare at the road signs. I sprint out from behind the trees, risking a look around from the middle of the road. I glance around the familiar street, leading into downtown.

"Yes, it is! Come on guys, we have to find Graydon!" I say excitedly. I run down the slope, past the nearest building: the wrecked structure of an old bank. I spin around to check if the other two are coming, but I'm suddenly blocked by a dark figure. I wildly back away. His boots don't bear the Queen's dreaded symbol, one of the dead giveaways of a Mordolus member, but he is dressed in their colors.

"Wait!" the man urges as the boys run over.

"Get away from my sister!" Isaiah shouts.

"Who are you?" I demand, holding up the phone light to see him.

"Are you okay, Ele?" Isaiah asks, pulling me further away. I nod, and Isaiah, full of anger-driven confidence, addresses the man. "What do you want?"

The man steps into the moonlight. I can barely see his face in the darkness, but I gather he's young. At first, I thought perhaps the phantom from the tunnel followed us, but now I see that the man standing in front of us looks nothing like him.

"I need to find Graydon," he finally says, and I look at him, confused.

"Why?" is all I can think to ask, though I really want to discover how he knows Graydon.

"I need to help him," the man says. "I don't know where he is, and I need you to show me. Who are you?"

"I'm Ele. How do you know Graydon? I'm certainly not taking you unless you give me a good answer for why you need to find him."

He looks annoyed but still responds. "He and some girl made a cure. I'm going to help them."

"Wait, he actually finished it?" I ask, joy and pride increasing despite my disbelief. He nods.

"But we found the cure! It already existed. The Queen was hiding it, but we found it," Isaiah says confusedly, revealing one of the vials they'd stolen. I'm not sure disclosing the cure to a stranger was the best idea, but it's too late now.

A look of shock, skepticism, and consideration falls over the man's face.

"I still need to find him," he says at last. I look him over, giving it some thought. *He better not turn us in.*

"Fine," I say. "Come on. We're going to find Graydon."

27
MARIE: MISTAKES

I sprint into the silent, empty province of Senneforte. A strange feeling tingles in my heart when I glance back at the Infirmary in the distance. I abandoned Ele, my parents, and my brother. But I can't go back. I won't take the chance of losing the opportunity to escape again. I'm finally free, and that's what really matters.

Half of the buildings have fallen into ashes, burned down after the Mordolus' raids. Businesses are destroyed. They're kinda lonely looking. Maybe the buildings are scared about getting burned down too. Makes me sad until I remember they're just stacks of bricks.

I need to come up with a strategy, ASAP. I don't have anywhere to go, and the only person I know is still out here is that dude Ele told me about. Not that anyone will be all excited to see me since I abandoned Ele. But he doesn't have to know, right? Anyway, it was her choice to stay for Isaiah. Not my brother, not my problem.

Everyone else left Senneforte before they built the walls. When I was, like, a little kid, I used to live in Erigate. I like it better in Willowmire. Not right now though.

I'm not as alone as I first thought. The Mordolus are everywhere. This street, too. I have to be aware of every sound since I can't trust my sight. The Virus has wrecked my eyes. I didn't start having vision problems until the Infirmary, so now being outside, I can tell how much it's deteriorated. It's kinda scary. Everything's blurry. I hope I don't go blind or something.

I'll find the medicine and go back for my family. It makes me feel better to assure myself. Then I won't be a traitor. I'm really looking out for what's best for them. I'm no use locked up.

I duck between two houses, trying to find somewhere to hide for the night. It's only the afternoon, so I've got time. It's started to rain a lot, and I end up soaked. Rainwater pours from the roofs of the houses, making everything a muddy mess. I toss my curly, saturated hair out of my face and survey the street. Darkness blankets the province like it joined Morzanna too and decided to suffocate me. Kinda creepy. I walk through the streets, drenched and alone. I'm about to lose my mind about these black biting flies. This is not as awesome as I'd hoped.

I spend hours wandering through the streets looking for food and shelter. Later, in the shadows of a tree, I hide from the storm. The sky growls with thunder like an angry beast, attacking the earth in the distance with claws of lightning. I watch the street of the neighborhood, waiting in vain to dry off a little until it gets dark.

My first roommate, Bella, and I used to spend all day in the Infirmary talking, playing Never-Have-I-Ever and Chopsticks, and scheming on how to get out. One time we tried knocking on the wall to see if we could get the attention of the people next door. It was super fun sometimes at the Infirmary. I miss Bella. I wish I wasn't alone out here in the cold, hungry wetness.

A figure emerges from behind the building. Crouched behind the large oak tree and confident I'm hidden from sight, I watch. Whoever it is looks around.

Eventually, three more people show up. They step into the open, just enough for me to see the faces of two boys and a girl in the glow of their flashlight. I'm practically blind, so it takes me a hot minute to recognize Ele, accompanied by two other boys and an older dude. Maybe one of them is Ele's friend. It's crazy she actually broke out. For once, before I do anything, I think it over. Ele might not wanna see me. I'll follow them secretly and see where they're headed. Honestly, it's kinda fun to sneak around.

I keep out of sight and watch the four closely. I slip in the mud, making more noise than intended. Shoot. The man glances in my direction, but I don't think anyone saw me.

I follow them until we reach a road called Gilded Way. Maybe it's called Gilded Way 'cause it's where all the rich people live. I look down the street and decide that's not the case. The houses aren't bad, but not top-tier. Most of them look like they've been here past their prime. Maybe it's called Gilded Way 'cause all the people who lived there originally got old and died, and it's like some weird symbolism of heaven. Or they just wanna glamorize the outdated homes.

I hide behind a bush, annoyed at the mud covering every inch of my lovely yellow high-tops. Ele and one of the boys, her brother I think, step inside one of the houses. It stands alone in the darkness, painted a blue-gray with an elegant porch in the front. It's the best-looking home on the street.

When I turn back to the other two, the kid boy has an odd look. The man's gone. Shoot. I quickly scan the scenery because, from the wrong angle, he might see me. The boy looks around like an anxious dog. I try to remember his name. It doesn't come to me. That usually means it's something generic or too long. Or my brain just decided not to remember it.

"Why are you stalking us?"

I jump around. The dude who was with Ele stares at me from a few feet away.

"Who are you?" he asks, stepping closer.

"It's none of your business," I say, backing away. "And, anyway, I'm not stalking you." I cross my arms uneasily.

"That's Marie! She ran away earlier! You are too following us, by the way," The boy says, walking over. The man looks at me. I shift uncomfortably.

"Who are you, then?" I ask.

"Atticus," he replies.

"What are you doing here?" the boy asks me. His eyes are kinda greenish, which is cool. They're like the color of partially dying grass. Honestly, they're his only good feature.

"I want to help Ele," I say quietly. "And how'd you know I was here?"

Atticus looks at me. "I heard you when—"

"I fell," I say, silently ridiculing myself.

Atticus nods. "I wasn't too worried. You didn't seem like a threat."

"Oh, well thanks," I say dryly.

"What happened to you?" the boy asks, looking me up and down. I glance at myself and realize I look like I've had a mud bath then rolled around in some leaves.

I shrug. "Camouflage."

I look around. Ele comes out of the house. She sees me from the porch.

"Marie!" Ele exclaims, running over and tackling me in a hug.

"I'm so sorry," I say, hugging her back. "I shouldn't have left you."

"It's okay," Ele says genuinely. "I understand."

Out of nowhere, I get a nagging thought. I'm sorry for leaving her or whatever, but I don't think I'd do much differently if I was in the situation again. I shake off the thought and convince myself I would do better and not abandon my friend. Loyalty. I'm gonna work on that. Well, try to.

Ele gives me a smile. "I'm glad we found you. I was getting worried."

"What, you don't think I would be okay on my own?" I joke, staring up at her.

"We're better together," Ele says, adjusting her teal headband. "We're going to find my friend Graydon. I don't want you out here alone."

"Okay, cool. At least you had a plan. Mine went fantastic as you can see," I say. "So I guess we're a bunch of secret rebels, escaping the Infirmary and hiding from the Queen! This'll be fun! Haha!"

Ele laughs. "It will be an adventure."

"Is that your brother?" I ask. The boy I saw with Ele earlier walks up.

"Oh yeah. I found him right after you left actually," Ele says with a broad smile.

"Hi! I'm Marie!" I say energetically. Isaiah looks friendly, I guess. He's blond too, but I think it would be helpful to announce the invention of the hairbrush.

"Hi, I'm Isaiah," he says.

"Ooooh!" I say enthusiastically. "You're the kid who got into the children's section! I seriously need to talk to you about that."

"Sure," Isaiah says.

I accidentally cut him off before he can say anything else. "Yeah, my brother's there. I'm going to make a plan to find him. His name's Axly."

Isaiah looks at me with a raised eyebrow. "Axly's your brother?"

I nod. "Yeah...Did you see him?!"

"Yes," Isaiah says, shocked. I'm bouncing and can't help it.

"When?! How? Where?!" I ask in the span of a second. "Was he okay?"

Isaiah nods quickly. "Yeah, he's pretty good."

Out of excitement, I impulsively hug him. My mind's racing twelve hundred bazillion miles a minute. I pull away and jump in circles.

"Eek! My brother's alive!" I say. Ele laughs at me. I try to calm myself when Atticus warns me I'm going to alert the Mordolus

As we get acquainted, they tell me about the cure. I'm so excited. No one mentions anything about how the Queen hid it from us so we should be really mad. 'Cause we don't want to ruin the mood I bet.

"So what's the plan now?" I ask, staring at one of the seven vials the boys retrieved. It's nearly the color of bubblegum, just lighter. I wonder if it tastes like bubblegum too. That'd be cool.

"I'm hoping Graydon will have some ideas, but maybe we could find a way to recreate it," Ele says as we begin walking toward where she says he should be. It's only a short way I'm told. But it's kinda annoying because Atticus keeps making us stop to make sure people aren't around or something. He's kinda boring.

As we get closer, there's a strong smell of smoke, and what I guess are white ashes coat the black pavement, getting thicker. I know

I'm not the only one who notices since Ele and Isaiah exchange glances. The Mordolus have been burning.

"The lab is right over here," Ele says, pausing and taking a deep breath. She runs around the corner of a house and gasps. I quickly run to see what it is. I stop. All that's there are ashes and charred wood.

"Uh, was that the lab?" that boy whispers to Isaiah. Isaiah nods. Ele stares in horror, and everyone's silent.

"It doesn't matter though, right?" I say, breaking the silence as we walk closer. "You found the cure already."

Ele shakes her head. "I hope so, but now all our supplies are destroyed, and now recreating the cure will be nearly impossible if we can't find more. And—" she pauses, and a shocked look comes across her face. She runs to the ruins.

"Ele, what is it?" Isaiah asks. Frantic, she looks around, kicking some of the charred boards.

"What if he was in there?" Ele asks, panicking. "Or he got captured?"

I step back. I don't wanna see someone who got burned up.

"Probably not. Let's check his house. It'll be fine," Isaiah says. I'm not sure he's as certain as he's trying to sound. Ele hesitates and turns.

"I'm going to text him," she announces. "Isaiah, where's your phone?"

Isaiah reluctantly hands it to her. Ele frantically starts typing.

"Ughhhh!" Ele groans. "It's not working! Apparently, now we can't communicate at all!"

She takes the phone and throws it hard against the charred remains in anger. There's a shattering sound.

"Eleanora Brooks!" Isaiah says. He runs and picks it up. The screen is cracked.

"Sorry," Ele says to Isaiah sheepishly. He does not look like he forgives her just yet. "We need to go find Graydon!"

Atticus nods. "We should leave this place."

"Yeah," that boy says. "They might still be around."

"Reece!" I exclaim.

He looks at me weirdly. "Yeah?"

I wave my hand. "Nothing, I just remembered your name. That's because I'm brilliant."

I follow them toward Graydon's house. It's quiet aside from Reece, who keeps asking about the safety, but I'm not really listening. I think he might be talking to himself, and it sorta creeps me out. I still haven't figured out who the heck Atticus is and why he's even here.

We reach the house, which is pretty similar to Ele's but smaller and more rustic looking. Isaiah runs up to the door and leaves it open, running inside. We all follow him.

"Graydon?" Isaiah calls into the quiet house. He runs through the building and leaves us in the empty entry room. Ele follows him. They eventually return, disappointed.

"He's not here," Ele says, tugging on a piece of her blond hair. No one says anything. I don't because a lot of unhelpful comments are trying to come out of my mouth.

"Is there anywhere else he could be?" Atticus says. "He sometimes leaves to locate supplies, and with the Mordolus so near, maybe they left the area to somewhere more secure."

"You have a point," Isaiah says. "Graydon would have noticed the Mordolus before they got close."

"You're right," Ele says. "But how are we going to find him? We can't just go searching the entire province."

"We can't contact him," Isaiah says, thinking. "But we can wait here. Nothing's gone. He'll have to come back sometime for his things if he's leaving."

"Say he was captured though?" Reece quietly interjects. "Will we wait forever?"

"I'll find somewhere we can stay in the event he never returns," Atticus says.

"I have a few tools and supplies at our house," Ele says. "It's a better start than nothing."

Reece watches out the window, wide-eyed. "Hey, someone's outside."

Ele takes one look out the window, gasps, and sprints outside. I leap out the door after her, assuming that means it's not an enemy. I stand on the porch while Ele stumbles down the steps. A boy approaches from the left. He looks Ele's age or older, dark brown hair, and tall.

"Graydon!" Isaiah says with a gasp.

A girl walks up behind Graydon. Orangey hair covers her face, and her fair skin is coated with ash. I stare in disbelief. There's no way.

"Bella?!"

"Bella?!"

28
BEXLEY: REUNIONS

Graydon and I arrive at the house about three hours after discovering the fire. We stayed at the house's ruins for a while then took a long route through fields and forests just in case the Mordolus were still around. A group of silhouettes gathers on the front porch.

"Who's that?" I ask, stopping as a zephyr of unease quivers through my heart. "Why is Atticus here, and who are those other kids?"

Graydon watches and doesn't respond. Stormy flutters inside the cage, and I set it down on the muddy ground. A blond girl leaps down the stairs and runs to Graydon.

Another girl comes rocketing out the door. "Bella!?"

Only one person has ever called me by that nickname.

"Marie!?" I exclaim.

"BELLA!" Marie shrieks.

She races across the yard and into my arms, and I hold her tight. "Marie! Oh, I missed you! How are you here? What's going on?"

Marie pats me on the back then squirms away. "I thought you were dead!" She fake punches me with a laugh. Shiny ringlets of dark brown hair hit almost at her shoulders. Her eyes are dark brown, studying me lightheartedly. "How are ya?"

"I'm okay," I admit, trying to figure out the right words to explain what happened. "It's a long story. Graydon and I had finally come up with an antidote, and it worked! But then it got destroyed in a fire."

Marie laughs again, and she's either psycho or I missed something. "It's okay! We found the cure! We have it right here! Morzanna already made it! She's been hiding it, and Reece and Isaiah found it in the Infirmary. They stole it!" Marie tells me quickly, bouncing.

"What? Really?!" I say excitedly, shocked with the same force as when Atticus told us Morzanna created the Maraloxis Virus.

"Yeah! And now we found each other!" Marie says. I'm as elated as she is. "I just can't believe you're alive!"

"I know, it's crazy!" I say, with a smile. "I'm not even going to ask how you got like this." I point to her mud-soiled clothes.

"Hey, it's been a rocky day. Escaping the Infirmary isn't a walk in the park."

Someone touches my shoulder. I spin around.

"Hey, Bexley."

"Isaiah!" I exclaim.

"So, you're not dead," he says.

"Oh cool, I hadn't noticed," I reply sarcastically. Isaiah laughs, his golden-brown eyes sparkling. His blond hair is a bit unkempt and wild like he's been off on some adventure. Given the situation, he probably has.

"So, you found a cure?" I ask, and he nods. "I should have known you'd be the one to get into that. Tell me about it later?"

"Yeah," Isaiah says. "So what happened? You just sort of disappeared."

"I don't even know how it happened. I saw a way to escape, and I just did," I explain. "A nurse sent me back to my room alone. I found a door unlocked, you know, the second one across from the Double Guard check-in area, and the guards had vanished! So, I left. I'm sorry."

"It's fine," Isaiah says as we follow the others, occupied in their own conversations, to the cover of the backyard. "That's the least messed up thing that's happened."

"I know what you mean. How could Queen Morzanna create the Virus *and* hide a cure?" I say despairingly.

"Create the Virus?" he asks.

"Oh yeah," I say. "That's what Atticus told us."

A rush of anger flashes in his expression, but it dissipates. "That's…insane. I guess if you think about it theologically, it's not shocking. Without God, we're unable not to sin. Sin leaves us totally lost. I guess with the Queen we notice how evil she is because it's affecting us," Isaiah says with a shrug.

"I suppose that makes sense. Do you really think that we can't *not* sin? That seems so harsh. I know some people who don't believe in God and aren't bad," I say.

Isaiah raises his eyebrows and looks at the ground. "Um, yeah. Pretty sure that's what the Bible says. At the first sin Adam broke the covenant with God. So all people are corrupted by sin. Aside from Jesus of course. I mean, common grace is a thing. They may seem alright on the outside, but without Christ…"

"I'm not entirely sure I agree. It's nicer to believe anyone can be good, or at least not evil," I say.

"Lies usually sound nicer, don't they?" Isaiah says abruptly, and I glance at the ground. "There's no in-between with good and evil. It's one or the other. It's better to know God's just by keeping his word and punishing evil. And that some people *can* be saved by his grace."

"Maybe you're right. So…how'd you get out of the Infirmary?" I ask. Isaiah starts to tell the whole story, all the way from Reece finding Marie and Ele in a closet to when they showed up here. I remember seeing Reece a few times before.

Having all my friends here brings a rush of happiness. As Marie tells me about her escape, I spot Graydon quietly talking to Isaiah.

"The Mordolus are taking action. They found out that the cure has been taken," Graydon explains. "And five people have escaped the Infirmary in the past few weeks. That can't have helped their unrest. They'll be coming to find us, and security will be increased for sure."

"How do you know?" Isaiah asks.

Graydon points to Atticus. "He's been watching them," he says. "We have to find a way to replicate this cure, which is way beyond what any of us can probably do. And how to give it to people. And we have to get everyone out of there. Maybe—"

"Okay," Isaiah interrupts. "Let's talk to everyone else about it later. Let's be relieved the cure exists and we have it."

"Are you even listening to me?" Marie asks impatiently, aggressively tapping a finger on my shoulder.

"Huh?" I say, refocusing. "Oh yes, of course!"

Marie raises an eyebrow. "Yeah, *sure*, Bella."

"Sorry," I say sheepishly, and Marie rolls her eyes. I got the nickname Bella after Marie forgot my name when we first met, so she made something up. It's a joke now.

My mind goes in circles with questions, and I twirl my charm bracelet in the same pattern. Maybe we should be worrying; who knows how long anyone has left, or how we'll give this cure out. All without the Queen finding out.

29
GRAYDON: WHERE DO WE GO FROM HERE?

Isaiah and Ele are back, Bexley found her best friend Marie, and we even have an antidote for the Maraloxis Virus. The fact that I had nothing to do with the current cure and failed the first time nags at the back of my mind. Beneath the ashes of anger, fear for my parents grows. Everything is so overwhelming. I should be happy.

Two years ago, our King Cyrus suddenly died from a heart attack. It wasn't until a week after the king's death, at the funeral, that his twenty-two-year-old daughter, Morzanna, appeared for the first time. No one knew she even existed. Apparently, he adopted her five years earlier and decided to keep it quiet. Until he died. It was legit—he stated much about her in his will. That's when Morzanna became queen. I remember hearing about it, but I was too young to worry about politics. Questions buzzed through our little community of Senneforte. But as King Cyrus's heir, Morzanna inevitably became queen. She's been in an unofficial trial period for the past few years. She did a decent job as queen. Everyone was skeptical, but the

Maraloxis Virus became a bigger problem. The two issues collided when she started 'helping' by locking people up in the Infirmary. If this really is a misunderstanding, then I get her not knowing what to do with all this. But it's been over six months, and besides the walls, Mordolus, and Infirmary, she hasn't done anything. It makes sense if she really did create the Maraloxis Virus. I'm still not completely sure she did. Atticus never explained where he got that idea from.

We haven't received any news from any of the other provinces of Willowmire; the once-was upper peninsula. Or any of the delegates. Ellismark's delegate, Fletcher Blaine, commented on ways to prevent the Virus' spread and potential outcomes in the beginning. He's Morzanna's spokesperson. I suspect he's aligned with her since he's spent more time with her than anyone. Either that or she's found some way to get rid of him, though Delegate Blaine has always been a little odd and uncertain, to say the least. Aspen Maddock, the delegate from the furthest west province, Ravimere, was rumored to have given the other vote for the Mordolus. Although, given the state of his province, it's not surprising he was blamed. The votes are split up by percentage; the monarch gets forty-five percent, and each delegate eleven. Kaylynn Sommerfeldt from Valerrow, the oldest delegate at thirty-three, was very opinionated and against Morzanna's queenship to begin with. I like her. Delegate Emerson Morin of the eastmost province, Lossaree, usually stays quiet until people are harmed. Still, we haven't heard a thing from any of them in months. Senneforte is the most rural of the provinces and placed between the other three and below Ellismark. It has an old-timey feel, blanketed in farms and nostalgic towns.

Ellismark is regal, crowded, and mostly city. It's very structured, uptight, and busy. Lossaree is all waterfront, a lakeside city, and truly beautiful. Ravimere is impoverished, the smallest and shadiest province, partially because it's so distant from Ellismark and close to Infrethia. Valerrow is a free and creative province, covered in street art, sculptures, and graffiti.

The sky grows into a dark ashy gray. A cool summer wind rips through the treetops. We stand outside the house, talking under the cover of a few creaking oaks. I try to listen, but I'm unfocused.

"Let's go inside and get out of the open," Atticus orders.

As we enter, I find the need to validate that the trashed house is not because of my poor housekeeping. Like most of the other ways I spend time, it's a safety measure in case of a raid. I choose not to paint my door, saving me from Mordolus fires, but leaving it liable to a break-in.

"Imagine having your own house!" Marie says, jetting into the kitchen. "Boy, oh boy, neat!" Marie's bouncing with energy. Her dark ringlets are a tangled mess.

Light leaks into the sky, fighting off the darkness outside. I've lost sense of time the past few days. I lean against the banister.

"Let's head back to our house," Isaiah says. "We can rest there for a while."

Ele nods. "That's a wonderful idea. There's more space and it's further from the Hunter's activity. We can discuss the cure tomorrow."

Her long hair is silky blond with chestnut highlights, held back by a blue satin headband. One strip of hair in the front is separated from the rest because she twists it so often. Her eyes are deep blue like the sky right before nightfall.

Frankly, I'm annoyed that I didn't help anyone escape the Infirmary. So far, I've basically been no help. Bexley had to risk her life to save me from the Mordolus. I'm pretty much useless.

For the next quarter hour, we head toward Ele and Isaiah's house. It's still decently dark, so we easily cross the short distance there through the woods without any trouble with the Mordolus.

When we get to the house on Gilded Way, an essence of familiarity surrounds me. Memories trickle back from my fading childhood. It brings back more thoughts about my parents, reminding me that our old house is gone. But this familiar house is still here. I found out Ele was captured last time I was inside.

When we're secure in the house, catching up, I feel better. It's weird to be around so many people again. The sun rises, and the air is fresh after the storm. Patches of golden light shine through the windows. The house is relatively untouched, but spirals of muddy footprints leave a cold reminder of what lurks right outside.

"So," Bexley says, toying with her mask, which she put back on following the fire. "What are we going to do to make sure no one gets sick while we're here?"

"It all has to do with how it's spread. My dad and the other scientists think the Virus is airborne. Which makes sense because of the types of common symptoms, and their similarity to the flu. But it's a neurological virus, which is why people have seizures and lose senses. That's probably why Marie has vision issues and Isaiah has headaches. Neurological viruses are also usually spread by air. It also makes it one of the easiest types of disease to catch because everyone needs to breathe," I explain.

"Oh, that makes sense," Bexley says, opening up Stormy's cage and letting him hop out and onto her hand.

"The Mordolus wear masks and gloves, and they probably know the best precautions. I think that's a pretty solid idea," Ele says, sitting down on the gray couch beside her brother.

"So if everyone just stayed away from each other, this wouldn't've happened?" Reece asks. "I would have been cool with that."

"Maybe. But either way, the Mordolus still would have taken people or found another way to destroy us. Honestly though, if we all had stayed completely away from each other, Senneforte would have crumbled anyway. It's just not a realistic solution," Graydon says.

"What about the masks and gloves? Do they help?" Isaiah asks. "Because we could wear them. But the Mordolus do and still get sick. They just have the antidote and cover it up."

"I don't know. There just wasn't enough time to figure out how to prevent it well. The Mordolus are also in very close proximity to infected people, pretty much all the time, so we can't really say," I say.

"You sound like your dad," Isaiah says.

I smile. "You're gonna think it even more in a minute because I have another thought. When I was researching, I read about the yellow fever epidemic. They thought the disease came from poor cleanliness in the city, but it was really caused by mosquitoes. During the Black Death, some people thought it was a punishment from God or that foreigners had poisoned their water, but the real cause was rats carrying infected fleas. What if we think the Maraloxis Virus is spread by air or touch, but it's really something completely different? What if the Mordolus wear all that to make us think it's transmitted that way, but it's just to throw us off? Then we all become sick much faster."

"That would be really crazy," Ele says with a sigh.

"It doesn't matter now though because it's too late to bring back the people who've died," Reece says tensely.

"But we have the cure, which we'll save until someone really needs it. In the meantime, we'll figure out how to get more," Isaiah says. "And we can save everyone who's left."

"Yeah, then go kick Morzanna right off her throne!" Marie says with a mischievous grin.

"So, we don't wear masks?" Bexley asks.

"What's the point? We have the cure and half of us are sick," Isaiah says.

"Fair. I do wonder how we will recreate the medicine if all our supplies were burned in the fire," Ele says.

"Maybe we could find more?" Reece says. He plays with the flowers from a dried arrangement on the table then glances around to see the reaction to his suggestion.

"It would work if we could go raid some laboratory or something. But, scientific supplies are one of the things the Mordolus takes, so the chances of finding anything are not great. Especially the ingredients. It took me weeks to collect them all. Now like half the buildings are burned, too," I say. "Anything valuable is hidden, stolen, or destroyed."

"I guess we'll have to find out where it's hidden. Maybe at that base or it's all been taken to Ellismark. But…if we all broke out of the Infirmary, why couldn't we get back in?" Isaiah says.

"What do you mean?" Ele asks.

"We know we can get in through the tunnels. We know they have everything we'll need since they made the cure. Might not even have to go past the abandoned hallways. They'd never realize we were there," Isaiah explains. "It's the perfect plan."

"You're suggesting we go back to the Infirmary and rob it?" Atticus asks. Isaiah nods.

"I don't know. They'll probably find out soon that we escaped and will be trying to figure out how. Besides, I don't really feel like going back there anyway; it's too risky," Ele protests.

"Well I can't think of any other way, unless, of course, we escape the province, which is even more dangerous and completely unrealistic," Bexley admits, petting Stormy through the rusted bars of his cage.

Atticus stares at the floor, deep in troubled thought. No one else says anything. I think that means we've reached a decision.

Leaning against the wall, I stare out the window at the sunrise. The horizon is an array of colors, and everything is shadowy. This picturesque scene attracts me. I used to be really into photography. I have literally no photographic memory. I can't form any pictures in my mind. Sometimes I can't even remember what my family looks like, and it's not just because I haven't seen them for so long. When I was younger, I took pictures of random things because I was scared I would forget what they looked like. I even kept a picture of myself in my pocket. I wanted to make sure I remembered what I looked like. Anyway, the shadows and sunshine look cool, and I'm sad I won't remember that beauty.

Suddenly, something moves out from behind the houses across the road. A surge of fear breaches my mind as I focus on the person. Draped in dark clothes, he looks emaciated. Sunlight glints off brutal scars on his arms.

It's still dark, but I can tell he's staring right at me. I want to look away, but it's like I'm entranced. He steps closer, enough for me to see his face, then disappears behind the houses.

Before retreating from sight, he turns to me. I shouldn't be able to hear what he says. The distance between us is vast, not to mention the layer of glass. The voices and sounds around me are all muted. The words of a distant conversation are confused inside my head. Reality slurs, which really creeps me out. All I can see is him.

"The Queen knows," a hissing voice says. It's like he's standing beside me. "The end is coming."

"Graydon?"

The haze shatters like glass. I stumble away from the window, knocking over the clay vase holding the dried flowers. It hits the ground and bursts into pieces. Everyone stares at me. Isaiah called me.

"What's up?" he asks. I stare at him, but words take a second to form.

"You didn't hear that?" I ask, peering across the road to make sure the person is really gone. Isaiah shakes his head. I point outside.

"Someone was out there," I say, terrified.

"Was it the Mordolus? A Hunter?" Isaiah asks, jumping up. I shake my head.

"I don't know. It was right over there. And he talked really loudly, so clearly…I don't know how you didn't hear it," I say.

"I don't see anyone," Bexley says, looking out the window.

"He disappeared immediately. Something wasn't right about him. It was…unnatural. He had so many scars. He said 'the Queen knows' and that the end is coming. You guys should have heard it." *Great, I'm insane.* Atticus stands in front of the door.

"What did he look like? It sounds like whoever I saw in the tunnels!" Ele says, horrified. "Do you think he followed us?"

"Maybe," Reece says uneasily, noticeably stepping away. I glance out the window one last time.

"Then we need to go somewhere safer! We can't be near him!" Ele cries hysterically. Reece tensely backs away, rocking and fearfully covering his face. Marie energetically bounds over to the window and curiously looks out.

"Everyone, calm down!" Isaiah demands.

"No, we have to go!" Ele exclaims. "If you'd seen him, you'd understand. You saw him, don't you agree with me, Graydon?"

I hesitate for a moment. "I guess. I don't know," I say. "I'm just scared he was serious."

30

ISAIAH: TRUST

An aura of fear and mystery courses through the room. Graydon sits on the brick fireplace with his head in his hands. Ele keeps her eyes fixed out the window. Atticus stands nearby, protectively silent.

I pace the room. This mysterious person is following us. And watching us. I don't like how he's making threats. I've missed him both times. By his physical description, I bet something awful happened to him.

"We should leave. If he's contacting Morzanna, the Mordolus could show up any second," Graydon says. Ele finally looks away from the window.

I nod. "Yeah. We could—"

"No," Atticus says firmly.

"'WHAT?" Ele says.

"Please, trust me. We need to stay here. Nowhere else is safer. We can't give in to fear and keep running. If the Hunters had shown up outside, it would be different, but we don't know who that was. There's no evidence that he is with the Mordolus," Atticus says. "We all need to stay alert, but, for your protection, we are staying at this house unless it becomes extremely unsafe."

"That's crazy! We can't hang around with a murderer outside and more murderers coming!" Reece says.

Atticus stands his ground. "We aren't leaving."

"Yes, we are!" Ele says fiercely.

Atticus looks her in the eye. "I am trying to keep you safe. Besides, I am an adult, and I know more than you. We *are staying* here."

Ele puts on her darkest glare and stiffly sits down in the rocking chair next to the fireplace.

The silence is tense, but Atticus doesn't let Ele win. "I'm going to make sure it's secure and no one's coming. We can discuss more when I return. Shut the blinds. Lock the door while I'm gone and stay inside." With that, he heads out the front door.

"Oh, are we really trusting him?" Bexley asks as Graydon locks the door and Marie covers the windows.

"I don't think we have a choice but to listen to him," I say.

"I trust him," Graydon says after a thoughtful minute. "He's helped us so far. Let's be wary, but I think he's safe."

"So, what if he isn't? We were just threatened and discovered, and Atticus is telling us to stay! Say he just went to get the Hunters?" Ele argues. "What then?"

"Good point," Marie says, perching on the arm of the couch.

"We'll watch. If he comes back alone, we trust him. If he doesn't, we leave out the back and head into the woods," I suggest.

"Well he's back now," Reece says, peering outside from the edge of the blinds. "Alone."

I go and unlock the door when there's a quiet knock.

"There's no one around," Atticus says, stepping inside and relocking the door.

"What now?" Graydon asks.

"I'm very tired," Bexley says.

"I'll watch while you rest," Atticus offers. "There's still a chance someone could show up."

I don't feel super excited about the idea. But I can hardly keep my eyes open. We have no choice. I say a mental prayer. *God, please don't let us get caught. But whatever you've got planned is good.*

"Fine," Ele says coldly.

I climb the wooden stairs. Heading to the right, I absentmindedly follow the usual path to my old bedroom. It's like jumping to a completely different lifetime. I change into some clean shorts and a T-shirt. Opening my closet, I collect some blankets and bedding. My guitar gathers dust in the corner of the room. I brush my hand across the strings. It's really out of tune. I pick it up and start to adjust it. When I'm satisfied with the sound, I strum a random song that pops into my head. It's been so long since I've played. My fingers are already sore.

"Weird, isn't it?" Ele says, walking into the room. I nod. She sits on my bed, staring out my only window at the trees.

"Do you think we'll ever come back here to live for real?" Ele asks.

I shrug and carefully place my guitar back in the corner. "Hope so." I set the blankets on the bed and sit beside Ele.

"Do you think we'll get the cure to Mom and Dad before it's too late?" she asks. We haven't had a ton of conversations about our parents. I just don't want to have to explain their state.

"We've got to get them out first," I say. Ele twists a strand of hair. I finally reveal that Mom had a seizure. Reece and I went on that crazy adventure to find her. Mom could've died. Ele doesn't say much.

"We've got to get more of the cure somehow," I add.

"I agree. Everyone seems okay right now, but you never know how long anyone has remaining," Ele says, gesturing to the rest of the house.

"Are you okay?" I ask.

She sighs. "For the most part. I think I was in denial for a long time until I got to the Infirmary, but I can feel it. I don't feel normal, you know?"

"Yeah," I say. The prodrome of the Virus is malaise. Then fatigue, followed gradually by more serious symptoms. In the middle stage, people get paresthesia. I sometimes notice the tingling in my hands. In the last phases, some weird things can happen. Paralysis, hallucinations, seizures. Mom's in the last stages.

"Sometimes I have chills, but for the most part I'm fine," Ele says.

"How's that rat bite?" I ask.

"Mostly fine. I hardly notice it. That was the strangest thing. Perhaps we scared the creature, or maybe it was terribly hungry," Ele responds. "How are you doing? You've been sick longer than I have."

I'm always sick more often than Ele. Maybe she has better immunity. She was probably infected around the same time as me, but I've got it worse.

"I'm tired a lot, and I have headaches," I say. "I've got one now, actually. It's not bad. At least twice a week they turn into migraines though."

"I worry about the others, too. Graydon says he's fine, but I don't know whether to believe it. Bexley is in the clear and improving since she had one dose of the cure, Marie only seems to have vision issues, and I don't know about Reece. I'm just so afraid," Ele confesses.

"Yeah," I say. "At least we have the cure. If someone gets worse, we can give it to them." Anxiety grows like a weed in an unattended garden. "We just have to keep going, Ele. We can't give in."

"I know," she says, flopping back onto my bed. "I just want to."

I stand. "God will give us the strength we need. Just have to trust."

"But it feels like when I just trust, nothing gets better so I have to fight on my own," Ele says.

"We gotta actively listen to God and rely on him. We can't expect to be able to just do absolutely nothing and God will fix our lives. We fight for what He promises. But when we can't fight anymore, He's there for us," I say. "We can't do this life alone."

"Right…I suppose," Ele says quietly.

We collect the last of the bedding and return to the living room.

"I'm SOO hungry," Marie says. We all agree.

"I'll see if I can find anything." Ele says. She heads to the kitchen.

"This is all I've got," Ele says when she returns, holding out half a box of pasta. It looks like the rats got into it. In the other hand, she has a metal water bottle.

"What's this?" Marie says, opening the bottle. She grimaces.

"Vinegar," Ele responds. "Of course, the power doesn't work, but maybe somehow we can cook the pasta."

"Oh, I know!" Bexley says. "We could soak it."

"That would work?" Marie asks.

"I don't know. Possibly," Bexley shrugs.

"You have water, right?" Graydon asks. Ele nods.

"A little, but we could always collect more from the creek," Ele says. She traipses off, returning with a bottle of rusty-looking water from the kitchen. It looks like it's been sitting around for a couple years.

"It's clean, I used iodine," Ele promises. "Bexley can try…whatever the plan is."

After applying an irrational amount of hand sanitizer, Bexley runs off into the kitchen. She returns with a metal bowl. "It might take a while," she says, mixing the pasta and water together.

We wait.

"Can I talk to you?" Graydon asks me quietly.

"Sure," I say. We go to the hallway. It's the first time in a month we've had a conversation alone.

He asks me about the Infirmary. I ask about the fire. He tells me about when he and Bexley nearly got caught by the Hunters. The conversation is almost normal. Almost.

Graydon pauses. He stares at me for a second. "You didn't hear anything about my parents, did you?"

I shake my head. "No. Which is okay, right? I mean, I wish I would've found them. But when some exciting death happens, everyone hears about it. And mom never said anything about them. She checks the death list often."

"That's mildly comforting," Graydon admits. He plays with the strings of his maroon hoodie. "And morbid."

"Yeah. Sorry," I say. I grew up with Graydon. His parents are like a second family.

"It's fine. Better than nothing. I'm good with it. My parents are dying, but hey, at least they're not dead yet. Thanks for looking," Graydon says. He's definitely *not* good with it. That's the thing about Graydon. He's like never honest about what he's thinking and feeling. It bothers me. I've known Graydon so long I've learned to read him. I still wish he'd just tell me what's going on inside his head.

"Why do you keep talking about hope?" Graydon asks. "Nothing's gonna get better."

"You don't know that," I say. "There's a point to all this. There are things coming that we have to fight for now."

"Maybe so. I just don't know if I can hold on until then," he whispers, turning away.

"Don't you dare give up, Graydon," I say. "We can't give up or hope really will fade. I can't be the only one who believes that. We have to have faith."

He starts down the hall. "I'll try my best."

In the dining room, Bexley still stirs. All that she has is cloudy water and a mess of uncooked pasta.

"Listen, it's soup!" she says, uncertainly.

"I don't like soup," Reece whispers to me.

"Since when?" I ask. "We had soup nearly every day at the Infirmary. You didn't complain."

He eyes Bexley's bowl. "Since *that* became soup."

Bexley jumps up from the table and marches into the kitchen. "I know what it needs! Salt!" She finds the saltshaker and dumps half of it in.

"That was a *ton* of salt. Maybe you should stop stirring it before it becomes something worse," Ele suggests.

"Can you get some bowls?" I ask Ele. Bexley forces us all to use hand sanitizer. When Ele returns, Bexley portions out the soup. Atticus refuses. I'm not sure if it's out of selflessness or disgust. Maybe both. Probably mostly the latter. He walks outside.

We all sit around the table. Marie drums her fingers on the wood. I stare at my bowl. Bexley rolls her eyes and takes a bite.

"It's, um, crunchy," she says with a forced smile.

Graydon tries it too. "It's not that bad," he says. "Kind of tastes like metal. And salt."

"Oh, well that's lovely," Ele whispers under her breath.

Graydon chews some more. "Whoa. A *lot* of salt actually. Like—"

"*Okay*, thank you for your input," Bexley interrupts frustratedly.

Everyone eventually tries it. Ele looks at me, disgusted. Soaking it did not help. No one complains much, though. Or talks because the crunching is so loud, we probably couldn't hear each other. I drink every drop of water from my bowl.

"Sorry, Bella," Marie says. "I don't think you have a bright future in culinary arts."

Bexley glowers. Two small braids crown her wavy auburn-red hair. The sunlight streaming from the glass door behind us brings out her golden highlights. Her silver charm bracelet portrays a fiery sun charm, a gold rose, and a platinum moon.

"At least we have something to eat," I say.

"I'm still hungry," Reece mumbles. "Is there anything else?"

"Unless you want the vinegar," Ele says.

Reece sighs. "I'll pass."

"You can have mine," Graydon offers.

"Really?" Reece asks. Graydon nods. He passes the hardly-touched bowl to Reece. "Thanks."

Still hungry, we decide on sleeping arrangements. Marie and Bexley were supposed to share my parents' room, but Bexley swears she saw a rat and forbids anyone from going in there. So they're sleeping in Ele's room. Reece will share mine. Graydon says he'll sleep on the couch. Maybe he's still holding onto the hope that he's not sick yet.

Reece has already found a notebook. Sitting cross-legged in the corner, he writes. He's really excited to have paper again. Reece glances up at me and silently nods for me to come. I sit next to him in the corner between the window and fireplace.

"I don't trust him," he whispers.

"Atticus?"

Reece nods. "I feel like he's hiding something. Acts all suspicious."

"If he is working for Morzanna, he'd have done something by now," I say. Reece taps the pen on the floor, thinking.

"How did he know that stalker outside wouldn't return? Odd coincidence. I don't think Atticus is part of the Mordolus. Just hiding things." Reece says, looking down at his paper.

"It is weird having a stranger around," I say.

"Well, half the people here are strangers to someone," he says. "I know the least people. I only know you. I like your sister, though. She gave me a notebook. Marie seems kind of sketchy, though. I don't like new people. Not to begin with at least."

"That's normal," I say, tilting my head. "In a way."

"I'm going to finish writing, you know, just in case Atticus murders us in our sleep. That way someone will know what happened," Reece says.

"You're crazy," I say.

Reece shrugs. "I know."

I'm super tired. Bexley's tearing apart Ele's room trying to find something for her and Marie to wear. Reece goes to bed. I stand in the kitchen and close the blinds above the backyard window. I bury my hands in my hair. I wonder if my parents are still okay. I'm wide awake. And still thirsty. Especially after consuming approximately five hundred times the daily value of salt from Bexley's pasta.

Atticus stands in the corner, watching the locked door.

I don't know how everyone else is surviving, but I need water. And I've been cooped up inside way too long. Two months too long. I open the cabinet below the sink and get out a pitcher. I'll get some water for everyone. I'm amazing like that. Atticus watches me, understanding what I'm doing. I pause to put on my shoes before heading outside.

It's a hot summer afternoon. Our big backyard is surrounded by trees. I follow a row of willows from our house down to the small creek. It's high because of the storm. I'll put iodine in it when I go inside. I'm not worried and go ahead and drink some. The water's cool and refreshing. I take a few slow sips. My head's already clearer.

Opposite the creek, there's a little cluster of trees. I don't wanna go back inside yet. I walk down there, leaving the water by the creek. Ele and I used to build structures out of sticks here. Then, Graydon and I would destroy them playing that we were convicts. Ele always told us that game was 'morally offensive'. She just didn't like being the victim. There are still remnants of some of our constructions.

"What are you doing?"

I spin around. "Jeez, Atticus, you scared me bad."

He shrugs. "Sorry."

"Did you follow me?" I ask.

Atticus shakes his head. "Not until you didn't come back."

I nod. "I have a question," I blurt out.

"Okay," Atticus says.

"Like, who are you?" I ask. "Why do you know so much about the Mordolus? How'd you not get caught like everyone else?"

"I'm not working for Morzanna. Never." He shakes his head and looks at the bare ground. "I've been trying to figure out what her plan is. I'm trying to find out why she would create this virus." He sighs. "There are just some things I can't share that explain my reasoning. As for not getting caught, I've learned over time," Atticus tells me. "Why?"

"You did offer to watch while we were all asleep. If you were working for the Queen it'd be the perfect time to act," I say, shrugging.

"I understand," he says slowly. "I hope you'll learn to trust me."

"Where's your family?" I ask.

"I'm an only child. My parents are dead," he says plainly. He's gotta be just a little over twenty. No family. That sucks. If I didn't have Ele, that could be me too. Maybe it was the Virus.

"Who was that earlier?" I ask.

Atticus stares at the oak tree to my right. "I don't know," he says. "We shouldn't stay out here in the open, and you should rest."

Atticus really isn't that bad. I'm not worried that he might be part of the Mordolus anymore. We can trust him. I'm with Reece though—he hides things.

Atticus and I walk back inside. It's cold in the house and damp from the storm. I'm tired enough to sleep. Besides, we're safe. For now.

31
ELEANORA: HOW IS THIS POSSIBLE?

After Bexley and Marie find something suitable from my dresser and I change myself, I head to the kitchen. Someone filled the water pitcher, and the iodine is out on the counter, so I know it's been treated. After downing a glass, I stop to fix my hair into a single long braid using the microwave as a mirror and then walk back to my room.

Atticus is stationed in the far corner of the dining room where he can see both the doors as well as the front windows.

"Hey." Graydon stops me in the hallway. "Lock your door," he whispers. "Just to be safe."

I nod. "Got it. Good night—er, morning."

Despite the trials of the day, once I'm in bed, I'm too tired to stay awake. I draw my blanket closer just to survey the multi-colored butterflies that bring back a lot of memories. I've had this blanket since I was probably seven, and Ms. Kassy, Graydon's mom, gave it to me at one of our sleepovers. When Isaiah, Graydon, and the dads go on bi-yearly camping trips, Ms. Kassy has my mom and me over all day to hang out then lets me stay for a sleepover. It's strange to think about those kinds of simple things anymore. Exhaustion eventually overtakes my consciousness, and I succumb to deep sleep.

I return to the backyard with my brother and Graydon, playing kid games and laughing. Only a few moments pass before the warm sun and careless chatter fades and the world becomes distorted into a dark pool of memories.

The images merge, forming the chalk-white walls of the dreaded Infirmary. The halls are empty and silent as I involuntarily walk forward, aware of every sound, although there are none except my own footsteps carrying me back past the door where Marie left me, through the dirty corridors, and to the pitch-black hall leading down to the tunnels. It seems to take endless hours, but somehow I don't have time to rationalize where I'm going until the darkness eclipses my vision.

Panic seizes my heart and comprehension sets in as I survey the dirt walls, which are illuminated by menacing, sourceless light. Smaller tunnels split off, the shadows shift on their own, and I'm at war with myself, trying to take control of my movements. *Please move! Please run! Just get out of here!* My feet are glued to the floor.

The same person who haunted me before steps out of the tunnel to the right, validating my fears. His sickly pale, shadowed skin portrays deep, severe scars. *I CAN'T MOVE!* My heart beats so furiously, it's like something is trying to break out of my ribcage, each throb a fist pounding against the atrium to escape the thing I fear is to come.

"What do you want?" I choke out.

"To kill you," he says, leaving just a few feet between us.

I draw a shaky breath. "Why?"

"I have to," he says matter-of-factly, walking around me in circles. He laughs lightly as if seeing me tense when he moves out of my vision range is entertaining. "Insubordination is a serious offense."

"Who are you?" I ask.

He takes a step back and draws a knife, looking at it a few times before holding it within an inch of me. The being inside my heart finally gives up trying to escape, and it takes me a minute to realize that's the sensation of a worryingly long palpitation. The light glints off the sharp metal that will any second pierce my heart.

"Merris."

I jolt up. Late afternoon sun rays still fall through the gaps in the curtains, painting golden lines on the floor. I rake a hand through my sweaty hair and take a deep breath, clutching my butterfly blanket tighter. *That was the most vivid nightmare I've ever had.*

My terrorizing dream leaves my hands clammy as I recall the fright. A shiver jars me, doubtlessly having no relation to the viral chills I usually experience. I'm normally not an overly nervous person, but this person my mind named Merris causes me anxiety I've never felt before. I feel out of control and absolutely hate it.

After a few minutes of attempting to return to sleep, I sit up. Bexley is asleep on a mattress on the floor like a princess, and Marie is sprawled out right beside me, limbs everywhere like a dying spider, taking up seventy-five percent of my bed. I push aside the pale pink sheets and go to turn on the strand of fairy lights wrapped around the headboard. Unfortunately the batteries have died. Bexley's bird stares at me from on top of my dresser.

I crawl out from under my blanket and wrap it around me like a cape, careful to be silent. I still end up tripping over Marie's yellow high-tops, and I glance around to make sure I didn't wake anyone. My room is a wreck compared to how I last saw it. The dresser drawers are removed, and clothes are strewn all over the floor, though I tried to tidy up a bit. From the clutter, I spot old schoolbooks, remembering that my first year of high school has been wasted. All the plants from my windowsill have been knocked off and spilled, and the only thing really still in one piece is the bed in the center of the room. Somehow our house has become like the others: destroyed and lonely.

After I was captured, I suppose that the Mordolus confiscated anything that was valuable, and the door was left open for hours, so I really don't want to know how many rabid creatures are hiding under my bed. I'm sure Bexley doesn't either.

A little wrinkled piece of paper lays on the floor amidst the mess, and I reach down to pick it up from the scattering of writing utensils dumped beside my desk.

Peace I leave you; my peace I give you. Not as the world gives do I give to you. Do not let your hearts be troubled, neither let them be afraid. (John 14:27).

My father copied the verse for me on this scrap card the first day Isaiah and I spent hidden in the attic—the first day the threat became real for us. I stared at the words inked quickly across the middle and the morning glory vines drawn around the edges through a blur of tears all day. I hold the old card carefully before stashing it into the pocket of my light purple sweatpants.

I stare at the empty wall across from me, remembering all my pictures and regretting taking them down since they're somewhere locked away inside the Infirmary now. I look at the floor, still marked with muddy boot prints, reminding me of the not-distant past when I was taken.

Bexley stirs, so I leave and walk through the vacant house, angry at everything. Graydon is asleep on the couch, but Atticus is gone. I tiptoe into the dining room and peek outside at the mountain laurels peacefully lining our fence. *My house shouldn't be destroyed. I should still be living here, with my whole family, happy. I should be going to high school and not having to worry about the fate of my family. I shouldn't have to deal with any of this.* As I head back to my room, the feeling boils inside of me, bubbling dangerously, and I worry that any moment, I'll overflow.

"What are you doing?"

I spin around to find Atticus standing in the hallway.

"What, can I not walk around my own house?" I ask in a harsh whisper. He doesn't reply. "And besides where were you? You would know if you'd been watching like you said you would."

I look at the ground. *It isn't the fault of anyone else here.* I'm not sure if it's anxiety, sleep deprivation, or hunger, but I feel irritable.

"I was checking outside," Atticus says, a little scattered. "You should be resting."

I shrug, feeling like a little kid still cloaked in my butterfly blanket, receiving ridicule from a parent—no, not a parent, a babysitter that really has no idea what they're doing.

"I'm fine, I've rested long enough," I say dismissively. Emotion brews dangerously inside me, and I know I should, but I don't try to suppress it. I want to feel its consuming burn.

My peace I leave with you. The words keep revolving around my mind.

I glance up at Atticus, for the first time observing how off he looks. Noticing my stare, he puts his hood back up with a shaky hand and gazes at the photo collage on the wall.

"Are you alright?" I ask.

He nods briskly, not looking away from the pictures. "Are you?" he asks and walks back to the living room without another word or waiting for a response.

I stare at the largest frame in the hall, a recent picture of my parents. My mother and father are nearly the same height. Her hair is trimmed in a pixie cut, and my father is as bald as I ever knew him. I dearly wish I could see them.

I saunter back to my bedroom and climb back into bed, attempting to remember my old life and trying to accept my new one. Trying to be at peace. Before long, I fall asleep again.

I'm back deep inside the tunnels. The strange lighting follows me around, and the walls seem to close in as ghostly noises whisper from the smaller tunnels. *Not again. It is just a dream, and I'm going to be prepared for this round. I need to be ready.*

Thankfully, I'm able to move around freely, and I sprint down one of the tunnels, hoping to find an exit. The passage seems to go on forever in a twisting maze, and before long I'm sure I'm thoroughly lost. It's dark, yet I know what's in front of me before I reach it.

"Wait!" someone screams.

Startled, I turn around and standing in the hall behind me is an old man. He stops so abruptly, his thin glasses fall off and crack upon contact with the hard dry ground. The short, round fellow is dressed in dark brown clothing and looks far too decrepit to be chasing after me without a cane at least, yet he doesn't seem older than sixty. Panting, the haggard man looks up at me and begs, "Please listen to me."

"Who are you?" I ask, apprehensive. *That's an awfully dumb question—this is my dream, so it must be someone I know or have at least seen…right?*

"No time to explain. I'm trying to help you. Please don't forget this," he says quickly, walking closer to me. I'm conflicted enough not to run since he seems sincere.

The old man looks around nervously as if expecting at any second something dreadful is going to happen. A blueish-green glow follows him and distorts everything around us.

"Let me show you something." He grabs my hand, and the tunnels fade out. The blue light swallows us, and I can't see anything but a sea of bright colors.

After a second of terror, a face flashes before my eyes. I take a step back, but I'm only wading through the airy blue-greenness. I see a young man, close to twenty, and instantly detect a fiery spark in his hazel-gray eyes. Nothing about it seems current, and it's like I'm watching a video. All I can distinguish in the background is the weird, dream fog, but the way his dark hair is ruffled suggests the moment was windy. I barely get a glance before the world is cast into darkness again, and I feel like I'm falling from a terrible height. Something about him is so familiar it disturbs me, but the picture and glow vanish instantly.

Again, a picture forms before my eyes; it's dark, cold, and sinister. The same person is shackled to a stone wall, bleeding from gashes on his arms and legs. Suddenly a whip comes down, and a violent scream shatters the image.

Moments later, I'm alone in the tunnel. *This is some crazy dream I'm having. I'll keep going down this passage and see if I can find anything.* The air becomes icy enough to make me freeze, and the tunnel looks darker. I stop suddenly and turn around slowly.

Merris.

Standing in the shadows of the tunnel, he watches me with a frosted gaze.

"I'm going to kill you," he says. I try to move, but my annoying dream paralysis comes upon me again, and I'm riveted by fear. Parts of the tunnel are still distorted in blotches of light as Merris nears.

"Yeah, I heard," I say. *It's a dream, it's a dream, it's a dream. I don't need to be scared. I'm not a fearful person—I'm the one who escaped the Infirmary.*

I'm the person who's brave enough to stand up to Mordolus guards. This is just a wild nightmare because I'm so tired.

"You did?" he asks. "So, you understand I'm real? This isn't just a dream, Eleanora."

Merris' murderous stare slowly breaks through my confidence. Eventually I can't stand it or the silence any longer.

"Why do you keep terrorizing me? How are you in my head?" I blurt out, petrified.

"The Virus," he states.

"What do you mean?" I inquire, my shoulders tense.

"I mean, if you could make a virus to infect thousands of people, why would you make it to just do one thing? I'm finding it useful. You've only seen the surface of what's going on," Merris says as I inspect all his injuries. I've never seen someone with so many cuts, bruises, and scars. Some of them are long since healed, but an unnerving number seem to be only days old. *Where did they come from?*

"What happened to you?" I gasp. Merris doesn't respond, a shadow rising in his countenance and a glazed appearance abounding in his eyes. He stares blankly at something behind me like for once he's the one immobilized.

"Starling!" he shouts suddenly, staggering backward and panting. I quickly swivel in that direction, but there's nothing else in the tunnel.

Merris instantly recovers, behaving like nothing had happened until his eyes fall on me. Suddenly, he changes, and a hatred darker than the deepest part of the tunnel settles in his eyes. He throws me against the wall, and I hit my head hard enough to taste blood.

"Your brother is doomed! I'll kill him as well!" he yells. Something strange happens with the light then there's a distant shriek.

That's the last sound I hear before awakening from my nightmare, realizing it was my own scream. This time, I'm certain that these dreams aren't fiction; Merris was definitely talking to me. And not only that, I'm on his murder list. A frozen, desensitized feeling denies the presence of my clothes and skin, penetrating straight to my very bones like a feverish chill.

Marie sits up. "Ele? What the heck was that?" she asks groggily, but I can't respond because I'm focusing on simply breathing. "Jeez, you look like you've seen a ghost."

Bexley wakes up too, standing from the floor and straightening her T-shirt and shorts, which are mine, before stepping over to the bed. "What's going on?" she asks in her high, silky voice.

"Ele?" Graydon knocks on the door, and as soon as Bexley unlocks it, he's by my side.

"Something's wrong with her," Marie states, jerking her head in my direction. I'm brought back to reality when Graydon places a hand on my shoulder, sending a tingling through the numbness I feel.

"What's wrong?" he asks. My stomach twists and my head spins with questions.

"It was him, the person you saw, Merris—he's in my dreams! Like for real!" I say.

"What?" Graydon asks. "How?"

I shake my head and quickly spit out, "He said something about the Virus when I asked."

"Are you sure it's real and not just a dream?" Bexley says. I nod quickly, wanting to retreat under the covers, pretend nothing happened, and wallow in embarrassment because I woke everyone up, but the fear is too real. The vision was too real.

"Absolutely, and he's planning to kill me—and Isaiah."

32
GRAYDON: MERRIS AND MORBID MISSIONS

Ele's face is painted with terror. She's confident someone's going to murder her. But it's pretty impossible to literally be *in* someone's dreams.

"Calm down," Marie says.

Ele shakes her head. "But Isaiah—"

"If you stop panicking and talk to us, we can figure out what actually happened," I suggest.

Ele dismisses me with a wave of her hand. "I just told you what actually happened, stupid!"

"Seriously Ele, what is wrong with you?" Marie asks. "You've never acted like this."

Ele gives her a sideways glance. "Merris is inside my head! He's threatening my FAMILY!" she says indignantly. "I'm freaking out!"

"Okay, deep breaths, girly," Marie says, patting Ele on the shoulder. Ele's gone completely insane.

"Did he say anything else?" Bexley asks.

"Yeah, he assured me he was really in my head. I asked what had happened to him, he got angry, and then I woke up," she recalls. "He also went all weird and said 'starling'."

"That's like a bird, right?" I ask.

Ele shakes her head. "Yeah, but I think whatever he was talking about isn't. I don't think *he* knew what he was talking about, like I said, he became strange and scared. I don't think it's a bird, anyway."

"Oh, I don't understand. How could he be in your dreams, Eleanora? There's no way," Bexley says impatiently. Ele plays with a piece of her blond hair, shrugging.

"I'm sure it was him," she says, shivering. Someone jogs down the stairs. Isaiah appears in the doorway.

"What's going on?" he asks. Atticus stands outside the door too.

"I don't know. She says she saw that creepy dude in her dreams," Marie says, pointing at Ele and hopping out of the bed. "Maybe she's got the Crazy Disease. I don't wanna catch it." At the word 'disease', Bexley steps back.

"The person you saw in the tunnels?" Isaiah asks. Ele nods vigorously.

"Yeah, Merris he said, and he's going to kill us," Ele tells Isaiah. Atticus freezes at her words.

"That's what he said," she adds, noticing the unsure look on Isaiah's face.

"In your dreams? That doesn't make any sense. It's impossible." Isaiah paces the room. Ele looks at each of us, annoyed.

"It was so weird but also so real. I'll prove it," Ele says.

"No need, just tell me exactly what he said. You're sure he said his name was Merris?" Atticus asks Ele. I talk to Isaiah by the door.

"This makes no sense," I say in an undertone.

"I know. She's acting really strange. I mean, maybe she's hallucinating or something," Isaiah whispers.

Ele jumps up and turns to Isaiah.

"I am not lying, and I am not hallucinating!" Ele shouts, her face turning bright red as she spins to me. "You heard him and we didn't, Graydon, and no one accused you of losing it!"

"You're right," I say.

"I think this might be a little more extreme!" Bexley interjects. "Besides, everyone knows that the Virus causes delusions."

Ele gives Bexley a particularly dirty look and glares at us. "I'm serious, and this is serious, so you need to believe me! People's lives are at stake!"

"But it doesn't make sense," Isaiah says. "Logically, someone can't just be in your dreams. You're talking crazy!"

Ele raises her hand to slap him, but Isaiah grabs her wrist with a cold look. I've never seen Ele upset like this.

"Okay, listen, Ele. I want to believe you," I interject. "I saw Merris too. It was unnatural, so maybe he does have...I don't know, some special power."

"Please just trust me," Ele says quietly, plopping down on the edge of the bed and looking from me to Isaiah to Atticus. "I promise you won't regret it."

"I believe you," Marie says easily, and Bexley shakes her head contemptuously. Isaiah looks unsure, but strangely, Atticus nods.

"Unbelievable things are happening right now. We have to go with what we know and trust each other," Atticus says. Ele picks up her blue headband from the bed, puts it on, and composes herself. She looks at Isaiah and me.

"Fine. I believe you," I say.

Isaiah nods, too. "So do I…I guess."

For the next hour we discuss Ele's vision.

"What do you think happened to Merris?" Reece asks, wringing his hands.

"He's crazy, it could be anything," Marie says, bouncing on the couch.

"But how is this happening to Eleanora? It doesn't make sense. Is there anything we can do?" Bexley asks, looking at Atticus.

"About this," he says. "No. We'll keep investigating the Merris situation when we can, and we all need to take extra caution and be aware. If Merris knows where we are, and he's making claims that severe, it's unwise to take it lightly. Maybe we should consider leaving and finding a safer location."

Ele gives him an I-told-you-so look. "Care to explain why you're just now coming to that conclusion?"

"No," Atticus says, surprisingly bluntly.

"Then how are we supposed to trust you if you're keeping secrets that affect us that much?" I say.

"I've protected you so far. I trusted Ele. I trusted you. I'm not required to share everything," Atticus says. "Unless something else surfaces, I think we should focus on the cure before we get too worried about relocating. We'll be better off if everyone is well."

On the coffee table in the center of the living room sit all seven small vials of the cure. It's not a lot. I guess each one is a single dose.

"So what are we going to do? Are we going to try and recreate it? Or are we going to steal it?" Isaiah asks.

"I vote to steal it! That sounds like waaaay more fun," Marie says, jumping up and down. That sleep did a lot more for her than the rest of us. Marie picks up one of the vials and turns it over a few times.

"Yeah, and more dangerous. If we try to recreate it, we only have to go back once to gather supplies, but if we steal it, we risk getting caught because we'll have to go back multiple times. We'll be relying on the Mordolus to keep making it. And besides, when they find out the secret cure is being taken, they won't leave it where we can find it. I think it's wise that we secure a way we can make it ourselves," Ele says.

"I agree with Ele. The abandoned hall probably still has some supplies we could salvage. They might never know we're there," Isaiah says.

"Either way, maybe it's too dangerous," Reece says, quiet enough I don't think everyone heard, watching Stormy and stroking his muted-blue feathers through the cage.

"We'll get the supplies. I have leftover tools from when I worked with the laboratory early on that we could use," Atticus says.

After everyone agrees, I wait for someone to suggest a plan or tell me what to do. The room goes silent. Everyone looks at Atticus, but he doesn't suggest anything else, so they stare in my direction instead.

"I think we could go back today and get whatever we can from the abandoned halls, and Atticus can retrieve the supplies he has. We can figure out tonight what else we'll need and make a plan to locate it," I say. "Besides, it will be better to get away from here if Merris is planning something. We can brainstorm a new hiding spot while we're out."

"Reece and Marie will help me, and the rest of you go to the Infirmary," Atticus says. Ele tenses.

"Okay," Isaiah starts. "Let's get ready."

Atticus exits out the back door again. Isaiah and I search for some lights and batteries to take since it's getting late, and the tunnel will be dark.

"Where'd Atticus go?" Isaiah asks when we meet back in the living room.

"I saw him go outside," I say. "I guess we just have to wait."

Bexley and Ele join us after they've changed and located backpacks for us all. Ele wears a pair of black jean shorts and a light gray hoodie. And, of course, her blue headband. Bexley's dressed in some of Ele's jeans, rolled up at the ankles, and an oversized muted dark green T-shirt. The last remnants of sunlight glint off her charm bracelet as she mindlessly twirls it.

We sit down at the dining room table, off from the living room and foyer. Bexley is at the head of the table, Ele is across from her, and Isaiah and I take the sides.

"It's weird doing stuff on our own," Isaiah says. "We've never done anything important without our parents before. I wasn't allowed to walk to Graydon's house alone. Now we're going on an adventure by ourselves."

"I wish we still had parents to tell us what to do," Ele says dismally. She undoes her ponytail and shakes out her fine hair. She has mild, shy features, displaced by a large, peaked nose. Her deep blue eyes are like wide pools of churning seawater. "I hate that everything is so dangerous and risky."

Bexley tenses. "What was that?" She glances around and looks nervously at the shelf behind her. "I feel like I'm always hearing things."

"Not another bird I hope?" I tease. She glowers at me then smiles.

"I didn't hear anything," Ele says.

"Today will be weird for me. I've never been to the Infirmary," I comment.

"Lucky you," Bexley says. Ele stares me in the eyes for an odd amount of time.

"When's Atticus gonna come back? I'm anxious to get going," Isaiah says, looking at the door. Ele nods subtly in Bexley's direction. She kicks Isaiah under the table.

"I don't know. It's strange how he just disappears. I wish he'd tell us why and how long until he'll return. Also, what are Reece and Marie doing?" Bexley says. I'm not listening very well.

"Bexley," I say cautiously.

"What?" she asks, noticing how everyone looks at her strangely.

"Uh, well…" Ele starts, pointing to the shelf behind Bexley.

Bexley closes her eyes and freezes. "Will someone tell me what it is, please?"

"Just don't move," Isaiah warns, pushing his chair from the table. "I'll try to scare it away."

A rat climbs across the shelf a few inches behind Bexley's chair. It's almost as big as the tall glasses on the ledge. Bexley has a fear of most creatures, especially diseased ones, and she's completely paralyzed. Isaiah picks up a thick cookbook from the top of the mantle and approaches it.

"You're joking. Isaiah? Eleanora? Graydon? Seriously, what is it?!" Bexley asks shakily, frozen. The gnarled creature stops stalking across the shelf and looks at us.

"Don't look," I say as Isaiah steps closer, preparing to throw the book.

"Well then tell me what's going on!" Bexley begs.

"Okay," Ele says calmly. A mischievous grin spreads across her face. "There's a big, ugly rat right next to you."

Bexley screams. She jumps up, sending the wooden chair crashing to the floor. Isaiah hurls the book toward the rat the same second, but it hits and shatters a glass instead. The startled rat jumps onto the dining room table. Bexley trips over her chair.

Isaiah groans, and Ele laughs until the rat leaps onto the left arm of her seat. She springs up, and the rat jumps to the floor and skitters off down the hall.

"RABIES! SALMONELLA! I'm going to get a disease!" Bexley squeaks.

"Where'd it go?" Ele asks, looking around. She's unfazed and glowers as she helps Bexley, who still trembles, off the floor.

"What just happened?" Isaiah asks.

"I don't even know," I say. The two of us just start laughing. Marie and Reece appear to see what's going on.

The back door slides open. Atticus has returned.

"You need to quiet down. I heard you outside," he warns. "Are you ready?"

Returning to reality, we all nod. I'm nervous. I've never been to the Infirmary, and it wasn't on my bucket list.

"Please be careful. And quiet," I tell Reece and Marie.

Marie nods dismissively. "Yeah, sure. I always am."

Reece doesn't seem excited and furrows his brow.

Atticus pulls me aside just before we leave.

"I'm putting you in charge. You're the oldest. If you think it's too dangerous, you bring them back immediately. Just be careful, and if anyone doesn't come back—"

"I got it," I interrupt with a nod. I'm worried and just don't like thinking about someone not returning. Now that I'm in charge…thoughts whirlwind around my mind.

"Sound good?" Atticus asks. I nod.

"Yep. We'll be fine," I say, pulling myself together. "It's not us I'm worried about anyway." Marie cartwheels around the living room. She crashes into the couch and crumples into hysterical laughter. "Good luck keeping that quiet." Atticus sighs deeply.

The moonlight's yellow glow illuminates the dark pavement, washed out by the reflective puddles from yesterday's rain. Isaiah, Ele, Bexley and I walk through the night air. The four of us continue on in silence. Isaiah uses the dim light from his phone to show us the way, commenting about how Ele ruined the screen. I don't really know how to get to the tunnels, so I lag behind. The Infirmary is in the heart of what used to be Delta, Michigan, just a few miles from Ellismark. We move through a field of tall grass and weeds. It's surrounded by trees. It's peaceful and serene with the twinkling stars in the sky.

"Is this really how you get to the Infirmary?" I ask.

"It's a shortcut. And yes, it actually is. We're not going to get lost. It's the way we came when we escaped," Isaiah responds.

Soon, wire fencing peeks out from behind the trees. The Infirmary. I almost can't stand going any closer. Fortunately, Ele and Isaiah lead us past it and into the woods on the other side.

"Is that the graveyard?" I ask, noting the dirty field next to the Infirmary.

"It is," Bexley says, grimacing. "I hate it."

"They're all unnamed. And the Mordolus are so careless about it," Isaiah says. Shadows settle between the mounds of haphazard clay. The desolate field voices the unjust murders that go on unpunished inside the Infirmary.

"It's disgusting to think that people we knew ended up there," Ele adds.

Bexley crinkles her nose. "Yeah, and I didn't want to think about that."

"That's what happened to Reece's mom," Isaiah says.

"I forgot about that," Bexley says softly. "Oh, I'm glad he didn't come with us."

"He doesn't talk about it a lot," Isaiah says.

"I understand that he doesn't want to talk to strangers about his dead mother," Ele says. "Truthfully, he's holding up extremely well."

"Sometimes, it's easier to just pretend hard moments never happened or some people never existed," I say.

"I think if it was me who'd lost my mom, I'd be scared all the time too," Ele says. "Especially of death."

"If God saves us, we don't have to be afraid of death," Isaiah says. "In fact, death leads us to life. I'm praying Reece learns to believe that."

The path leads deeper into the woods. Soon, it opens into a field. A peaceful stream trickles from behind the trees.

"This is the tunnel," Isaiah says, sneaking toward a giant hole in the ground. I carefully stroll to the edge. It leads downward and splits off into multiple smaller tunnels once it levels out. Ele twirls a strand of hair. We turn on our flashlights and step down the steep path.

It's dark and damp. Weird thinking the Infirmary is above us. That's where my parents are trapped. A shiver threatens to rack my spine at the prospect of Merris lurking down here too. I don't like it.

"So does anyone know how to get to the Infirmary from here?" Bexley asks.

"We follow this main tunnel basically the whole way. We should be able to figure it out," Isaiah says. Adventure radiates from his tone. We set off down the cavernous tunnel. For a quarter hour, we get on fine. Then the main tunnel splits. All of us stop when we hit the fork.

"Which way?" I ask.

"It's this way," Isaiah says confidently, examining the two passages and pointing to the right. "I remember."

Ele nods. "I think it's that one too."

The dirt passages make me feel trapped. We follow the right one for a while.

"I don't remember it going up. It led down for a long time, then up, so we should be going down first, right?" Isaiah says when the ground begins to incline upward.

We stop, and I ask, "Should we go back?"

"I don't know. We could go a little further to make sure. It might just be like this for a little while, and we forgot," Isaiah says.

"I think we should keep going before turning all the way around," Bexley says.

We continue up the tunnel. Ele looks around nervously. I'm not sure what I feel. I need to make sure everyone's safe. Isaiah glances around the tunnel, unsure.

"What is that?" Bexley blurts. I hear it too. We all freeze. There's a distant crackling, gravelly sound. It almost sounds like—

"Is that digging?" Ele asks. Before anyone can respond, there's a muffled voice. It's coming from the ceiling of the tunnel. The sounds grow nearer. Soil rains down from the tunnel ceiling. Bexley squeals, but Ele quickly hushes her.

"We need to go," Isaiah says.

Light suddenly pours in. Isaiah drags me into the darkness of the other side of the tunnel. He turns off his light, and everyone else follows suit. The voices are close. The gaping hole in the tunnel's roof grows larger. On the other side of the tunnel, Bexley and Ele hide. We're trapped. If we move, we could be seen from above. Isaiah quickly motions for everyone to stay quiet as we scramble against the tunnel wall.

"What's that?" a man's voice calls.

"I don't know," another, closer, says. More earth falls into the center of the tunnel.

"Let me see," the first says in an annoyed tone. I hold my breath, crawling as far into the darkness as possible. "Looks like a cave or something."

"Yeah, why do you think it's there?" the first asks. "That's the third cavity we've found."

"A natural formation," the second says. "We should probably back up before the ground caves in."

"It works. Saves us time too."

There's shuffling above. The hole is big enough to illuminate most of the nearby tunnel. I can only hope they don't look down again.

"Bring it here."

A second later, there's a thud; something falls into the tunnel. Bexley clamps her hands over her mouth to suppress a scream. Ele quickly shields her face. I don't look. A glance at Isaiah's horrified expression confirms my worst fears. We aren't under the Infirmary. We're under the graveyard.

Three more thumps follow. I cover my face with my arms. I can't describe the stench. Isaiah backs up even further; it's like he's glued to the wall, eyes shut. I think I'm going to throw up.

We wait until the two voices fade completely. Everyone's silent. I keep my eyes set on the ceiling. Ele lets out something between a gasp and a sob. Shielding her face, she quickly turns and stumbles down the tunnel. As quickly as possible, I follow her. Once we are far down enough, Ele lets out an angry yell and kicks at loose stones, clenching her fists. Isaiah drops to his knees and stares at the ground, placing a hand on his head and ripping the other through his hair. I don't know how to react. Sitting silently beside the wall, Bexley crosses her arms and wipes her teary eyes.

No one says anything for a long time.

Bexley twirls her charm bracelet and whimpers. "How could they do that?"

"I wish I hadn't looked," Ele says, horrified. I can't be gladder I didn't. The heartlessness of the two people makes me feel sick.

"We need to go on," I say, remembering that I'm supposed to be leading this. We can't mourn in the tunnel all day, no matter how fitting it may be.

We finally tread back to the forked tunnel.

"Not to be insensitive," Isaiah mumbles. By the waver in his voice, I can tell that he isn't. He's just as shaken up as the rest of us. "But at least we made it out of there without being seen. Sorry, I guess that was the wrong tunnel. At least we know this one's right. It takes us to the opposite side of the Infirmary."

Ele takes a stone and draws a big 'X' on the tunnel we just left.

This tunnel brings us to the tile floor in less than half an hour.

"We need to keep silent," Bexley whispers as we climb the steep, muddy staircase. I'm actually in the Infirmary.

We walk down the hall to the closest room. Inside, it's mostly empty besides a couple cluttered tables. The four of us search through the mess of trashed equipment. I don't find anything still useful. It's strange how they have so many science materials here. We move to the next room. It's smaller but looks more promising. Isaiah kicks through a pile of broken glass and metal. In the back, there's a large cabinet. It takes a while to get the corroded hinges to cooperate, but I finally wrench it open.

Rusted tools are piled in the bottom. Chemistry tools. We can still use them. All the glass items are shattered, and I have to be careful not to cut myself while sorting out the metal pieces.

Isaiah finds a collection of small bottles. Most of them are empty, but one is chloroquine. The cure is pretty simple, but that means everything has to be perfect. No leaving out things or substitution. Ele picks through a few piles but ends up just sitting in the corner. She looks exhausted.

Bexley sends her a few venomous looks and whispers, "Lazy."

"Is Ele alright?" I ask Isaiah, quietly.

"I think so. This whole Merris thing has kind of messed her up, on top of what just happened."

Suspicion pricks my mind. We found chloroquine, and there were a ton of empty bottles of oseltamivir. I open a crate. Several small glass vials lay in the bottom and half of them are crushed. Pink sand coats the contents. Fairy dust. None of it's salvageable.

"I think I know what this is," I say.

"What?" Bexley asks. "What are you talking about?"

"The abandoned halls. I think they were making the cure here," I say.

"That would make a ton of sense," Isaiah says. "And that's good. Better chance we'll find what we need."

In the next room, Bexley finds a whole shelf with ingredients. Favipiravir, more chloroquine, oseltamivir, dexamethasone, and one half vial of fairy dust. All ingredients for the cure. It might be enough to make one batch if we can locate the last few items. Bexley postulated that she spilled about a half teaspoon of the mysterious powder in the base mixture.

"This is the seventh room," Ele says. "Should we go back now?"

"Oh, I think we should search one more. No use coming all the way here just to leave without doing a thorough search," Bexley says, and Isaiah agrees with her.

The next room is completely destroyed. I can't step anywhere without trash crunching beneath my feet. Morzanna's M is scribbled all over the furthest wall. Isaiah finds an alcohol burner in a crate. I cut myself more than once, but, after searching through the glass, I find three salvageable beakers. Ele seems to have drifted into sleep for a minute crouching wearily against the wall as we finish packing up.

"Do you think this will be good enough?" Bexley asks me.

"I hope so," I say. I don't want to tell her that since we didn't find any more fairy dust, this will barely be enough to make a dose. I'll figure out what to do on my own. I'll come back by myself if I have to.

Suddenly, Ele jolts awake. She leaps to her feet.

"We have to go now!" Ele says, too loudly. "He knows we're here! He's coming!"

She picks up two backpacks and shoves one at Isaiah. Shouldering the other, she runs out of the room. "Come on!"

I take the last two backpacks, even though Bexley offers to carry one. We follow Ele.

"It was Merris again! Somehow, in my dreams, he can locate me!" she explains.

"What? How?" I ask, running down the steps to the tunnel.

"I don't know! I still don't know how he's in my dreams to begin with!"

Isaiah takes out one of the flashlights as we head deeper into the tunnel. Eerily, I think I hear footsteps behind us. I don't look back though. I can feel a stranger's presence.

We make it out in time, just as when I'm sure Merris is nearing us. Panting, we sprint into the woods. We stop in a hidden spot under the dense forest cover.

"He was definitely there!" I say, out of breath.

"I know I could hear him!" Isaiah agrees. "It was so weird!"

"I didn't hear anything. Are you sure?" Bexley asks, collapsing onto the ground.

"Yes! Of course, Bexley! He was telling me he knew where I was! He said I kept showing him!" Ele's trembling.

"Well, we need to get back. Far away from there," Bexley says. We all nod. I can barely see the ground, so I dig through my backpack until I find my flashlight. We sneak back through the streets of Senneforte.

When we return to Ele and Isaiah's house, I can hardly believe we made it. I don't have time to feel relieved that we didn't die. I'm immediately aware that the others haven't arrived back yet. We unpack all the supplies and look over what we have. I'm really glad I believed Ele before. Merris *is* in her dreams.

Half an hour later, the door opens, and Atticus, Marie, and Reece step inside. I can tell they've had quite an adventure too.

33
REECE: THEY'RE LOOKING FOR *US*?

Marie, Atticus, and I slink out the back door a few minutes after the others head off to the Infirmary. We go the opposite direction, and Atticus warns us to keep quiet as he leads us down the road. A cold, night wind whips through the empty streets and sweeps across my skin. Occasionally, Atticus orders us to hide somewhere, or wait while he checks to make sure it is safe. Apparently, the night isn't any safer, except maybe the enemy can't see—but that's our disadvantage too. Atticus won't even let us use a light, and I'm scared. When Atticus said he was taking Marie and me, I internally freaked out. I just want to stay with Isaiah. Atticus is sketchy, and Marie is too loud—and they're both strangers. We cross a highway overgrown with dandelions and jog through town.

"You two wait here. Be quiet," Atticus says, leaving Marie and me hiding behind the window of a trashed bookstore in a shopping strip.

"Yeah, just like the past twelve times we've done this. 'Cause, ya know, I might forget and make a ton of noise," Marie grumbles. She gets up, but I stay beneath the window.

"They're going to see you!" I whisper, glancing up at the window.

"Well, let's close the blinds," Marie says, bounding over to the other front window while I close the ones above me.

"I'm still staying here," I say.

"Fine by me. Be boring," she says.

"Atticus isn't going to like that we aren't staying hidden," I inform her. "And by we, I mean you, because I'm staying right here." I gesture to the floor.

"Whatever. No one's coming, and we'll be quiet!" Marie says, motioning for me to join her. "Come on!"

Cautiously, I stand and follow her through the building. Panic's nagging voice reverberates around my mind, warning me of all the possible dangers. But for some reason with Marie, it's easier to shut those thoughts down, which really isn't a good thing.

Six-foot shelves form lines down the center of the store. Several of them are knocked over, spilling dusty books across the floor. Full of wonder, I gaze at all the books, thinking about my room in the Infirmary that's covered with my writings. The 'I HATE THIS PLACE' scrawled permanently next to the window I'm especially proud of.

"We're going to get caught. This is too dangerous. They'll see us, and we'll be stormed by the Mordolus—and then we'll get captured and die," I mumble quietly.

Marie stops. "Are you talking to yourself?"

I look at the ground. "Uhh…yeah."

She snorts. "That's weird. Didn't realize you were doing it, did ya?"

I shake my head. Marie laughs, turns the corner of a shelf, and disappears. "Oh cool!"

By the time I find her, she's balancing at the top of a ladder, trying to climb onto the top of one of the shelves. She stands up, grins, and gestures for me to join. "Come on!"

"Um, how about no," I say, hating the thought of Atticus coming back to *this*.

"This is SO cool!" Marie says, walking along the shelves like they're a nice sidewalk on a sunny day.

I follow her from the ground. "Be careful please."

"I'm fine, don't worry," Marie replies. She does a cartwheel then laughs when I gasp out of dread. "I've done gymnastics for five years; I'm not going to fall. I have good balance."

"That doesn't mean the shelf does," I remark. "You shouldn't risk it."

"Listen Reece. Take risks. It's fun," Marie says. I don't think it's necessarily a good piece of advice. She smugly glances around.

"I'm gonna jump," Marie states.

"What?" I ask.

"I'm going to jump to that shelf," she says, pointing to the next row gleefully.

"No! You're going to fall and die!" I say.

Marie smiles. "I won't. But you can catch me, alright?"

I shake my head. I don't think I could catch *anyone* with these toothpick arms, and that would definitely be embarrassing. But what would be worse is if Marie fell and cracked her skull open. What would I do then? And what if Atticus never came back?

Marie leaps to the next shelf. She sticks the landing, but the bookshelf she jumped from wobbles like the first domino in a run. Suddenly, both shelves capsize, and Marie disappears into a mess of books.

"Marie? Are you okay?" I ask worriedly, climbing over the toppled shelf.

There's a laugh, and Marie pops out from the mountain of books. "SO fun! A book did hit me in the face. Ouch. But that was epic!"

"You probably just alerted every member of the Mordolus in Senneforte that we're here!" I say, a burning fear building in my chest. *We're going to die. We're going to die.*

"Oh shoot. Sorry. I forgot. But what are the chances that there are actually members close and interested enough to investigate?" Marie says, grimacing and shoving away some of the volumes. "Hey, are you gonna help me get out of this mess or what?"

I wasn't always so scared of everything. About a year ago I started noticing how real things were and the world scared me. The

Virus didn't help, and my mom dying definitely didn't. I hate how my face burns when I'm afraid because people notice, and that only makes the problem worse.

Marie walks back to the front of the store, and I follow her.

"I guess maybe we *should* just wait until Atticus gets back," Marie says decidedly.

"Great idea," I deadpan. We crouch behind the window as I stare at the mess we just created. Actually, the mess *Marie* just created.

Marie gets up after five minutes and strolls over to the cash register.

"I wonder how you open this," she says, knocking on it. "Usually, they already are because the Mordolus raid everything. This one isn't."

"There's probably a key," I say. "That's usually what a keyhole is for."

"Jee, don't have to be so sassy," Marie says. "Duh, a key would work, but this will too."

She reaches onto the counter and grabs a heavy book about biology. She hits the register with it so hard the sound echoes through the whole building.

"Marie!" I whimper. She smacks it again before I can stop her, and the drawer pops open. "Be quiet!"

"Whoops. Honestly, I'm no good at not making noise, but seriously we're fine. Look, it worked!" she says, and I jump up and walk over.

"So it hasn't been raided," I whisper, staring at all the money in the dented box. Surrounded by plain designs, tiny numbers list different information to be used in each of the separated post-America countries. After the division, USA currency was exchanged for a neutral option.

"Nope," Marie says, reaching in and grabbing several twenties. "Hey, remember when people actually cared about this stuff?"

"Yeah," I say. "Money's not useful anymore."

"I think the only person in Willowmire who even thinks about it is Morzanna," Marie says. "Well then."

Marie takes a piece of paper money and tears it in half. "She isn't getting any more." Then she laughs. "This is fun."

"Isn't that illegal?" I ask uneasily.

"Is it?" Marie says, ripping some more. "Cool! I haven't done many illegal things yet!"

"That's a good thing, right?" I ask.

"Who cares? Ditch the laws," Marie shrugs. She jumps up on the counter and tears another one. "Because we don't really care if Morzanna dies," she rips another, watching the matching halves of a ten drift onto the floor.

"Or if she hates us. Because she already does." She takes another handful. "She can't even keep us locked up because she sucks! Hahaha!"

I hand the money to her from the box, and Marie keeps destroying it, throwing it up in the air and cackling.

"We hate you, Morzanna!" she says, just loud enough to make me cringe. She goes on. "Because Morzanna is a liar, a thief—"

"And a murderer," I add.

"Yeah!" Marie rips more, throwing handfuls of coins at the window.

Just then, the door flies open. Marie drops the money she's holding, and I slam the drawer shut.

"What is going on here?!" Atticus demands, staring at the overturned shelves, destroyed books, and maimed money on the floor.

"We got bored?" Marie suggests, and Atticus glowers.

His hazel eyes bore into my conscience. "You're going to get caught!"

"That's what I said!" I blurt, blushing guiltily.

Marie throws a quarter at me and jumps down from the counter. "Don't act like you didn't help! I just got carried away."

"You two better get it together, or you're going to end up killed. This isn't a joke." Atticus says seriously, eyeing Marie. "Lives are at stake, and right now we have an advantage and a chance we didn't before. If anyone gets captured by the Mordolus, we'll lose valuable help, time, and—most importantly—hope. It might not seem like it matters, but what we do now is going to have extreme consequences. We're all that's left. I know it's a lot to ask, but you're going to have to be mature and remember that. Now come on."

"Sorry," I say as Atticus walks us back outside. I hate the silence that follows. Marie doesn't seem bothered though. But the next time we're told to wait and hide, we don't move or say a single word.

After an hour of walking, we come to the street. By now, I'm exhausted. I hate the Maraloxis Virus.

After five minutes of waiting for the all-clear, Marie and I follow Atticus to one of the houses. Climbing the stone steps, we walk through the wooden front door into the empty room. A dirty fireplace is set in the wall adjacent to the door, but I don't think it's been used in like a hundred years. Pieces of glass dust the floor from broken bulbs in the cobwebbed light fixtures.

"You can talk now—quietly," Atticus says.

"Finally!" Marie says softly. "So why is it so dangerous around here anyway?"

"It is everywhere. But there's a base a mile away. The Mordolus use these roads a lot," Atticus explains. "That's why we have to hurry. They don't usually use the roads at night unless they are transporting something, but we don't want to risk it."

"Why wouldn't we want to see that?" Marie asks with a mischievous smile as she peers out the window. "We could discover their secrets."

"Because it's unsafe," Atticus impatiently explains. "Especially with you two."

"If it's so dangerous then why do you live here?" I ask.

"It makes it easier to watch them. Since I was alone, it was safer," Atticus says.

"I haven't gotten us caught yet," Marie points out.

"Yeah, *yet*," I say automatically. Marie scowls.

Atticus leads us to a room down the hall. The building is empty and sort of creepy. All that's in the corner are some wooden chests. I open one and find a bunch of vials and bottles. Most of them have varying fluids in them: different colors, different textures, and different densities. Marie digs through the chests until she finds a thin blanket. She shoves it in the bottom of the bag to protect the glass and starts stashing the containers in her backpack. I carefully fill my backpack, which I think someone left for me as a joke because it's covered with bright unicorns and glitter. Ele apologized and said it was all she had, but none of the girl's backpacks had pink sparkles.

"Alcohol," Marie reads from a plastic bottle. "You drink?"

"No, Marie, it's isopropyl. You can't drink that; it would make you sick. I'm underage anyway," Atticus says. I never would have guessed he was under twenty-one, but it doesn't shock me.

"I'm kinda sick of laws. They don't matter, and the government doesn't keep them either," Marie says and tosses the bottle into her backpack. She picks up another vial from the bottom of the dark wood chest. I notice an inscription on it; a swirly engraved 'M'. I don't say anything, but I tense. Maybe I shouldn't have decided Atticus wasn't part of the Mordolus that fast. *Why else would he have something with Morzanna's symbol?* I take a deep breath and try not to make assumptions. He could have found it or something.

A second later, Marie zips up her backpack and dashes out of the room. Just as Atticus and I pack up the last items, she sprints back into the room with a startled look.

"Someone's coming," she blurts. Marie leads us out of the room and down the hall, and we look through the single window in the first room. A truck halts right outside across the street, and twenty Mordolus members file out. Hunters and guards swarm the street.

"Stay quiet," Atticus says, carefully opening the window an inch, turning the muffled voices outside into coherent words.

"Hurry, we have to find them!" one of the older guards with a thick southern accent yells. "We only have tonight before we have to tell the Queen we can't find them!"

"We've already checked the entire Infirmary, and they've vanished!" another calls.

"Dead or alive?" a younger girl with a shrill voice asks.

"Doesn't matter!" the accented man says, pointing people in all directions. The girl smiles as she nocks an arrow before bounding off toward one of the buildings.

The guards and Hunters scramble to check all the houses. Atticus stares out the window with growing concern, and Marie grinds her teeth. A fire of anxiety flames inside me, and it's like I'm being smothered by its smoke. *We're gonna get caught, we're gonna get caught, we're gonna get caught.*

"We have to leave," Atticus announces, running into the other room and bringing the other backpacks. He hands one to me, earning points because he intentionally gives Marie the unicorn one, and leads us quickly to the back door, motioning for us to stay silent. We run through the backyard, past another house, and to the other street parallel to the one the Mordolus are exploring.

"What are they doing?" I ask breathlessly as we duck behind a fence. "I thought you said they don't come at night?"

"They don't. Unless, I guess, five people suddenly go missing from the Infirmary," Atticus says.

"Oh," I say, with a surge of realization.

"Wait. They're looking for *us*?" Marie asks. Atticus nods and leads us past the line of houses and into a dense forest. "Great. Don't you love being tracked down by murderers?"

"Won't they eventually find where we are?" I ask, ignoring her. "I assume there are other squadrons out. If they're checking the whole province, they'll eventually find Ele and Isaiah's house too, if they haven't yet, right? And Merris tipped them off about where we are!"

"We have to get there and hope the others are back. We need to find somewhere else to hide. At least until tomorrow when they have to inform the Queen. After that it won't matter. We need to find the others quickly," Atticus explains. "I hope they got everything they need because no one's going back to the Infirmary."

We race through the forest. It's dark, the ground is swampy, and my feet are soaked. Shadows dance across the forest floor as the moonlight finally shows through the clouds. Twice, I nearly trip over a branch, and I stumbled through some thorn bushes back there. Most of the time, all I can see is the pink glitter on Marie's backpack. Time drags on, and I want to ask if we're lost, but Atticus kind of creeps me out so I don't. Marie chuckles at me when I jump because a squirrel darts out from the underbrush.

Finally, we break from the trees and reach a road again. We follow the path into the country neighborhood. The others have returned from the Infirmary.

"We have to go," Atticus tells Graydon the instant we get back. "They're looking for you, and we have to find somewhere else to go."

"Where can we go so that they won't track us?" Graydon asks. "There are so many of them, and there are limited places to hide in Senneforte."

"I don't know."

Ele explains her latest dream. This time they all heard Merris. Apparently, he can tell their location, and I bet that's how he located us at Isaiah's house to begin with.

"Whenever I sleep, he appears in my mind and he can somehow figure out where I am," Ele says. "I don't know how he's doing it, and I'm worried he might know where we are currently."

"But if he has only talked to you in your dreams, he must not be able to find us unless you're asleep," Graydon points out, returning to the group.

"You're right. Eleanora will just have to stay awake until we figure out how to stop it," Bexley says sensibly.

"How long will that be?" Ele asks, twisting a piece of hair.

"A couple days. A week maybe," Graydon postulates. "Could be longer, depending on whether or not we can locate your dreams' cause."

"We'll focus on that after we find somewhere to hide," Atticus says, interrupting the conversation.

"Any ideas?" Isaiah asks.

"I don't know where we could hide that they won't eventually locate us," Ele says dismally.

"Oh, there are plenty of places. Whether or not they're safe, livable, or accessible, I'm not sure," Bexley says.

"Well, they can't search everywhere, right? I mean, here for sure, but we know they've already looked some places, so what if we went somewhere they've already checked?" Graydon says.

"Like hide-and-seek tag," Marie says.

"What about the elementary school?" Ele asks.

Marie screws her face. "Why there?"

"It's pretty far away from the Infirmary, so there should be fewer Mordolus members around, and it has this huge basement with places to hide if it came to that," Ele says.

"What do you mean by hiding places?" Bexley asks.

"Like hidden rooms, the attic, the crawlspace, and a place behind the water heater that leads outside," Ele says.

"She's right. Also, last time I saw the school it looked secure," Graydon says.

"It sounds like our best option," Atticus says.

"Let's try it," Isaiah agrees.

"Pack up everything fast," Graydon says, picking up the backpack with the cure and going to zip it shut. He freezes, wide-eyed. He starts frantically searching the bag.

"Graydon?" Bexley asks.

He holds up a single vial. "Where's the rest of it?"

"What?!" Ele says, jumping up and snatching the backpack. After pawing through it, she announces, "It's gone!"

"Did someone move it?" I ask, panicking. "Or take it?"

Everyone freaks out, searching for the other six vials. We look all over the house. Nothing. It's really gone.

"Either one of us is lying, or someone else came here while we were gone. There's nothing we can do about it now," Atticus says. "We still need to leave."

Solemn, we quickly pack up everything, including our single dose of the cure, and head toward the abandoned school. I bring a couple of Ele's notebooks.

It's a long, quiet walk through the countryside roads.

"Is that it?" Marie says, running up ahead after we exit the woods. She stops at the top of the hill ahead and looks out. "That's not good."

Several hundred feet away, beyond the schoolyard, sits the school building, but not abandoned as we'd hoped.

"I think we're going to have to come up with a different idea," Bexley says.

"Wow Bexley, how profound," Graydon says sarcastically.

"Aw, come on, wouldn't a sleepover with the Mordolus be fun?" I say, in a cold joking tone. The school's doors are open, several trucks are parked out front, and there are at least two members of the Mordolus outside.

"First the cure goes missing, and now this? Why does the one place I suggest end up turning into a Mordolus post!" Ele groans.

"There, there, sister, your ideas can't always work out," Isaiah says, patting Ele on the shoulder.

"I feel stupid," Ele laments.

"It's okay, Ele, because no matter how lame you are, you'll still be awesome just because I'm your brother," Isaiah consoles with a smirk.

"You're an idiot," she replies. "But I do feel better now."

"See?" Isaiah says smugly.

"Actually, it was because I was reminded no matter how dumb I feel, you'll always be dumber," she says with a vindictive seriousness. Isaiah slaps her shoulder playfully.

"So, what's Plan Two?" Graydon asks.

"We get away from here now," Atticus says firmly.

"That's a good idea," Marie says as several more Mordolus members step outside. We retreat into the nearby forest to forge another scheme.

"Now what?" Bexley asks, but no one answers for a while.

"How long ago were you in the tunnels?" Marie asks suddenly.

"We left about an hour ago," Isaiah replies.

"That's the same time I heard the man say that they had already checked the Infirmary!" she says excitedly.

"What do you mean?" Graydon asks.

"If they already checked there, at the same time you were in the tunnels, they must've either checked them, or not know about them!" Marie explains.

"I get it! So we can hide in the tunnels!" I say.

"No! Not again," Ele cries. "Maybe they know Merris is guarding them, and that's why!"

"We'll be fine as long as you don't fall asleep. The tunnels are pretty endless. He can't find us if we hide," Graydon says. "And, if we need something else from the abandoned halls, we'll be right where we need to be."

"We need to go back now then," Atticus announces.

So we set off for the tunnels, where, hopefully, we can find safety.

34

ELEANORA: HUNTED AND HAUNTED

The golden sun rises like a dragon, spitting fiery rays of sunshine through the province to devour the cold bite of night. A layer of smoky haze blankets the ground in its wake. It's only been an hour since I was following this same path, hoping I'd never have to return. The prospect of hiding out in the tunnels doesn't comfort me, yet I'm heading back to the Infirmary.

As we walk through a dewy patch of asters near the tunnel entrance, I play with a section of hair, tugging on each flaxen strand. *Merris is waiting for us down there. We're going closer to someone who made death threats to me and my family and can also reveal our location to the exact person we are hiding from. Smart.*

Standing at the tunnel's tenebrous edge, terrifying images flicker through my mind, and a chill claws up my spine. A cold sweat breaks on my palms.

A cool breeze ruffles Reece's sun-lightened, brown hair. He crosses his lanky arms, clenching his hands in an effort to feel secure as he peers down beside me. A longing and incomplete maturity radiate from his pale green eyes.

I stare into the abyssal darkness, nothing there to stop the monstrous tidal wave of fear building inside me. We start down the steep, muddy slope into the tunnels.

The wavering beam emitted from my flashlight reflects my unease as I glance over my shoulder again to make sure everyone is still with us. I internally beg for someone to break the silence with conversation, but I can't bring myself to speak.

Have peace.

The words spontaneously spring into my mind, and, for once, I don't fight them but embrace the tranquil feeling. Fear of vulnerability and submission to the words was what has led me to reject them, but courage thrives in the calmness of my soul now. I believe the promise I tell myself: *we'll be okay.*

It's like everyone's been telling me; the chances of Merris finding us if I stay awake are very small. We'll be okay if we focus on replicating the cure. My instinct would be to treat everyone here, but now that we only have one vial left, we must save it for an emergency. No one's illness has progressed to such a state yet.

As Atticus leads us deeper into the labyrinth of tunnels, we must be hundreds of feet below the Infirmary. In the case that the tunnels are discovered, the more hidden we are, the better chance we have of staying hidden. Although my backpack feels full of bricks rather than batteries, I shudder at the thought: *what if the flashlights die?*

It doesn't help that Reece is walking next to me mumbling aloud the same fears.

"We can't need to go further," I protest, examining the tunnel that looks akin to all the rest we've been walking through for the past half hour. Aside from the trails of flashlight beams that cut through the shadows, the darkness seems thick enough to touch.

"Soon," Atticus assures me. "Why don't you talk to each other? You've been silent the whole time."

"Yeah, because we don't want to attract creepy people," Reece whispers, shining a flashlight around the tunnel and, consequently, in my eyes.

"There aren't—" Atticus sighs. "That's not going to prevent people from finding us."

"Yeah, just like that comment isn't going to help *anyone* feel better," Reece replies.

"I can't help reality," Atticus replies.

"Whatever. But I'm staying on sketchy-people watch," Reece says quietly. "Ya know, so we don't die, or something worse."

"Or something worse? Worse than dying?" Marie asks.

"Yeah," Reece says. "Imagine being driven insane by lifelong torture and kept in a cell until you don't recognize yourself or remember your own name. Oh, or watching everyone else beheaded and brutally murdered while you slowly bleed to death yourself."

"That's morbid," Marie replies, playing with her light.

"Thanks, I try," Reece says.

"That went off the deep end," Graydon says, walking up beside me.

"Yeah," I say with a shrug. "Personally, I'm trying *not* to think about things like that."

"Neither," Graydon says. His eyes are like dark ponds of melancholy clouding any way for me to detect what he's thinking. "It is safe here, though. Merris won't find us, and we'll be fine."

Not with me here. If I fall asleep, everyone else is going to be in danger. Maybe I should have stayed behind—I'm just a liability, I think.

"I'm just scared." I admit. "I know I shouldn't be since it's not going to change anything except drive me crazy, but it's hard to control."

"I get it," Graydon says.

"I'm having these dreams, weird voices in my head, ghost feelings, seeing potential apparitions—honestly, sometimes I think I'm going crazy," I confess.

"Well, I don't know why that's happening," Graydon says. "But I'm sure you're not going crazy. I've had my doubts, but mad things are happening, and we just have to go with it."

"Doubts regarding my sanity?" I say.

He grins. "Truthfully…maybe? Okay, only for a minute."

"Jee, thanks for your confidence in me," I tease. "But I understand what you mean. It's all weird, and I have a feeling it's just going to keep going that way, too."

"We'll figure it out. I'm sure," Graydon says, but I'm not certain either of us believes it.

"I'm scared of dying," I blurt.

"Honestly, same," Graydon says.

"I mean, I know about God, and I trust him and all, most of the time. I just don't know…I don't understand what's going on or how it could in any way be good. I'm having a hard time believing. I feel out of control, and I wonder how through all this, God could still be there and allow it. Actually, I understand *how* it can happen, I just don't get *why*," I say, reaching into the pocket of my athletic shorts and touching the Bible verse note from my father. I should simply throw it away—let it fall to the muddy tunnel floor and be covered up with dirt until it decomposes. It only reminds me how confused I am about the world and frustrated I am with life…but it's one of the last reminders I have of my family, so I leave it in my pocket.

Graydon is silent for a second and stares at the floor. "I get the feeling. But the thing is, we don't know because we don't need to know, right? We just have to trust. It's hard. I know it is."

"I'm not sure if I have enough faith to keep trusting," I admit. *Is God really still there? And does he really care about us?*

"Well actually, all this happened because of sin. It's the grace of God that we're all still alive right now," Isaiah interrupts from behind us. "You don't have any faith of your own. It all comes from God. He gives us as much as we need."

"Isaiah, thanks, but this is not your conversation," I say. "I'd like to talk sometimes without being preached at."

"There's a lot of things wrong with that statement. But whatever. Continue on in your theological wrong…ness," Isaiah says, marching up to the front of the group.

"I'm sorry, Graydon, for spilling all my issues," I apologize.

He smiles and shakes his head. "It's okay, I can take it."

I know he can because he always has, but no one can be strong on their own forever. The earthy path grows wider and eventually splits off in two directions.

"Which way?" Reece asks timidly.

"Be quiet, I'm thinking," Isaiah says, inspecting each direction.

"That's shocking," I say, and Isaiah glowers.

"I know which way we should go," he announces, standing at the fork. He gestures to the right. "This way."

"Why that way?" Reece asks, holding onto the light like it's a lifeline.

Isaiah shrugs. "Because I have a feeling."

"Last time you chose, it didn't go well," Bexley points out, but she's ignored.

My brother always walks around like he's the main character of an adventure story and you'd expect any second he'd slay a great beast and come out unscathed, except for an exacerbated ego. It's annoying.

Freshwater drips from the cavernous roof, and my flashlight glints off several pools of reflective water. Suddenly, the tunnel opens into a much wider passage, almost resembling a room.

"See guys! This is perfect!" Isaiah says, a smirk growing across his face. "You have to trust me. I'm always right."

"Ha!" I accidentally scoff. "Atticus, what do you think?"

"We'll stay here," Atticus says.

"I have no idea how to find the way out from here," Reece says, a crimson flush of fear freezing over his complexion. "Please tell me someone does?"

Atticus nods, which I'm glad about. We remove from our backpacks most of the lights and set them up around the room; a variety of flashlights, LED candles, nightlights, basically anything we could scrounge at home.

A rush of dizzying exhaustion swirls around my brain, mixing with a concoction of dread as I ponder how long we might need to postpone sleep. I'm calculating hours as I sit down on the driest side of the tunnel, leaning against an earthy wall. A sharp pain spiders through my head from a bruise above my neck. I do a double-take, not remembering where it came from, and it leaves me wondering. I take off my aquamarine headband and fix my hair, hoping to look a little less tired than I feel as I watch everyone else collapse. I long to sleep as well, but I desperately resist the urge despite the wave of lassitude that overwhelms me.

Marie bounds over and plops down next to me. "I'm gonna make sure you don't fall asleep."

"Thanks," I say.

Marie takes a deep breath. "Listen Ele, I'm sorry I left you. I kinda regret it."

"I know, and it's okay. I'm not saying I agree with your choice, but I totally understand the reasoning. If you hadn't left, everything might be different now, and I'm just glad it all worked out in the end," I say. "I just can't figure out what's wrong with me. How is Merris getting in my head? How is he finding us? It's like some cursed witchcraft."

Marie doesn't respond for a second and plays with some stones on the ground. "Wait Ele, tell me again exactly what he told you."

Marie always manages to put things together and figure them out, and I'm glad for any help because right now I'm pretty desperate. I tell her again about the dreams, hating having to relive them in my head in the very place they were set.

"And I asked what happened to him, and he got upset and…"

I freeze, lightly touching the bruise on my head with a wave of horror.

"What is it?" Marie asks.

"I don't know. I hit my head in my dream, but I didn't realize, until now, that I have a bruise there."

Marie stares at me. "You don't think he can really do that though, right? I mean, how?"

"I don't know. I've been asking 'how' about a lot of this stuff, but it could explain why Merris can find us. If he can somehow interact through dreams on some physical level, he may see my surroundings," I say, terrified. I don't mention it, but inside I'm sick with fright. *If that's true then he could have killed me before, and I could be dead right now.*

"It makes sense. But I had another thought. He said that it was somehow related to the Virus, yeah?" Marie asks, and I nod. "If it has something to do with the fact you have the Virus, then if we cure it, maybe he won't be able to do anything to you."

A shoot of hope springs up in my heart. "That does make sense!" I exclaim. "How did you think of that?"

Marie shrugs and smiles. "I'm brilliant, Ele. When were you going to realize it?"

"Also, you weren't there, but when we ran out of the tunnels after I saw him again, Bexley didn't see or hear him, and all the rest of us did. She's the only one who's ingested the cure so far!" I say.

"But why can't he see us, too?" Marie asks, gesturing to everyone else.

"I don't know, but he must not be capable because he would have discovered us by now," I say with a deep breath. "For some reason, I must be more susceptible. So that means if we're cured, we'll never have to worry about Merris again."

35
MARIE: THE CURE

"Let's give you the cure, and the smart people can start working on making more for everyone else. Then Merris won't find us," I say, thinking. "We don't have long until you'll fall asleep, or until the rest of us start having problems with Merris."

"I know, I just hope we can truly create more doses from what we have," Ele says. I stand up, dusting off the dirt from my athletic shorts. Reece is fast asleep, and Bexley and Isaiah might be, too. Graydon looks like he really could use a few more days of rest. Atticus is watching the tunnel. We need to get to work.

Once everyone's roused, I start explaining. "We need to work on the cure, so we can, ya know, get rid of Merris and stuff. And we never know when someone will find us, I mean, someone has to know about the tunnels. Merris does," I say, clasping my hands together. "So we gotta be ready for them."

"And you figured that all out on your own?" Reece says admirably.

"Well, sort of. Parts have been circulating my train of thought for a while," I say.

"So basically yes," Ele says with a smile.

"How does the Virus have anything to do with visions and mind stuff?" Isaiah asks.

"I don't know, but the Maraloxis Virus does target the nervous system and brain," Graydon says. "As Marie said, let's finish the cure and find out later."

"So since Ele has the Merris-can-find-us-and-kill-her-any-second issue, let's give her the cure," I say. "That way she can finally chill for a while."

Graydon hesitates, and Isaiah shifts a little. Bexley glances at the final vial laying on the floor of the tunnel.

"But there's only one vial left," Reece points out. "What if…" He doesn't finish.

Ele looks around. "It's fine, I can stay awake until it's finished. I'll be okay."

"No, Ele, you should take it," Graydon says finally. "We can't risk Merris discovering us."

"But what if there's an emergency and we need it? That's why we saved it to begin with," Bexley interjects. "We can just work quickly."

"But—" Graydon starts, but Ele interrupts, "I'll be fine." After that, it's a full-blown argument over whether Ele should take it or not. Graydon and Isaiah say she should; Bexley and Ele argue she shouldn't. I think she should, but I don't wanna get involved.

"Guys!" Ele shouts.

Atticus stays out of it until it continues to escalate. "Stop! This isn't helping anything. Let Ele decide how she feels about it."

Everyone goes quiet and stares at her. "I refuse to take it. If you really want to help us all then start on the cure. I promise I'll be okay," Ele answers.

"Whatever. Where *do* we start then?" Isaiah asks, looking at Graydon.

Graydon nervously looks at the floor, running a hand through his hair and pacing. "I really wish I knew."

"Where did the notes say to start with the base ingredients?" Bexley asks.

"I don't know! I can't remember anything, I never can—I can't do it," Graydon says, turning away.

"Whoa, calm down, bro," Isaiah says. "You can, and we'll help. I'm sure Ele remembers part of it, and I do too."

"But what if I forget something and mess it all up?" Graydon asks anxiously.

"Graydon, you can do this. You've studied those notes for weeks, and I know you can remember them. Just focus, and tell us what to do," Ele says encouragingly. "We can work together to figure this out."

Graydon takes a deep breath. "Okay. We need to get everything set up first. But you're not helping us, Ele."

"Wait, what? Why?" Ele objects.

"Because if you refuse to take the cure then you have to focus on staying awake, not making yourself more exhausted," he says.

"I agree with that," Bexley says.

Ele sighs and relents, "Okay, fine."

"Someone should make sure Ele stays awake too," Isaiah says.

"No one needs to babysit me, I'm fine," Ele interjects.

"Yeah, but we can't really risk that," Graydon adds.

Graydon, Bexley, and Isaiah start setting up and arranging the test tubes, flasks, and chemicals to begin crafting fresh doses of the cure. I get to hang with Ele.

"Will you be alright?" Atticus asks Ele. She nods. "I'm going to keep watch. Don't fall asleep, and neither of you do anything stupid."

"Excuse me, that last part was unnecessary," I comment, putting my hands on my hips.

"Was it?" Atticus asks. I know we're both thinking about the time at the bookstore, so I decide to shut up.

I'm not exactly sure how you're supposed to help keep someone awake. I mean, I have a few ideas, but I don't think Ele will appreciate them.

"Hey, Reecey, come help me," I beg.

"Fine," he says.

"Guys, relax, I'm not suddenly handicapped because I have to stay awake for a few days," Ele says.

I look at her and raise an eyebrow. "Just a few days? Hasn't it already been one?"

Several long hours pass by. Ele's getting super tired. I'm sooo bored and pretty beat myself. Meanwhile, with three people mixing and measuring, they've already started the process of making the base. Apparently, Graydon conjured up most of the steps he was worried he forgot, and Isaiah and Ele are filling in the blanks. This stuff confuses me. I've had to keep Ele from trying to help them too much. That will not help her situation. She resorts to writing down with a rock everything she remembers from the notes as legibly as possible on the dirt floor. I haven't seen Atticus for hours. I guess that's a good thing.

"How's it going?" I ask the others. Bexley stirs something, and Isaiah crushes up some white pills. I wonder how and why they know what they're doing. I guess they're just smart or really weird. Maybe both.

"It's okay," Bexley says, brushing her wild auburn hair out of her face. "We still have a long way to go."

"We're going to figure it out," Graydon says for like the twentieth time today.

"Great." This is going to be a long few days then for all of us. We still need to find a more permanent place to stay, and I haven't eaten anything since we left Ele's house.

"I don't know what to do," Reece tells me when I head back.

"You're supposed to be helping Ele stay awake," I say.

"I know, but we just finished our *seventeenth* game of tic-tac-toe. And I had to talk to a—ugh—*stranger girl*. Besides, I'm hungry and tired. What else am I supposed to do?" Reece asks desperately.

"I don't know. I'll talk to her for a while. Go find something else to do," I suggest.

"What's gonna happen after this?" Reece asks.

"I don't know, Reecey. Stay alive, fix Willowmire," I reply.

"That's crazy. We can't just *fix* Willowmire. What about Morzanna and the Mordolus?"

"Wow, your optimism right now is radically high," I respond.

"Your sarcasm is radically high," Reece says.

I roll my eyes. "They'll finish the cure, I know it, and we'll work from there."

Reece stares at me a second before leaving, mumbling to himself about this being too risky. He's a weird kid but kinda cool. I hurry over to the other side of the room to Ele. She's petting Stormy.

I'm careful not to step on Ele's notes. Her handwriting is super neat, especially for being drawn into dirt. Each letter has fancy swirls. My handwriting looks like a four-year-old's. I don't know how the heck she can write like that. Isaiah walks over.

"How ya doing, Ele?" he asks.

"I am *fine*. I'm more worried about you guys. I'm not even doing anything!" Ele says, and Stormy takes that moment to escape from her grasp.

"Don't complain. I have a bad headache, and I really don't want to stare at the tiny lines on a beaker or risk burning myself with boiling chemicals, but that's twhat I've gotta do. And you have to stay here and keep yourself awake," Isaiah says. "You don't need to do anything that will make you more tired. You know that stuff makes you drowsy super-fast."

"*But,* with another person, it'd go faster," Ele says. I watch Reece desperately try to catch Stormy while Bexley glares at Ele like she wants to bore a hole through her skull.

"Any more people will be too many," Isaiah counters.

"I could take your place for a while!" Ele offers.

"Then accidentally fall asleep, and we die?" I point out. Ele scowls at us.

"Seriously, Ele. Don't fall asleep, and make sure Merris doesn't find us," Isaiah says. "That's a really important job."

"Ugh." Ele sighs venomously.

"She's in a bad mood," I inform Isaiah.

"I can tell."

Ele takes a breath. "I'm sorry. I just want to be helpful. There's some ibuprofen in my backpack if you need it, Isaiah. I'll stay here."

"Thanks," Isaiah says, nods, and then leaves.

"Hey, I bet you could help them out!" Ele suggests to me. "I feel like I'm causing too much drama, and maybe you could prepare the containers for each dose or take my water bottle and wash the dirty tools."

I think it over. "Sure, I'll help them if it will make you happy. You wait."

Ele looks a little more content, so I go off to see if I can help. Their whole setup on the dirt floor looks a little strange. If someone asked, "where'd you get the cure?", and we said, "Oh yeah, we made it on the dirty floor of a tunnel," it would sound a bit weird.

"Need any help, Bella?" I ask, plopping down next to her. Stormy's back in his cage beside me. It's an odd cage for a bird. It looks like something you'd put a rabbit or a guinea pig in. Bexley stirs together some mixture and keeps adding watery stuff.

"I don't know, honestly," she says quietly. "Oh, I don't actually know what *I'm* doing."

I look at Graydon. "Need any help?"

He glances up at me. "Sure. You can measure this out." He hands me some sort of bottle of gray chalky powder and tells me to pour it into some beakers. "Fill it to the two-milliliter line."

I feel like I'm going to mess something up. I'm trying seriously hard. I almost spill it like eighty-six times though.

I pick up one of the beakers and tip the bottle to pour some of the powder. I think I filled it to the right place. Close enough, at least. I really can't see a thing. I had to squint for like five minutes to find the right mark. Maybe not the best job for someone half-blind.

I set the finished measurements down beside Graydon. I glance down at his ankle. A brutal, reddish line runs vertically across the skin. Weird.

"What's that?" I ask, impulsively touching it. "Is that a scar?"

"Not personal space, that's for sure," Graydon responds, yanking his leg away.

Bexley shoots me a reproachful look. I shrug. "Just wondering," I whisper innocently.

It takes me like twenty minutes to fill all the vials. Basically forever.

Graydon suddenly sets down the glass breakable thing he was mixing clear liquidy stuff in. "We can't do it," he says, dragging a hand across his face. "I don't know what I'm doing, and we're missing vital ingredients. I told you about when we made the cure the first time, it was only because we found that weird powder stuff. We have to have it. And we don't have enough. Give Ele the cure, or whatever. Let's just give up."

"Graydon, chill," Isaiah says, setting a beaker of rust-colored liquid on the flamey candle thing that they use to heat stuff. "We don't have it yet, but we aren't stuck down here forever. We can find it, we just have to have everything else ready. We'll figure it out."

"I'm sorry," Graydon says, glancing up and taking a deep breath. "But do you think Ele's gonna last that long?"

Isaiah shakes his head. "She's gonna have to."

Bexley and I exchange glances, but neither of us says anything.

"I mean, she's my sister, and thus she can do anything," Isaiah says brightly. "You know, because I'm amazing."

Graydon rolls his eyes but smiles, and Bexley shakes her head. I finish my job and kinda feel like I'm just getting in the way, so I go back to Ele. She asks how it's going, and I just tell her good.

"I'm going to go for a walk. A short one," Ele says, standing. She brushes her hair out of her face and ties it into a loose ponytail. Her blond hair is her best asset, and her nose is definitely her worst.

"I've been sitting so long I might fall asleep if I don't do something. I don't want to go alone though."

"I'll go with you. For I, Marie Luna Hale, shall protect you from the evils of the tunnels below," I say with a dramatic gesture. I pick up a rock like it's a weapon.

Ele laughs, and we walk out of the roomy place and into the nearby tunnel. This isn't exactly a nice stroll. Sort of like a trek through a creepy cave where you meet a monster, and Ele insists we *both* bring a flashlight, just in case.

"Where are we going? Not like, right now. After we finish the cure part, I mean," I ask, kicking some rocks on the ground.

"I don't really know. I guess after a while they'll give up looking for us. We may be able to find somewhere else above ground," Ele says.

"Yeah. How are we going to get everyone out of the Infirmary? And then we'll have to figure out how to leave the province," I say. Ele shrugs. "Maybe then it'll be easier to give the cure out. But it's going to be hard with Morzanna."

"We'll figure it out. I mean, we not only created the cure but found and stole it, and escaped the impossible Infirmary and now are hiding under it," Ele says confidently. "How hard can it be if we've already accomplished so many impossible things?"

My assurance peaks a little.

I wonder what time it is. Isaiah has a phone, so I can ask him when we get back. Ele and I walk, but the tunnel gets boring. My imagination is underwhelmed.

"What was that?" Ele says suddenly. I don't know what she's talking about, so I shrug. She freezes. "It's him!"

I look for a moment, confused. There's a metallic clink. I guess my vision's still getting worse because it takes me a few seconds to see the tall person in the shadows like twenty feet away. He's super thin and ghostly looking. Scars. That's gotta be Merris.

"Oh, that," I say. "Shoot."

Ele whimpers nervously then gets a weird look and tenses. "Give me that rock, Marie!"

"What?!" I ask. Ele quickly picks up some stones from the ground. Her face is red.

"I'm done being scared." She throws one of the rocks at Merris. "Leave me alone!" Ele misses by like five feet and groans.

"Stop following us, you creep!" Ele throws another rock, still majorly off. I look at her like she's insane, which right now, I'm wondering if she is. I've spent most of my time recently with Bella and she's predictable, but Ele's a surprising gal. She's getting more frustrated by the second, and Merris isn't fazed. He seems numb, blank, and mechanical.

"Don't be stupid, Ele! We need to go!" I warn. Ele stumbles backward, her eyes fearfully fixed on Merris.

He tilts his head and smiles sardonically. "You're afraid."

"No duh, Sherlock. Wouldn't you be if some freak was stalking you?" I blurt out, then whisper to Ele, "Let's get out of here." She nods and runs off down the tunnel. Merris takes a few steps forward, and I take that cue to follow Ele as fast as possible. I risk a glance behind, and Merris still stands there, watching us.

"You'll fall asleep soon enough," he says. "Then I can get what I want."

Ele cringes. A few minutes later, we return to the cavernous room, panting.

"That zombie-dude found us," I say.

"Merris—he's not far away," Ele coughs out between breaths.

"We should leave before he finds this place," I agree, pointing at the ground. "Someone should go find Atticus. He won't see him if he comes 'cause it was in the other tunnel."

"What?" Isaiah asks.

"I don't think he followed us," Ele adds. "But we need to get out of the tunnels. He'll find us here. Are you finished yet?"

"Nearly, I hope," Graydon says.

"It's fine. We just need to get out," I say, turning.

Suddenly, Atticus returns. I'm about to say something when someone stumbles down the tunnel behind him.

Reece stares, an expression of unbelief flickering across his face. "Jess!"

36

ISAIAH: THE HAVEN

"Jess! You're okay—and you're here!" Ele exclaims. Ever since Jess helped us escape, we've wondered what happened after she disappeared. Now, she's here in the tunnels. We rush over to her.

"I'm glad you all are fine as well," Jess says with a smile. "I never thought I'd find you."

"What happened?" I ask. "How *did* you find us?"

Jess takes a deep breath to calm her wild breathing. "I stayed to lock the door to buy you some time. Afterward, I knew I couldn't get caught, so I had to find a different escape without chancing leading them to you. I saw you come down here, and I took the other hall. When I heard over the intercom that they were searching for you and that they knew one of us had helped, I needed to get out before they checked the cameras and found out it was me, and I didn't have long. You don't want to know what they would do if I got caught, so I did the only thing I could think of. I watched the camera footage but couldn't figure out where you all vanished to! I searched a while before

I found the door and spent a day down here looking," Jess explains, straightening her coat. She's still wearing her light gray nurse outfit.

"Thank you for helping us," Ele says. She looks at the ground. "And sorry for hitting you."

Jess laughs. "It's fine." She looked mean at the Infirmary, so seeing her laugh is really weird.

"Marie almost didn't believe me when I told her you helped us," Ele says. "We were all so shocked. Oh, and this is Graydon."

"And I'm Bexley, by the way," Bexley comments with a wave. "I've seen you before."

"I'm really glad you're here, Jess, but we have to leave," I remind everyone.

"I know. When they found out you had escaped the Infirmary, the Queen wasn't pleased. They began a lockdown, and those two kids who helped you," Jess looks at Reece and me and exhales. "The Queen had them killed."

Reece yelps. "What? You mean, that girl, and River—they're dead?"

"They knew about the cure and helped you escape. It's not the first time something like this has occurred," Jess says flatly. She clenches her fists. "Morzanna doesn't take lightly insubordination. Nor should we take lightly the casualties of her rule."

Reece takes a step closer to me. River and that girl are *dead*. They sacrificed themselves for us. And maybe something bigger in the end. Reece looks at me, flushed. His wide, bleary eyes reflect what I'm feeling. I remind myself of truth. *God is good. This is His will. Christ is my hope.*

"The Mordolus concluded that you must be hiding somewhere after they failed to locate you. They're combing the Infirmary to find out where you escaped, and I worry they'll discover this place," Jess says, looking at where we've been working on the cure replication.

Marie nods. "Not just that. It's Merris."

"Who is that?" Jess asks.

We give her a very brief synopsis.

"I was not aware of the Maraloxis Virus enabling any sort of mind tricks. I'm not surprised; there is much that remains a mystery to me even now," Jess says, tossing a black braid over her shoulder. "I've never heard of dreams like Eleanora's in all my time at the Infirmary unless it was caused by a Virus hallucination."

Ele bites her lip and shifts a little.

"I saw him!" Marie interrupts. "Graydon did once, too. And I'm definitely not hallucinating. That dude is super creepy."

Jess gives a slow nod.

"So how'd you locate us all the way down here?" Graydon asks.

"I was still looking for you when Atticus found me," Jess says.

"Anyway, we need to go now. Soon, someone or another will find us, and we need to get somewhere secure," Bexley says. She swirls her charm bracelet.

"She's right. If Merris is around, we have to leave," Atticus says.

"He can tell Morzanna our location. He hasn't yet, but he could," Reece adds. He sways nervously. "And then we'll be dead. Like River."

"Where can we go then?" Graydon asks. "I thought this was basically our last option."

"I'll show you," Jess interrupts. "There's a safe and hidden place, but we must hurry."

"Awesome!" Marie says. "Let's get moving, folks. I'm SOO ready to be outta here."

"Let's start packing," I say.

I hope we don't have to stay in hiding long. I hate it. It kills the fun of the adventure. It's also annoying to have to put everything for the cure away. I carefully wrap each vial, bottle, and tool in paper and all the excess fabric we can find. Graydon stashes everything into the backpacks.

"Guys?" Ele says shakily. I spin around.

Someone stands in the tunnel. Wintery terror snakes across my skin. He looks like part of a horror movie cast in costume. Mutilated arms extend from beneath his gray cloak. He has a ghostly presence. Merris. Atticus freezes.

Ele hoists one of the backpacks onto her shoulder. She disappears down the other tunnel. Marie looks, jumps up, and runs. Reece looks like he's seen a ghost and bolts. Bexley shrieks and grabs the birdcage. She drags Graydon with her. I stand, overwhelmed with curiosity. I'm finally seeing him.

"Atticus?" I ask. He just stares with a horrified gape. "Come on!" I say. Merris strides closer. The part I hate most is how silent he is. I didn't think Atticus would be more scared of Merris than us. I guess I'm wrong. For once.

"You two need to come on!" Jess orders. She scoops up the last of the unlit candles we've been using.

"Sorry," Atticus says, breaking from his daze, still disturbed.

Atticus wasn't just trying to assure us when he said he remembered the way out. The path is steep and winding. I hope wherever Jess takes us is legit. If Merris catches up and follows us, he could reveal everything to the Queen. Or whatever nightmare of his own he's got planned.

Whenever I glance back, I feel like Merris has to be following us. But maybe I'm just scared. When we finally emerge from the tunnels, we stop for a moment.

"Where is the place, Jess?" Marie asks.

"This way. We can't let anyone follow us," Jess responds. She takes the lead and dashes off into the woods.

We follow her into the forest. Once we're within the thick wood, it's calmer. Merris didn't follow us out of the tunnels. Just like last time. It's strangely unsettling.

I run into spider webs the whole way. Once, Bexley freaks out because she almost steps on a black snake. I have no idea where we are.

"How much farther? I'm so tired," Reece mumbles to pretty much no one. Even though we're pretty sure Merris stayed in the tunnels, Jess takes a long winding route. She pauses often to scan the surroundings.

Then we get to a clearing. An old building is nestled among the trees. It's big, shaded by a thick canopy of trees. Bigger than a house but not two stories tall. Sun rays shimmer through the branches. Jess guides us toward the building. Thick ivy and vines grow all over it. On the other side of the clearing is a small patch of turned-up dirt. I think it's a garden. A sad garden.

"This the place?" I whisper.

"I think so," Reece replies.

Jess gets out a key at the entrance. Strands of wire are wrapped in designs around a pole bent over the doorway. It's the only thing different from a regular building. The wire looks like guitar string. It reminds me of my guitar. I was a hyper kid and playing chilled me out. I did sports summer camps with Graydon, but I've always been more interested in music.

"Here," Jess says, handing each of us but Bexley, who already has one, a face mask. "A precaution."

She opens the door. The huge room is bright. The gray paint on the walls is scratched and chipped. Rafters run along the tall ceiling. There's a big wooden table in the center of the room with an open kitchen on one side. Tall storage shelves create a wall enclosing some homey furniture. Doors line the wall adjacent to the door.

"What is this place?" Ele asks.

"It's a meeting place and a safe house for the survivors," Jess tells us. "A few others, including myself, created it to be a refuge for anyone seeking help. We have been trying to bring the cure here and treat those we've rescued but have been unable to. The other members are either working undercover like me or performing some other job to keep our mission running. Most of them aren't here now. We call this the Haven. Morzanna doesn't know about it, either. She had no idea until now that there were any traitors."

Atticus shifts from one foot to the other. "You're sure it's safe here?"

"Of course, we're very careful," Jess says. "We're picky about who we bring back, for obvious reasons."

"I hope so. If anything happens—" Atticus starts, shooting a protective glance at us.

"It's safe," Jess says. "I know we had a weird introduction, but I wouldn't bring any of you here if it wasn't as protected as possible during this time."

"Listen, we've all had weird introductions," I say. "I'm pretty sure like none of us met under normal circumstances."

"Yeah, Marie just fell out of a closet," Ele says.

"Graydon scared me to death," Bexley adds. She looks at the leafy ground. "And I threw a piece of glass at him."

"We thought Reece was part of the Mordolus!" Marie says, bouncing.

"Yeah, and Atticus kidnapped Bexley and knocked me out," Graydon recalls, marginally less enthusiastic.

"I'm sorry. I was trying to help you," Atticus apologizes again. Jess raises an eyebrow. "Let's not discuss that right now."

Reece crosses his arms. "So Jess, you worked at the Infirmary. How can you not have the cure?"

"They have extremely efficient security. We're not even allowed to leave the Infirmary without being searched. I wasn't ready to sacrifice my identity to take any. We hardly had access to it to begin with. I tried to secure a recipe or discover what ingredients are used and what the process is, but very few know. In fact, only a handful of technicians crafted the antidote and supplied what we have. Since I did discover some of what was in it, I focused on collecting those things, although I haven't made it past that step. However, we did manage to bring a little bit of the cure back once undetected," Jess says. "Other than that, we've only managed to steal minor medical supplies we critically needed."

"Does the cure have a name? Like we keep calling it that, *'the cure'*, but what is it actually titled?" Graydon asks.

"It's called sulfavirdoton, but the generic name is raxoxin," Jess says.

That's where I get lost. Too many science things. Too many other waaay more interesting things around us. There's a staircase down to our right. The doors across from us *beg* to be opened. I want to explore so bad.

"So you're like rebels of the Queen?" Bexley asks.

Jess nods. "Basically. We call ourselves Auxillia."

Marie crinkles her nose. "What kind of a name is that?"

"It means peace in Quxillith," Jess says.

"In *what?*" Ele asks.

"You've never heard of Quxillia?" Jess says.

"My dad's coworker's brother was a member of it and was killed," Graydon says. "That's about all I know."

Bexley raises her hand. "I have! My sister told me about them. During the Separative War, a group formed to try and stop it, but more importantly to protect the people getting hurt. They rescued civilians stuck in the worst parts of the war. They saved a lot of people. That is until they were all killed during the battle at Washington D.C."

"That's right," Jess says. "They were targeted as being a radical religious group for their belief in Christ. They formed a simple and secretive language called Quxillith. Their own name, Quxilla, means help, the specific type of help or care, reflecting the servanthood of Jesus commanded in the Bible. During the D.C. battle, they came quickly to protect the citizens of the city. They were killed in the crossfire that separated our country."

"That's crazy. And now you guys are sort of doing the same thing, right?" I say.

"In a way, yes. Right now, we're helping people stay alive. Our secondary goal is to find a way to terminate Morzanna's rule and restore the province," Jess says. "We have also helped some people escape the Infirmary."

Bexley gapes. "Really? Wait…"

Jess nods. "I was the one who left the door open. You weren't the first one to escape. The Mordolus never found out either. I would mark them as dead, so no one discovered the breach."

"Can I join? I want to be a part of a secret gang, sneaking around the Infirmary, saving people! Maybe I'll even meet the Queen. Ugh, I'd give her a good kick if I did," Marie pipes up.

"It's not a gang," Jess remarks.

Marie's still deep in thought. "Waaaait, are there rules?"

"I don't know about joining. There's a lot to happen before we delve into that. And yes, actually," Jess says. Marie rolls her eyes. Jess ignores her. "We must have rules in order to maintain our safety. We always aim toward not hurting anyone, no matter what, and—"

"Um, but what about you dragging me and Ele around? That wasn't exactly nice. And what if someone's gonna kill you?" Marie interrupts.

"I was getting to that," Jess says impatiently. "For minor things like that, everyone has agreed we do what we have to. But, if anyone comes back with real blood on their hands, they have to confess and have a reasonable justification."

"Sounds like a weird, pacifist cult to me," Reece mumbles. He's clearly less enthralled than the rest of us. Thankfully, Jess didn't hear.

"Reece," I whisper. "They're going to help us. You can go back to the tunnels with Merris if you'd like."

"But what if someone doesn't confess or doesn't have any reason for why they did what they did?" Ele asks.

"I hope that doesn't happen," Jess says. "But actions would be taken."

Bexley plays with the moon charm on her bracelet. "How many people are in Auxillia?"

"Almost ten, but it varies. Right now we also have four guests apart from you," Jess says.

"Are you the leader?" Atticus asks.

Jess shakes her head. "More like second in command. Our leader isn't around a lot because it's not safe."

"Well, where is this leader at other times?" Ele asks.

"They have a secured location outside of Morzanna's knowledge and some access to additional resources and occasionally limited access outside Senneforte. There are several other members that remain at this place with our leader to assist in other endeavors. But anyway, let me show you around," Jess says.

Jess shows us the Haven. The larger room for meetings and meals, and the doors lead to guest rooms. Jess says downstairs they have more bedrooms, but that area is off-limits. She doesn't go out and say it, but basically, the other guests are not at all well. They're quarantined.

Someone comes running up the steps from the basement. Winded, the boy stares at Jess. He's around eighteen, but he seems small for his age. The boy has curly brown hair and sparky eyes. He gives off an air of friendliness that makes me both comfortable and uncomfortable. He gapes for a second then it fades into a smile.

"Jess! You're back!" he says, running over. "Did something happen? It's early—whoooa, who are you?"

Jess shakes her head. "I just brought them here, Ledger. Most of them are from the Infirmary. They're staying with us now. They have raxoxin, and they know how to make it."

The boy looks at us in awe. Refreshing considering no one believed us at first.

"Whoa," he says, wavering. I decide he's having a greater internal reaction. He just stares at us for an uncomfortable amount of time.

"This is Ledger Grove," Jess says. "Our caretaker for the sick."

Ledger bows, smiling. "Well, to be honest, it's really because I'm not good at not getting caught," he stage-whispers. "But yes."

"He's also the only one who's recovered from the Virus without raxoxin. We don't know how, but it was a miracle. Other than I, Ledger is the only one who can safely be around the sick," Jess explains. Graydon gives me an odd look. *How is that possible?*

"I–Wait. How'd you escape from the Infirmary? That's crazy. Did Jess help? Wait, nevermind, you can tell me later. So, you guys really have raxoxin?" Ledger asks.

"Yeah," I say.

"Cool!" Ledger says excitedly. "Well as the caretaker or whatever, I know how much we need it. It's crazy. So many of them—yeah. You wouldn't believe it. I've seen things." he shakes his head. "Almost everyone's sick. Some of them even died, it's—" he stops when Jess gives him a look. "Well, I get carried away," Ledger restarts. "So who are you?"

We start introducing ourselves.

"I'm Isaiah," I say, shaking his hand.

"It's a pleasure," he says. "So, who's that guy?" Ledger whispers, jerking his head toward Atticus. "I feel like he's giving me the silent treatment."

"He's always like that," I say.

"Ah, well, I guess that's good. We always need someone attentive and wise. I, for one, am lacking a little in some of those areas. He does need to lighten up a bit though," Ledger says, grinning. I laugh awkwardly, realizing he's still shaking my hand.

"Well, I have patients to attend to," Ledger says a moment later. "Nice meeting you."

"Pleasurable introduction, lad," he says to Atticus and claps him on the back before descending the stairs again. Atticus looks disturbed.

"I'll tell you more about Auxillia later, and introduce you to some other members, but it's important to finish this cure soon. For Ele," Jess says.

I forgot about that for a second. Everyone at the Haven is relying on us now too. I glance at Ele. We've gotta hurry.

37
GRAYDON: FINALLY

Right after we arrive at the Haven, a safe place for survivors, Bexley, Isaiah and I jump back into completing the Maraloxis Virus cure. We were given false assurance when Bexley and I first developed the antidote. Then what we had vanished from the Brooks' house. I'm almost scared to feel the levels of hope building up inside me.

Isaiah and I set up while Jess takes Bexley to look through the Haven's storage for ingredients. When they return with a few vials of the pink powder, I falter with relief. We've got everything we need—except maybe time. Ele documents all the steps so we have a concrete path for next time. Jess helps us as much as she can, but there isn't much to do. The steps aren't hard. It's just a matter of having time for the process.

Marie goes manic with exhaustion, so Jess has her help set up our rooms. Later, Jess prepares us a hasty meal of rice and canned vegetable soup. Atticus paces the room and keeps checking outside. Pretty soon, Reece falls asleep at the table. Sunlight highlights every scratch on the only strip of window above the door. The rays are golden orange. It's sunset.

Ledger pops upstairs to check in. "Whoa, is that fire? That's so cool. So you really know what you're doing? 'Cause if it was me, I'd have no idea what to do. That's probably not helpful. Whoa, what's that sparkly stuff? Is it glowing?"

"It's a type of mineral that counteracts something in the Virus and is a crucial ingredient for raxoxin," Jess explains.

"Whoa," he replies, fixated on the fine, glittery sand. "This is so absolutely awesome."

My hands tremble. With a rush of doubt, I wonder if the cure will even function right, or if it was too rushed, or I forgot something. I fight to stay focused as I doggedly add a combination of pantothenic acid and magnesium to the mixture, heating it to exactly two-hundred degrees. Ele looks even more exhausted now. Jess mixes her a cup of instant coffee, and she looks a little revived afterward. It's been over thirty-six hours since we slept.

"No, you're supposed to use this," Isaiah corrects Bexley, handing her a vial of liquidized dexamethasone.

"Oh, I thought it said to use the black one. Yeah, I see now," Bexley says, mumbling about Ele's notes being difficult to read.

I stir the mixture of chloroquine and dexamethasone Bexley crafted over the alcohol burner until it starts to simmer. Jess hurries off to find more oseltamivir in the basement. She secured some supplies from the Infirmary, even though she couldn't get much raxoxin itself. Only once did she successfully steal any, and they used it immediately to save someone.

We've been here four hours, and it's dragged on. We had to dry out the magnesium precipitate, which took an hour even with a hairdryer. I overheated one of the mixtures, which set us back too. This is only the beginning though—barely enough doses for us. I'll be making this concoction until I'm ninety at this rate. Pushing that thought away, I focus on reality. The cure is nearly complete.

I'm barely conscious of what my hands are doing, but eagerness keeps me awake. Reece sleeps on the floor, and Marie finally got delirious then crashed on the bench. Isaiah keeps laying his head on the table. A headache from strain and exhaustion threatens to intensify as I stare at the notebook, everything we remembered from my dad's notes in intricate, swirly letters. Ele watches longingly and offers to read the last few steps.

"Hurry up and add the fairy dust," Bexley says with impatient excitement.

"Fairy dust?" Isaiah asks, staring into the beaker of foggy liquid.

"The powder," I say, handing him the rosy beaker. He measures out eight full portions and mixes it with the rest of the solution. The realization sets in: we've finished the cure.

Weirdly, the shower of relief brings fatigue. I almost don't care about the raxoxin. Almost.

Jess stares at the cure with awe, comparing it to the vial recovered for the Infirmary. "That looks right. I can't believe this! You're the brightest kids I ever met!"

Isaiah smiles confidently.

The second Bexley wakes up Marie, she's jumping with enthusiasm, and it's contagious. For once, Reece's expression is free from fear, and he even joins Marie in bouncing around the room.

Ledger runs up from the basement at the news.

"I think we should give Ele the original one," I say, a tiny bit of doubt still intact. "From the Infirmary. Just to make sure."

Jess nods and carefully measures the correct portions of about twenty-five milliliters. We measured what was in the vial from the Infirmary to discover the dosage amount. She hands Ele the Infirmary vial first and then gives ours to the four of us.

When I receive mine, uncertainty and hesitation overwhelm me. I shove the cup back in Jess' hand.

"I can't take it, Jess," I say. "Give it to one of those people Ledger was talking about, or one of you have it. I'll make more for myself later."

She shakes her head and hands it back. "Take it. You've worked hard enough. Be at peace. Besides, you need to be well if you're going to make more for all the rest of us."

I relent and take it. The sour rose-colored liquid has a sandy, gritty texture. So whatever the powder stuff is doesn't dissolve. That's at least a clue.

I'll be more excited tomorrow, but I'm too exhausted and it's too surreal now.

"No more Merris," Ele says with a bright smile.

Isaiah gives me a high-five. "Good job, Gray."

Joy is exhausting. I'd rather rest in the fact that, hey, I'm not dying anymore, and neither are the others. I know we'll all feel a lot better when the raxoxin starts working.

"This is amazing!" Jess says with exhilaration. She carefully stares at the leftover portions of the antidote. "Our leader will be so happy when she hears!"

"You mean the leader you won't tell us about?" Reece asks causally.

"Not won't, *can't*. It's for safety reasons," Jess explains. "Someday, you'll know."

Despite my weariness, I promise Jess we'll make more of the cure for everyone at the Haven as soon as possible. At least I will. We reserve an emergency dose, and Ledger takes the final one left to give to someone downstairs. We confirm that no one besides us has ever known about Merris. I wonder if it had something to do with being in the tunnels. The mystery remains of why Ele was attacked more. I smile, confident in our current welfare. Maybe we'll be okay. Maybe my parents will live. Maybe we're safe. Maybe hope has paid off.

Jess shows us to two rooms across from where we entered. Each room has a few beds crowded inside. When Reece, Isaiah, and I enter our room, I collapse on the bottom bunk. I don't bother to change clothes and barely stop to take off my shoes. A lightness glitters through the air. Minutes later, we're all asleep, too drained to stay awake a minute more.

38
BEXLEY: SAFE HERE

The patter of gentle raindrops draws me from my deep sleep. Excitement whirs in my chest, but tranquil relief subdues it. Physically, I feel like I've been hit by a train, but mentally, I'm calmer than I've been in a long time. Peaceful rain falls outside, the kind that makes you never want to get out of bed. Ele and Marie are both still asleep across the room.

Our bedroom is small for three beds, which take up almost all the floor space. Mine's in the corner, half under the picture window. Ele and Marie's are on the other two walls opposite the door. A soft chirping draws my concentration to the wooden nightstand between Ele's bed and mine. Two black eyes peek out from behind downy, blue feathers as Stormy tilts his head at me. I smile and open the cage, allowing Stormy to hop onto my hand. Currant-red curtains hang around the picture window behind my bed. I gaze out the glass, taking in the forestry sights.

We're safe here at the Haven—even though it smells like mildew, and I worry about the diseases that might be hidden in my sheets. At least I'm here and not in the Infirmary.

It's so odd to not have to worry about the Mordolus, or the Virus, or whether I'm going to find somewhere safe to sleep or something to eat. That thought makes me more aware of the hunger pangs assaulting my stomach.

People are talking outside the room. I can't figure out what they're discussing. I'm guessing the topic is us, and they must be the rest of Auxillia. Maybe they arrived during the night or earlier this morning if it is still morning. It's bright enough now it could easily just be a rainy afternoon.

Seeing Ele and Marie stirring, I rise, sneaking across the small room. I stop to sprinkle birdseed in Stormy's cage and return him. I enter our bathroom to examine, somewhat regrettably, my appearance in the mirror. I throw my hair into a bun to try to conceal how oily it is then wash my face. I still wear Ele's borrowed clothes, but I doubt she'll want them back because of the stains and tears they've accumulated. Her jeans barely fit me; she's slimmer and taller than I am. Staring in the mirror, I realize I look ill and pale since I haven't eaten well in months. If I wasn't so hungry and curious, I'd stop and take a shower. There are still remnants of ash on my skin. But I like to take my time bathing, which I can't enjoy with this excitement nagging me. I open the door as quietly as possible, stepping out into the cold middle room.

Jess is surrounded by six other young people. They sit at the long wooden table in the middle of the room. A slight blush creeps onto my cheeks when I realize they are all surreptitiously peering at me.

Rain pours onto the roof, sounding like pebbles on metal; it's coming down heavily now. Jess waves me over, and I amble over to her. I slide onto the bench beside Jess, trying not to draw too much attention to myself. Everyone's chatting, which is nice, so I don't feel awkward. On Jess's other side is a girl wearing a simple face mask. Her small, blue eyes are shy like she's hiding behind her glasses and long black hair. She'd been talking with Jess a second before. Her skin is pale, and she looks weak but kind. I know instantly she's succumbing to the Virus. Next to her is a younger freckled boy. The kitchen is adjacent to the table, and there's an open window and doorway leading in. A sandy-redheaded girl strides gracefully from the kitchen, and I do a double-take.

"Everyone is so happy about the raxoxin. They're all amazed by you guys. I told them not to be overwhelming, in case you thought they were ignoring you. They all understand what it's like to be the new one," Jess says. I don't respond as an avalanche of shock leaves me speechless. Jess looks at me, worried as I blink over and over again. "Are you alright?"

I let out the breath I was holding in a surprised laugh. "Hadley?"

The redheaded girl looks over at me, confused. She opens her mouth in surprise and gasps. I spring from the table, ignoring everyone's stares. Hadley runs from the doorway and throws her arms around me. I can hardly speak.

"Bexley!" she chokes out.

"Hadley! You're okay! I thought you were locked up!" I say.

Hadley nods in agreement. "I can't believe you're alive!"

My sister pulls away, grabs my hands, and leads me to the far side of the table. Her brown eyes glisten, and a smile spreads across her perfect face.

"How are you here?" I ask.

"Jess brought us. She found Hallston and I after you were taken to the Infirmary. We promised to help them, and Jess let us stay. We have been working mainly on locating a safe supply of raxoxin," she says, still taking in shaky breaths. "But how are you here? Jess said she's never been able to rescue anyone and bring them directly back from the Infirmary."

"I escaped, and, actually, she did help me. I found some friends, and they already had the cure; we met up with Jess later. It's a really long story!" I laugh, overjoyed.

"I couldn't believe it when Jess told us that some kids had located the antidote, but my sister? I still can't believe you helped with it!" Hadley says, dramatically throwing her hands up.

"Oh, Hadley, I'm so happy," I say. "Where's Hallston?"

"She's coming later. She's out in the city working. Hallston was here last night but had to leave! I'm sure she wouldn't have gone if she knew you were here!" Hadley exclaims, resting a hand excitedly over her mouth with a smile. An Argentine, jade ring is on one hand, and the other wears a silver twisted wire one with an emerald pendant—I made it for her last year.

I never realized how much I missed my sisters. I didn't know what happened to Hadley and Hallston after my capture. When it occurred, I was actually running to my friend's house to make sure she was still safe. They caught me on the roads and threw me in the truck.

Several months after Hadley was born, my parents adopted Hallston from Senegal. People always ask why on earth they adopted a newborn when they had a baby of their own, but it's a rude question for our family. They always told me God gave them Hallston, and His timing is perfect. Hadley is only a month older, so they've basically been regarded as twins their entire lives. I was born seven years later and became the classic, spoiled little sister. Thankfully, I grew out of it. Hadley is outgoing and kind; Hallston is protective and serious, and I'm somewhere in the middle and the most adventurous.

For the next hour, time melts away as I catch up with Hadley.

"So after Hallston and I came here, we began a new mission. At first, we were out looking for food and supplies, but we ran into a family out on the street and brought them back with us to the Haven. Jess wasn't thrilled, but after some debate she decided that we could help in another way. It sacrificed some of our security, but saving lives is worth it. We convinced her to let us bring people back. Naturally, they are all infected with the Virus, and we've been doing our best to treat them. We're certain that one of our members, Zia, has the Virus. She's been quarantined for several weeks, and just last night she was able to come out due to our new supply of raxoxin. We've all been exposed at some point, but as you know it's difficult to tell, and no one else is showing symptoms yet. Ledger is a special case; he recovered from the Virus without a cure. We don't know how, but he was almost as sick as Zia after he arrived at the Haven and fell ill, but a week later, with minimal treatment, he improved. We even tested him to make sure, and somehow it was negative. No one can explain it, but Hallston says it's a miracle by the grace of God. As common viruses go, he shouldn't get it again, so he takes care of the other patients. Jess also helps, having received sulfavirdoton undercover at the Infirmary. And now we can do even more with the cure!" Hadley says with a surprising squeal that makes me jump. I'm grappling with the impossibility that Ledger recovered from the Virus without the antidote. Could there be others that get better as well?

"How have you kept people alive until now?" I ask. Surely they have some way, or they would be just as sick as the people in the Infirmary.

"Honestly, I don't know," Hadley says. "We can give them treatment for symptoms. We make elderberry glycerites and have many disinfectant measures to prevent ourselves from contracting it from our guests. Ledger is certified in first aid and volunteered in geriatrics after high school, so he's the most qualified to provide medical help here. Jess is fairly capable too since she learned a lot at the Infirmary. We bring people here, help and feed them, and offer to let them join our group. That's where most of us came from. It started with Jess and our leader, then Hallston and I, and now there's over ten of us."

"But what if someone doesn't join and leaves to tell the Queen about this place?" I ask.

"I hope they won't, Bexley, and I don't think they will. We helped them and unless they're wicked, I don't think they would betray us. Anyway, there's nothing we can do to keep them here. If we forced them to stay, we'd be no better than the Queen. It's all a battle of judgment on whether to bring someone here to begin with," Hadley says, spreading out the wrinkles on the pleated skirt of her pink and red plaid dress.

The rain has stopped sprinkling on the roof, and the door to our room opens. Ele stalks out looking like she needs another year of sleep. Marie, however, looks like she's had too much rest and comes bounding over to us like a caffeinated rabbit.

"WOW! I was BEAT! I can't believe I slept later than you, Bella! I feel SO energized! It's so cool here!" Marie says, smiling. "Is this your sister?"

Hadley and I both have slightly wavy, auburn hair, and round face shape; the only difference is I have light blue eyes, and she has brown. Late at night in the Infirmary, Marie and I would talk about our families, sometimes reminiscing until we fell asleep. Those memories of our days there were fun and hopeful, yet they leave a terrible feeling, and a thick, black shadow has settled over the memory.

"Yes! This is Hadley," I say, excitedly.

"I'm Marie!" she says enthusiastically. "That's cool you found your sister." Marie grins and shakes Hadley's hand.

When everyone gets up, I'm busy introducing people to my sister.

"Oh, so these are the kids you met in the Infirmary," Hadley says when I introduce her to Isaiah and Ele.

"Yeah, kind of," I say, explaining how we all met.

"Well, really nice to meet you," Hadley says. "I'm sure everyone's hungry."

"Heck yeah!" Marie says, bouncing. "I'm STARVING!"

My sister smiles, heading for the kitchen. "I'll go start working on breakfast."

The Haven is exciting. Marie runs around looking at everything. Eleanora, Isaiah, Graydon, and I sit at the barstools in the kitchen while Hadley fixes breakfast and chats with Zia, the girl with the long hair and glasses.

"I think that cure is working. I haven't had a headache at all this morning," Isaiah says.

"I can't believe this place existed the whole time," Eleanora says, straightening her teal T-shirt and rigidly running a hand through her hair. She plays with a crystal earring. I think we're feeling the same way about our clothing and hygiene at the moment. There might be a battle over who gets to take the first shower.

"Yeah, it's crazy," Isaiah says, scrolling through his phone. I'm not sure what he's doing since there's no Wi-Fi or phone service. I think, for Isaiah, his phone is a security thing. Also, he gets fidgety if he doesn't have something to do.

"Wouldn't it have been great if we knew about the Haven a month ago?" I ask.

"Definitely," Graydon says, toying with the strings of his hoodie. He glances around before leaning in closer. "So, we're trusting Jess?"

"Do we have a choice?" Ele asks.

"No, not exactly. But shouldn't we be cautious?" Graydon restates.

"We could. But why not just let go? We have no control. There's nothing we could do if, say, Jess turned out to be a true Mordolus member. So let's just go with it and trust," Isaiah says.

"I suppose that's logical. And anyway, my sisters wouldn't be here if Jess was dishonest," I say, taking out my bottle of hand sanitizer, one Ele gave me at their house, and applying it to my hands. It's nice, sort of springy and floral. It makes me feel cleaner and hopefully it's strong enough that I smell better until I can take a shower—priority one right after breakfast.

"You're going to ruin your hands using hand sanitizer that much," Isaiah says.

I put the bottle away. "Hygiene before health."

"Doesn't that sort of defeat the purpose?" Graydon asks. I shake my head with a grin.

"FOOD!" Marie screams, sprinting to the bench as Hadley begins to set out bowls.

We walk to the big table in the meeting room. The rest of Auxillia slipped out, and Jess explains that they're preparing to go work either at the Infirmary or out in the province.

I'm ravenous. The Infirmary's bland soups and stale bread hardly count as a proper meal. I haven't eaten much since my escape either. Hadley serves everyone oatmeal and fresh bread. I'm surprised we don't deplete their entire food supply.

"Good morning!" Ledger says, emerging from the basement.

"How is everything?" Jess asks, helping clear the dishes.

"It's okay," Ledger says, uncertain. "It'll be better when we have raxoxin for them."

He doesn't voice impatience, but guilt surges within me. People are dying without the cure in this very building.

"What's up, bro?" Ledger says to Atticus, holding up his hand for a high five.

"Hi," Atticus says. Ledger frowns after he's left hanging.

I don't think Atticus is exactly adept at friend-making. I have to admit, Ledger is trying very hard in what Isaiah told me is his attempt to make Atticus lighten up. It's amusing.

Ledger tilts his head and stares at Atticus. "Whoa, you're not even that old."

"How old did you think I was?" Atticus asks. Ledger shrugs.

"I don't know, older. But you're like nearly my age, huh? I'm almost nineteen! But anyway—whoa, what's that?" Then, Ledger's gone, leaving Atticus looking thoroughly uncomfortable.

A few minutes later, Jess introduces us to the remaining members of Auxillia before they have to leave.

"This is Zia Locks," she says, pointing to the girl with long black hair. Zia waves in a timid, but friendly manner, readjusting her glasses.

"And this is Gabby Shorsee." He's an average-looking boy, the one who had been sitting beside Zia and Hadley earlier. An easy smile paints his freckle-spangled face.

Violet is younger, blond, and outgoing. There's an older boy who's a bit intimidating and loud named Bentley.

The next day, Hallston returns. Her sable hair is plaited in boho braids, and a confident smile glows across her dark skin. Hallston seems so much older now.

The week goes by alarmingly fast. Jess tells us to take a little time off working on the cure to have a break and make sure this version truly works, and no one argues. I even spend time making a new cage for Stormy, repairing my charm bracelet that has gotten a bit tarnished, and hanging out with the others. My sisters try not to be away too much, and only when they leave do I remember our parents and the many others still waiting in the Infirmary. But we do have a successful antidote.

We've all become much closer friends here at the Haven. Marie and Reece spend the majority of time together and like to cause trouble. Nothing serious of course, but *very* annoying. I've tried talking to Eleanora, but she seems to want to hang out more with Graydon and Isaiah. She and Isaiah don't look very similar, but they have the same voice. Ele's is gentler, and Isaiah's lower, but they're still so alike. I have to admit, sometimes I envy Ele. Her soft blond tresses fall to her mid-back, held back by a teal, shiny, silk headband. Calm blue eyes give voice to her deepest desire: peace. Well, that and the blueberry pie Hadley's preparing, and she's eyeing longingly. Hadley manages to make our meals not quite as detestable as they could be since the only food we have is either a preservable that's meant to last the apocalypse or on the rare occasion a plant someone found or harvested from the unsuccessful garden.

I don't see Atticus much, but he still makes daily checks to make sure everything's secure. He seems different in a good way. Maybe Ledger's cracking through his silence.

We asked about the other guests, but their rooms are in the basement. Ledger said they were too sick to come up and to just focus on the cure. We aren't allowed to go down there since they're quarantined.

Everyday Isaiah, Ele, Graydon, and I work a bit on the cure, but I have to admit progress is slow. No one really wants to work on it, and it seems the rush has dissipated some. Most of the time I just procrastinate doing it since almost everyone's been treated here and we're simply trying to build up a supply until we exhaust Jess's ingredients. Graydon works on it the most out of any of us, but I think he actually enjoys it. We work step by step, with certain people who are more gifted taking over the challenging areas. Graydon gets stuck doing most of the exact heating and tedious mixtures. My favorite part is filling the vials. Eleanora usually takes on combining the chemicals and mixing them for long stretches until they reach the right consistency. Isaiah does whatever he's tasked with.

"Can I help you guys?" Gabby offers one day while we are preparing to begin concocting another round of doses. "I can read directions. I'm sure I can learn."

"Yeah, actually that'd be great," Isaiah says. "How'd you end up here?"

"I'm the second kid of four, and we're all two years apart. Two of my brothers left with my dad before the lockdown. My mom, youngest brother, and I were going to join them later, but my brother got sick. Really sick. My mom was desperate, and that ended up getting them both caught. Honestly, it was probably good. My brother was—is—super sick and really needed medical attention," Gabby explains. "Bentley and I knew each other so he contacted me and that's how I got here." After that, we have a fifth helper for our antidote production.

It's strangely become quite like a family here. And best of all, we have a home. It's something I've missed; just having somewhere safe to be. But it all seems dismally temporary, and I wish it would last forever.

39
ELEANORA: FOR THE BETTER

"Oh sorry!" Bexley calls, chasing after a blur of blue and silver fluff. Stormy escaped her attempt to catch him by taking flight at the last moment, sending her crashing into me as I was walking to the bench to sit down.

I roll my eyes, plopping down at the huge wooden table to stare at the red notebook in front of me. I borrowed it from Reece, and as I fill the sheets I'm becoming increasingly more aware of how long it's been since I've done any school. As I begin to pen lines, black ink leaks onto my hands. It reminds me of before all this when I would practice calligraphy in my spare time or the margins of my schoolwork. I love how you can make words with one definition confer something completely different just by giving them an extra swirl or sharp edge. I would write things I loved in thin print, some bulleted if they were school-related, or bold lines for something important. Before we left our house to head to the tunnels, I packed a few of my favorite pens to bring, though unfortunately none of them are true calligraphy pens, and I'm using a sparkly blue one now.

Where did the Virus come from?

Why is everyone following the Queen?

Why is the Queen doing this?

Was she really behind this all?

What really happened to King Cyrus?

How do we get the cure to everyone?

What do we do about Morzanna?

How can Merris access our minds?

How do we stop this all?

I've started writing down my thoughts to try to figure them out. There's something alluring about crossing things off a list, although I haven't gotten to that phase yet. Thankfully, the time here at the Haven has helped me summon more ideas about how we could get through this, which I write down on a significantly shorter list. I've realized I spend far too long thinking and complaining instead of trying to actually do something active about my problems. As I flip through the pages, the rows of unanswered questions seem endless.

"Stormy, come down!" Bexley calls, frustration filling her airy voice. Ledger helps her attempt to coax Stormy down. The bird stays perched on the top of the tall metal shelf as Bexley runs to get a chair to stand on. I stifle a laugh as Bexley finally seizes the bird but ends up falling from the wobbly plastic chair. Ledger catches her, but Stormy bolts out of Bexley's hands in a mess of feathers. Eventually, she wrangles the bird and scolds him as she returns him to his cage, which consists of a perfect golden metal bent into an elegant dome, decorated with little shiny wire butterflies. I'm envious that Bexley managed to make it from the meager strands of wire she acquired.

Bexley is really obsessed with Stormy, and I've started to think the bird might be better off than most of us with the number of trinkets Bexley provides for him. Bexley's Stormy obsession has officially gotten to the annoying phase. The amount of time I have to spend with Bexley and sharing her room has been grating my nerves for days—that, and the constant underlying anxiety about my parents' health has made me irritable.

Ledger sits down on the bench across from me, tiny blue feathers peppering his telegrey T-shirt. Since Jess can't work at the Infirmary anymore, the two of them take turns with the sick. Ledger was a bit reluctant at first, but after we treated half the patients with sulfavirdoton, he relented. Violet reported that after Jess' flight, the Infirmary cracked down on staff regulations. She also informed us that she had heard no talk of the tunnels, meaning the other Mordolus members know nothing of them.

"Whatcha doing?" Ledger asks, glancing at my notebook.

"Writing," I say, nonchalantly.

"Cool. Writing about wh—whoa, what color are your eyes?" he asks.

"Blue?" I answer, absentmindedly blinking.

"Cool. Most people have brown. I do. Did you know only two percent of people have green eyes? That's like one in forty people. One in fifty, I think. Wait, do you think someone could have red eyes? Or maybe purple?" Ledger asks, looking at the table.

"I'm not sure. Reece has green eyes, I think," I say, dusting specks of blue glitter from my fingertips.

Ledger looks up at me. "So sorry, I got distracted. What were we talking about?" I simply shrug and hide the book under my arm. I don't really want to explain the doubtful plans I've been surmising.

"So whe–hey, have you seen Gabby?" Ledger asks.

"No, not since this morning," I reply.

"Do you like the Haven?"

I nod. "Yes, it's so much better than the Infirmary."

"I bet," he says. "I love it here—there are so many people, it's safe, and it's in the woods. I lived pretty much in the middle of nowhere, so it's homey to me in the forest."

"I can imagine," I say, thinking. "So, do you agree with all of Auxillia's beliefs?"

"Yes. When I first came, I didn't. I didn't believe in God. But Gabby and Jess and everyone told me about Jesus dying for our sins, ya know, the gospel. It took a while, but I came to believe. I realized what a miracle it was that I got better. God gave me another chance. So I'm giving it back," Ledger says with a smile. He glances behind me. "Oh, hey, Isaiah."

Isaiah sits down beside me with a bored expression. "Hey."

"What are you doing?" I ask casually.

"Nothing." Isaiah shrugs. "What are you doing?"

"I was talking to Ledger before you interrupted," I respond.

"I didn't interrupt! I literally just walked over here. But forgive me, Ele," Isaiah says sarcastically. "Hey, that's a cool blue pen. Can I have it?"

I snatch it off the table and shove it in the back pocket of my jean shorts. "No. It's mine, and it's going to stay mine. Why do you have to ask for things just to be annoying?"

Ledger looks at both of us. "What's up with you two?"

"We're siblings," Isaiah states plainly, but Ledger seems confused.

"You don't have siblings, do you?" I ask, taking off my headband and staring at it.

Ledger shakes his head. "No."

"You won't exactly understand then," Isaiah says.

I shoot him a reproachful look. "Rude."

"You're one to talk," he mumbles.

"Isaiah Ever Brooks, you are way ruder than me," I say, and Isaiah rolls his eyes.

"Eleanora Fawn Brooks," he says in a sing-songy voice. "At least I don't get lost in my own house."

"That only happened once, and I was really little!" I retort. "Well, at least I brush my hair."

Isaiah glares at me and instinctively touches his blond, unkempt hair that sticks out in every possible direction and is in vital need of a trim. "I do! It just doesn't usually look like it. I think I look fine. I'm not vain like you."

"I wasn't the one who got detention for stealing things from people," I mutter.

"You have to admit, Ele, it's a cool skill," Isaiah says, holding something up. He twirls my glittering, blue pen with a smirk. I absolutely hate it when Isaiah takes things from me, and he knows it. A nagging feeling burns in the pit of my stomach.

Seizing the pen from my brother, I open my mouth to rebuke him, but then glance at Ledger and suddenly remember he's been here the entire time. "I'm so sorry, Ledger. You see what we mean though."

"It's normal. We love each other, but we hate each other," Isaiah adds as if it's some awful medical condition.

Jess climbs up from the basement, sprints over to Zia and Gabby, who just walked in from outside, and starts talking to them in a serious tone, but I can't hear what she's saying.

Ledger follows my gaze then says immediately, "I've got to go." He dashes to the basement, ignoring my asking, "What's wrong?"

The only other time something like this happened occurred several days ago when two Auxillia members didn't come back on time. After a nerve-racking twenty-four hours, one of them returned, the girl Violet, informing us her counterpart Bentley had been captured. They work undercover, similarly to Jess, at the Infirmary. He'd been caught after stealing some of the cure to treat a six-year-old boy within the children's section, and Violet says he'd been taken to the Queen to be thrown in prison—or worse.

Don't think about that, Ele. If this occasion is anything important, Jess will inform us. I gather my writing instruments and return them to my backpack in our room.

Isaiah talks to Atticus in the kitchen, so I join them.

"Are you gonna join Auxillia?" Isaiah asks Atticus as I stand beside my brother.

"The Haven is safe," Atticus replies. "But I'm not interested in joining Auxillia."

"Atticus, do you believe in God?" I ask.

"No," Atticus says.

"Why?" Isaiah questions, tensely leaning against the counter. Isaiah is very serious and bold about his beliefs, and he's not afraid to jump into any argument to defend them.

"There's no proof for it. My aunt was a Christian. When my mom was dying, she told me if I prayed then God would save her. If God exists, He doesn't listen. If God is all good and created everything, why is there evil? I could never find any reasonable answers. Most evidence pointed away from God's existence, at least in the terms Christians believe. It seemed like Christians had to work really hard to find some answer to their beliefs. It just isn't plausible to me."

"Uh-huh," Isaiah says slowly. "Firstly, your aunt's a heretic. God doesn't work like that. God isn't just swayed by every word we pray. He already has a plan in place, but He listens to our prayers. Evil is a debatable topic, but I like to think about it like light and dark. Dark isn't a *thing*, it's the absence of light. Same with evil being the absence of holiness."

"It's not enough proof for me," Atticus says with a shrug, leaving to head outside.

"I'd love to talk more about this!" Isaiah calls after.

"Isaiah, I'm not sure the way to win people is by offending their aunts and forcing explanations," I say.

"I'm just trying to tell him the truth," Isaiah says, gripping the countertop.

I head back to the meeting room and walk over to the left corner where the table is set up with all our supplies for making raxoxin. Bottles, beakers, and vials containing the different liquids and powders fill half the table. A thin notebook that holds all the steps for creating the cure stands open against the burette. In the week we've been here at the Haven, we've made seven doses of the cure. We used it first to treat the people in the basement. Although, their recovery is slow and hard, and it seems the sicker the individual, the longer it takes to heal.

I sit up straight and take a deep breath, stretching out the ache in my back. After two hours, I've been staring too long at chemical measurements, so I extinguish the alcohol burner and pour the cure base into a vial and cap it.

I run to our room, exchange my flip-flops for a pair of ankle boots, and dash outside. There's a small shady portion of clear grass outside the girl's bedroom window that Atticus has deemed sufficiently hidden for us to visit. It's beside a wall of mountain laurels, and once I saw a deer grazing only a few feet away through the glass.

I walk through the thick grass, and scorching afternoon sun rays tingle against my skin. Variegated vines swirl all around the Haven walls and intertwine themselves around every possible surface. To no one's surprise, Bexley sits under the window, with Stormy's cage right next to her, talking to Graydon and Isaiah. She wears dark denim shorts and a pristine white T-shirt, accompanied by a pair of knee high gladiator sandals. I glance down at my cutoff jean shorts, faded blue T-shirt, and ankle boots I've been wearing since the Infirmary. Bexley is about the same size as Hadley, so they share clothes, but I'm too tall, and the only clothes I can wear are Hallston's, and she doesn't have much style, just practicality. I considered asking for new attire, but the only two people who go out to forage the province anymore are Hallston, which could be an offensive request, or Gabby, and I'm not asking a boy to locate me clothes. I'm simply doomed. *Eleanora, you need to get over yourself. You're being stupid. People are still dying, and you're worried about clothing!* One of the things that really gets to me is that Bexley just seems so flawless all the time. I mean, she always looks nice, she's kind to everyone *except me*, and I've rarely seen her do anything embarrassing, and if she does, she plays it off super well. I'm not perfect or anything. This morning while I was brushing my teeth, I got a little too ambitious and somehow stabbed myself in the eye with my toothbrush. I had to stay in the bathroom for an hour so no one would ask what was wrong with my eye and I had to tell them it was from a toothpaste assault. It was bad.

"It's so weird," Isaiah says as I walk up. "To be here and know so many people are still dying. Wrong, ya know? And there's nothing we can do about it."

"I know. I want to find my parents. At least everyone, except Marie, has their siblings," Bexley points out. Graydon looks down and nods.

I sit down on the grass between the two boys. We were confined inside for so long that now we spend a lot of time outside, usually just hanging out under the morning shade of the trees for as long as it lasts, then suffering through the afternoon heat.

"Oh, hey Eleanora, you followed us," Bexley observes with a fake, irritating smile, and I grit my teeth, returning it with one just as vexing.

"Yeah, well sometimes I'd like to spend time with my brother too. Crazy, I know," I say, blinking a few times. Bexley tosses her wavy, red hair and doesn't reply.

"I wonder if there's anything we can do about the people dying right now?" Graydon deliberately continues, probably noticing the growing tension. I'm pretty sure he accentuated the word 'dying' on purpose, and it brings me back to reality.

"Well, what I was going to say was we'll just have to keep making more of the cure or rat-oxen or whatever it's called," Isaiah says.

"It's raxoxin," Graydon interrupts.

"Yeah, that. And, hopefully, Jess will give us a better plan soon," Isaiah says.

"Oh, I really hope so," Bexley says.

I rip out a few blades of grass, overwhelmed with the feeling that we're wasting time. The prospect that I'm unable to do anything leaves me feeling helpless.

"I'm going to the garden," I murmur, hopping up to walk over to our little, meager plot of vegetables. I kneel and start to pull some of the numerous weeds growing around the edge of the tilled square. The only things growing are wilted radishes, bitter lettuce, and a few carrots. However, it's wonderful to have some extra way to support ourselves. Caring for it has given me something to do during these afternoons. I wonder what will occur when winter comes, and we are overcome with the cold winds and frosted grounds. Will the last remnants of life and hope for us wither like our last crops?

I sprint inside and, seeing Isaiah's phone and headphones sitting on the table, I grab them and head back outside. To prevent Isaiah from discovering I stole his phone, I wander into the woody section behind the Haven. There is a strong, thick oak tree growing a few hundred feet away from the building that I saw on our journey to the Haven.

I finally locate my tree: it's perfect, with low thick branches and sturdy limbs that my childhood taught me to recognize for good climbing. Shoving the phone in my pocket and putting the headphones around my neck, I start my ascent into the foliage. Once I find a nice spot, I sit on a branch, type in Isaiah's passcode which he doesn't know I know, and press play on my favorite rock playlist. I take a long, deep breath, block out my worries, and focus on the familiar emotions filling my heart. *It's going to work out for the better.*

Later, Isaiah, Marie, Reece, and I sit at the wooden table in the main room on the eve of a relaxed afternoon, enjoying the intermittent pattering of rain on the windows. Graydon is focused on organizing and cleaning the raxoxin-crafting-area, and Bexley helps Hadley make lunch since Marie's been teasing her about needing to improve her cooking skills ever since the pasta event. It was a pretty scarring meal, and even Isaiah jokingly advised her to go easy on the salt.

"Ele, why'd you play that?" Isaiah asks exasperatedly as I lay down a fourteen on top of his one.

"Don't judge me," I say as he gathers the cards and adds them to our stack. "I've been playing Rook longer than you have."

We always played Rook with extended family, and I learned to play before I was seven. My cousin and I always teamed up and played our grandparents, and we won nearly every time. Isaiah was too wild as a kid to play any card game, so he didn't play until he was eleven and became competitive and determined to beat me.

Isaiah shakes his head and plays another one, glowering at me from behind his cards. "If we lose, it's completely your fault. I've only lost twice in my whole Rook career. You're messing it up."

When it's Reece's turn, Marie looks around the room seriously. "Okay Reecey, think sunshine and my favorite shoes."

"Marie!" Isaiah says. "That's cheating!"

Marie shakes her head. "No, not really."

I stare at her and raise an eyebrow. "You *literally* just told him to play yellow."

She opens her mouth to reply, but Reece sets down a red card and cuts in. "Marie, stop cheating. It's fine guys. I don't even have yellow."

Despite Marie's rule-breaking, it's the first time she or Reece has ever played, and Isaiah and I win the game. Hadley and Bexley finish cooking just as I begin to put away the cards, and I'm amused to see it's the same infamous meal. Bexley smiles as she serves out the pasta dish made with canned vegetables and sets the plates out on the table. The rest of the day is so calm my mind wanders all the way outside the Haven, to and past the very Infirmary itself, and through the walls of Solstice Keep.

The night comes, and Marie sits cross-legged on the rug in the living area with her head propped on her hands, listening. For pajamas, she's wearing a pair of pink leggings and an oversized T-shirt that I believe was given to me, which explains why it's big since Marie is a very small person. Marie tends to 'borrow' things if she finds them laying around. Reece sits next to her, pretending not to be paying attention, turning his green notebook over and over. Graydon is across from them, reading aloud from a storybook. He's wonderful at reading out loud. When we were younger, he would even add unique voices for the characters, but he stopped when we got older.

"And Chalky the marmot never tried to make friends with Kona the coyote ever again," Graydon reads, closing the book. "The end."

"Um, whatcha doing?" I ask, walking over.

"A bedtime story!" Marie says excitedly, kicking her heels against the floor.

"Marie, aren't you a little old for bedtime stories?" I laugh. "Especially *Chalky the Marmot*? I'm pretty sure the last time I heard that one I was six."

Many of Willowmire's children have heard the stories of Chalky, an albino marmot with unrealistic digging abilities. He lives in a burrow next to Lake Michigan but often makes grand adventures to far away countries.

Marie gasps and wags her finger at me. "Ele, you are *never* too old for Chalky. Right, Graydon?"

"Sure Marie, it's a classic," he says lackadaisically, handing her the book and tiredly playing with the strings of his hoodie. "It's always riveting when he digs a tunnel and accidentally pops up four countries away."

"See Ele. He's like almost four years older than me, too," Marie remarks.

"It's called sarcasm, Marie," Reece says.

"Whatever. My parents always read me and Axly stories at night. Anyway, goodnight! I'm going to bed," Marie says, jumping up. It's only eight, but she likes to go to bed early, which enables her very energetic, premature rises in the mornings.

Marie pats Graydon and Reece on the heads then jumps on my back, nearly knocking me over. "Don't worry, Ele, I'll try not to wake you up if I have any nightmares about Kona chasing me. Hey, how 'bout a piggyback ride to bed?"

"Nope," I say, gently letting her drop to the floor. "I gave you one yesterday."

Tossing her shiny curls back from her face, Marie chuckles and runs off to our room, Chalky the Marmot under her arm, humming a song that sounds suspiciously like something from a Barbie movie.

Isaiah perches at the table, wearing a pair of headphones, and leafs through a Bible with an expression of hard concentration. I have to applaud my brother for his dedication, although it prompts me to wonder if he intentionally does it in an effort to one-up the rest of us in some aspect, which is something he would do. I'm a bit ashamed of my own neglect of my faith, and I'm still toying with my beliefs. I've never endeavored to personalize my family's beliefs or clarify my own until recently. I'm still torn, and I wonder if I'll ever find rest from my internal conflict.

"Where'd she even find that book?" I ask, sitting down on the couch. I love Marie, and she always finds a way to make things fun, but when she's gone things tend to relax.

"I don't know," Graydon says with a shrug. "She threw it at me and said I had to read to her."

"Marie's something else," I say, smiling. "She is only twelve though."

"Hey, what do you mean 'only twelve'?" Reece interjects at the prospect that I might have insinuated something bad about his age.

"Nothing. Just that she's younger," Graydon clarifies. "She's socially allowed to be extra."

I think back to when I was twelve, and it seems like forever ago, in a different, simpler world, yet it was truly only two years back. Everything's changed, but something inside me advocates that it will eventually be for the better.

40
GRAYDON: SAFE…OR NOT?

It's been ten days since our arrival at the Haven, and things are somewhat peaceful. Especially late when it's quiet. It's pretty cool that I get to have a sleepover with my best friend every night.

"What do you guys think about Atticus?" Isaiah asks randomly, sitting on his bed. "He hardly talks. Don't know much about him."

"He's weird, but I've decided he's not *as* sketchy," Reece says, leaning over the rail of the top bunk.

"He's kind of like you, Reece," Isaiah points out. "Quiet, suspicious, reserved…"

"Maybe." Reece shrugs. "I heard he's from Ravimere."

Ravimere has a bad rap for being a poor, crime-ridden province. It's dangerous, and kids at school said if you went there, you'd get mugged. I don't think it's all bad, but there's some validity to the stigma.

"Hey, I have a question," Reece says. "Why doesn't anyone talk about the fact that Ledger recovered from a fatal disease without raxoxin?"

"It's crazy. I want to know why. And how. And if there are others who had the same thing happen," Isaiah says with a groan. "I just want to know *why*. Why *everything*."

"Jess said he was only sick for a few weeks. They only gave him over-the-counter medicines. So, what's different?" I ask, laying a hand on the bunk bed.

"One clue is that he didn't get sick until he got to the Haven," Isaiah says.

"So it could be something about the Haven, or something's wrong with everywhere else," Reece says, drumming his fingers against the wall.

"But then there's Zia," I say. "She didn't get sick until the Haven either, and she definitely wasn't recovering even after two months. She would have surely died without the cure."

"You know what I noticed? I watched people in the Infirmary. I spent days in the check-in area scanning the death list. I saw people come in. I saw what they looked like. Nothing close to how they were a week or two later. They got so much worse, so quickly," Reece says.

"I mean, the care there sucks, but it's not that bad," Isaiah says, intensely staring at the gray ceiling.

Reece nods. "Something weird is going on."

"And if we can figure out what it is, maybe we'll be a step closer to saving our families," I say. "I wish I could ask my dad. I'm sure if I could talk out everything we've discovered, he'd have some solution."

"Same. My dad's a doctor, and he worked mostly with emergency situations, but he's dealt with this kind of stuff before," Reece says.

"When I was younger, I thought it would be so cool to be a doctor," Isaiah says then shudders. "But I can't do blood."

Reece looks up. "You know what I wanted to be?"

"What?" I ask.

"One of the people who changes the bulbs in streetlights," Reece says.

"That's odd," I say with a laugh.

Isaiah snorts. "Um, is it an actual job?"

"I dunno, but I figured someone had to. Then I could people-watch at the same time, but never have to speak to anyone," Reece says wistfully then peers at me. "What about you?"

"When I was really young, I wanted to be a tattoo artist. Until I realized they weren't the kind you put on with water," I admit. Both of them laugh at me.

"I already have a tattoo," Isaiah says, staring at the small, purple ink mark on his shoulder from the virus test.

"I got green," Reece says. "Thankfully."

"Mine keeps spreading and getting darker. You think they'll fade?" Isaiah asks.

"I'm not sure I'll live long enough to find out. I'll be lucky to make it to eighteen," Reece says with a defeated sigh.

Isaiah jolts up. "What do you think's gonna happen? You'll just kick the bucket one day?"

Reece shrugs. "Do you know how easy it is to die? And there are so many ways. You could get attacked by a dog, or go into anaphylaxis, get carbon monoxide poisoning…then, that's it."

"Those kinds of things don't happen fatally to most people," I say.

"I mean, it's true. God could just have it planned for you to die at any time. But still. You're twelve, Reece. Don't start planning for your death. It's really concerning," Isaiah says.

There's a loud knock on our door. "Can I come in?"

It's Ele. Isaiah groans. "Yeah, I guess."

Ele opens the door. She wears an oversized T-shirt and biker shorts and holds a toothbrush and toothpaste. Her fair eyebrows are low, and she frowns. "Can I use your sink? I need to brush my teeth, and Bexley's been in the shower for *forty-five minutes*. I'm just trying to go to bed."

I shrug. "Sure."

"Thanks," Ele says and saunters into our bathroom.

"Make it fast!" Isaiah calls after her.

Reece takes a pen and one of his notebooks from under his pillow and starts writing.

A few minutes later, Ele walks out of the bathroom. "Well, goodnight. And thanks."

She leaves, and Reece keeps writing for some time. Isaiah hums to himself and looks idly at his phone. I lay on my bed and trace the floor with my hand.

"It would be cool to have a sibling. I mean, I've gotten kind of used to having other humans around. It's strange because I don't really like people," Reece says randomly. "Graydon, do you ever wish you had siblings?"

I freeze. Isaiah shoots me an odd look then says lightly, "Of course he does. Just like sometimes I wish I was an only child."

"All the time, Reece," I say.

"I had three dogs for siblings. Daphne, Patch, and Rusty. Daphne only had two and a half legs, and Patch was missing both eyes. Rusty had complications from distemper. We had a cat for a while, but my mom was allergic. It was bad because she worked at a pet store. Our neighbors were cat-hoarders, so we just dumped ours in their backyard. They didn't notice. It was fun," Reece says quietly. "I guess all our pets are probably dead now."

"Well, maybe ones with no legs or eyes," Isaiah jokes, and Reece smiles a little. "Sometimes I wonder about extended family, friends, and people I met like once, but still it's just weird to think about them being…dead," Isaiah says, running his fingers across the cracks on his phone screen.

Reece rocks back and forth, and the bunk bed rattles. "Sometimes I feel like the Haven is the eye of the storm."

"Yeah," Isaiah says, finally putting down his phone. "Maybe it is. But I still have hope."

"It'll all be fine. We'll figure it out," I say. "Either way, we should probably stop thinking about these kinds of things at night, or we'll never fall asleep."

"Graydon's being a dad again," Isaiah teases, flopping back onto his pillow.

I roll my eyes. "Shut up."

"I'm tired," Isaiah says, glancing at the clock on the mostly empty bookshelf. "And it is nearly eleven."

"That's early," Reece whines. "But fine. My mom didn't like me to stay up late. She said it was a bad habit and would probably mess up my brain or something." He loudly jumps from the bed to turn off the light. I crawl into the bottom bunk, and Reece climbs back up the ladder to the top bunk.

Isaiah sits up abruptly. "Do you guys even know what the date is?"

"I…I honestly have no idea," I say. "Why didn't you check your phone?"

"The date's been blocked," Isaiah says.

"I think it's August twenty-ninth," Reece says. "There's a calendar downstairs in Hadley and Hallston's room."

"How do you know?" I ask.

"Marie," he replies. "She's the snoopiest person I've ever met."

"Yeah, well you're up there, too, Reece," Isaiah comments.

"No, I just pay attention to everything and eavesdrop. I learn just as much, and I'm not doing anything suspicious. You can find out so much about people by just listening" Reece mumbles. "I used to do it all the time at school."

"What, stalk people?" Isaiah asks. "Because that's creepy."

Reece sighs. "No, Isaiah, you're missing the point."

"Whatever," Isaiah says.

When the room's silent, I find a lot of things to think about. Mostly discomforting things. Maybe I can do some investigating tomorrow. Maybe if I can get Jess or Ledger to take me down to the basement, I'll unearth more clues.

The clock reads two thirteen in the morning. The room is quiet, and moonlight that streams in from behind the blue curtains casts shadows on every surface. Isaiah is still asleep across from me. Our bunk bed is super rickety, so I know every time Reece moves, and it's been still. I detect more voices from behind the door. As quietly as possible, I climb out of bed. I trip over one of Reece's notebooks then cross the room to the door and listen.

"When did it happen?" someone asks. Might be Hallston, but it's hard to tell.

"This morning. Everyone was out here so nothing could be done," says another vaguely familiar voice. There are footsteps, and someone cries softly.

"So we're not telling them?" Atticus says.

"They don't need to be burdened any more with these things. It's why we insist they stay up here," Jess says, her voice wavering.

Atticus agrees. At this point, my curiosity and concern rise, so I open the door enough to peek out.

In the meeting room, the lights are out except for the kitchen's pale yellow overhead fixture. I eventually identify Jess and Atticus, and I surmise, Gabby, Zia, Hallston, Hadley, and Ledger. All I can hear is Zia still crying. The door outside opens. I shut the bedroom door and wait so I'm not seen by someone entering. By the time it's two twenty-nine, it's completely silent and I haven't uncovered any more info, so I slowly push open the door. Someone sits at one of the barstools in the kitchen.

"What are you doing out here?" Atticus asks. *As if he isn't hiding something.*

"What's going on?" I say, walking over. I cross my arms as a chill rips across my bare skin. Atticus wears his usual, plain, dark clothes. He must have at least ten pairs of black jeans.

"Nothing," Atticus replies, staring at his glass of water as I sit at another stool. "Everything's fine."

"Sure," I say sarcastically. "I heard all that about hiding whatever from us and that something happened."

He sighs. "I don't want you to tell the others."

I nod quickly. "Deal."

"There's been a tragedy," Atticus says. He won't look at me.

"What do you mean?" I ask uneasily.

He shifts away. "Someone died today."

Inside my heart, a painful sensation of shock grows. Swords of reality murder the sense of security I've built up at the Haven. "Here?"

Atticus nods.

"How? Who was it?" I ask, fighting to keep my voice level.

"It was a little girl; she was sick. It was the Virus," Atticus says. There was a younger girl the one time Jess allowed us to visit the basement. Other than that occasion, all the other guests have remained quarantined and will until we're certain the raxoxin has been successful. A tidal wave of guilt crashes in my chest.

"That doesn't make sense! How? Jess said they were getting better! We've been making more of the cure! We—" I start.

"This is why we didn't want to tell you! That girl had been on the verge of death for weeks. Even with the cure, she didn't have a chance. Raxoxin isn't a magical antidote that can heal everything. Some of them are too far gone," Atticus says. I know that it's the truth, but I don't want to accept that we might end up finding some of our family in that state.

"But what about Bexley? She was pretty sick too. We gave her the antidote and immediately—"

"I'm not sure it did. It's possible she was hoping so much that it would work, she convinced herself it had before anything actually happened. Luckily, she recovered, but it probably wasn't as instantly effective as you thought. That's why I was skeptical about it," he says. Horror simmers inside me.

"Why are you keeping it a secret?" I ask quietly, gently kicking the leg of my seat.

"They're kids. So are you, but you asked," Atticus says, gently stroking his grown-out beard. "You're older, anyway. It doesn't change anything if the others know or not. We've taken care of it."

We need to start making raxoxin faster to build up a supply and plan to rescue our parents. Like, now.

"We are going to start thinking of ways to escape the province and to rescue everyone, so don't worry about that," Atticus says like he knows what I'm thinking. "Just don't tell the others. When things are unclear, guilt and fear can become a monster."

That hits me painfully, and I finally nod.

"You should go back to bed," Atticus says, pushing my barstool away from the counter with his foot.

"Okay," I agree, realizing it's still super early in the morning. I'm wide awake now.

I walk back to our room, my head spinning with a whirlwind of questions. *Is the sulfavirdoton going to work? Will we ever win? Can we just give up?*

I open the door, rereading the Bible verse posted on the wall outside our room; *For God alone my soul waits in silence; from him comes my salvation. He alone is my rock and my salvation, my fortress; I shall not be greatly shaken. (Psalm 62:1-2).*

We need salvation right now. We really do. I step inside.

I pick up Reece's notebook, so I don't stumble again and place it on the nightstand before climbing into bed. *But if I give up, they die. My parents die.* And I'm not going to let that happen.

"What's wrong with everyone today?" Ele asks at breakfast. Ledger hasn't even come up from the basement today. Gabby went down there, too. Zia looks like a sad puppy as she sweeps the floor, hiding behind her long, black hair.

"I don't know. They are probably overwhelmed about the plan," I say nonchalantly, tracing the grain of the oakwood table.

"What plan?" Isaiah asks, looking up from his plate. I wonder if he's also trying to identify what might have been combined to create this strange, homogeneous meal. Thankfully, Hadley has a talent with spices or else everything would just taste like a metal can. The texture's still a little off-putting. I only take a few bites before opting for a piece of fresh bread sitting at the center of the table, which is sweet and chocolaty with hints of cinnamon.

"Yeah, what are you talking about?" Ele asks, pushing aside her empty bowl and taking a slice of bread as well.

"To escape the province and get everyone out of the Infirmary," I say matter-of-factly.

"Really?" Marie says, springing from the bench. "That's great!"

"Why do you know?" Reece asks suspiciously, setting down an empty glass.

I shrug. "Overheard it last night."

I don't tell them about what *caused* the decision. I know it will make everyone feel better to know something good is happening.

"Were they gonna tell us?" Reece asks, annoyed. "Or just wait until the last minute? I knew the people here were sketchy." He shoots Zia a judging look.

"Probably eventually. Maybe there's a reason they haven't told yet. But hey, now you know," I say. That stifles the conversation, and everyone seems more content now. Maybe they'll lay off asking any more questions, too.

Ele stares thoughtfully at the wall for a few seconds. "So do you think King Cyrus' death had anything to do with Morzanna?"

"Honestly, I've wondered. I mean, I wouldn't put it past her," Isaiah comments.

"We know she created the Virus and withheld the cure. Oh, and let's not go there with the Infirmary. She's obviously a murderer," Bexley adds, twirling her charm bracelet. "If she wanted to be queen, she could just kill her father and be done with it."

"Well, how do we get rid of her then?" Ele asks abruptly.

"We can't just get rid of her, Eleanora," Bexley says, picking up her half-constructed earrings she's crafting from wire. They're swirling hearts, beaded with red glass orbs and wrapped in copper strands.

"Can you just call me Ele?"

"Okay," Bexley says, twisting the metal strands. She glances at Ele with a smile. "*Eleanora.*"

"Good grief," Marie says.

Ele grits her teeth and crosses her arms. "I really don't care."

"Can we get back to the conversation?" Isaiah asks annoyedly. "No one else really knows what we know that Morzanna has committed. Even if they did, I'm not sure the people can do anything. Someone with authority would have to deal with it."

"Who? King Alaric?" I say sarcastically. King Alaric is the ruler of Erigate, our closest neighboring country, formed from the lower peninsula. Willowmire has nearly entered war with Erigate over the ownership of land and the Great Lakes and whether we should be aligned.

"Yeah, right," Reece mumbles. "I mean, he dislikes us enough he might be perfectly fine with getting rid of Morzanna. Right before he takes over Willowmire, orders Erigate's military to slaughter half of us, then banishes everyone else to Infrethia.

"What about tyrannicide?" Marie suggests excitedly. "I learned that word in history!"

"No! We can't just murder Morzanna," I protest. "Imagine what would happen to Willowmire if we had no ruler. It would be anarchy."

"Yeah," Isaiah agrees. "But I haven't heard that King Alaric is doing anything about the Virus yet. Maybe he just doesn't want it to spread to Erigate, which I get. When we tell everyone about the cure and the Queen, they probably won't even believe us. It'll be the scandal of the century. I don't know what or who will take over Willowmire. It won't be Morzanna. Chances are if she's gone, Erigate will easily take over."

"We can't just go to Alaric and say, 'Hey, the Queenie is a mass murderer, and we need you to dethrone her for us real quick but not attack us'," Marie says.

"I just wish we could know what's going on outside of Senneforte," Ele voices with a sigh. "Why isn't someone coming to help Willowmire?"

"We haven't heard anything from the outside since like…ever since the Virus. It's in Ellismark, we don't know anything about Ravimere, Valerrow, Lossaree, or anywhere in Erigate," I say.

"Unless Ellismark went into lockdown too, it's safe to assume the Virus has made it to the other provinces in Willowmire," Bexley says, trimming off the last bits of excess wire.

"What about the delegates?" Reece asks.

"I don't know. Delegate Hettler is trying, but without the other votes, she can't do anything. The Mordolus hasn't touched her yet, but she's unable to communicate outside Senneforte either. The other delegates have been silent for months. I'm scared Morzanna's going to find a way to stop Hettler sooner or later," I say.

"It wouldn't be unlikely that Morzanna released the Maraloxis Virus in the other provinces, and they're as locked in as we are," Bexley says. "If alliance was possible, the delegates would have surely come together and stopped her already."

"Well, we're gonna starve soon if we don't get out of here," Isaiah says.

"Yes, that's true. The garden isn't yielding much, and there's no reliability in what can be found in the province," Ele says.

"What about hunting or trapping?" I say.

"Good idea. Is there anything we could catch?" Isaiah asks.

I tilt my head. "Well, maybe, but I know we could catch mice at least—"

"Ew, ew, ew! Please do not even suggest that!" Bexley squeals, recoiling from the table.

"Sometimes it's what you can find or starvation," I say with a shrug.

"I would eat a mouse!" Marie says with a big grin. "Would you eat a mouse, Reecey?"

"It wouldn't be my first choice," he responds quietly.

"I think we've gotten a bit off topic. We have a time-sensitive problem to discuss here," Ele says. "Morzanna has our families trapped."

"Well, you know, there are adults here. You are kids. You don't have to deal with all this alone," Jess says, walking over.

"A lot would be different without us. We want to help," I say.

"Oh, and besides, you're not that much older," Bexley says.

"I'm twenty-four. A little time can make a significant difference depending on the circumstances," Jess says, smiling and laying a hand on the table.

"Yeah, see Isaiah, it does matter that I'm a year older than you," Ele says.

Isaiah rolls his eyes. "Eleven months and twenty-three days. Not a year," he retorts.

"You round up. Of course, I would know that because I'm older," Ele teases.

"Doesn't matter if you're immature," Isaiah snaps back.

Ele gasps. "Excuse me?"

"I'm with Isaiah; this whole fight is kind of immature," Bexley interjects. Seriously, if looks could kill, Bexley would be six feet under from Ele's deathly glare. Isaiah looks taken aback, too.

"Getting involved in a sibling conflict. Good luck with that," I comment to Bexley.

"Well, at least I don't spend ninety percent of my time talking to a stupid bird!" Ele explodes.

"Sad you're comparing caring for an innocent, helpless creature with torturing your brother," Bexley says.

"I am not!" Ele replies.

"Will you two stop? You're being so annoying," Isaiah groans.

"I'm waiting for Eleanora to finally grow up," Bexley answers. Ele stays silent, slaps her palms on the wooden table, pushes herself up, and stomps off to their room.

"See, you can't even finish a conversation without having to leave because you're so petty," Bexley taunts. She doesn't seem perturbed by the shocked looks on everyone's faces.

"At least I'm mature enough to stop an argument this ridiculous," Ele says. Bexley purses her lips, then gets up and walks off in the other direction, chagrined.

"What was *that*?" I ask, turning back to Isaiah.

"I honestly don't know." He looks as stunned as me.

Neither of the girls return. Despite what Atticus said, yesterday's events leave me inclined to focus on raxoxin this afternoon.

"No, Marie!" Reece says from across the room. "We are not doing that!"

"You're SO boring! It'll be great! Come on, Reecey-boy," Marie says, laughing as the two of them run off to the kitchen. Most of their conversations consist of Marie coming up with a screwball idea, and Reece refusing until Marie annoys him enough and he decides it'll be fun.

I pour three milliliters of chloroquine into an oseltamivir and phosphate mixture over the alcohol burner. A few minutes pass before it begins to simmer, and I stir so it doesn't burn, watching the thermometer closely. Bexley walks over to me.

"Hey," I say. "What's up?"

"I need you to go get Stormy from my room," she says with an eye roll.

"Why can't you?" I ask, organizing the vials on the rack.

"You know why," Bexley says. "I don't want to talk to her…or even see her."

"Why didn't you ask Marie?"

"I did. She said I was being dumb and needed to get over it because we're all stuck here together and on and on," Bexley says with a wave of her hand.

I agree with Marie. Bexley twirls her bracelet, fingering its three charms. One is a fiery copper wire sun. The next is a silver rose, and the last one is a golden moon.

"What's with the bracelet?" I finally ask.

Bexley looks down at it. "Oh, everyone in the Kamryn family has one. Well, we also give them to good friends. Each person has their own special charm. Mine is the sun," she points to it, holding up her wrist. "And this one is my grandma's," she points to the rose. "And my aunt," she gestures to the moon. "When someone dies, each person adds a charm to theirs, whoever's it is. It's weird, I know. The person who takes the bracelet off the person's wrist gets the original, and everyone else gets one made. Like I said, it's a family thing." Bexley puts her arm down. "I don't have any originals, thank goodness."

"That's really cool," I say. *In a sad and kind of morbid way.*

Bexley gets back to the point. "Soooo, will you get Stormy for me?"

"Fine," I relent. I cap the bottle and walk to the kitchen to put it in the freezer. It's nice to pause mid-process and take a break. The Haven has a generator, so we have power, and a well that supplies clean water.

When I open the door to the girls' room, Ele sits on her bed reading a book. This is only the second time I've been in their room. Marie thinks it's fun to be annoying and enforce the 'no boys allowed' rule. Apparently, it's one sided because multiple times I've caught her snooping in our room.

"Oh hey, Gray," Ele says, looking up. The butterfly blanket my mom gave her is folded at the end of the bed.

"Hi," I say rigidly.

"Whatcha doing?" she asks, as I walk over to the nightstand where Stormy's cage is placed. I reminisce about the day Bexley and I found him—the day we found the final ingredient for the cure.

"Getting Stormy for Bexley," I say.

"Come on, you're ruining my plan." Ele smiles evilly and closes her book, an old copy of *Anne of Green Gables*. "See, I'm helping Bexley with her bird addiction. I think she has an idol problem."

"Don't hate the bird because you're mad at Bexley."

Ele shakes her head. "I'm not. If anything, I feel bad for him. Poor birdie has to be around Miss 'I'm perfect and I guess that means being a brat'."

"Ele."

"I'm sorry, but honestly, she's getting soooo annoying," Ele says seriously.

"In case you forgot, there's a fatal virus going around, and our families are still stuck in the Infirmary dying," I say.

"You're right." Ele sighs. "I know I'm being dumb."

"I understand that you don't like her, but this is a really insignificant issue," I say.

"You're right. I'm really sorry. I don't know what's wrong with me. I'm being horrible," Ele confesses.

"You guys were fine before we got here. I've never seen Bexley be mean to anyone else," I say, staring out the window at the robins scampering through the English ivy.

"She annoys me so much, and I don't know why. It's like she's always trying to replace me. We just don't get along." Ele sighs, defeated, ripping tiny pieces off the frayed spine of her book. "I can't imagine being friends with her."

"You can be friends with anyone," I say after a long semi-awkward silence. "You just have to consider what real friendship is. You shouldn't pick friends by choosing which people you like best, or who can help you, or who will be easy to get along with. You find real friendships by looking at everyone and asking yourself how you can serve them. It's about sacrifice. Not everyone will end up as your best friend, but at least you've been an example for them. There are still going to be hard people. We shouldn't just shut them out or return their negativity. Maybe you won't be friends, but at least you've done what's right. People can change. I'm not so great a friend at times, but I think we all should try."

Ele doesn't respond.

I pick up Stormy's cage from the table and walk toward the door. "Come with me."

"Fine." Ele tosses the book onto the windowsill. "And thanks for the pep talk. I feel a lot less like I want to murder her now."

I smile. "That's good. And you're welcome."

The two of us step out of the room.

"HEY!" Marie comes bounding over. She slaps my arm and scowls. "Bad. No boys in our room. It's illegal."

"Sorry," I say.

"Now you're indebitted to me," Marie says with a grin.

I stare at her. "Sorry—I'm what?"

"He is not, and it's in-*debted*, Marie," Ele says.

"Whatever," Marie says. "He owes me. And you know what that means?" She points at Graydon, pumping her other fist and beaming. "Chalky every night for the next week! Haha!"

"Marie, you're special, you know?" Ele says, laughing.

"Yes, yes, I'm wonderful," Marie says, bowing before cartwheeling away with a maniacal laugh.

Ele shakes her head. "She's wearing my shorts again."

Bexley sits in the corner of the room, working on something else with wire strands. Looking across the room, Ele groans. She takes an enormous breath, snatches the bird cage from me and marches over to Bexley. She holds out the cage rigidly.

"I am sorry," Ele says tensely. Bexley stares at her. The second Bexley reaches for the cage, Ele basically drops it and leaves before Bexley can reply.

I shake my head and return to the corner table. When Atticus enters, he gives me a look. I guess he noticed I doubled the amount of time I spend working on the sulfavirdoton. I retrieve the bottle from the freezer when Ledger emerges from the basement.

I run to the table and take the vials from the rack. "Ledger?"

"Hey, Graydon!" he says. "Whoa, you finished all that?"

I nod, handing him the three new vials of raxoxin completed today. I thought that the more cure we have stocked up, the less stressed Ledger will be. And then maybe he'll agree.

"Thanks!" he says excitedly. "I don't know what would have happened without you guys here! Actually, I do. I don't want to think about it though."

"Yeah," I say, taking a deep breath. "Ledger, can you take me downstairs?"

Our visits to the basement are very limited. As in I've only been down there once before, just to peer in the door. It's mainly to prevent the spread of the Maraloxis Virus, but I'm not sure it matters. We should be safe after being cured, but this virus isn't typical. We can't take unnecessary risks. We may still be susceptible to it. But I need to know the state of what's happening downstairs.

"Well, you know—" Ledger starts.

"Yeah, but I really need to. I want to see the others," I interrupt.

"Alright, fine," he agrees.

As we descend the stairs, dread sinks in like a heavy, thick fog. Silently, Ledger leads me through the dim stairway and to the last room on the hall. I count four other doors before it.

"Try to be quiet while we're here," Ledger says as he hands me a facemask to put on. "Some people's recovery is hard."

Ledger pushes open the door. A sick feeling rolls in my stomach. *Someone died here yesterday.*

The wide room is weirdly still. There's a morgue-like icy silence. Three metal dividers separate the four beds. *There shouldn't be an empty bed.*

In the single-bed division next to the wall is a lady who seems about my parents' age. A book lays open on her lap, but she's fast asleep. In the next divider is a middle-aged guy with balding, gray-speckled hair. Both are pale and sleeping, so they're still pretty sick. Two silent, brown eyes stare at me from the last bed. Pained eyes. I smile as Ledger leads me closer to the old woman.

"Hey, Ms. Waller," Ledger whispers, prompting me closer. "This is Graydon."

"Hi," I say, vaguely recalling seeing her a week ago.

"He's one of the kids who made the cure," Ledger explains, kneeling next to the bed. Ms. Waller just stares at me. She reaches out a shaking hand, gesturing me closer.

A sweet smile spreads across her dark, wrinkled face. "I remember. Thank you." Her voice is quiet and hoarse.

Through a rush of intrusive thoughts, I nod. "You're welcome, Ms. Waller."

Why couldn't I have made the cure sooner? I glance across the room to the empty bed. *That little girl could have lived.*

"Are you feeling alright?" Ledger asks Ms. Waller.

I walk across the room and run my fingers over the cold sheets of the single, lonely bed. *That girl is dead from the Maraloxis Virus.* I try to take a deep breath, but it gets caught in my lungs. *Someone's dead because of me. Again.*

"Graydon?" Ledger asks. I spin around. "What are you doing?"

"Nothing," I say with a tense shrug, pushing away the emotion building inside me before it gets out of control.

"Maybe we should leave," Ledger suggests.

I don't argue and force myself to say goodbye to Ms. Waller. I take one last glance at the empty bed and draw a shaky breath.

"Whose room is that?" I ask as we walk down the hallway, gesturing to one of the doors and ripping off my mask so I can breathe again.

"Hadley and Hallston's. And that one's Jess, Violet, and Zia's," Ledger says, pointing. "And that's Gabby, Bentley, Atticus, and my room."

"I didn't know you guys all shared a room," I say. The thought of Atticus and Ledger sharing a room is funny.

"Yeah," Ledger says.

Jess is talking to Gabby and Zia in the kitchen when we get to the top of the stairs. Gabby and Zia spend a lot of time here at the Haven. Zia is still recovering from the Virus, but the treatment is giving her more energy every day.

"Jess, we can't leave the province. But we've exhausted almost all the places to find food and supplies," Zia says worriedly. "Winter is coming and what little we're harvesting from the garden will be gone."

"I know. I can talk to our leader and see if there's any way she can help us. We just have to keep looking," Jess says.

Gabby runs a hand through his black hair and slaps the other on the counter frustratedly. "But we aren't finding anything."

"We can't leave the province. We have no other choice," Jess says quietly. "We have to make it work and pray."

Bexley and Isaiah are talking on the other side of the room. I told Isaiah how I was going to ask Ledger to take me to the basement. He shoots me a smile. I return it and walk to the door. I step outside into the sun, but I don't really feel it. Maple trees line the front side of the Haven, choked out by tons of wisteria blooms. What's the point when I can't fix the things that are wrong? Life is just a cyclic whirlwind of pain and failure. I walk to the edge of the woods and stare into the vast, shady trees. Years ago, I memorized verses in Sunday school. I'm honestly shocked that one resurfaces now.

If I say, "Surely the darkness shall cover me, and the light about me be night," even the darkness is not dark to you; the night is bright as the day, for darkness is as light with you. (Psalm 139:11-12).

I take a deep breath and walk back to the Haven. Maybe everything can be okay.

41
REECE: THE BEST WE CAN DO

It's been over two weeks since we arrived at the Haven, and time's gone fast. Finally, the entire Haven is Virus-free and recovered. Two of the three other guests decided to leave the Haven and set out on their own, but the one lady stayed. Ms. Miranda seemed sketchy at first but turns out she has three kids in the Infirmary and wants to try to free them by helping us. She took up the position of spy, returning every few days with news on what's happening outside the Haven. I'm always anxious about what she'll tell us, but so far there hasn't been much.

Everything about the Queen has been quiet, but lately I've heard talk about forming a scheme. A few nights ago, I overheard Isaiah and Graydon whispering about it in our room. They thought I was asleep, but I'm a seasoned eavesdropper.

"It's been two weeks, and we're safe from the Virus. We're just waiting around! We need to do something! People are dying. We need to make a plan to rescue them," Isaiah whispers.

"I know. But I told you—they said they were!" Graydon says.

"Well, they're taking too long. Tomorrow, I'm talking to Jess about it. If they aren't planning anything soon, I'm going to," Isaiah announces.

I don't like to talk to people about feelings, but one day Hadley asked me, and I admitted how scared I've been. I'm sure she wasn't shocked because no matter how hard I try to hide it, everyone knows I'm a nervous wreck.

"The biggest battle of life is not out there, in the Infirmary, or within Solstice Keep. The hardest battle is, and always will be, here," Hadley told me, laying a hand on her heart. "Sin, despair, and fear will always war inside us. It's a hard enough conflict to keep us fighting for our entire lives. We must trust that God will protect us from the curse of sin and pray that He'll save us from the battles outside ourselves as well."

"I feel like every part of me is screaming something different," I painfully admitted. Her answer keeps running through my head:

"The mind will always want what's safest for itself, and the heart will always want what's most satisfying to its feelings. But the Holy Spirit can show us what's best for the soul, which is often contrary to what the flesh desires," Hadley replied. "We always have hope that through Christ, no matter how much we fail, a King intercedes for us."

The other members of Auxillia spend a lot of time away, and I've noticed that they aren't bringing back any supplies.

I keep track of all the happenings in my notebooks. I like the corner of the meeting room between the metal storage shelf and doorway for writing, and that's where I am right now. I'd rather write my problems down than talk to someone about them.

Marie comes and sits near me, trying to read what I'm writing. I lean away so she can't. She ties her curly hair into a ponytail and kicks her yellow high-tops against the floor. When I don't pay attention to her, she slides on her stomach into the empty bottom shelf and stares at me.

"Can I help you?" I finally ask.

"When's your birthday?" she asks.

"February," I say.

"Yes!" Marie says to herself, pumping her fist and nearly hitting her head on the second metal rack. "That means I'm the youngest kid in the whole entire Haven! Ya see, my birthday is in May. May seventeenth."

"What does any of that have to do with anything?" I ask, signing my name at the bottom of the page beside the date, 8/30/2038. I put *Reece R. Ashford*. My middle name is Raven, but I don't really like it that much because it sounds like a girl's name. Reece is already a boy-girl name, and people get confused.

"Being the youngest, I get special privileges. I get to be annoying. And everyone has to be nice to me," Marie explains excitedly, rolling off the shelf onto the floor in front of me.

I roll my eyes. "Yeah? Well, what about respecting your elders?"

"What are you writing?" Marie asks, ignoring my question.

"Random things," I say.

Marie makes a weird face. "Why?"

"Because." I shrug. "I like to."

I've always liked writing and used to create stories when I was younger about my family as animals in an alternate dimension. I like journaling and poetry more now. In our room in the Infirmary, I wrote all over the walls, which was even more fun because the nurses and guards hated it.

"Can I see?" Marie asks, reaching for the book, but I shut it.

"No," I say.

"Come on, Reecey," Marie pleads. "Please?" I shake my head and clutch the book to my chest, staring down at the green cover. Green's my favorite color, so I was thrilled when I found this on the bookshelf in the living area. I deliberately back away from her.

A door slams down in the basement, and Jess marches up the stairs. Her black hair separates in two braids like it always was at the Infirmary, and a remnant of the seriousness returns to her face.

"What's she doing?" I mumble to myself.

"Let's go see!" Marie says, jumping up. She snatches my book, sets it down on the metal shelf, and yanks my hand.

"Ew, don't touch me," I say automatically, shaking her off.

"Get over it and come on!" Marie calls, already halfway across the room.

Jess gathers everyone for our first official meeting. Everyone's here; all Auxillia, including that new lady, our whole group, and Atticus.

"It seems that not many people are left in the province that haven't been taken to the Infirmary. At the rate people were taken there, knowing some fled Senneforte, and the fact we haven't found anyone in weeks, I'd assume we're all that's left in the province," Jess says as we all sit around the big table.

"Yes, except Delegate Hettler's allies," Atticus says.

"Of course," Jess says. "Still, there are few of us remaining."

A hollow, anxious feeling crawls inside me. I wonder what happened to those people who got the cure and left the Haven.

"What do we need to do?" Hadley asks.

"We need to figure out a way to get out of the province. Now that we have a supply of raxoxin, we need to find somewhere we can create it quickly and where there are more people to help us. And for us to help," Ledger says quickly.

"But how? And what about everyone still here in the Infirmary?" Hallston asks.

"Out of all the people there, I'm sure someone can help us figure a way out," Isaiah suggests. "Maybe we could distract the Mordolus, or disable the wall's defenses, or dig a tunnel underneath or something. Our best bet is to see what we have to work with."

"So, we free as many people as we can from the Infirmary, escape the province, then give them the cure. We can work on giving it to everyone else after that," Marie says.

"That could be a lot of people," Gabby reminds us. "The Virus could have spread to all of Willowmire by now."

"Or we could just escape the province and figure out the Infirmary thing later," Marie suggests in a way that makes me think that's her preferred idea.

"No! We can't just leave our families trapped," Graydon protests.

"Oh, I guess the main thing we need to decide now is how we'll get everyone out of the Infirmary," Bexley says, fiddling with her charm bracelet. Her lovely, pink smile seems misplaced in her round, pale complexion. Her blue vibrant eyes and light red-toned eyelashes strike me. "And we can figure out how to escape the province later."

"That might be the only feasible solution," Zia says quietly. She doesn't wear a mask anymore and moved in with the other girls so Ms. Miranda could have her room.

"We could use the tunnels to get in," I mumble.

"Yeah, maybe, but it would seem odd if suddenly there were strange people in the Infirmary, all coming from a specific hall that's supposed to be off limits. They might, or totally would, notice," Graydon points out. Heat spreads across my face.

"What if we just get caught?" Ms. Miranda asks. Her shoulder length brown hair is striped with gray.

"Then we can escape through the tunnels," Ele mutters, thinking.

"So, you think we could safely use them again?" Bexley asks.

"Nothing's safe anymore. But if we don't try, we don't have a chance," Isaiah says.

"Most of us could pretend to get caught. It's unlikely they'll catch on, but if they do, we'll just have to do our best to return safely," Jess says, and everyone seems surprised at how many risks she's willing to take.

"Won't they test us and find out we don't have the Virus? We wouldn't be able to get in, and they would discover we are the ones who stole the cure since everyone else is sick," Graydon says.

"I don't think they even test anymore. We can fake the marks," Hadley says softly, referring to the tiny tattoos they give people when they're tested. Hadley's like everyone's mother. She always seems super interested when someone speaks. She makes me feel like I could tell or ask her anything. I like Hadley; everyone does. "I think that even if they do a test, they'd still take us inside. If they don't suspect the cure, they might bring us inside to ensure our infection," she finishes.

"It'll be risky," Ledger says.

"It's the best we can do," Atticus says.

After the evening meeting, we hang out in our room with the addition of Ele. Marie already went to bed, and I'm pretty sure Bexley's taking another endless shower. We just need a minute to chill and not think about all the not great things going on right now. I sit on the floor, listening to their memories of times before the Virus.

"Remember, it was you, Graydon, Olivia, and me," Ele says to Isaiah. The two of them lounge on Isaiah's bed.

"Yeah," Isaiah says. "Olivia said I was an idiot for trying."

"We all thought it, but Ele and I aren't as straightforward as Olivia," Graydon says, chewing on the strings of his hoodie.

"Okay, as a kid, it seemed like an amazing idea, especially since you guys advised me not to," Isaiah says, putting his phone on the charger. "About five minutes later though, jumping out of the tree into the pool didn't seem like my best plan."

"You got a cut by a branch and freaked, remember?" Graydon says.

"Yeah, then nearly drowned," Isaiah says.

"Graydon had to save you because Olivia and I were laughing too much," Ele recalls then jokingly adds, "I've always been a good sister, haven't I?"

"You did that, Isaiah?" I ask. Isaiah does some dumb things even now. He can be a showoff at times. Most times, actually.

"Yeah," he replies, shaking his head.

"Uh-huh, and we've been acting like it was when he was little, but it was two summers ago," Ele adds. "Right before Olivia moved to Ellismark."

"Who's Olivia?" I ask.

"She was a friend from church," Ele says.

"Hey, Isaiah, wasn't that the same summer you decided to cut your own hair?" Graydon asks, laughing.

"Okay," Isaiah says, putting up his hands. "I was young."

"Someday, we'll show you pictures, Reece," Graydon says.

"Hey, speaking of haircuts," Ele says, side-eyeing Isaiah. "It's time to cut that mane."

"That's rude," Isaiah says. The truth is, he really does need one, and it probably wouldn't hurt Graydon or me, either.

"Sorry if you're offended, but I'm just looking out for you," Ele defends. "Hadley could do it. She trimmed mine," she suggests, pointedly tugging on a strand of hair.

"Didn't notice," Isaiah says with a shrug.

"I know," Ele replies sourly.

Isaiah rolls his eyes dramatically. "Well *sorry*. Wow, I think your hair, that you cut a meaningless amount from, looks great," he declares. "And I'll talk to Hadley tomorrow, to appease you."

"Thank you," Ele says, hugging him. Isaiah responds by telling her to get off. "Remember when you and Graydon blew up the backyard with some of Mr. Madison's chemicals?"

"That happened more than once," Graydon says.

"The good old days," Isaiah says wistfully. "Let's share some of Ele's past?"

"Sure," Graydon says, grinning. "Like how many times she got in trouble at school for being mean and violent."

"What'd she do?" I ask, surprised. Ele doesn't seem like a scary person, and I just assumed she was alright because she's Isaiah's sister.

"Attacking, biting, hitting, hair-pulling, screaming," Isaiah lists off. "Not gonna lie, everyone was afraid of her. And I had to live with Senneforte Elementary's monster."

"Thank goodness she grew out of her mean phase," Graydon says then whispers jokingly, "Mostly, at least." This comment earns him a pillow to the head.

"Did you ever do anything stupid or crazy?" Isaiah asks me.

I stare at the wall and shrug. "Well, I became friends with you, and I guess that could fall into either category," I deadpan. Isaiah pretends to be offended, and Ele and Graydon laugh.

"Like I said earlier, I only had dogs to hang out with and barely survived private school. I didn't have many opportunities," I say with a shrug. "Well, there was this one time when we were at a lake house with my whole family, and I got fed up with my cousin Celeste, so I put salt in her drink." I shake my head. "But then she punched me."

"That's unfortunate," Ele says.

"My mom got really mad, so she said I could push Celeste into the lake," I say. "It was pretty much the highlight of my childhood."

"Your mom sounds awesome," Isaiah says.

I take a long, deep breath, thinking. "She was. What do you miss most about life before everything?"

"Easy," Ele says, braiding a section of hair and letting it fall out again. "Family: time with my parents, long conversations with Mom, and Dad helping me with homework. I also miss getting to go to work with my dad at Kindell's on the weekends. That's the department store he manages."

"I miss the freedom we had," Isaiah says. "But I try not to miss too much. I want to be content with life now."

"That's hard," I say.

"We have so much," Isaiah says. "Besides, there are still memories. I'm content with having God as my hope."

42
MARIE: BLADES AND BLOOD

On the last day of August, we have another meeting. Sitting at the gigantic wooden table, we start chatting.

"If we're going to break into the Infirmary, we'll need weapons, supplies, provisions, and information—items we don't have right now," Zia says. "Mainly, we need somewhere to flee to."

"I agree. After we rescue everyone, there's no way we can come back here. We're going to have to find somewhere that can accommodate more people," Gabby says.

"You guys said we are already running low on supplies, and there's no way we can hide that many people, probably anywhere," Graydon says. "What's your suggestion?"

Jess and Gabby glance at each other.

"Ellismark," Gabby says.

"What?" Ele asks. "I know we were talking about escaping the province, but that soon? I mean, I'm all for it, but how?"

"I don't know," Jess says. "But we can't stay in Senneforte forever. Eventually, whether or not everyone survives that long, they'll find us. They'll hunt us down, and we've already seen what Morzanna will do."

"Yeah, but still, how the heck are we going to do that?" I ask.

"We fight," Jess states. We all look at her. "They're destroying us most by trapping us in Senneforte and preventing us from seeking help and locating resources. We get past the barrier; we earn freedom."

"What?! That's gonna be so dangerous!" Reece whimpers from beside me.

"I agree with Jess: we have to stand up and fight. We can't let Morzanna keep getting away with this," Atticus says.

"But do we have to *fight?*" Hadley says clearly, tucking a wisp of red hair back into her Dutch braids.

"Isn't there anywhere that they haven't set up as well? Could we find a way there? You know, a loophole in the wall?" Isaiah asks.

"Maybe, but I doubt it," Jess says. "Even so, after we get out, there's no telling what we might discover outside the province."

"The only way out is the gate, which is guarded, and all the rest of the province is fenced with wires and cameras lining every post," Hallston warns. "Even scouting out a breach would be unnecessarily risky. We'll likely have to fight to ensure our success."

"So we go up to them, fight until they decide to let us out, probably die, then we go where exactly?" Reece asks quietly.

"No. That definitely wouldn't work," Jess says and pauses.

"Is there any way that you could get *anyone* past the gate? I mean, you did work for the Queen for a long time, longer than anyone else," I suggest to Jess.

"I couldn't personally make it due to being recognized, but maybe, with planning, we could get two or three people out without them catching on," Jess responds, thinking. "But we have no idea what it's like beyond the province, and they might not even be of help to us."

"What use would it be getting out a couple of people while everyone else is still trapped?" Graydon asks.

"What if someone could go and help us from the outside?" Ele asks.

"That's a great idea!" Ledger adds. "Someone could go in disguised and try to get information, or even get the gate open, and then everyone else could get through. Wait—well, I guess it doesn't matter, we could find out. And then—"

"It could work," Gabby interrupts, trying to keep Ledger on track. "Bentley told me since they hardly open the gate at nighttime, they decrease the patrol. That hour would work best."

"When I was undercover in Ellismark for Mordolus orientation, I saw the gate house. It would be accessible if we could get someone out there," Violet says. It's pretty cool having Violet inside to get info.

"I don't see a better way," Atticus agrees.

"I have extra uniforms from the Infirmary, and I bet we could come up with a believable story," Jess thinks.

"And we could always get Atticus' car," Bexley suggests. "It's still at the lab. Graydon, where are the keys?"

"I left them at the Brooks' house," he says. "But I know exactly where they are. On Isaiah's dresser."

"That could be super useful," Gabby says.

"I think I have an idea," Jess says. "We send in a group on foot to start working on raising the gate. Soon after, we send a second group in the car carrying as many as we can to start working on locating a place to stay. We could also find a way to smuggle some of the children that we'll in theory rescue with them. If we could perhaps make some modifications to the vehicle, we could make a hiding place that they wouldn't discover during inspection."

"And what about everyone else?" Zia inquires.

"After the gate is open, they will have to fight," Jess says. "But we can do our best to arm them and use surprise."

"Sounds solid to me," Isaiah says.

"I agree," Atticus says.

"Who would go in the first group?" Jess thinks aloud. I immediately throw my hand in the air.

"I'LL GO!" I offer, jumping up and down. "I want to, and I know tons about that kind of place! Pleeeease! Please! Please! PLEASE!"

Jess stares at me for a second. "You're right, and it was your idea. But I would discourage you from going, and I hope you understand the danger that will be involved."

"I do, and I still wanna," I say.

"Wait, you're going to let a kid go into Ellismark?" Atticus asks.

Jess sighs. "I guess so. I want to give the kids the opportunity to help, and Marie is right. They are the only ones other than me and Violet who have been inside the Infirmary, so it will be helpful to have someone with experience. I don't really like the idea, but this is serious, and we're all going to have to work together—even the children."

I bounce up and down excitedly, my yellow high-tops thumping against the concrete floor. *I'm going to Ellismark. Hehe.* Even if no one else does, at least I'm gonna escape. I'm trying hard to do it for the right reason, but I feel a little selfish like the day I left Ele. Whatever.

"Who else? I would go, but that likely wouldn't end well," Jess says. Reece shrinks like he's scared someone's going to ask him to go. Ele, Isaiah, Atticus, Hallston, Graydon, and Gabby put their hands up.

"No! You're not going unless I am!" Ele tells Isaiah.

"And I'm not sending three children into the most dangerous situation yet," Jess states. "Marie only gets to go because she volunteered first."

"Seriously, Ele?" Isaiah says. She nods stubbornly, and he rolls his eyes. "Fine, I guess neither of us are going because *you're* not going without me."

"Jess, I'm going," Hallston states, her tone strong with determination.

Jess agrees then examines the remaining volunteers. "I think I might have something else for you, Atticus. I'll talk to you about it later if that's alright." Atticus looks at her suspiciously, but nods. "Graydon,

I don't want to endanger any of you unless necessary. We will send Gabby."

Graydon glances at me. I smile back as widely as possible. "Okay," he agrees, disapprovingly.

Hallston, Gabby, and I are going to Ellismark. I bounce a little.

"Jess, we still have to discuss supplies. You said there's probably going to be a fight. Hopefully there are going to be a lot of people, and we can't have them all unarmed. The Mordolus will be everywhere, and we never know if we'll have access to anything in Ellismark. We can't go completely unprepared," Hadley mentions.

"You're right. We are going to have to locate supplies," Jess realizes.

"Well, there is a base we could rob," I say.

"The one that's super dangerous," Bexley reminds me.

"Yeah, but it also has everything we'll need. I don't think she's saying we go in and take it over, but we could steal what we need," Isaiah interjects.

"Honestly, that could work," Hallston says.

"They have to have weapons," Ele agrees, nodding.

"We're going to rob the base?" Reece asks. "When?"

"If we're going to rescue the people of Senneforte in time," Jess glances around. "We have to go soon. Today."

"All of us?" Reece asks, turning red. He's always blushing.

"No, not everyone. Now, Atticus, tell us everything you know about the base," Jess says.

When it's time to leave for the base, I'm jumping with eagerness. Atticus explains that there are several ways to get in. He's going to tell us more on the way. Gabby's been there before too. Hadley made us wear boring clothes to blend in or something. I couldn't find anything black, so I just stole a random T-shirt from the boy's room. I don't get to wear my fav yellow high-tops because apparently they draw too much attention. I wasn't the only one to lose a staple clothing piece. Ele isn't wearing her teal headband.

"Once we get to Sunlit Street, I'll show you the base, and we can make a plan," Atticus says. He leads us through the dusky province. Atticus, Gabby, Ledger, Hallston, Graydon, Ele, Isaiah, Bexley, Reece, and I are the ones going on the mission. Hadley's not really cut out for this, so she stayed behind to watch over the Haven. Zia's feeling better, but she still suffers from long-term symptoms. Yesterday, Hallston found an intact weapon safe downtown, so Jess is going to take tools and check it out. She's also going by to pick up the keys and car.

Even though we're going to steal weapons, we bring what little we had at the Haven, just in case. I touch the cool metal of the kitchen knife Hadley gave me.

We follow the road in silence. It's vaguely familiar from the one time Reece and I came with Atticus. I see that one bookstore, noticing the blinds are closed and the door is still ajar. I tap Reece on the shoulder and nod to it with a grin. He just shakes his head.

A sign reads Sunlit Street. The eight of us carefully follow Atticus. He looks up ahead, signaling for us to come. I remember what he told us originally. They don't use this road at night unless something's up. Thankfully, I don't think we've done anything yet to attract attention. It's completely silent, except for me in my loose rain boots skipping alongside everyone. We pass by Atticus' house. Ahead, the row of houses ends, and the road leads into the woods. A building looms at the dead end of the road. Atticus slowly brings us to the edge of the wood, and we're careful to stay off the road and out of sight. We crouch beside a thick, fallen tree. Water seeps into my black leggings from the dew-soaked moss. Gross.

"So what's the plan?" Hallston whispers.

"We've got two options. The front entrance is out of the question. We can go in through the loading bay where they fill the trucks. We'll be right where we need to be, but I'm sure it's guarded. There's also the back entrance. There's a small door, probably less guarded, but we'll have to find our way to the supply room and out without being seen," Atticus tells us.

"There's risk either way; I suggest we go with the loading bay," Ele says from beside me. "It's far more direct and we know what to expect.

"But what's the point if we get caught? If we go in through the back, we have a better chance of not being seen because it's not as guarded," Bexley counters. Ele rolls her eyes.

"Let's take a vote," Graydon suggests. Everyone nods. "Who votes for the loading bay?"

I raise my hand. I look around and start counting: Hallston, Ele, Graydon, Atticus, Gabby. Including me, that's six out of ten.

"So we go through the loading bay," Gabby says. "Will it be locked?"

Atticus nods. "Of course."

"What do we do about that?" Isaiah asks.

"We steal a key, right?" I ask. Everyone looks at me. "You said there'll be guards who have keys, and we have some weapons."

"She's right," Hallston says slowly. "I'm going to wait on the road and watch for incoming vehicles. I'll find somehow to contact you or stop them if one heads your way."

Atticus studies me then agrees. "Okay, we're going to split up. Half of us will go inside; everyone else will be in charge of packing everything up, and we'll have two people on lookout," he pauses, thinking. "Ledger, you and Bexley are on watch. Graydon, Ele, Marie, and Reece, you're coming with me inside. Gabby and Isaiah, your job's packing everything up. Everyone fine with that?"

We all nod. Reece doesn't, but maybe it's because he really didn't want to be here in the first place.

Hallston heads out in the other direction. We move toward the building. It's an average sized warehouse with a massive garage. At least twenty trucks are stationed outside, and two Mordolus guards are positioned beside a fat door. That must be the loading bay. The road leads right up to it. The base is in the center of a field, surrounded by woods. We leave the trees, and Atticus motions for us to crawl, using the shadows for cover. I'm even more soaked after wriggling through the dewy grass. Atticus stops about a hundred yards away. The lights from the base ruin our cover for the last bit. I can imagine Atticus is planning. I lay on my stomach in the grass. I shiver as a giant spider scampers across my hand. Eww.

Slowly, Atticus stands, and, when the two guards turn away, he runs the final stretch. He waits beside the wall of the base, hidden. Isaiah does the same, and when it's my turn, I sprint as fast as I can to join them. Everyone eventually makes it over. Atticus motions for Ledger and Bexley to stay there and wait. Bexley repeats the message because Ledger was distracted staring at the sky. Atticus draws his knife, indicating to the rest of us to do the same. I glance at my kitchen knife that might have even been used this morning to make breakfast. How wonderful.

"This is crazy. We aren't going to have to, you know, fight anyone, right?" Reece whispers to me shakily. I'm surprised Reece even came, but he didn't want to go with Jess either.

I shrug. "Hope not, but we gotta listen to Atticus."

"Huh, that's a first for you," Reece replies. I elbow him.

"Hey, wanna hear something weird?" I ask quietly as Atticus watches the two guards from behind the wall.

"Sure, but make it fast," Reece says.

"When we were at Atticus' house to get the supplies and stuff, I went to explore. I saw something in the dining room. There was this giant picture of Morzanna," I whisper. "Huge. It freaked me out. I ran out of there, and that's when I saw the Mordolus outside. Isn't that kinda creepy?"

Reece stares at the sky. "Well, yeah. Why didn't you tell me earlier? We've been living in the same building with Atticus for a month!"

I shrug. "Why would he have a big fancy picture of Morzanna if he hates her?"

"You guys wait here. Gabby and I will take care of the guards. Be ready when we call," Atticus says and steps out from the hiding place. Gabby's right behind him. I get bored and bounce a little. About three minutes later, Gabby breathlessly returns to get us. Around the corner, Atticus holds up the key and approaches the door to the supply room.

"Where are the guards?" Reece whispers. "Where'd you get the key from?"

"They weren't expecting us," Atticus says. "The second guard had the key."

"Tied them up on the other side," Gabby says, nodding to the left.

"Isaiah, go get Bexley and Ledger and have them watch from over there by the last truck," Atticus says, fumbling with the lock. Isaiah nods and runs off to fetch them. The lock clicks open, and Atticus and Gabby lift the heavy door. As my eyes adjust to the darkness, I gape. There are shelves lined with boxes and crates filling the vast room. If I was in a cartoon, I'd probably have stars for eyes or something bizarre.

"Bexley and Ledger are watching," Isaiah says, returning. Gabby nods and climbs up into the supply room after Atticus. Ele,

Reece, Graydon, and I follow. The ledge is several feet off the ground, and I almost can't climb up. I hate being short sometimes.

Isaiah and Gabby set the backpacks out on the edge of the bay.

Ele searches along the wall until she finds the light and turns it on. The boxes are labeled and stamped with Morzanna's insignia.

"Reece and Marie, you're on weapons. Graydon, Ele, you know what we'll need for sulfavirdoton. I think it's that way." Atticus points then gestures over the back side of the room. "There's a door over there somewhere, so watch it. Keep your weapons close and pay attention." Then he disappears in the other direction.

"Come on, Reecey," I whisper, heading toward the wall of weapons. I giggle with excitement. They're hung up on hooks with more lying messily in boxes and crates on the floor. We reach the wall, and I stare at the options.

"Do you think they have any guns?" I ask.

"Umm, those are illegal, remember? Also, none of us would know how to use one," Reece says.

"Well, I've seen the Mordolus with them before," I say. "They must store a few somewhere."

"That's really scary to think about. This is going to be heavy to carry back," Reece comments. I nod, picking up two tinier but equally as stabby daggers.

"Go smaller. That way we can take more," I say, taking an empty box and loading it with several knives. Reece quietly helps me, constantly gazing around.

I drop a dagger, and the metallic echo rings through the whole room. Reece cringes. We carry the box back to where Isaiah and Gabby are. They wrap each blade and stash it into the backpacks. Almost the whole time Reece mumbles about it being dangerous.

"You're talking to yourself again," I inform him.

He stops. "Sorry."

We walk back through the storeroom, and I gaze at the tall shelves. They're stacked with dark boxes and so crowded I can't see to the next aisle. It's maze-like. Cool.

"I'm going to Ellismark, I'm going to Ellismark," I sing quietly.

"You're actually excited about that?" Reece asks.

"Uh, yeah," I reply.

"Well, I'm not," Reece says. "It's gonna be dangerous."

"You're not even going!" I remark.

He shrugs. "I know."

"Aww, Reecey, are ya worried about me?" I ask, batting my eyes.

"Yeah. I mean, I guess," he says, then smiles. "And everyone else who's stuck going with *you*."

"Shut up." I fake punch him. "*I'm* going to help rescue everyone."

Reece doesn't respond for a minute and studies me. Something obscure in his pastel-green eyes makes me uncomfy. "Or do you just want to go so you know you'll escape? You didn't actually volunteer so you could help, did you?"

I take a deep breath because I was not expecting that. Reece is a surprising kid.

"No," I blurt.

"No as in you wanted to help, or no as in I'm right?" Reece asks. I hesitate.

Before I get to respond, I hear something. It's a strange sound coming from the back of the supply room.

"What's that?" I ask.

"I don't know—" Reece gets cut off by someone yelling far off. It's Ele.

"Something's wrong," I say immediately.

Reece nods. "We should go help them."

"You're right," I reply. I'm not scared, but I don't exactly want to risk my life for whatever's happening. Everyone for themselves, right? If I go now, I'll be able to get away and be fine. But Reece is right. They're my friends. We should help. Besides, if Graydon and Ele die, who else will read to me or give me piggyback rides? "Let's go!"

"Wait, I said we should, not that we had to! I want to help them, but I'm scared," Reece confesses, panicking. He divulges a lot of things when he overreacts. "What are we even going to do?!"

"Help them!" I say. "I don't know how yet!"

"I don't want anything to happen to Ele and Graydon," Reece says quietly, wringing his hands.

"Same! So let's go figure out what's going on! Don't be stupid and come on!" I order.

Without waiting a second longer, I sprint off toward the scream. I really should have taken one of the knives from back there. I reach for my only option—the one I brought. I run through shelves and stacks of supplies.

"Ele?! Graydon!" I call again. They're right up ahead. Rounding the corner, I reach for my lousy knife.

In the back edge of the supply room, surrounded by shelves of what must be ingredients for raxoxin, I see them. Ele and Graydon are cornered by two Mordolus guards. The door Atticus warned them about is open.

"Let them go!" I scream, jumping out from behind the shelf and diving at the guards. He catches me by the shoulders. The other kicks me into the corner with Ele and Graydon.

"Are you okay?" Graydon asks, helping me up. I nod, favoring my side. I look down and realize the knife's completely bent out of shape and unusable. I throw it to the ground, noticing Ele and Graydon's weapons are gone, too. Both the guards are armed with sharp daggers. We're also trapped. This is not good.

Ele grabs my hand and holds her breath. I look down at my feet. I always wanted to pet an elephant before I died. Too bad.

When I look up, one of the guards starts hollering. He's clutching his upper arm, writhing. A Mordolus knife falls and clunks when it hits the floor. Golly. Somebody stabbed the guard.

"Reece," I whisper. "Dang." The other guard closes in on us, holding up a big ol' sword. I try to see what's happening. The injured guard approaches Reece, roaring. Reecey's backed up to the wall across from the line of shelves and catches my eye. The guard raises something. That's a knife.

"Wait, stop!" I say, but it's too late. Graydon looks horrified, and Ele gasps. Reece stumbles back. He freezes, staring at the guard. Blood runs from the knife's target on his shoulder. Reece gets a strange, kinda distant look. Quickly, he yanks out the knife and whimpers as it clatters to the ground and more blood splatters onto the floor. He puts his hands over the wound and takes a few steps back. Then, he collapses.

"Reece!" Ele shrieks, charging at the guard. It doesn't go well. The other guard throws her to the ground. She hits hard, falling on my bent knife, cutting a brutal slice across her leg. I grimace.

"Eleanora!" Graydon calls. "Ele?" I think she's unconscious.

The guard and Graydon stare at each other like they're about to face off, and I'm scared. I glance at the other guard. His arm is slick with fresh blood. *He's gonna kill Reece.*

"Stop!" I demand. Suddenly, Gabby bounds in, wielding one of the swords Reece and I were rummaging through. The guard over Reece turns to Gabby. Atticus comes rushing from the other side of the warehouse.

I run to Reece. "Dude, you're full of surprises," I say.

"I'm gonna die!" he gasps half-consciously with a sob. "I can't—I feel dizzy."

"Chill out. Breathe. You're gonna be fine," I say. Except right now he doesn't look that fineish. Blood leaks from the wound in the middle of his right shoulder. At least he's still breathing. I can't believe Reece attacked the guard.

Graydon sprints over and kneels beside us. Reece is out.

"Is Ele okay?" I ask.

"She's alive; I checked," Graydon responds. He breathes super heavily.

"What do we do?" I ask.

"Find something to stop the bleeding," he says, thinking. "He shouldn't have taken out the knife."

"Want me to put it back in?" I ask, eyeing the bloody metal a few feet away.

"What? No," Graydon says. "He'll bleed out if we don't do something though."

I take off my jacket to use. Graydon helps me, hands shaking, but the blood soaks through. Graydon closes his eyes for a minute. He's either praying or gonna pass out too. Praying's a good idea, and I silently do the same. I don't know what the heck to say because I've never done this before.

"Please, Reecey-boy, don't die," I whisper.

With the guards taken care of, Atticus throws his weapon down, kneeling beside Reece. Gabby lifts Ele, who's still unconscious, from the ground. With one glance, Atticus quickly picks up Reece. I stand, dazed.

"Come on, Marie," Graydon says urgently and grabs my hand. I glance back. The two guards are dead, lying on the blood-streaked ground. I follow Graydon. I'm so scared. We've got to get back to the Haven now.

43
ELEANORA: RESCUE

A throbbing headache crashes in my brain, sending aches slinking through my whole body and a hissing ring to bounce against my eardrums. My fingertips graze soft, cottony sheets and the air is beautifully cool. My mind refuses to form coherent thoughts no matter how hard I try, but I finally haul myself from pained delirium into consciousness.

The ceiling is smooth and gray, and the bright white light and stars in my vision instantly make me nauseous. *What is going on? How am I here? Where is this anyway?*

"Ele?!" someone says. "You're okay!"

I lift my head, and it weighs more than a boulder, sending new pain spidering through my skull and a ringing in my ears.

"Ledger?" I say hoarsely, putting a hand on my head. A thunderclap resounds inside my head, and I peer over the edge of my bed to find it's only Stormy fluttering inside his cage. I'm back in my room in the Haven.

"How are you feeling?" Ledger asks, bounding over to my bed. Every sound is exacerbated and excruciating, but I force myself to sit up.

"Not fantastic, honestly," I admit.

"Jess guesses you have a concussion. She also said your leg will take a while to heal, but won't need stitches or anything extreme," Ledger explains courteously quieter, nodding.

"My leg?" I ask, quickly throwing aside the blankets to reveal my leg, which is tightly wrapped in white bandages from knee to mid-thigh. The stinging is awful, particularly when I move.

"Oh, sorry. I guess that happened after you were already out. That must be weird for you," Ledger says before explaining what happened from the time I was injured.

"Isaiah came and got Bexley and me, and when we got there, you two were not looking good," he finishes.

"You two?" I whisper to myself. Then the realization sets in, sending my heart racing at least a thousand beats per second. "Oh my gosh! Where's Reece? Is he okay?!"

"It's okay! He's alive," Ledger assures me. "He's a lot better. It was bad before. Seriously. Blood everywhere—nevermind. Honestly, we thought he was going to die."

"But he's okay now, right?" I try *not* to imagine Reece bleeding out in the middle of a Mordolus base.

"Yeah, we think so," Ledger says. I sigh and reach for a tangled strand of hair.

"Where is Reece? And everyone else?" I ask.

"The boys' room. Everyone else is fine. Tired and shaken up, but fine. Oh, wait—I promised I'd come get them when you woke up," Ledger says, thinking.

I glance out the window, shocked to notice sunlight streaming inside, painting the ground and window a refreshing gold. "How long was I asleep for?"

"Not long. A few hours maybe. It's just now morning, the same day. Well, I guess it isn't the same day then. Technically, it's the day after," Ledger replies, looking outside too, and for a second he just stares at the robins pecking beneath the windowsill.

He looks back at me. "Whoa, sorry. Ugh, I keep getting distracted. I have ADHD."

"It's okay. Isaiah does too, so I get it," I say.

"Really? Anyway, where was I? Oh yeah. I'm going to go get the others. They'll want to see you. I'm really glad you're awake now, Ele."

Ledger leaves the room, and I fall back onto my pillow. *Everyone else is safe and alive, and so am I. We're going to be okay.* My hand grazes the familiar soft fabric of my butterfly blanket, and I pull it tighter around me. I stare at the picture next to the door; a scenic wildflower background painted with black lettering. Whenever Hadley goes out in the province with the searching group, she brings back furnishings for the Haven, and this one is a Bible verse:

I have said these things to you, that in me you may have peace. In the world you will have tribulation. But take heart; I have overcome the world. (John 16:33).

It brings me a bit of comfort because right now I'm feeling awfully keyed up and worried. *If I can truly let go of this world, would I really have peace in all situations? If only I could bring myself to it, if only I could trust.*

Suddenly, the door opens and Isaiah, Graydon, and Marie step in.

"Ele!" Isaiah exclaims, running over to hug me. "Are you okay?" I pat my brother on the back to let him know I'm in pain and squeezing me is nice but not helping the problem.

"I'm fine," I say, which is questionable. I really consider adding, *other than the fact my head feels like a bomb went off, and I'm scared any second I might throw up on you, I'm great.*

Isaiah kneels beside my bed, his hair even more of a mess than usual. "Not mad at me?"

"No," I reply, propping myself up further. "Why? What did you do?"

"You don't remember waking up earlier?" Graydon asks me. "You were in a daze the whole journey back, and when we arrived you were a lot more conscious."

"You were so mad and wanted us to leave you alone. Isaiah was trying to talk to you, and you told us all to shut up, then just blacked out," Marie says.

"I don't remember that at all," I admit, massaging the back of my neck. "That's so concerning."

"I'm so sorry, Ele. We shouldn't have gone near that door. And been more aware. It's my fault, but I'm glad you're okay," Graydon says, walking over to the side of the bed. "You're sure you're fine, though? I mean, I'm sorry Ele, but you don't exactly look fine."

I just stare for a second then glance at the mirror on the wall above Bexley's bed. I nearly gasp aloud at my reflection because it looks like I haven't slept in at least three years. My complexion is completely flushed, and my hair isn't even describable, but I'd probably use some of the same adjectives for a bird's nest. I really want to crawl under the bed and pretend that they never actually saw me looking like this.

"I mean, I'm alright," I say with a nervous smile and subconsciously reach up and try to fix my hair, hoping to look a little less like the complete madwoman I saw in the mirror.

"We were worried for a while," Graydon responds, playing with the strings of his hoodie.

Marie jumps up on the end of my bed, her wild curls bouncing. "Ele, that was insane! It might not have been your *best* idea, but that's okay! How's your leg?"

"It's okay. Not too bad," I respond, smiling. "Someone bandaged it well."

"That was Hadley. Oh, and I put your boots back in the closet, too," she says, kicking her yellow high-tops against the floor. "So, what'd you go and almost die for?"

"I don't know," I say with a shrug. "I was scared and worried about Reece, so I made an impulsive decision. I guess that's how it works, right? Something bad happens, and you do things you never would have expected of yourself."

"Well, it was pretty courageous," Isaiah says, avoiding eye contact, and I smile.

"Hey, Marie, what happened to the 'no boys in the room' rule?" I ask.

"I revoked it under the current circumstances," Marie says, standing on the bed and patting Isaiah and Graydon on the heads.

"We didn't mean to abandon you. Wrong timing for breakfast," Isaiah explains, swatting Marie's hand away.

"It's fine," I say. "Did you guys bring anything back from the base?"

Graydon nods and shrugs simultaneously. "Yeah, not a lot though. Ledger helped the four of us carry everything we had packed up so far. Just a few weapons and like half the ingredients we need for the cure. But, good news, Jess' excursion was successful, and the car waits just outside the woods."

At least it wasn't a complete failure, but now we've got to figure out another option. We can't try to escape Senneforte with no supplies, and we can't go back to the base again. I ask, "What's going on with Reece? Ledger explained only a little of the situation."

"He needed stitches. Jess had to do it," Graydon tells me, fidgeting.

"What? How?" I ask.

"When we got back, Jess had arrived about ten minutes earlier, so she made Atticus take Reece straight to the boy's room while she ran downstairs. Ledger was too scared to do it. Jess poured some alcohol on the wound, took a needle and thread, and literally just stitched it up," Marie says, pretending like she's holding a needle and sewing the air in a disturbingly casual demonstration. "It was crazy but kinda cool."

"I couldn't watch," Isaiah says, grimacing. "I came in here with you, Hadley, and Gabby. Graydon had to explain what happened."

"They gave Reece something so he would stay relatively unconscious. It was like ketamine or something. Ledger used an injection for blood loss too. He was in hypovolemic shock. I think he might still be, but at least the bleeding stopped. Thank God it didn't cut a vital artery, but the knife fractured his upper rib," Graydon explains. "Atticus was super upset about it all."

"It was pretty nerve-racking," Marie agrees with a shrug.

I nod, taking everything in and still battling my headache. "When do you think he'll wake up?"

"Dunno," Isaiah says. "I'm guessing it's gonna be pretty brutal."

Isaiah's probably right; I feel terrible, and I didn't even get stabbed or almost die from blood loss.

"Yeah," I agree as a wave of dizziness comes over me, so I lay back down. The movement sends a jolt of pain up my leg, and I cringe.

"You okay?" Graydon asks, but his words are a little slurred. I nod, but all my muscles begin to ache as I brush the boiling skin around my cut, and all I get out is, "My head hurts."

"Jess left some medicine or something around here," Isaiah says. He gets up and walks over to the table, picking up a pill bottle from next to Stormy and inspecting the label.

"Here." He hands me two of the small red pills, and Marie runs and gets me a glass of water. As soon as I choke down the pills, the pain begins to dissipate. Isaiah speaks to me, but I miss it as the room becomes strangely distorted. The glass in my hand seems too heavy, and I hear it clank with a splash as it hits the floor. I thought that was just ibuprofen, but immediately drowsiness sets in, and before I can fight it, I fall asleep.

When I wake up, the room is so dark I can't see the door. Across the room, Marie is asleep on top of the covers still wearing her outfit from today, with one leg hanging off her bed. I lean over and turn on the red lamp on my side table. I look down, and Isaiah lays on the floor right next to my bed. He sleeps like a sea star, and I don't get how anyone could breathe on their stomach. Graydon dozes in the chair beside the door. The past few days have been especially exhausting.

I stare at Stormy, asleep on his bird perch, the events of the past day running around my head like a wild stampede. It seems so unreal and, eventually, I fall back into a light sleep.

Pain ricochets around my head as I fight off sleepiness, and, for a second, nothing registers.

"Ele?"

I sit up so fast I nearly leap out of bed.

"Oh, sorry," Graydon says quietly, standing a few feet from me. "I have a message from the other room. Reece is awake and has been for a while. They wouldn't let me in, though."

In a moment, Graydon rouses the other two and delivers the news.

"We've got to go see him," Isaiah says, standing and stretching.

Marie leaps out of bed so loudly I'm pretty sure everyone in the whole Haven heard. "Yeah! Come on!"

They start toward the door, and Graydon reminds them he wasn't allowed in. Meanwhile, I throw my legs over the side of the bed and wince. Biting my lip, I take a deep breath and cautiously stand up.

"Eleanora!" Graydon warns. "You're going to hurt yourself!"

I dismiss him, but then a rush of lightheadedness nearly sends me toppling to the concrete floor. Isaiah quickly grabs my arm before I fall.

"I'll be okay," I say, limping across the room.

"Oh, and guys, remember this is Reece. Don't say anything that's gonna freak him out," Isaiah warns as we head to the door.

Marie runs to the boys' room and pauses outside the door for the rest of us.

A strange nervousness hangs in the air as Isaiah softly knocks on the door before opening it. "Jess? Ledger?"

I hear Jess and Ledger arguing, Reece whimpering, and things clattering. Graydon peers over Isaiah's shoulder and pushes the door shut with a grimace. "Let's take that as it's a bad time and come back later."

"What's happening?" Marie asks, shifting.

"Just trust me. It's not a good time," Graydon says.

Marie drops her shoulders, and we all stare at each other. Behind us, footsteps echo from the stairwell, and someone squeaks.

"Ele! Why are you up? You're supposed to be in bed!" Hadley admonishes, running over to me and grabbing my arm gently to steady me.

"She doesn't listen to anyone," Graydon comments.

Hadley glances at the door to the boys' room. "Come on. You all need to rest. We can't have Ele getting worse or any of you sleep deprived. I can come get you at a better time."

She helps me limp back to the girls' room, the other three following us. I slip back into bed, trembling as Hadley examines my injury.

"You've made it bleed again," she says, shaking her head.

"I'm sorry," I say, although I'm not sure why I'm apologizing because it's my leg that feels like it's being chopped in half.

Hadley fetches a brush from the dresser across the room. She gently brushes my hair then separates it into two French braids, similarly to how she usually has her long ginger locks. Between her perfect complexion, wavy hair, and soft brown eyes, Hadley is exceptionally pretty, and likewise, Bexley is easily a lot better looking than me. *How can Hadley be so nice and Bexley so awful?* I didn't miss how Bexley was the only one who didn't come visit me, not that I care. I'm not even sure where she is. *Maybe we left her at the base. That would be wonderful.*

"Is there anything I can get you?" Hadley asks, breaking me from my vindictive thoughts, and I only request water. I wonder if the medication is wearing off because a dull, nauseating pain returns to my head.

"How are you feeling?" Isaiah asks me.

"In pain, but I'm okay," I respond.

"Sorry. There's always going to be suffering, I guess. It's part of the curse of sin. But there's hope to be found in Christ. Things will work out for good," Isaiah replies. "I'm praying for you and Reece. We're gonna get through this."

For an hour, we all just miserably wait, barely speaking to each other, though, for me, it's somewhat refreshing to sit in silence.

"I'll go check on the situation and come and get you if it's okay," Hadley says. "Although, I really think you should stay in bed, Ele."

"I promise I will," I say. "*After* I see Reece."

Marie plops at the foot of my bed, and Isaiah and Graydon sit on one of the others. I twirl a strand of hair, waiting until Hadley returns.

"It's okay now. They gave him medication that should help ease the pain," she tells us.

Marie charges out of the room, almost knocking over Hadley. Telling the other two to go ahead, Hadley helps me stiffly stagger to the doorway.

"Ele?" Atticus comes over to me from the stairwell. "I'm really sorry," he says.

"You were the one who saved us. I don't know why you're apologizing," I say.

Atticus doesn't reply, and Jess opens the door to let us inside the boys' room.

Reece lays on the single bed under the window. It's Isaiah's bed, but I'm sure my brother gave it up since Reece had the top bunk. Reece's face is ashen, and his cheeks are blood and tear stained. I subconsciously check to assure myself he's breathing, but it's hard to tell because he's shaking so severely. Isaiah kneels next to the bed, the same he did for me, and so does Marie, while Graydon and I stand on the opposite side.

"Reece?" Marie asks, lightly touching his good arm with a surprising amount of concern. His breathing seems worryingly shallow, but finally his eyes flicker open.

"Isaiah? Marie?" Reece whispers slowly, dazed. He yanks his arm away from Marie and groans.

"Yeah," Marie says. Reece's light green eyes make his sickly pale skin even more noticeable, and I really try not to look at his bandaged shoulder.

"Reece, that was so brave. I'm proud of you," Isaiah says. Reece exhales and gives a languid nod.

"Man, you look bad," Marie says with a frown.

"Thanks," Reece replies sarcastically.

"Does it hurt a lot?" Marie asks.

"Of course not, Marie," Reece murmurs. "Imagine getting stabbed and it hurting. That'd be crazy."

Marie smiles and rolls her eyes. Isaiah looks like he wants to say something, but instead, his eyes flicker around the room, and he blanches. Blood is everywhere: on the floor, the sheets, Reece's skin…Ever since we were kids, Isaiah has had a real fear of blood, and he looks sicker than I'm feeling. Anytime he or someone else would get a cut or anything, he'd run away, screaming.

"Atticus?" Reece asks quietly, and Atticus takes a step closer. "Thanks. I kind of remember you bringing me here. I guess you aren't sketchy after all."

A rare smile subtly spreads across Atticus's face.

"Aww, no," Reece mumbles to himself.

"What?" Graydon asks worriedly.

Reece looks down sadly at his bandages. "This is my writing arm."

"You can learn how to write with the other hand," Marie suggests.

Reece closes his eyes and grimaces. "Maybe. It hurts to breathe. Am I going to die?"

"No, of course not!" Jess interjects. Reece sighs. "You'll be fine after you have some time to recover."

"Hey, Reecey," Marie asks. "What was it like to, ya know—" She slashes at the air. "Slicey someone?"

Reece sighs again. "Scary. I can't really remember. I'm tired."

"Would you like us to leave?" I ask quietly. He subtly gives a slow nod. Marie hangs her shoulders but doesn't argue.

"But Isaiah," Reece whispers, tiredly putting a hand over his eyes. "Stay, please?"

"Okay," Isaiah replies.

"Marie can, too, if she's quiet," Reece adds, and she immediately brightens.

Jess remains to monitor, and Graydon accompanies me back to my room.

"Are you okay?" Graydon asks as I climb into bed. "I sort of thought you were gonna pass out back there."

"I felt like it too, but I'm okay now. Hadley was right; that wasn't a great idea, and seeing Reece like that makes everything so real," I admit.

"Yeah, I get it," Graydon says, sitting beside me. "But honestly, I'm just glad you two are alive." A long silence lingers between us.

"What's this going to change about the rescue mission?" I finally ask.

"I don't know. We have to wait at least until Reece is somewhat better and you've recovered. I'm not sure if it's going to change anything about us, though," he says.

I screw my face and look at him. "What does that mean?"

"When we got back, Jess, Atticus, Hadley, and Hallston all kept talking about how they should have never taken us and we're just kids. Hallston was mad, and I'm surprised she didn't go back to the base and take on the Mordolus on her own, but she was more focused on getting here. You know Atticus, he acts kind of weird sometimes, but I think he cares about us. A lot. He kept apologizing to Jess and asking if he could help. Hadley was crying. It was chaotic," Graydon tells me.

"So you think they're going to try and protect us by not letting us help?" I ask.

He sighs, then nods. "Yeah."

"But it's not going to! There are not really that many people here, and besides Jess, Violet, and Bentley, no one's even been inside the Infirmary. They're going to need our help!" I argue. "If we fail, we're probably all going to end up dead. With the antidote, we're a threat. We know too much. Getting caught will be a lot more severe than we thought. After what happened yesterday, I know. But we can't stay here until everyone else is dead without raxoxin, and right now we're trapped. If we don't get out of Senneforte, we'll all be doomed." I reach to twist a strand of hair, but the braids prevent me, so I drop my hand.

Peace I leave you; my peace I give you. Not as the world gives do I give to you. Do not let your hearts be troubled, neither let them be afraid. (John 14:27).

The words from the note my father gave me return to my memory. I want to reject them, to not have to think about it, and darkness builds up inside me. *What do I, what can I, really believe about God during this time? How can I ever have true peace when things like this happen and keep happening?*

"I don't like the idea of us going into danger, but it's necessary," Graydon resumes, breaking me from my internal conflict. "I was pretty upset about Jess agreeing to let Marie go on the Ellismark mission. I don't understand why I couldn't go instead. But…we're all going to have to play a dangerous part. With the Virus killing everyone in the Infirmary, why wouldn't Morzanna go ahead and murder them all? They're vulnerable enough. I just don't understand what she's planning."

I take a deep breath. "I think the way to find out will be to get out of Senneforte. If we go to Ellismark, chances are we'll find out something. It's odd, but I just have a feeling."

"We *will* find out someday, whether or not it's after we're dead," Graydon says, staring at the floor.

"Don't say that Graydon, we're not going to die."

"It's true. You were nearly killed, Reece almost died, and if we make it to Ellismark, what happens then? What if it's, I don't know, a trap? Who knows, we could all be murdered the second we leave the Haven. I just—I have a feeling we aren't all going to get out of this," Graydon says grimly, running a hand through his hair.

"I seriously hope that's not the case," I say.

Graydon looks at me, and his eyes flicker with fear. "Me too."

The next several days drift by like slow storm clouds bringing in anything between a serene drizzle and a violent thunderstorm. I learned that we did not, in fact, leave Bexley at the base after all and that she was helping out more so we could take time to recover. After Hadley found out how badly I was feeling, she forced me to stay in bed for three days. Marie was bored since she didn't have anyone to hang out with and picked me some black-eyed Susans from the woods, which made me happy. I love flowers. The only caveat was she forgot to put them in water, and they died in a few hours. Isaiah picked more before she found out and put them in water that time. My bruises have faded to light blue, and my cut is almost healed. I still get a lot of headaches and dizziness when I walk around, but I'm getting better.

The first couple of days for Reece were rough, since not only was he recovering from a stab wound, but also a fractured rib, all with little medical help, but now he's significantly better. Hallston said it was the grace of God he didn't get an infection and is recovering so quickly.

We're yet to bring up the plan for rescue and escape, but the unspoken question settles beneath the air, likely to surface soon. Atticus and Hallston have been working diligently on the car, and they've started crafting a hiding spot inside the backseat, carving out a place in the glove box, and raising the floor in the trunk. Isaiah went to work with them one day and told me that they've collected all kinds of tools and have taken everything apart to reconfigure. He guesses there will be room for two kids under the backseat, and a couple beneath the floor.

Jess calls a meeting one night, and for the third time, we all gather around the table in the meeting room.

"We need to discuss the plan," Jess states. "The attempt to rob the base didn't go as we expected. We're just going to have to go with what we have and pray it will work out. I spoke with our leader yesterday, and they agree with the idea."

One of Jess's best qualities is always being able to plan and manage all the crazy going on. Her hair is also perfect, a raven black, shiny, and thick—it even beats Hadley's.

"We're still going through with it?" Atticus asks, and Jess nods slowly.

"We have to, or we're worse off than before. We knew there was a risk, and there is for this too," Zia says quietly, readjusting the thin frames of her round glasses. She tucks a long strand of black hair behind her ear.

"We still have some final plans to make, but most importantly, we need to choose a date, or this is never going to happen," Hallston says.

"How much time will prep take?" Bexley asks as I run a hand through my golden hair, still wavy from being braided.

"Several days, at least," Jess says, thinking.

"So we can go after that," Isaiah says. "We need to do this as soon as possible."

"We can't just rush into things," Hadley interjects.

"But the longer it takes, the more people die. Every day, hundreds of people, just in the Infirmary, are dying without raxoxin. Not only there, the Sanatorium, and the other provinces of Lossaree, Ravimere, and Valerrow, too," Gabby reminds us. "The truth is, either way, people are going to die. But we have a better chance to do this than wait. Honestly, I don't think any of us could live with the guilt of waiting until everyone else dies. I'm willing to risk my life, rather than discarding theirs."

Gabby's right: this isn't about us, it's about the entire country of Willowmire—and maybe the world.

"We should decide now, huh?" Marie says.

Everyone looks at each other, but no one says anything. I glance at Reece, his arm still in a sling, and remember what it was like to watch him get stabbed, wondering what will occur if that or worse happens to anyone else in this second foray.

Reece looks at me then takes a deep breath. "I think we should go in a week."

Everyone looks at him. "Most of us have family waiting. We have the remedy, and I know if we wait, they could die too. Imagine what would happen if we went there and found out it was too late. That's what happened to my mom, and I don't want it to happen to anyone else. Besides, Morzanna already knows we're out here after the base raid. She'll be looking harder for us." Reece says, and a blush creeps onto his cheeks. He looks uneasy, waiting for their response, but I give him an affirmative nod.

"Okay," Jess decides. "Okay. You're right. We'll do it. We aren't people without hope and faith. We will continue to pray for the Lord's guidance, and trust that He will be with us in this fight. A week from today, we're going to rescue everyone."

44

ISAIAH: THE CHILDREN

"Everyone needs to be out of the Infirmary by midnight," Jess announces. "Join your group and make sure you're all fully prepared. Say a prayer for success and protection today. It's time to head out."

We're going to rescue everyone from the Infirmary. It's exciting to think about finally saving my parents. Last night, we were assigned jobs. Reece wasn't supposed to go on the mission. Ledger says it's going to be a long time until he's fully healed. It's only been two weeks since he was stabbed by the Mordolus guard at the base. His wound has mostly healed, but the broken bone hasn't. Reece convinced Jess to let him go though. I was surprised. Mostly that he wasn't begging *not* to be involved. Jess agreed that Reece could go with Hadley, Ele, and Marie.

Gabby and I are a team. Our job is the children's section. We've gotta rescue as many kids as we can. I wish we had more people. But we don't. Besides, fewer people are less suspicious.

"Are you sure you want to go? You can stay here and join Ledger and Violet. It'll be safer," Jess asks Reece as we make final preparations.

"I'm fine," he says.

"Do this," Jess says, raising her arm. Reece only gets halfway. "How does it feel?"

"It hurts," he says. "So I just won't use this arm. What do you think I'm gonna have to do? Knock someone out or something?"

"Okay," Jess agrees. "I thought you said it was painful to breathe."

Reece rolls his eyes. "Okay, I won't breathe either."

That comment surprises me. Reece doesn't usually sass anyone but Marie and me. Jess doesn't look amused. Reece smiles at her. "I'm joking. It doesn't hurt anymore."

Graydon helps me. We finish packing up our supplies: a light, Violet's stolen keys from the Infirmary, and weapons we got from the base. I put my phone in the inside pocket of our bag.

"Do you think you and Gabby will be able to make it out with just you two?" Graydon asks in an undertone.

"We've thought it through. I think we will," I reply. "I'm good at this sort of stuff."

Graydon shakes his head. "I wish I could do something more important."

He picks up the backpack. Graydon joins Zia and Jess. They're taking our supplies to the tunnels. Graydon's going because he knows the way, and Jess can't go inside the Infirmary because of her betrayal.

We drew up maps together of the tunnels and Infirmary. That way no one gets lost, and no one doubts. We all packed up our things to take when we leave the Haven to wherever we run to. Ledger, Violet, and Ms. Miranda will bring them to our meeting place in the tunnels. Everyone going has received a dose of raxoxin, so we're good. We don't have to worry about contracting anything at the Infirmary.

Jess calls everyone outside at seven-thirty. I'm jittery. Adventure fills the outside air. Pine trees sway in the wind at the edge of the clearing.

"Alright, well, see ya tomorrow!" I say to Reece. He nods slowly.

"See you, Isaiah," he says.

"Be careful," I say.

"Yeah, I'll try not to get stabbed again," Reece jokes, crossing his arms and gazing at the setting sun.

"Great, you do that," I say. "Worried?"

He shrugs with his good shoulder. "Not as much as usual. I'm scared but excited."

"Really? Where'd all this bravery come from?"

"I don't know. After everything, I've changed. I'm tired of being afraid all the time. You taught me about things…you know, about God and hope. About life and death. No one told me stuff like that before. I didn't think much of it, but then I almost died. I had a long time to consider, and I decided. I'd rather be dead and brave than alive and a coward," Reece says awkwardly. "And honestly, it's weird. There's freedom."

I try not to act shocked. That makes me super excited though. *And it was all because of me.*

"I'm proud of you. But I'd rather you not, ya know, die," I comment.

Reece smiles and blushes a little. "I'll try."

"Remember, God will take care of us. It's all for His glory. We'll go to heaven if we have faith," I say. I give him a quick hug. Surprisingly, he doesn't act repulsed. "There's nothing to fear in Christ."

I turn to my sister. We're all dressed in the oldest, dirtiest clothes we have so that we look like we've been surviving the province for a while. Ele wears tattered jeans and a shirt so stained, I can't even tell what color it was. Her hair has a similar look. Jess told me to wear this pair of khaki pants. First, they were way too long, and second, I don't even wear long pants. Ever. Shorts only. Especially in the summer. I fixed both problems last night by just chopping off the bottoms. I'm smart like that.

"Wow, you look great," I say sarcastically.

Ele slaps my shoulder.

"Be safe. Don't do anything stupid," she says seriously then hugs me. "Love you."

I smile and nod. "I never do anything stupid. That's your job."

Ledger comes bolting outside to say goodbye to Gabby. Then, we head into the woods. We're all going to end up at the Infirmary. We're gonna be caught in different places. That way it's hopefully less suspicious. It could have been weeks since someone was found. We can't risk them catching on. We'll be caught by different squads. They won't announce the new patient numbers until tomorrow. No one has the chance to put the facts together.

We head north. Gabby and I run until the Haven is way out of sight. The trees are sparse here. The only sound is the crunch of fallen leaves. Gabby knows the way. I don't. I have to walk quickly to keep up.

"Where are we going?" I ask.

"Somewhere the Mordolus will be," Gabby responds.

I swat a holly branch out of the way. "So, anywhere," I say.

Gabby nods. "We'll go this direction until we find them."

The forest is open. The exposure is weird after a month at the Haven. I feel like any second the Mordolus will pop out from the trees and take us.

"How much farther?" I ask after some time. I kick some mud from my boots.

"The woods should break shortly," Gabby replies.

After clamoring through the forest for an hour, we step out onto a small grassy slope. It leads toward a road. Abandoned buildings haunt it. Shattered windows. Doors crossed in red. It's creepy. It gets dark and cold as we follow the road. I hardly recognize Senneforte Middle School right across from the high school. It's completely overgrown. If we can get to the main road, we can stage our capture, easy. It's dead silent. I uneasily listen for the Mordolus.

"See those buildings?" Gabby whispers. He points toward a cluster of businesses: a car shop, post office, and jewelry store. They sit side-by-side across from the road. I know this place. The Mordolus come through here a lot.

"We're going to wait over there, okay? It shouldn't take long," Gabby says. I nod.

Hidden in the small alleyway between the post office and jeweler's, we wait. Twenty minutes pass. Then, a familiar crackling breaks the silence. A truck is coming. I'm scared. We have to wait for the right moment. Gabby peeks behind the wall. He gives me a nod. We silently agree on a plan. The vehicle's creak is near the alley.

I take off running, sprinting straight across the road in front of the vehicle. I don't take my eyes off the woods across the street. Gabby runs the other direction, down the road. The vehicle stops. Voices and footsteps increase. I risk a glance behind me, forcing myself to not run for my life. Someone chases me. It's an older man. He looks mean. That's just a Mordolus thing. Jess was the same way. I thank God it's not Ash chasing me. He might recognize me. I hate Ash. Ever since the day I was captured. The memory haunts me. Ash took me from home. He tried to tell me my parents hated me and left me alone to die. He hurt me. He tried to break me. Guess I was stronger than he thought.

I stumble over some rocks, lost in memory. The Hunters chasing Gabby and me close in. A commotion grows from the road. They caught Gabby. The wood's edge is right in front of me. I force myself to fake fall onto a cluster of big stones. My arm hurts. A pair of hands wrench me from the ground. My heart lurches.

I channel all my hate. I fight like I would if this were real.

Gabby waits in the back of the truck. I'm thrown in. Gabby's leg bleeds badly. His black hair is disheveled. A bruise forms on my arm. At least it looks more believable.

"How'd that go?" I whisper.

"No problems yet," Gabby replies. He wipes some of the blood from his leg. "Keep up the act."

We sit on the dirty floor. The ride is jostling. I wonder who'll get there first. Ele, Marie, Hadley, and Reece are closest to the Infirmary. I think they were going to try and get caught near the elementary school. Hallston, Bexley, and Atticus are the furthest. They could be caught before they get there, though. Jess, Zia, and Graydon should've already been at the tunnels by the time we arrive.

We drive down the road for thirty minutes to the Infirmary. I get fidgety. I listen to the muffled conversation of our driver and his companions. When I first came to the Infirmary, the line of people filled the entire gated area. The parking lot is empty. Everyone has already contracted the Virus or died. I can't forget the horrifying field next to the Infirmary. It's just dirt and rot. Hardly any graves are empty. They're all unmarked. So many have been lost.

The truck comes to a halt. The gate closes behind us. Two men open the truck door. They drag Gabby and me out into the large, fenced parking lot.

"Let us go!" I seethe, kicking my guard in the leg.

"Stop it!" he yells, spinning me around. He slaps me across the face. The guard holds me even tighter. Gabby and I struggle less as they haul us closer so they won't lock us in the Hopeful Rooms.

The Infirmary door shuts. Glistening, white walls surround me. Unless the plan works, we're trapped. Volleys of sickening cries attack my ears. The third guard signs us in at the desk.

"What are your names?" she asks.

"Gabby Shorsee."

I give my arm a yank. I hesitate. "Ledger Grove."

She writes on the paper, opens a drawer in one of the filing cabinets, and slides our paperwork into a folder. The other two guards take us to a room.

"Good job," Gabby says. He gives me a high five. "You alright?"

I touch the burning bruise on my cheek. It does hurt, but I don't want to seem like a wimp. I wave my hand. "Yeah. We need to get out of here."

Gabby takes a sheet off one of the beds. He cleans the cut on his leg. "Why'd you fake your name?"

"I've been here before. I thought they might know my name since I escaped," I say, satisfied at my cleverness.

"That's smart," Gabby says. "I wouldn't have thought of that."

"I know, I'm pretty amazing," I say, followed by a little wrench of guilt. I really need to start working on my pride issue. "I mean, thanks."

The second we arrived I knew the security had been improved. More cameras are secured to the ceiling. More guards. More locks. Thankfully, our door is open.

We wait a few minutes to be safe. Gabby and I step out of our room. When we reach the dirty halls, the two of us break into a run. We head to retrieve our supplies from the tunnel entrance. I jump to the foot of the stairs. Gabby steps down behind me. I search the dark ground.

"Found it!" I say. I grasp the backpack and hoist it onto my shoulder. No one else has been here yet. All the supplies still lean against the tunnel wall.

"What was that?" Gabby says. He stares into the dark tunnel. Footsteps. I'm not imagining it. Maybe Merris, or the Queen, or the Mordolus are guarding the tunnels. Maybe they already caught the others. Gabby fishes a dagger from the bag and holds it ready.

"Relax, it's just me!" a voice calls from the darkness. Gabby puts the blade away.

I drop the backpack. "Graydon? What are you doing?"

"I'm coming with you. I brought the girls here, showed them where to go, then sent them back to get the other things. I've been waiting for someone to come for an hour. Seriously, when you're down here alone, it's unnerving. I was just checking out the tunnel," Graydon says, starting up the steps. Gabby and I follow him.

We reach the door out of the abandoned halls. "I was worried about having just two of us," I say. "Thanks for staying." I'm glad Graydon's here. It's safe to say I'm his best friend. It's crazy we've known each other for over ten years.

"Where is it?" Gabby whispers, as we step into the hall.

"This way. A lot of people tried to get in. It's heavily guarded," I say.

Stepping through the familiar hallways and doors, I lead Gabby and Graydon towards the children's section. There are a lot less people. I try not to think about what that means. We pocket all our items and shed the backpack before we enter the busy hall.

I stand in front of the locked doors of the children's section. Children's brutal cries echo through the eerie halls. They have more nurses to care for the children. We certainly won't blend in. The three of us stop and hide behind the wall.

"Isaiah, what are we doing?" Graydon asks.

"Just a second," I whisper. Footsteps resound from behind the door to the children's section. As the door opens, two nurses walk out, alarmed.

"We're missing a patient. We need to check the whole Infirmary. The Queen will not tolerate another breach," one of them says. They run off down the hall. That had to be one of us who helped them escape. We're that much closer to getting caught.

I take out a pilfered key and unlock the door. Three members of Auxillia worked here. Jess, Bentley, and Violet. Jess stopped, and Bentley was caught. So yesterday, Violet stole all the keys we'll need. She won't be coming back here again anyway.

"Let's hurry," Gabby says. Graydon glances to make sure the nurses are gone. We run.

I know this place. I came here to treat some of the sickest children. Back then it was easier to get in.

Along the wall, several hallways led to the right. They're categorized by age, oldest to youngest. I glance up at the cameras. That's new. We only have a few minutes—at most.

"Where do we go first?" Gabby asks.

"We should get the older children. They can help with the younger ones," I decide. Taking the first hall, we stop at the second door. I glance up at the sign. *6-9.*

Other rooms line the same hall. This one is the common room for the children. Most of the older kids will be here. I'm not as worried about them. There are fewer nurses. Often, the older kids will take care of each other and the younger ones. It's cool and sad. I open the door. We step inside. The room is big but crowded and loud. *Very* loud.

About fifteen kids are inside. They notice us instantly. A silence falls across the room. Like everywhere else, it's filthy. There are no toys or anything. It's just an empty, depressing room. The children all have a pale, feverish look.

"Who are you?" an eight-year-old boy asks.

"I'm Isaiah," I say. "We broke into the Infirmary to help you. If you come with us, we'll help you escape."

"We're going to help you get out of here and find your parents." Graydon adds, eyeing the backdoor where the nurses could enter from any second.

The children exchange glances and start to protest.

"Are you that kid who's broken in before? With the medicine?" one asks.

"Yes, I am," I say.

"It's okay. We're going to help you recover too," Gabby says, sporting an easy smile.

The kids are still confused. They keep asking questions. I have to tell them to come and ask later. Thankfully, most agree.

"Where are we going?" asks one of the girls as we lead them out back to the main hallway.

"You'll see. Somewhere safe. We're leaving the Infirmary, that's for sure. We've got to hurry so we can rescue some of the other children," I say.

"Thank you for helping us. I'm Bridget," the girl says. "I'll try to help too."

The procedure is similar for the next room. *3-5.* The younger they are, the harder it gets. We haven't seen a single nurse. Either they're short-staffed, or something else is attracting their attention. Something that might have to do with my sister.

"They're going to save us!" Bridget says. She gently takes the crying child's hand.

We leave the room empty. I feel so exposed. We lead the party of children to the last hall. The cameras are running. The children are screaming. This is not good.

"This better be fast," Graydon comments, eyeing the kids.

Only one room left. I silently pray no one will come. That the nurses will stay away. So far, I think it's been answered the way I want.

There's no way the Mordolus would leave a room full of sick babies alone. And they'll have to be carried, so we can only bring as many as we can hold. It's an awful thought. The youngest ones, less than a year, are kept in a section of the ICU. We won't be able to save them today. But we will come back. Someday.

I listen carefully at the door to the room. I'm shocked to hear no nurses inside. I slowly push the door open to confirm. No one. Graydon, Gabby, the oldest kids, and I rush inside. After a moment of chaos, each person holds at least one child. Then we're out of the room.

"Alright, please be quiet!" I say to everyone. I try hard to get the screaming child in my arms to quiet. "We've got to hurry! This way!"

Graydon makes sure no one is coming while I lead the children toward the door. Gabby helps all the stragglers. I peek around to see if the door is clear. The doors to the children's rooms are internally locked. This one would be externally locked to keep the family away. For once, we have a clear shot at making it.

"If we hurry to the tunnels, we'll be okay!" I say to Graydon as I open the door. I quickly motion the crying, screaming group of children into the foyer between the halls. As Gabby steps through the door, I slam it shut. Another door opens. There's a gasp. Someone must have gone to check on the children. And discovered the room was empty. *Their fault for leaving them unattended.* But that isn't the problem now. They're coming.

"Hurry!" I call. I run down the hall toward the tunnels.

"Oh no," Graydon says. A nurse stares at us from the doorway. I can't hear anything over the children's voices. He turns and runs off down the hall, pulling out his phone to call backup.

"It's okay! We just have to get to the tunnels now! We'll be safe there," Gabby says calmly. Several of the children burst into tears. I'm panicking. How are we going to get out of this? *God help us.*

"Over here!" I call. I usher them down the hall toward the tunnels—further away from the crime scene. I'm just praying over and over that they'll be quiet. Thankfully, at the end of the hallway, the noise dies down. That's when the nurse returns with help to the other hallway.

"They were right here! Check the other halls!" he says. If we can get them quickly to the tunnels before we're found, we might make it. If they can be quieter.

"Hey!" another voice says. There's a commotion. I glance at Graydon. He's pale-faced as he motions the children further down the hall. Confused, I search for an explanation.

"Gabby," he whispers. I gasp. He's not here.

"Here," Bridget says, taking the child from me. She somehow balances both children in her small arms. I nod thankfully. That's my signal to do something. The hallway clears, and Graydon leads the children away. I sprint back. The children's voices fade. I peek around the wall.

Gabby is held back by two of the guards. The nurse who alarmed them watches, arms crossed tightly. He stands beside another who interrogates Gabby. The group is only feet away. I stay hidden. I can't risk getting caught. But I have to help Gabby.

"Where are the children?" the other nurse screams. "How did you infiltrate the children's section?" Gabby glares. He shakes his head.

"Tell us!" one of the guards demands. Gabby refuses again. They continue to ask him questions. They want to know where the children are and what he was doing, but Gabby stays quiet. One of the Mordolus holds him back now. The other gets impatient.

"I won't tell you!" Gabby finally says.

The guard slaps him furiously. "How did they escape?!"

"He's obviously not going to tell us, and we're wasting time! We have to look for them!" says one of the men holding Gabby. The nurse nods in agreement. They drag him down the hall. I don't know what to do.

"Take care of him and search the area. I'm going to begin lockdown and check the cams," the female nurse orders.

The two guards throw Gabby to the floor. Anger spreads into a wildfire inside me. One guard pulls something from her coat and hands it to the remaining nurse. A deafening noise reverberates around the hall, hammering against my head. Gabby collapses.

My brain freezes. Despite the silencer, the gunshot still rings in my ears. Gabby is motionless. I gaze from the blood pooling on the floor to the gun in the nurse's hand. That can't have happened. There's no way.

"Block the hallways to the children's section and call someone to take care of this," the guard says, tucking the handgun back into his belt. Then, the nurse and guards run off down the hall in the opposite direction. Gabby lays still on the ground. My hope for his survival grows weaker every second. This can't be happening.

I just stand there. Firearms were banned and confiscated by Morzanna before the Virus outbreak. I guess she just took them for her own army.

I take the risk and run over to Gabby. I can't hear anything but my own pounding heart. I roll him onto his back. I can't comprehend what I see. My hands are stained red. *Blood. People can survive getting shot in the head, right?* I quickly check for a pulse. Nothing.

God, please don't let him be dead. He can't be dead. But as I gaze at Gabby's lifeless body, I force myself to accept reality. It's like poison seeping into my head. Gabby's dead. An ache burrows into my chest. I only realize I'm really crying when there's coolness on my bruised cheek. The children need to get to safety. Someone will come. I choke back a sob, stumbling to my feet. I stare at his pallid, freckled face. Gabby was a Christian. That's a comfort.

"God is good. This is His will," I whisper. "Thank you, Gabby," I mutter. With a final glance, I run as fast as possible toward the tunnels.

"Come on, everyone! This way!" Graydon quietly orders up ahead. I catch up with him. He glances at me, worry brimming his eyes.

"What happened? What was that sound? Where's Gabby?" Graydon asks quietly. I shake my head.

"He's gone," I whisper. The older children look at us.

"What?" Graydon asks, scared. He lays a hand on my shoulder. "Isaiah, you're crying?"

I hold up a bloody, shaking hand. He stares, wide-eyed. I feel sick. Very, very sick. And dizzy. Numb. "He's dead, Graydon," I say. "They shot him."

Graydon looks away, shocked. Actually saying it makes it real. Gabby *is* dead. The longer I stare at my hands, the more the world tilts. *Blood.* It's just a red blur. I'm gonna faint. A coldness on my hands brings me back as Graydon dumps a bottle of water on them and washes away the blood. I shake the sense back into my head. I unsteadily scramble to the very front of the group, taking back the child from Bridget. There's an empty feeling in my chest. *God, just let this all work out. I know it will. Help me remember that.*

Axly clings to my free hand. "What's going to happen, Isaiah?"

"We're getting out of here. Safely," I say. I guide the children toward the tunnels. We'll make it to safety, and Gabby just sacrificed himself to get us there.

45
REECE: DAD?

Ele, Marie, Hadley, and I enter the gates to the Infirmary an hour after leaving the Haven. The staff members question us about our exposure, but the four guards skip the Virus testing, and it makes me feel a ton better. I didn't want to get stabbed with a needle again, and I was scared they would find the mark from my first test. It's green, which is the color for June, so that would be a dead giveaway. Isaiah's right; mine's spread to the size of a dime over time.

We're dragged inside the doors, and I bet we're the first ones here. A nurse at the entrance quickly writes something down, nods, and hands the paper to the guards. They take us through the entryway, past the shadowy obituary pillar, and down the hall. The white hallways close in around me.

Hadley puts up no fight, but Marie, Ele, and I holler and struggle against the guards to be realistic.

"Hey, wait!" Marie protests as the three of us are each thrown into one of the small dark rooms. I stumble back, and the door slams shut, separating us. They're the Hopeful Rooms. Hadley isn't caged. Probably wise of her not to fight like us.

There's a loud groan from behind the wall to my right and a banging sound like someone kicking the door from the other.

"I'm trapped, I'm trapped, I'm trapped," I mutter, a steady stream of intrusive thoughts crawling into my brain. I rip a hand through my hair, gripping the dirty wall. A sharp pain slithers through my chest and shoulder. We'll be stuck in here until they decide we're tame and hopeless enough to let out.

"I'm going to be okay," I say. Panic rakes an icy talon across my throat, and a fiery heat spreads across my face.

"I'm going to be fine. I'm going to save my dad. Marie and Ele are right in the other rooms, and we're going to be let out soon," I tell myself. "I'll be okay."

But there are still people dying. There's still an insane queen. There's still a country ready to attack us. There's still a deadly virus. But, there are also survivors. There's a cure. And there's hope.

I pace the room to try to relieve the pain in my shoulder. I wish Isaiah were here. I hope he's okay. I've never tried before, but right now I'm scared, so I pray. If God really has this all worked out, I need help right now to trust His plan. I have no idea what to say. *God, are you real? Can you help me now? Keep Isaiah safe. He deserves it because he always trusts and stuff. I know I'm not the best person, but I'd like to not get hurt again too. And find my dad today.* I want to know more about who God is. I wish I had more proof of Him being real. All I know is what Isaiah told me. I want the fearlessness and hope Isaiah has. I've been trying to be good, but it's hard. Isaiah said faith is what's most important, so that's what I've been working on. The truth is, I really didn't want to believe that God and sin were real at first because that would mean my mom….my mom didn't know the truth, or at least didn't believe that she needed Jesus to save her like I do now. Isaiah explained to me what happens to people who don't believe and know they're a sinner when they die. Hell. I hate it. Just because I ignore the truth doesn't make it not true. But I don't care. I can't handle the thought of my mom being *there*.

A long half-hour passes, and it's quiet, so I think we're the only captives in these rooms.

The door opens, and a tall, thin, older woman calls me outside. She unlocks Ele and Marie's rooms. She guides us through the hallways, and I carefully internalize the excitement growing inside me. Pausing, the nurse looks down at a clipboard and carefully scans it.

"We don't have a lot of space," she says then looks at Ele and me. "Are you two siblings?"

"Yes," Ele responds, nodding, but I'm wondering how the nurse could mistake us for being related. Although, now that I think about it, we do look more alike than, say, Marie and me. Ele's hair is lighter and straighter than mine, but I guess some of our other features are similar. Getting put in the same room will be good, and we can get to the tunnels faster. We'll join Hadley there.

"The door is unlocked," Ele says, checking the handle after the nurse drops the two of us off at a tiny room and takes Marie upstairs to a different one. "We'll meet Marie at the tunnels as soon as possible.

You say you know which rooms are my parents'? I don't want to be distracted from the job, so let's make some progress before we go find them."

Ele sits on one of the creaky, metal-framed beds and drags a hand through her tangled, blond locks while I pace the room to get out some nervous energy.

"If that's what you want. This room is close to the tunnels," I say, thinking. "We just have to follow that hallway. There are no cameras in here either. If we wait a few minutes, it should be safe to go get our supplies."

"How will Marie and Hadley find the tunnels from inside?" Ele asks. "Do you think they will be able to locate them from the map we drew up?"

"I hope so. If not, we can split up and look for them. They should be able to find the general area," I say.

After we retrieve our things from the tunnels, Hadley, Ele, Marie, and I are supposed to bring as many people from the unrestricted areas as we can. Compared to the others, we have a simple job, but a zephyr of unease still blows through my mind.

I open the door cautiously, and Ele and I leave the blank bedroom. I keep glancing over my shoulder after we climb past the restricted section's red-taped barricades to make sure we haven't been seen.

A strange coolness chases away the nervous heat from my face as I open the hidden door to the abandoned hallways. We climb through the narrow secret entrance and down the stairs to the mouth of the tunnel.

"There you guys are," Marie says, shining a flashlight around the stairwell and standing beside Hadley. She bounces up and down, an excited grin spreading across her copper countenance. "I waited like foreverrrr. And I got turned around getting here too. I left the second that nurse dropped me off. I got stuck in this room with these two weird ladies. I'm telling ya, they got too much of the wrong kinda medicine or something. I was out of there the second I could."

"Well, Marie," Ele says as I take away the light before Marie leaves us with permanent vision damage. "*We* were trying to be safe."

Marie shrugs with a wave of her small hand. I glance around the clay passage walls.

"Isaiah's been here. The others haven't made it yet," I observe, staring at the supplies laying on the tunnel ground.

"I hope they arrive soon," Hadley says, straightening her light brown jacket.

Marie picks up her knife and shoves it into the homemade sheath on her belt.

"I really hope you don't need that," I say, eyeing the blackwood hilt.

"Just for safety," Marie says, patting the leather scabbard and covering it with her coat. "This is so cool! We're like superheroes! We should've had Bexley make us some fancy-schmancy badges or something."

We climb the stairs again and walk back through the abandoned hallways.

"Where should we start?" Marie asks quietly. Ele shrugs as we follow the hall back until we cross the barricade to the unrestricted areas.

"Why not here?" Hadley suggests, stopping at the first door to the right.

"Alright," Ele says, twisting a piece of hair. Suddenly, the lights dim for a second.

"It's midnight," I say, thinking. "Jess is going to be worried. We're supposed to be back soon. That also means fewer guards, but they're the worst type. Like Ash."

"I think we sorely miscalculated how long this mission would take," Hadley says, tossing a ginger braid over her shoulder.

"Since we weren't even the last ones to get supplies, I don't think it's going to be just us who don't arrive on time," Ele says, lowering her volume so as not to draw attention. "So how are we going to do this? Take turns bringing them back to the tunnels?"

"That works," Marie shrugs.

"I'll go first," I offer, crossing my arms and double-checking the ceiling to make sure no cameras point toward us.

Ele nods and, with a quick look around and swift knock on the door, opens the first room.

Two beds sit adjacent to a window across from the door. One girl stands in front of the window, staring longingly at the moonlight.

The second girl lays in bed and flicks her head toward us as the door opens. They're both young, about Zia's age, twenty-five.

"Who are you? What are you doing?" one with darker hair asks, sitting up straighter in her bed, a terrified expression settling over her pale face and pink cheeks.

"I'm Ele. We came to get you out of here. We're going to help you escape," Ele says.

"My name is Hadley. I am part of an undercover group. We have secured a path out of here," Hadley explains.

The other girl turns from the window and coughs weakly. "Won't we be caught?" she asks, tossing her peroxide blond hair with dark, grown-out roots.

"We found a secret way out. Tunnels under the Infirmary," Marie says, rocking onto her toes. "We've got to hurry though."

"For real? What's the point? To leave and die more miserably?" the other girl says from her bed.

I shake my head. "No. We have a cure! We can give it to you, but you have to hurry!"

The girls exchange a wide-eyed glance.

Marie sighs. "If you're gonna come, hurry up!"

Ele shoots Marie a reproachful sideways glance, but the blond girl helps the other out of her bed.

"I hope everything you said is true," the brown-haired girl says as we cross the room to the door.

"It is. I promise," I assure her as a wave of stranger-danger tries to overtake me, but I push it away. "Come on, I'll show you where to go."

As I return from showing the girls to the abandoned halls, I meet Marie taking three other people there too. We make it through the next few rooms alright, but Marie starts getting annoyed because it takes a few minutes to wake people up, explain everything, and convince them to come with us. Hadley's pretty good at talking things out. We only have to hide a few times when a nurse checks on a patient or a guard passes by. Marie and Ele aren't as accustomed to hiding as me. I'm pretty much a pro at it from years of practice, so I'm always scouting out hiding spots.

Of the thousands of people who are in the Infirmary, we've taken like *maybe* twenty to the tunnels in an hour. This is only Section One of three. We'll never get to the others and barely make a dent in this one. While I think about my dad and Isaiah's parents, fear wells inside me. The icy swell grows as I wonder if we'll find them before it's too late. I really want to see my dad.

Marie throws open the door to one of the rooms and walks inside. She starts our routine spiel as Ele and I follow her inside. Hadley is walking the last person to the tunnels.

"Hi, I'm Marie, and I'm here to rescue you!" Marie say. Ele freezes.

"Ms. Kassy?" Ele cries, immediately throwing herself into the woman's embrace.

"Eleanora!" the lady with long, wavy, brown hair says, standing up. Ele and the woman stare at each other, joy glittering through the room. Releasing Ele's hand, the woman runs outside and jogs down the other hall. She returns with a tall, brunette man.

Marie leans over to me. "Who even is that?" I shrug.

"Mr. Madison!" Ele exclaims then notices our confused expressions. "These are Graydon's parents!"

Shock obscuring both our expressions, Marie and I look at each other.

Marie laughs and looks at the woman. "Ohh, haha! We're pretty lucky, huh?"

"I'm Kassy," the lady replies, a lovely smile spreading across her light face.

"Madison," the man says. Marie elbows me.

"I'm Reece," I say quietly, looking from the lady to the man.

"Where is Graydon?" Ms. Kassy asks.

"He's helping too!" Ele says, excitement still vying at the edges of her mouth.

Ms. Kassy throws her hands over her face and laughs softly. A bright smile grows across Mr. Madison's face, one similar to Graydon's, and they share those dark, secretive eyes that make me sort of sketched out. It's probably just me though; I over-analyze people.

Ele begs to walk them to the tunnels, explaining everything during the trip, and Marie and I get back to work.

Two rooms later, all four of us end up in the tunnels at the same time. There are a ton of people there, and it's super loud since they're all talking and trying to figure out what's happening. Mr. Madison's got it figured out and explains, urging everyone to quiet down. Hadley remains with the group to answer questions and explain our story. I get overwhelmed in here fast; Ele, Marie, and I hurry back up the stairs. I look around carefully then climb out into the hallway. It's crazy how the restricted area's warnings don't faze me anymore.

"It's one," I gasp as the lights flash on and off twice.

"Yeah?" Marie says. She's not getting it.

"They're going to be sending out the night nurses to do a check-in!" I say, heat crawling into my cheeks. "They're gonna find out people are missing!"

"We need to hurry then," Ele says, twirling a piece of hair. We run back to the hallway, and I glance to the very end.

Room 30.

"Ele! You're parents!" I say quickly, feeling too many conflicted emotions to sort through them. I motion for them to follow me. Turning the corner, I head for Room 37.

"What?" she asks, her eyes widening as we run to the door.

"This is where your parents are! It's time to rescue them."

Ele gasps as I throw the door open. Tendrils of excitement work their way through the mess inside my head. Ele's mother basically treats me like I'm her own, especially since my mother died.

"Eleanora?" a familiar voice says. Ele tries to speak but sort of chokes and runs to her mother. I don't say anything while the two embrace. *She's okay, she's okay, she's okay.*

"Come on, Marie," I say, running across the hall.

"Mr. Brooks?" I ask, opening the door to Room 49.

"Reece? What are you doing here?" he asks, rising. He's weaker and more tired looking than when I last saw him. His roommate is gone now, one way or the other. I'm trying to analyze how much Ele's parents have changed and apply it to the last time I saw my dad.

"Ele's out here! Come on!" I say, gesturing for him to hurry.

Ele reunites with both her parents in the Infirmary hallway. Ele laugh-sobs and tries to say everything at once. Jealousy simmers in my stomach.

"Reece!" Mrs. Brooks says weakly, embracing me, one arm still around Ele. She needs the cure, bad. A strange longing tingles in my heart. I have to find my dad.

"This is great and all, but the night nurses are coming!" Marie warns, impatiently tapping on my arm. Ele nods, but I swat Marie away as suffocation sets in. I want to just run through every room until I find dad, no matter the consequences. *We're never going to find him. He's going to die. I'm going to die.*

"We should probably go back," Ele says reluctantly.

"No!" I blurt out, wanting to curl up on the floor and cry. Cry forever. Cry until it's okay again. I throw my hands over my face, a frenzy rising in my chest as I take short, insufficient breaths.

"Hey," Marie says, grabbing my wrists so I look at her. "Chill out. You're fine. We'll find him eventually."

I yank my hands away. "Just a little while longer?" I beg.

"I don't know. The nurses are coming, and we don't have long to get back," Ele says hesitatingly. "I think—"

"STOP!" I say. My mind churns. "I'm going to find my dad."

So, I take off. I just run. "Dad!" I call, over and over, throwing open doors and running like I'm mad, ignoring every questioning occupant that isn't him. "DAD!"

I think someone's following me, and it could be the Mordolus. I could get caught. I'm *never* going to find my dad. I need somewhere to hide.

There's a nice-looking broom closet up ahead, so I take it. Turns out it's not a broom closet, it's a medical storage room. I crawl behind a fancy giant first aid box. I have totally lost my mind. It takes a few minutes of deep breathing to calm myself to rationality. *God's got this under control.*

"Reece? Reece?!" Marie calls from outside. If they're looking for me, it must be safe. I head for the door.

Nearly the second I open it, I get smacked in the face.

"Are you stupid, Reece?! What'd you go and run away for?!" Marie demands, wielding our hand-drawn Infirmary map.

"I'm sorry. I got overwhelmed," I say quietly.

"Now is not the time for breakdowns! We gotta go find Ele and get out of here!" Marie says. "Come on."

My mind clears as we run down the hallway. Ele meets us right around the corner from where we left.

She sighs. "I thought you guys got captured."

Marie shakes her head as we make it back to where we left Ele's parents. "Nope, we're good, but Reecey here nearly got us locked up."

My face burns.

Suddenly, an unfamiliar voice rings through the hallway, and I turn to look down the adjacent hall. A nurse runs through the corridors, opening doors, and wildly dialing a number on her phone when she sees they're all empty.

"They escaped!" she screeches.

"We need to go before they come!" Ele says urgently, escorting her mother down the hall and grabbing Marie's hand. Mrs. Brooks' roommate joins us too. "If we hurry, we can make it," Ele announces.

I nod, and the five of us run past the nurse and toward the tunnels. I glance back and see that she isn't following us, but footsteps close in all around. We cut across the main medical hallway, where they do most of the basic, daily treatment.

That's when the alarms start to blare. The lights flash over and over. In seconds, the halls are packed with people wondering what's going on. Ele and Mr. Brooks help Mrs. Brooks as we cross the hallway, struggling to push through the crowd.

"Reece?"

I freeze, the lights making my eyes see psychedelic. I slowly turn around like a blow has knocked all my senses away.

"Dad? Dad!" I exclaim, staring down the hall through the crowd. I don't know how. I don't even know if it's real, but there heading toward me is my father. I'm so shocked, I can't even move.

"Reece!"

Before I can think, I find myself wrapped in his arms. Ignoring the soreness in my shoulder, I hug him tighter. He could have met the same fate as Mom. I might have never seen him again. At least, that's what I've been telling myself. But he's okay.

"I missed you so much," I say softly.

"I can't believe I found you! I heard the alarm and wondered what was going on!" Dad says, his calm tone bringing a rush of assurance.

"We're rescuing you, Reece's dad!" Marie announces brightly.

Dad stares down at me, eyes twinkling, then at Ele and Marie, and hugs me again.

"Come on, guys!" Marie calls, and we follow the final, dingy hall.

"Where are we going?" Dad asks.

"The tunnels are over here!" I say, quickly opening the hidden door, favoring my arm. Ele is careful to shut the door tightly, and we run through the abandoned halls and down the flight of stairs.

The tunnel is illuminated by several flashlights; all the people we rescued are ready and waiting for us.

When we get there, Hallston runs up to us. "You guys got out! Did you see Bexley?"

Marie shakes her head. "No, we almost all got caught! Bella's still in there?"

A worried look spreads across Hallston's face, and she shakes her head before running past us up the stairs.

"This way!" Ele orders, motioning for everyone to follow us. There's a chance they'd find the abandoned halls, so we need to be long gone by then. We planned a meeting place within the tunnels, and Jess said we'll figure out the next steps there.

"Why didn't the nurse follow us?" I ask, confused.

"She practically collapsed on the floor from hyperventilating, didn't you see?" Marie says as if it were funny. "I don't think anyone else saw us." I swallow and nod.

We walk through the tunnels in search of the meeting place. It's a little pool we passed before. It's in a large open area and should fit everyone.

The four of us are bombarded with questions. Ele catches up with her parents, I talk to dad, and Hadley assists the most ill. So, Marie gets stuck with everyone else, trying to explain the tunnels, how we rescued everyone, and what's even going on to fifty people.

"You just happened to find this place?" Dad asks.

"Yeah. We used it the first time we escaped. A lot's happened, Dad, it's going to take so long to explain," I say, crossing my arms to help alleviate the pain in my shoulder that's rapidly spreading to my chest and down to my hand.

"Once we get out of here, we're going to have all the time we need," Dad says with a smile.

Something hangs on my conscience, and a sudden current of fear floods my mind. I know what it is.

"Dad. I—I mean, Mom–you know she's…dead? I mean—"

"I know, Reece," he interrupts.

I look up at him. "What?"

"I know," Dad repeats solemnly. "I know how she was when we got here. I knew that there was no way she would have survived for this long. I'm a doctor, Reece, I know when someone's dying. I wondered about you too, but…"

I nod, a familiar feeling of loss prickling my heart. Dad puts a hand on my shoulder—the good one, thankfully. Another event I've gotta explain later.

"Okay, everyone, I'm sorry, but can you just shut up? I'm only one person, and I can hardly take all this," Marie says as she's being questioned about the cure's discovery and replication. Ele's eyes widen with horror, and she quickly goes to fix Marie's statement and explain our situation to the score of people.

Marie walks up beside me. "Jeez, all those people kept asking me the same questions, all at the same time. Like what the heck?"

I shake my head at her and smile, but then a new realization sets in. Marie didn't find either of her parents.

Ele, Marie, and I lead the others through the labyrinth-like passages, only stopping to dispute which way to go. We're in one of these spots, and Marie goes down one path to see if it leads up, down, or level. Suddenly, a shriek echoes through the passage.

Ele and I exchange uneasy glances.

Dad springs toward the tunnel to listen and looks at me. "Is she alright?"

"We'll go check!" Ele says, nodding to me, and we run down the path Marie took.

"You think she's okay?" Ele asks, holding the light as we clamber deeper down the tunnel.

"I don't know. It is Marie. She sometimes yells for no reason," I say, trying to hide the fear in my voice. The ground slopes further down, and it gets colder.

"Marie?" I call. A light flickers ahead. The two of us sprint toward the source.

Ele screams, and I freeze.

Around the bend, Merris holds Marie tightly by his scarred arms. The second Ele sees Merris, she drops the light.

"I'm going to get help!" Ele says and runs back up the tunnel.

Marie struggles in Merris' grip while he remains completely silent. She ends up saying some shocking things to him, thrashing. I don't know what to do, so I just stare for about thirty unnecessary seconds. My old best friend, Cowardice, kicks in, and I want to bolt.

"Don't be stupid! Do something, Reece!" Marie hollers desperately, pulling me back to the real world.

Have courage. You are not alone.

I look around the passage quickly. *I can do this.* On the ground nearby lies the light Ele dropped. The one Marie had taken to investigate is broken on the floor, extinguished. With a deep inhale, I grab the light, turn it off, and the tunnel disappears into darkness. I can't see anything, and it's scary, but I sprint to where Marie and Merris struggle. Marie shrieks, confirming their location through the shadows.

Though I expected it, the complete darkness leaves me disoriented. I quickly recover, knowing I have to take action. I *can* overcome my fear. Like a new sense has awakened, I perceive the two of them right in front of me. A new feeling surges up inside me, and I sense my opportunity to make my move. Using the moment of distraction, I find Marie's arm and kick Merris in the leg as hard as I can. His grip falters, and I yank her away using all my strength. I'm shocked by my miraculous success. Maybe I can get out of this. Marie pulls her arm away from me, and the three of us are left in complete, separated darkness. I search the floor until I find the light again and turn it back on, just in time to see Merris standing in front of me. I scramble away, but he chases me across the tunnel and grabs me. I drop the flashlight and claw at his arms as I find myself locked in his tight grip. I kick and fight with my good arm, strength flourishing inside me. Merris drags me down the tunnel while a surprising inner force of courage controls me as I try to wrench away from him but fail. The light rolls across the ground, aiming toward the wall so it gets pretty dark.

"Let me go!" I cry, struggling and trying to get away from him, but I can't; he's too strong. An unbearable pain rips through my shoulder, and I try to scream, but Merris has me in a chokehold.

Suddenly, Merris lets me go with a shout before his footsteps fade into the darkness. I stumble away. The flashlight is picked up. With a metallic clank, Marie drops her knife. She covers her face with her hands and for once in her life looks completely terrified. Her hands slide away, and we both look at each other, shocked.

"Now I know," Marie says solemnly.

"Know what?"

"What it's like to slicey someone," she replies with a shiver. "Bleh."

Less than a minute passes before Ele comes back.

"What happened? Where's Merris? I heard the scream and came back because I knew we didn't have time, but—" Ele gasps. "Are you okay? I'm so, so sorry! Are you guys alright?"

Ele runs over, looking at both of us with horror. I shrug, too shocked to speak. I stare at the blood-sprinkled ground, noticing it's purple-tinted and speckled with silver.

"Seriously, what happened?" Ele asks, holding up her hands and picking up the light from where Marie dropped it at her feet.

"Merris finally let me go. But then he took Reece, and then I remembered my knife, and—" Marie stops, and a sick look spreads across her face. "It was only his arm."

Ele just gapes. "Oh my goodness."

"Reecey saved me. He was a real hero," Marie says. I blush and turn away, looking down the dark tunnel Merris descended.

"We need to leave now. Merris could return or contact Morzanna. Everyone's going to be worried, and Jess expected us back hours ago," I manage to say.

"You're right. Merris can probably mentally talk to Queen lady or something, and she'll send someone to take us down," Marie says and shivers. "That was the weirdest thing ever."

She picks up her weapon and returns it to her belt.

When we come jogging up the path, our parents crowd around us.

"Reece? What's going on? Is someone hurt?" Dad asks, running up to us. "Is that blood!? What happened?"

"It's not mine. We're fine," I say, calming myself. "Don't worry, we're alright."

"You're sure you're all okay?" Dad asks. I nod quickly, and we explain what happened to Dad, Hadley, Graydon's parents, and the Brookses, who all heard Marie's first scream and watched us leave. I don't even know where to start with Merris' telepathic capabilities.

"Everything's fine!" Mr. Brooks announces to everyone. "We need to keep moving."

At some point my shoulder injury hurts so bad, I can't hide it anymore. Marie tells an overtly gory version of the story, leaving all the parents horrified. Dad goes off and pleads for someone's extra clothing or something. Ms. Kassy gives him her jacket to make me a sling.

We finally arrive at the pool. There are a lot of children. I hear them from a long way away. Isaiah immediately comes over to us, and I'm just glad to know he survived. Jess is extremely relieved when she sees us.

I'm really proud of myself for making it here. For having the courage. All this time, my panic I was sure was protecting me was really killing me from the inside. Those fears have been eating away at me. Destroying me. Lying to me. That's how anxiety is—it's a trap. I guess the only remedy for it is truth. Truth and hope.

With my dad, somewhat safe here in the tunnel, I feel happy. With faith in God that He's gonna take care of me, I'm complete.

46
BEXLEY: TIME'S ALMOST UP

Atticus, Hallston, and I arrive at the Infirmary later than anticipated. We suspect that since there are fewer people left in Senneforte, there are also fewer Hunters roaming after they noted the decrease. Our delay could have been because I'm with Atticus and Hallston, and both of them were painfully cautious. Hallston said we couldn't get caught too close to the Haven, or it'd be suspicious, and Atticus argued we should hide and let them find us. It took us nearly two and a half hours to be discovered.

Standing in the hallway outside the abandoned hallways and tunnels, the three of us go over the plan again. I reach into the backpack and check that everything's there. The smooth plastic of the flashlight. The rough leather sheaths of the daggers. It's all here.

"We better act quickly," Hallston says quietly. "They'll be aware of our plot soon."

None of the nurses walking around even acknowledge that we're out at night. The cool air is an icy wave crashing against my bare skin.

"Where are we headed?" Atticus asks, peering around the next hallway. He gestures to Hallston and me that it's safe to pass.

"Follow me," I say, pointing down the hallway. "It's this way." We pass by signs labeled "Double Guard" and "restricted areas" and take the hall opposite them. The bold, red lettering lists penalties for breaking the area rules.

Responsibility lays its heavy hand on my shoulders. I'm the only one who's been inside the Infirmary. I have to really consider what are the safest and smartest options.

The eeriness of the kenopsic halls is unusual. Hallston keeps glancing at me, and I know she's worried. There's tension between her and Atticus due to their similarities: leadership, protectiveness, and stubbornness.

Our footsteps are like the tick of an invisible clock counting down the seconds until we are caught. My plan is to head to the areas upstairs, further from the tunnels.

"Over here," I whisper, turning down one hallway. It's exceptionally dirty, although nothing here is particularly clean. Ghostly cobwebs hang from the ceiling.

"Are there always so few guards?" Hallston asks.

"No," I say uneasily. "It's never like this."

The truth is, something must be going on, and I know exactly what it is. We don't even get to the first room on the hall when the lights dim and brighten repetitively.

"What's that?" Atticus asks, playing with the edge of his black hood.

"Oh, I don't know. It's not good," I reply. The lights keep flashing, and my intuition tells me that the others have been found out.

"We should leave," Hallston says quickly.

"What? We haven't even done anything!" I argue, shaking my head. "What about our parents?! Oh, we can't go now!"

"If we get caught, it won't matter," Hallston states, but I put my foot down. "Bexley Paige Kamryn, if we have any chance of getting out of here, we need to leave now! Let's hope the others found them," my sister says.

Hallston's right, and soon the silence is broken by yelling and clambering clanks. It's no use arguing with my older sister.

Atticus takes the backpack from me and hands Hallston a knife wrapped discreetly in thick burlap. He grabs one himself and returns the bag to me. Failure sinks in as we start off for the tunnels. We didn't help anyone at all.

Suddenly, a loud alarm begins to beep. I've never heard anything like that in the Infirmary. Instantly, the rooms open as other patients exit to see what's going on. I swirl my charm bracelet around my wrist and get an idea.

I take out a weapon myself, stash it inside my baggy purple shirt, and tuck it in before anyone can see.

"Hide those," I say to Atticus and Hallston, eyeing their knives. I toss the backpack into the corner of the hall. They both do as I say, and, in seconds, the hallway is so packed with people, we blend in easily.

Pushing through the bustle of people, we make it to the check-in area undetected. The Mordolus order people back to their rooms, but the patients are searching for answers. Signs point to the Double Guard, Emergency Care, and the dark death pillar or obituary, and I remember the days when I considered this home. Isaiah and I even created a way to help patients more effectively.

"Oh wait," I whisper as shock hits me with such force my heart falters. "Hallston, go on to the tunnels. I need Atticus' help. It'll be quick, I promise."

Hallston studies me skeptically, and so does Atticus.

"Oh, please," I beg. Around us, the nurses rush about, trying to direct patients back into their rooms and secure the exits. Hallston eyes Atticus like she's entrusting him with my life, nods, and runs off.

I weave my way to the hallway leading to rooms 90-110, and Atticus follows me. When we leave the main hallway, I break into a run, fighting my way through the bustle, searching for the room.

"What are you doing, Bexley?" Atticus asks. Time is wasting away, and I'm too busy reading the signs on the door to respond. *Eighty-nine, ninety, ninety-one...*

"Ninety-two," I say aloud, stopping so abruptly I almost trip. I open the door, praying he's still here.

He's not. The boy Isaiah and I worked so hard to keep alive is gone.

"He's gone," I say, freezing in the doorway.

"Dead?" Atticus asks.

"Possibly," I say sickly. "But…there is one other place we can check. Oh, I hope he's there."

"Where?" he asks.

"Hospice," I respond, looking out into the narrow hallway where people bustle by.

Atticus pointedly looks out the door at the chaos.

"If we hurry?" I plead.

Atticus sighs and takes a step out the door. "If we hurry."

I think as fast as I can—and run even steadier. It's not exactly 'hospice', since this whole place really is, but more like a place for the unconscious, brain dead, and hopeless cases during their final senseless time, just before death. I hear they only have a few people manning it.

Nurses and Mordolus leaders rush around, flying through the halls, forcing people back into their rooms and making phone calls. They probably couldn't care less about us since they're focused on securing the Infirmary. Their emergency procedures backfired, paving an easy path for us.

After following signs, I burst through the hospice door, unprepared. Rows of silent beds are pushed together and packed into the room. The room is saturated with the stench of chemical-covered death. Atticus steps closer to me as I force myself to browse the beds.

Several are covered completely in white sheets holding multiple bodies piled for burial.

"We need to be fast," Atticus warns, strolling over to the door again and peering out.

I cover my nose with my hand and search. Finally, I spot him in the far corner, my hope renewed. He's still alive. I think. I dash over to the bed, panting. His freckle-spangled face is nearly as pale as the walls

I bound over to the bed, fearing we'll be discovered any second. He's still breathing.

"Hurry up, Bexley!" Atticus urges, standing in the doorway and looking out to the hall. "They're coming!"

"Help me then!" I say. With a nod, Atticus gingerly picks up the sickly boy.

I hurtle through the door to hospice, and we head toward the tunnels. I run ahead, checking each corner for the Mordolus. People eye us curiously.

I stop abruptly at a corner, listening to a company of passing guards. They say something about missing patients before sprinting past us. Voices echo off the halls ahead, and I'm certain any minute we'll run into a nurse or guard that stops long enough to consider us. The hidden door appears. I wrench it open and help Atticus with the boy through the narrow entry.

Noises collide with the silence from both sides as we enter the tunnels. The crowd that had previously been here is gone, but they're not far ahead. Footsteps echo closely behind us, and I think the guard might be within the abandoned halls. Oh, I hope they didn't discover the hidden halls.

"Are you alright?" Hallston asks. She must have waited behind for us and lays a hand on my shoulder, leading us further into the tunnel.

"Yeah," I say, relieved. Mud clings to my shoes as we walk through the tunnels.

"We were almost caught," Atticus tells Hallston. "Your sister is brave but reckless."

Atticus looks down at the boy we rescued. So do I and grimace; he looks like the poster child for the last stages of the Virus. Pale, feverish, unconscious, thin. Atticus checks his shoulder. There's a faded green mark, which indicates a June test. No one lasts longer than four months. His maximum time to survive this illness is almost up.

"They may have found the abandoned halls," Atticus continues. "Whether or not they venture down here, we need to get to the meeting place quickly."

"Everyone else just left. Marie, Reece, and Ele are leading the others there right now. I caught them right before they left," Hallston tells us.

"Hallston?" I ask as we walk through the quiet tunnel. "Did you see our parents?"

Hallston looks down grimly and shakes her head. *They probably were there, and she missed them. Or perhaps they never got caught. They could still be at home.*

"Bexley, who is this?" Hallston asks, looking at the torpified boy I risked our lives for.

"I wish I knew," I reply.

I can still sense the others up ahead. My legs ache, and the effect of a missed night of sleep combined with an exhausting morning bears down on me.

Finally, a small pool of water glistens on the floor of the tunnel. The silence of the tunnels amplifies the noise growing ahead of us. As we enter the room, there's hardly space to walk. The crowd of survivors is chaotic but hushed. The cavernous room is about the size of the Emergency Care room in the Infirmary, but in this instance seems much too small to hold the large group.

"You're finally here!" Jess says, greeting us.

"Yeah, sorry we're late. It didn't go quite as planned. We ran out of time," Hallston says defeatedly.

"It's okay," Jess says. She glances at the boy we rescued and frowns. "Here, there's a man over here, Roland, he's a doctor. Ledger's helping too. They're treating the other patients, but this is far more urgent," Jess says, leading Atticus to the other side of the room. "We have a small supply of sulfavirdoton left. We've been keeping it under wraps, though."

When I turn around, Hallston is gone, and I feel a bit awkward among all the strangers until someone screams at me. "BELLA!"

Marie bounds over, more excited than I've ever seen her. She jumps so high I think she might burst through the tunnel roof.

"You're finally here! Guess what?! Guess! Guess! GUESS!" she says, bouncing in circles.

I raise an eyebrow. "What?"

"MY BROTHER IS HERE!!" she screams. A young boy around five runs over to Marie. This is obviously her brother; they have the same curly hair, bright brown eyes, and small but strong frames.

"This is Axly," Marie explains, and he waves at me.

"Hiya," Axly says with a grin.

"I'm Bexley," I say, smiling. "I'm so happy for you, Marie!"

"I've got a ton to tell you, Bella!" Marie says.

"I know, so do I," I say and pause. "But I've got to talk with Jess."

Marie nods, a little disappointed until she and Axly go bounding around the tunnel, hand in hand.

I scan the crowd for Jess, simultaneously holding onto the hope of seeing my parents. I spot her talking to some adults and wait until they walk away.

"Are we leaving soon?" I ask.

"We're forming a plan. We will have to wait until all of the medications have been handed out to the sickly. I have Atticus on guard now. Merris also knows our location, so we shouldn't linger. Thankfully, from our other encounters, it seems Merris may not have a quick way of contacting Morzanna," Jess assures, avoiding looking at me. "We'll leave as quickly as we can. I see us sending off the first group to enter Ellismark within twenty minutes."

Needing to clear my mind, I hurry over to where they are treating the patients. Ten desperately sick people await their turn with the doctor. I spot a man kneeling beside one of the patients, carefully giving out small cups of liquid medication that Auxillia brought to ease the patients' discomfort and strengthen them for the next phase of our escape. This must be Mr. Roland, the doctor, and my assumptions are confirmed when Reece calls him "Dad". Oh, how wonderful it is that Reece has been reunited with his father. The similarities are apparent; tall and lanky with fair brown hair and tensely alert but trapped-in-their-own-world expressions.

"Is he going to be alright?" I ask Ledger, who stands right next to the boy we rescued.

"Don't know. We'll have to wait and see. We gave him the cure," Ledger responds.

"It doesn't seem to be having the same effect as it did for the rest of us," I say despondently, aware of how much worse the boy looks since a few weeks ago.

Ledger shrugs. "It depends on the person."

"I suppose," I say, playing with my charm bracelet.

"He'll probably be okay," Ledger says encouragingly. "Oh, by the way, Graydon has your bird. I brought him from the Haven."

"Oh, thank you, Ledger."

"Do you know where Gabby is?" he asks.

"No, I haven't seen him," I say.

"Okay, let me know if you do." Ledger looks behind me. "Oh hey, Isaiah!"

Isaiah trudges over to where we're standing. Weariness wells in his coppery eyes. He looks simply awful.

"Hey," I say softly, offering a hug, which he takes.

"Hey. How'd it go?" Isaiah asks me tiredly as we walk over to a quieter spot.

"Okay. It took us forever to even get to the Infirmary, and the only person we could bring back is half-dead," I say, watching all the children running around and a couple reuniting with family members or acquaintances. The sight is heartening. "I'm a little disappointed but trying to be thankful that we had any success," I say. Isaiah is sort of wobbly and pale. "How'd it go for you guys?"

Isaiah hesitates, a troubling look flickering across his face. He looks away then says drearily, "Pretty awful."

I follow his gaze across the room. Zia sobs in the corner, and I bet this is why Jess seemed off.

"What happened?" I ask instantly, my heart racing.

Isaiah tells me everything that happened and about Gabby's ruthless murder. The reality of the danger sets in. That could have been Isaiah or Graydon.

"Are you okay?" I ask. I can't imagine witnessing that happen to someone.

He shrugs and stares at his hands for a long time. "I'm sort of still in shock. It's surreal. I'm going to be honest, when we got here, I nearly passed out because of the blood. I kind of freaked. I've never experienced anything like that before. I literally watched someone get murdered." His words are cold, blank, and shocking like icy rain. I give his hand a reassuring squeeze.

"I'm so sorry, Isaiah. Is anyone going to tell Ledger?" I whisper, heartbrokenly. "He and Gabby were best friends."

Isaiah glances at him and slowly shakes his head. "I don't want to, Bexley. I *can't*."

"It's okay. Maybe it's better to let things settle first," I reply. Thankfully, Isaiah's parents are safe, but I'm not sure that compensates for the tragedy.

Right after our conversation, I find Graydon. I need to check in and get Stormy. He assures me he's fine, and I believe him. Both of Graydon's parents were rescued.

"Please, try to remain as quiet as possible! The noise could carry to the Infirmary, and we could be discovered if we aren't careful to conceal our location," Jess announces, and the noise begins to die down more.

Weaving through the crowd to locate my sisters, I spot a woman. She's middle-aged with medium-length brown hair and big, distinct eyes. She races around, frantic, looking for something or someone. I make my way over to her.

"Excuse me?" I ask. The woman spins around, panting. "Do you need help with something?"

"I'm looking for my sons. I need to find them!" she says, still surveying the crowd.

"Okay. I'm Bexley by the way," I say. "If they're here, we'll find them."

"Arlene Shorsee," she says with a nod.

"What do they look like?" I ask.

"One is eighteen, and the other's fourteen. They both have dark hair. I have to find them! You must help me!"

I follow her, trying to help her as best I can, but it is hard to look and keep up. I haven't seen two dark-haired teenaged boys yet, and there are only about a hundred packed in the tunnel. Chances are they aren't here, just like my parents.

I lose Ms. Arlene, but she was headed for the right side of the room. Suddenly, there's a scream. That's where they're treating the really sick people. I want to slap myself from realization. The boy I rescued from hospice is her son.

"Camber!" she cries, kneeling next to him. "Camber? Camber? He's still alive, isn't he?"

"Yes, he's alive," I say. Ms. Arlene nods gratefully and stays there for a minute, tears welling in her big eyes. She gazes back over the crowd and jumps up.

"I have to find my other son! I've got to find him!" she says, clasping her hands together. "Gabby!"

I freeze, recalling a memory from the first day at the Haven. *And this is Gabby Shorsee.*

"Wait," I say, before I know what I'm doing, and run to her. A sick feeling grows inside me. How many eighteen-year-old boys named Gabby live in Senneforte? How do you tell someone their child is dead?

I lead Ms. Arlene over to a quiet corner. I don't know what to say, so I just explain everything how it is. She silently crawls back to

Camber sobbing. She weeps, and I wish there was something I could do. I'm so bad at this. *Why couldn't Hadley have told her?* She would have anesthetized the pain and explained in the gentlest way, and all I did was go in with the raw truth, stumbling over my story like trying to do surgery with a butter knife.

I leave Ms. Arlene with Camber and return to Jess after I see Graydon motion for me to join the group forming around her.

"We need to set out immediately. Remember, we'll send in the first group to pose as Mordolus guards on foot and try to raise the gate or plan another route for us. Then, the group in the car will enter. By then, hopefully the way will be easy for the remaining fighters to enter with weapons. We still need to send you in," Jess says, looking at Hallston and Marie. Almost everyone is here, except Reece, who's helping his dad, and Hadley, who's with the children. There are a man and a woman, definitely Ele and Isaiah's parents. Their mother looks a lot like Ele and shares some mannerisms. There's another lady, dressed in Infirmary clothes but somehow has an elegant look. Her gorgeous, long, brown hair almost shimmers, and she stands with a tall, familiar-looking man. Those are Graydon's parents; I met them earlier.

Jess clears her throat. "Unfortunately, we need someone else to go to Ellismark in the first group."

"I'll go. I volunteered that day, too," Graydon says quietly, and his mother gasps.

"Graydon!" Ms. Kassy cries. "You could be killed!"

He looks at her. "I *have* to go. We all will be if someone doesn't. I promise I'll be okay."

Mrs. Pierce exhales and subtly nods.

"Thank you," Jess says solemnly. "We've already elected the youngest children to travel in the car. There is an older lady who must ride and an extremely sickly man. We need a capable driver and another passenger."

"Jess, what about the boy—what about Camber?" I ask.

"We are trying to figure out what to do about that," Jess says. "He is far too sickly to play a Mordolus member. Hallston said there may be an extra hiding spot for him."

"Can my mom be the passenger?" Isaiah asks earnestly.

"Certainly," Jess says, and before Ms. Leona can protest, she adds, "I was going to suggest it due to her condition. For the driver, I need someone who can deal with the guards, locate a place to flee to once having entered Ellismark, and keep the passengers safe."

Graydon's parents share an interesting look.

"I believe I can do that," Ms. Kassy says.

While the two groups dress in their Mordolus attire, Hadley lays out the plan for the crowd once again in case anyone missed it on the journey to this place. As the time to leave nears, I wish the best for our escape. Jess hands out weapons, especially to those who are with the older children who can't be hidden in the car. As we start our way out of the tunnels, surreality increases. We will flee to Ellismark today.

Soon we see the familiar grassy field, exiting the tunnels, hopefully for the last time. Surrounded by thick trees, the clearing provides a temporary safe place. The clear night sky seems to beckon a successful mission, and hope sprouts amidst the mire of our world.

Jess and the other three get ready to go; they need to leave ahead of the rest of us. Jess is going with them as far as she can without being seen and will return when the time is safe to bring us. Marie hugs her brother goodbye, and Ms. Kassy and Mr. Madison embrace their son. I quickly run to Hallston, giving her one final hug, then I watch them disappear within the forest.

47
MARIE: THE GATE

Hallston, Graydon, Jess, and I head for the gate between Senneforte and Ellismark. Before we came, Jess gave us lots of instructions. There's still junk we've got to figure out when we get there, but the plan's mostly laid out: we get the gate open for the others.

"Remember, you have two hours, and then at four-thirty, I'll bring everyone to the gate. You've got to have it open by then so we can get into Ellismark. It's got to be dark, so they'll still have the night guards out and we have a better chance of surprising them. You've got this," Jess says as encouragingly as she can. Hallston nods, and Graydon just looks nervous.

Jess motions to us to follow her.

Slipping between shops and behind houses, we only occasionally see a Mordolus truck on the paved roads to or from the gate. We've gotta be super careful. Crossing the street is an event. If we'd brought Atticus, we'd never get there.

A truck creeps up the road. I can see the gate from my hiding spot, and it casts a black shadow over the streetlights' beams. The truck stops just outside the massive doors. They have big lights set up around the checkpoint. The gate is almost as tall as rooftops. It's made of sturdy metal, solid, with super sharp spikes. It's sick to think that the Queen's allowed the Mordolus to trap people. Graydon's rigid, and I know he's thinking the same as me. *Shoot, how are we going to do this without getting killed?*

But the gate gives me hope. Hope for escape. I've been kinda obsessed with the idea since *forever.*

"Please be careful," Jess tells us as we stand under the archway of a hotel entrance. On the other side of the building is the huge street going to Ellismark.

She pulls Hallston aside to talk with her. I straighten the big ol' black coat that Jess gave me. I tighten my belt a little more because these pants are gigantic on me, and I don't wanna accidentally lose them. She brought us clothes from their time in the Infirmary, so we'll blend in. I've got Jess's outfit, Graydon has Bentley's, and Hallston is wearing Violet's. Jess also used mud from the tunnel walls to try and make us look older and to fit our story that we've been sent to Ellismark from grave-digging duty. I was kinda sad to see my favorite pair of yellow high-tops go, again, for stupid rain boots. Atticus painted them with the Mordolus symbol for our costumes. I always wear my yellow shoes because they're comfortable, and I got them last year before school started. My mom bought them for me because my brother Axly told her in the store they were perfect for me because I'm always happy and bright like the sun. They make me think of my family and remind me to stay radiant.

Graydon and I wait until Jess and Hallston return. I peek out from behind the wall of the building.

"Ready?" Hallston asks. I glance at Graydon, and we both nod. Hallston steps out into the street. Jess gives me an encouraging smile then hides behind the wall. She's gonna wait to make sure we get in then go get the others.

I feel really exposed on the road. I think about our disguises. Graydon will probably be fine 'cause he's fifteen and already like sixty feet tall, but I still look twelve. Maybe they won't be able to tell in the darkness.

Graydon nudges me, and I realize I've been staring behind to see if anyone watches us.

I keep my eyes on the ground from then on. The road is cracked and dusty. I'm silent, and with Graydon and Hallston to my right, I'm closest to the open street.

The road goes uphill, and the gate is near the top. The land levels out there and only a few buildings stand.

The structures are mostly stripped and painted over with red so I make a game of figuring out what they once were so I don't have to look at the Mordolus. Some of them have scrappy looking graffitied protests against Morzanna. Reading them, I learn some new words I probably shouldn't use.

A few Hunters stand nearby, leaning against the wall of a dilapidated shop. I think they're guarding the gate. I step closer to

Hallston and Graydon to feel more secure. Hallston would do anything to keep me safe. Graydon's kinda like everyone's big brother.

"There's no one left here! We seriously are stuck on gate duty? Ugh," A middle-aged Hunter woman with crooked teeth complains, kinda annoyed. There's a small flock of Hunters standing against the wall of one of the buildings. "Morzanna better let us transfer to Ravimere soon. It's getting boring here."

A younger girl nods, watching the road like a hungry vulture, clutching her silver bow tightly. "I agree. They'll have new prey there," she says with a wicked laugh, fingering the sharp tips of a couple of her arrows.

Graydon tenses, noticeably looking in the other direction.

"If only we could convince her that there's no one left and we've completed our task," the older woman says. The other girl hisses. I walk past them and shudder.

A loud croak fills the air. The large bronze-colored gates open to let in three guards. I just see a lot of Mordolus members in my glimpse beyond the doors.

I don't notice we've gotten to the gate until I receive a kick to get my attention. The ground seems like a safer place to look than potentially making eye contact with one of the Mordolus. Yuck. I quickly look up. I kick Graydon back just for the heck of it.

We stand in the well-worn path in front of the security area. Several guards are stationed at the large gate. A man stands in front of us, and obviously he's got authority. He's holding a tablet. The dude looks kinda judgy. I don't know why, but with the gate and stuff, I think about the door to heaven. But I don't expect it to be dark like it is right now, and the device dude is way too grumpy to fit the bill of heavenly gatekeeper. More like the door to the *other* place. Now all I can think of is that I'm about to walk into hell. That's just *awesome*. Maybe it's foreshadowing.

"Names?" he asks. Graydon and I wait for Hallston to take the lead.

"Diane Brewer," she says, blankly. He looks at his tablet and nods slowly. When it's my turn, I stare into space for a second.

"Name?" he asks.

"Uh, Violet…" I say. "Violet Andersen."

Our identities are taken from the Infirmary. Violet hasn't been found out yet, and Hallston and Graydon's were stolen. The man looks at his device and nods.

"Solomon Rey," Graydon says.

Hallston talks with the guard. I study him. He's got pale skin and hair a shade even lighter. A scraggly white beard hangs limply from his pointy chin. He has big front teeth and a hunch.

"That dude looks like Chalky the marmot," I whisper to Graydon.

"Shut up, Marie," he replies but struggles not to smile. I giggle.

After a few more questions about what we are leaving for, everything seems to go as planned. Apparently, we're going to the Ellismark Infirmary, the Sanatorium, and we're here at night because we just got off our shift at the Infirmary. We don't have a vehicle because we're going to stay in the Ellismark barracks until tomorrow and go with their group. The man is about to let us in, but then he looks us up and down and scowls with his rodenty face.

"What happened to you guys?" he asks, looking at our pieced-together costumes.

"Excuse me, that's rude," I say, before thinking. Hallston gives me a warning look.

"What are you, twelve?" the man says, glaring. I scowl, and Hallston subtly wags her head, but I'm triggered.

"I look good for my age," I state factually, straightening and holding my head higher.

"I'm sorry, are you going to let us in?" Hallston asks politely. The man grumbles and presses a button on the screen of his tablet.

There's a loud metallic sound. The gate begins to open. I glance back at the man for a second. He's staring thoughtfully at us. My heart races and the gates part. I take a step forward, excited. That second, I see the man whisper something to several of the guards. That's not good. I glance at Graydon. He must've noticed too.

"Hallston?" I say nervously when the guards approach us. She doesn't respond, or at least I miss it because someone screams.

Someone runs through the gate. Suddenly, everything is chaos. There's yelling and running around. I even lose the guards. Dang.

"What's going on?" I whisper to Hallston, straining to see through the sudden garrison of guards in the darkness.

"Someone just escaped," she says, surprised.

The three of us stand, stunned. A few guards have already caught whoever it is and drag her inside. I gasp.

It's Jess.

I'm shocked. Jess's been captured. And everyone's distracted. Jess looks up, nodding urgently toward the gate for us to go. I freeze.

"You're a traitor, Jess!" Someone yells. Jess is dragged away down the street. Graydon and Hallston stand there just as dumbstruck as me. Again, Jess gestures for us to go. She doesn't even struggle against the guards. I smile weakly, hoping that will suffice for thanks. The gate is closing. Hallston nods to Jess and pulls me inside Ellismark. The gate slams shut just as the three of us step through. An eerie silence follows.

I try to make sense of what just happened. Jess must have seen the guards. Our original plan didn't work. We never would have made it without her. And Jess sacrificed herself to be a distraction.

Their words still swim around my head. The Queen is ruthless. What's she gonna do with a traitor? Probably like what happened to those two kids who helped Isaiah and Reece. Golly.

I can't believe it. We escaped Senneforte. It isn't hills of wildflowers, glistening waterfalls, and oddly clean, singing animals. Everything has a ghost towny look like Senneforte, but it's way more cityish. It's not Dante's Inferno, though, and the starry, clear sky is cool. Lights line the whole paved road in front of some other super clean, modern buildings. Some have been modified to be used by the Mordolus. Large structures are all around us. I remember as a kid coming to Ellismark and walking among the streets thinking these must be the tallest, biggest, shiniest buildings in the world. There are a lot of the Mordolus out. All eyes are on us. Graydon pulls me behind a building, followed by Hallston.

"We have to hide until everything calms down," Hallston announces, glancing around.

"Wait, what about Jess? Is she good?" I ask, ducking further into the shadows.

"I don't know. I hope so," Hallston says.

"What if she's not? What if—" Graydon starts.

"Then she couldn't get back to warn the others," I interrupt.

"She could be dead!" Hallston says frustratedly. "She sacrificed herself, and you're worried about if she'll make it back? I'm worried about whether she'll live!"

"Of course I'm worried about her!" I snap, bitter at her words. "I was the one who said something about it first. If she can't get back, and they don't come, what she did will be for nothing. We know she got caught, so she can't get back and tell everyone to come here."

Hallston straightens. "You are right. I'm sorry. Let us pray for our friend Jess first."

"Alright," I say with a shrug.

"Father, help Jess. Protect her if it is your will and keep her faith strong. Thank you for providing us with her to help us and for allowing us to succeed so far. Thank you. Amen," Hallston says.

"So will the others know to come anyway? Do you think they'll at least send someone to check if Jess doesn't show up?" Graydon questions, nervously playing with the hilt of his dagger.

"I hope so. We just have to be ready if they do. We have to get the gate open," Hallston says, patting the wall. "Jess said two hours. We need to be ready then. It could be more, but we're sticking to the plan."

After a short talk, we decide I'll go and scout. I glance out from our hiding space. There are still some guards around, but I can work with it. I step out into the street.

So many lights. It's crazy how Ellismark is so bright with electricity, unlike Senneforte. The road goes miles past the gate in a straight line. It separates both sides of the street. A few feet away in the middle of it is the bell tower. It has fancy carvings. The bell's made of shiny, black metal. That's the Tarrivel Bell.

For emergencies, the Tarrivel bell is supposed to summon everyone to Ellismark. Not very many people come because it's streamed on TV. The bell's really loud and others are rung in all the other provinces to go further. I always wonder how the bell could be so loud and reach the other provinces. The Tarrivel Bell's only been used once in my life. It was after Cyrus Nixon's death. My parents left me at home with a babysitter to go to the meeting. It took over a day because it was so crowded with the people who did go in person.

I follow the wall, pulling my jacket closer around me. It's kinda cold at night. I stay crouched and hide whenever someone's near. There's a door in the wall on the other side of the road, next to the gate. I can't get close enough to check it out or investigate where it leads. Looks important. I watch from behind a wrecked vehicle beside the road.

"Hey, what are you doing?" someone says behind me.

I turn to find a girl. She's not a ton older than me. Probably seventeen. She stares at me suspiciously with big brown eyes. She has that shiny metallic-y bow. It's that Hunter girl. I swallow.

"You're not supposed to be this close to the gatehouse," she says, pointing at the door.

"Yeah," I say, terrified, nodding. She tilts her head.

"Sorry, I'm going," I announce clearly, standing. The girl shrugs.

"It's alright. I can tell you're a new convert," she says. I smile. *Ewww.* "The gatehouse is off-limits for safety reasons."

I nod. "Got it. I was just curious."

"I'm Shirla, by the way," she says. "Have you been assigned a position yet?"

I raise an eyebrow and tilt my head. "Uh, no?"

"That's weird, they usually do it at orientation. You should be a Hunter. It's the funnest job," she says with a grin. "Hope to see you around...?"

"Ma—err, Luna," I spit out.

"See you around, Luna," Shirla says with a smile. She turns and walks off. My heart races like crazy. I start walking back to the others. My legs feel like playdough.

A Mordolus guard stalks up the street across from me. I freeze. Behind her facemask and complete black attire, it's hard to tell. I only recognize her because of her curly, fake, blond hair that's so stiff and brittle it might break off if the wind blows the wrong direction. She always wore that kinda old people makeup with too much powder which made me wonder what the point was. It's my fifth-grade teacher Ms. Doddridge. And she's a Mordolus guard. She was nice. *How could she have joined the Mordolus?* That's weird. I walk away in case she sees and recognizes me. That'd be bad. I'm supposed to be at least sixteen to be a Mordolus member.

I cross the street and stare at the ground, thinking. I've gotten out of Senneforte. I'm safe. I can leave now and find somewhere to hide. Reece was right. This was my plan; get out of Senneforte and run away. If I stay, I might get hurt. I might get captured again. I can escape for good now! *I'll leave and be free.*

"Am I really going to do this?" I whisper to myself. "Yeah, guess I am."

Before I can talk myself out of it, I take a deep breath and step away from the gate. I walk down the street toward the Tarrivel Bell. A Mordolus guard watches me from a building nearby. He stares at me for a long time. I try to keep walking normally until I get too creeped out. I run down a street between two tall buildings across from the bell. I look out into the road. The guard didn't follow me.

"Marie?"

I spin around and look down the path. "Graydon?" I whisper.

"What are you doing?" he asks. "You took so long, Hallston sent me to find you."

"That guard was watching me," I make up. "I had to act like I was going somewhere else and came here. I was about to come back, but I had to make sure she wasn't following me."

"Okay," Graydon says, and we start walking down the alley. "What happened?"

I explain about the gatehouse and skip the parts about Shirla and running away. I'm ashamed of it. Now that I think about it, I can't believe I was going to leave Axly like that.

"There are so many Mordolus members out here. It's like they're nocturnal," I say.

"That, or it's a lot worse in the daytime," Graydon says.

The two of us find Hallston a few minutes later, and I relay the information again.

"We need to get to the gatehouse then. That's how we'll get the gate open. They'll have another control for it in there. We've got to have perfect timing right after we see the second group enter," Hallston says.

"How long's it been?" Graydon asks, absentmindedly wiping some of the dirt from his face.

"At least thirty minutes," Hallston says. "That doesn't leave us long."

"Yeah. Someone will also need to be watching to know when they arrive," Graydon adds.

"If we're too early, the Mordolus catch us before they get through. If we're too late, everyone will be waiting around," I think aloud.

"But it would be helpful to know when they come, even if it doesn't change anything, or if they arrive earlier than we anticipate," Hallston says.

We decide that Graydon will be on lookout, which I'm glad of because it sounds boring. Hallston and I have to figure out how to get the gate open. Yay.

Graydon leaves to find a place to watch, heading up a set of stairs to the top of the wall. Hallston and I head toward the gatehouse. I remember that there's a guard there, and that Shirla told me members are to stay away, and tell Hallston.

We stop behind some trees nearby. There are very few actual living things here. Like plants and animals and stuff. This is pretty much it. All the other ground is paved or bare, dry dirt. In front of us is the only open grassy area, and then the wall and gatehouse. To the right are the buildings and street we came from, and to the left are more trees. I watch a few guards talking, standing near the gatehouse door. There are three of them. I wonder if the gate house is locked and if there are more guards inside. Or how we do this and not die. That's also important.

"What are we gonna do?" I ask Hallston, watching the area from behind our leafy hiding spot. I pull some leaves from my hair. A stick pokes my side.

"I don't know. They're not leaving anytime soon."

"Well, I don't know either," I say. "I'm scared."

Hallston looks me in the eye. "There's no reason to be scared when we have God to protect us and carry out His plan. We need to trust no matter the outcome. I pray we will overcome this evil, but I'll give my life before I let you get hurt."

She stares at the gate, her dark eyes full of determination. "Have your knife?"

"Um, yeah?" I answer.

She looks at me for a second. "You trust me?"

I slowly nod. I'm totally freaked out, but I trust Hallston more than a lotta people.

"You go to the gatehouse. I'll distract them. Try not to act suspicious. I'll follow you, and if they say anything to us, just try to get to the gatehouse and leave the guards to me," Hallston orders. "Remember, we're Mordolus guards too."

"Okay," I agree. We step out from behind the trees.

The guards watch us, but I try to keep my head forward. I focus on the door to the gatehouse. Everything's silent. Instinctively, I touch the hilt of my dagger. It's a proper one this time.

I try to focus, but suddenly, I hear a loud creaky sound. That's the gate opening. Then I see someone on top of the wall waving like a crazy person at me. Oh, that's Graydon. The second group must be in. They decided last minute to play that they're going to pick up new recruits to help with the Infirmary breach.

"What are you doing?" One of the guards asks as we approach the gatehouse. I don't have time to get distracted. We've only got like thirty minutes max now. We're so close to the door. He walks toward us. He's got weapons. I don't say anything. Hallston signals for me to keep going and turns to talk to the guard.

Without another thought, I run to the door. I throw it open, and surprisingly, it's not locked. I jump inside, slamming it behind me.

I crack the door open a sliver and stare out in time to see Hallston hurtling toward me. I quickly get the door for her, shut it, and fasten the lock. I can't hear a thing over the voices outside. Hallston spins around.

"You two stay there!" she says, brandishing her knife. I turn around, taking in the room. It's small, like the size of my bedroom. Most of the space is taken up by crates of spare parts. Wires and cobwebs hang from the low ceiling. I take in a deep breath, startled by the presence of two Mordolus members. My mind blanks for a minute, so I wave to them. They look at each other, confused. Hallston walks over to them with her knife out. I grab mine and follow her.

"What are we going to do?" I whisper. One of the two, a woman with very dark hair and rosy cheeks sits in front of a table. On the table is what looks like a weird computer, wired to gears that spiral along the right-hand wall. The other is a younger man. He looks scared.

"I'll deal with them, and you figure out the gate," Hallston says, collecting a sizable dagger from the table. I think that's the only weapon in the room. At least I hope so.

I nod. Hallston takes the two people over to the other side of the gatehouse to make sure they don't try to take us down or escape. Before me is a whole table filled with electronics to open the gate. I stare, completely confused.

"Hallston, I don't know what I'm doing," I say, trying a few of the buttons. Nothing happens. We don't have much time until the outside Mordolus get inside to us. Hallston signals to me to watch the Mordolus members and hands me a second knife. I kinda just stand there holding them as Hallston takes her place at the controls a few feet behind me.

Noise comes closer to the door. The two guards. They're talking calmly, I hear a jingling, and then…laughing?

"They have another key," one of the gate people whispers to the other.

"Hurry!" I warn Hallston. "I think they're coming!"

"I know," Hallston responds. I frantically look around for something to help. There's a pile of heavy crates in the corner. I dash over and try to move them in front of the door. A few seconds later I realize this isn't going to work. My hands and arms ache, and I've only managed to move two of the crates.

"Help me!" I demand the two gate people who watch me struggle. They both look at me defiantly.

"I have a knife!" I announce. The two hesitantly begin to drag boxes, and I keep my blade ready.

"We shouldn't do this," the woman says. The other dude just nods.

Outside, I hear muffled conversation. The door is blocked, and all I can do now is wait. The lock clicks. The door vibrates. The crates won't hold long. The guards outside talk, and I shudder, realizing they've called for help. We're trapped.

A second later, there's a loud sound outside. It startles me so much I nearly drop my dagger. I'm confused until I realize what it is.

That's the gate opening.

I run over to Hallston, grinning. She got it to work.

"What now?" I say, pointing to the two people.

"We'll have to fight," Hallston decides, taking back the other knife.

I barely respond before a loud crack interrupts me.

Suddenly, the door flies open. The crates tip over and scatter across the room, spilling tools and replacement parts. Two guards from outside walk in. Instantly, I'm approached. The four people surround us; two guards and two gate people. I dunno what to do.

The gate's open, but we're trapped. I wonder if everyone else is here yet. Maybe I'm proud of myself for coming and doing this. Or maybe I regret it. I'm not sure.

I wait for Hallston to do something first. My impulses don't always have the greatest result. The dark-haired woman walks over and begins to close the gate. I grit my teeth.

I listen to the gate close and fight back the pain in my throat. One of the guards grabs Hallston roughly, and she loses her dagger. The other walks toward me. Anger burns inside my head. I'm going to die either way. Holding my knife, I run toward the guard holding Hallston.

I'm smart enough to know that there's no way I'm actually gonna kill someone, so I barrel into the guard. He stumbles, and I shove the knife into Hallston's hand. Apparently, she's not a wimp when it comes to self-defense. Then there are just five of us left.

If I hadn't seen the other guard pull a gun, I'd have a bullet hole through my head right now. I lay on the floor trying not to get shot, and Hallston wrestles with the guard for the gun. The gate lady grabs Hallston by the waist and tries to yank her away. I crawl across the floor to retrieve Hallston's knife. I guess I am gonna have to stab someone. Just as I stand up though, the gun goes off. That gate dude drops, writhing and screaming, before going still. We all just stare for a second, and the gate lady and guard look astonished that they accidentally killed one of their colleagues. The gate lady runs out the door. I don't have time to stop her, not that I could. She's probably getting help. I quickly pick up one of those empty crates and throw it right at the guard. Hallston gets the gun away. I use my favorite tactic, which is ramming people in the stomach, and the guard crashes into the gate mechanism with a loud bang. The device cracks and crunches. I cringe. He recovers and shoves Hallston to the ground, grabbing me and knocking my knife out of my hand. I'm dragged to the door, and Hallston struggles to sit up.

"Get away from me!" I scream, kicking harder. "Let me go!" The guard just holds me tighter.

Suddenly, he drops me. I hit the floor, the guard's arms still wrapped around me as he lays writhing and choking. Blood pours from a wound on the guard's chest. Ew. I hurry and stand up as he crumples.

Graydon stands in the doorway holding a knife. His eyes drop with a look of horror as the guard crawls away and collapses in the grass. Graydon steps back, dropping the blade and covering his face. My heart throbs hard.

"Oh my gosh!" I say, covering my eyes and turning to Graydon. "Thanks!"

So far, the field looks Mordolus-free, but not for long. Those two Mordolus people got away. Graydon looks like he's gonna pass out.

"Hey, thanks. You just saved me," I repeat, picking up his knife and handing it back to him by the hilt. Graydon nods, not taking his eyes off the guard. He stumbles over to the grass, staring at the blade in his hand.

"Deep breaths," I say. "We've got this."

He nods again. "I'm good, sorry."

The stars fade from the sky. I quickly run back to Hallston.

"You good?" I ask, holding out a hand to help her up.

"Yeah," she says, standing. New hope grows inside me. "Are they here yet?"

Graydon looks up. "Don't know. I don't think so."

"Can you get the gate open?" I ask Hallston.

"I'll try," she says, looking hopefully at the destroyed machine. I nod.

"Let's go," I say, dragging Graydon by the hand.

We have to run, and a lot of guards swarm toward the gatehouse. We barely make it through the street. I follow Graydon as he leads me to a steep, brick staircase. I don't dare look back. I'm sure we're being followed.

At the top of the wall, it's narrow. There's no railing either. I'm afraid a strong breeze might send one of us falling to our deaths. At least we're the only ones up here. I wait nervously for the gate to open.

Graydon and I scan the province, standing on the brink of Senneforte and Ellismark.

"That's a lot of guards down there," I comment.

"Yeah. Hallston," is all Graydon says. I know what he means. She's still locked in the gatehouse. Where all the Mordolus are headed. I desperately search for a familiar person.

No one.

"It's definitely been two hours," I say, disheartened. "Jess didn't get back."

"Marie," Graydon says suddenly, urgently pointing just as I turn to leave. In the darkness of the streets, there's a flashing light.

That's when I see them in the darkness on the Senneforte side, ready to fight their way into Ellismark. Ele. Bella. Isaiah. Hope and excitement break through the dark situation. Even though the gate isn't open for them yet, we've had success. I wave down at them and turn to Graydon. "They really made it."

48

ELEANORA: SLAUGHTER AND SURPRISE

I stand hidden behind a building beside the road leading up to the wall between Senneforte and Ellismark. The daunting gate stands out against the fading starry sky, feeding all at once into the monstrous anticipation, fear, and excitement growing inside me. Our path to Ellismark is clearer than it's ever been, if only Marie, Graydon, and Hallston succeed in opening the gate for us very soon.

We received the news that the first group made it inside Ellismark to work on raising the gate and to make our way to the entrance. I don't know how it happened, but I felt it inside my head that they had succeeded, and Jess wouldn't be arriving. I felt some strange, supernatural urgency to come and that no one would be coming to call us. Multiple people agreed that they'd sensed something similar to me, including Bexley who likes to take every chance possible to prove I'm insane. It's completely crazy, but I couldn't talk myself out of the odd intuition. But an issue remains: the gate is not open, and we are currently still trapped in Senneforte. Perhaps we were all wrong.

Atticus, though, who was stationed to make sure the second group taking the car successfully passed the vehicle inspection and entered Ellismark, informed us when we arrived a few minutes after their entry that they had made it safely inside. They smuggled seven children in secret interior hiding spots and hid Camber behind the engine compartment. Things are looking hopeful.

Bexley's hair whips around in the crisp wind, and Isaiah stands by my side on the dusty, uneven ground waving his phone flashlight as the three of us stare up at the barrier. The signal works. I quickly wave to Marie at the top of the wall, and jumping up and down, she returns it, gesturing for us to come. Graydon stares at me through the metal spikes and barbed wire, jaw set and eyes narrow, before smiling weakly. I glance over at Isaiah's phone, and the time reads 4:27 a.m. We're early, but not by much. *Please, gate, please open.*

I run off to summon the others, hoping each second I'll hear the creak of the gate sliding open.

"What's going on?" Atticus asks when I return to the large alley between two clean-white, futuristic apartment buildings that serve as our waiting spot.

"The gate is still closed, but Marie wants us to head up to the street. Graydon was there, too, but I didn't see Hallston. Maybe she's working on it," I report. "Now is the time to get out of hiding before we are discovered in this alley."

Atticus nods, throwing back his hood. "Okay."

He orders everyone to follow me. *Graydon's right; I have a feeling we're not all going to make it through this alive.* Knowing that the car made it in assures me that my mother is safe. Our biggest fear was that the secret hiding locations would be discovered during the inspection, but it seems Atticus and Hallston are truly amazing.

Metal clangs as I draw my weapon along with everyone else. We have to fight for our lives and for everyone else. We have to fight for our freedom. Streetlights glint off the polished steel blade, causing a cloud of unease to swell in my heart and an earthquake of fear to tremor through my hands. *Are we really doing this? Are we really standing up to the Mordolus like this when only a few of us are strong enough to fight?*

I freeze behind empty crates stacked along the road next to Isaiah, drawing in a deep breath. A chilling wind blows through the air, sweeping dry fallen leaves across the dusty ground.

"You ready, Ele?" Isaiah asks after taking a deep breath.

"I'm not sure," I admit, toying with the cold metal hilt in my hand.

"I mean to be free," Isaiah says, his golden-brown eyes wide.

"To be free, yes, but I'm scared," I confess, peering up at the guards stationed outside the gate. In minutes, they will know we're here.

"We'll be free," Isaiah reiterates with confidence clearer and stronger than usual. "Whether we make it through or die. I'm gonna keep trusting. To die would be scary, Ele. Heaven would be cool though. I'm not afraid. I don't have to be."

"Isaiah," I say, fighting back the pain in my throat. "Please don't die."

"I'm not planning on it," he says.

"I don't know if I'll be free," I admit.

"What do you mean?"

"I don't know if I can trust or be free because I'm not sure if I trust God. I don't know if I can really submit to that. I don't know if I'm saved," I say. "I just don't want to die."

"You know the truth. You know the truth about God. Salvation isn't just about not dying. It's about living for God. It's knowing that God is holy, and we aren't. It's trusting that Christ has paid the price by His love. It's not about us," Isaiah says. "We need freedom from our sinful selves first. And only One Person can give that freeing forgiveness: Christ. I know this sounds awkward. I know a lot of what I say about God is hard for me to communicate. I still have to say what's true. God will still use it. Please trust, Ele. Believe."

After I fail to respond, he whispers a breathy, "Ready?"

I throw my arms around him one last time, still unsure, but say, "Yes."

Isaiah steps forward, out from behind the crates into the street, and, with renewed courage, I follow him. I force myself to keep walking as the guard at the gate sees us and gives orders. I glance behind me and everyone else is coming, too. *The gate is still closed, and they've seen us; how will we make it through this?*

Ten guards are suddenly at the gate yelling at each other, and more are appearing. A tornado of bravery and adventure destroys the anxiety in my stomach. *Morzanna has to be stopped, and this is the beginning of her downfall.* One of the Hunters draws a sword and gestures for the other guards to surround us. Although firearms are a rare commodity for even the Mordolus, I'm sure they will obtain some soon.

Adrenaline surges through my veins, inciting a new rush of energy. The haft of my knife digs into my cold palm. The Mordolus call for help, which is good; we caught them off guard.

The quiet street erupts with sound as the fight ensues. First blades crash together, and the first wave of panic hits. Instant chaos falls over the entrance to Senneforte as the rebels and Mordolus collide. I suppress my growing anger, reminding myself of my personal goals: *get through, try not to die, and don't kill unless completely necessary. Will I even be able to if the necessary time comes?*

I'm broken from my thoughts by a series of piercing screams, and I glance around to take in the situation. Black outfits with red embroidery separate the Mordolus from us, along with their increasing numbers. No one's beside me now, I spin around just as one of the guards approaches me. My legs fail to keep me steady, and I quickly analyze my future opponent and search for a way to get the upper hand. She's bigger, stronger, and way older than me, and my dagger doesn't even compare to her gleaming sword. I take a sharp breath and wait for an opening.

My knife is heavy in my hand, and before I can make a direct plan, she strikes. I dodge the attack and end up on my knees in the dirty street. *I'm definitely going to die.* I jump to my feet and shriek as the blade nearly takes off my head. I recover and brandish my dagger but feel far from intimidating. The woman raises her sword again, but this time I'm more prepared and block it. The second the metal collides, I drop my dagger as a harrowing pain tears through my arm. I can't feel my hand enough to pick up my weapon again, and I shake my wrist to try and bring back some sensation. *I'm actually going to die.*

Blotches of fear blur my vision when there's a clash of metal again followed by an agonized scream as I watch my adversary perish right before me. A lengthy second passes before I can believe I'm still alive or what I saw. The guard's body crashes to the ground at my feet, painting the ground sanguine. Atticus reaches down and removes a knife from the corpse.

When my nerves recover enough, I bring myself to say, "Thank you."

Atticus nods and tosses back his hood, leaving a trail of blood across his cheek. "Be careful, Ele. Keep your weapon close and help the others."

I nod as he disappears, forcing myself not to look down again and run. *Oh my gosh, how am I alive?* The memory is just a blur in my mind, and I grimace, trying to suppress the growing guilt and move onward. *Where are all these guards coming from? How are things going for Marie, Graydon, and Hallston with getting the gate open? But, if we can't get into Ellismark, none of the Mordolus can get from there to here either.*

I push ahead through the crowd, making my way closer to the gate and hoping to see Graydon, Marie, or Hallston with news.

I step over the mutilated body of a Mordolus guard, trembling so much I can hardly walk. I glance over the crowd, my whole body freezing and my heart beating double.

"Where's Isaiah?" I whisper to myself with horror. *I have to find him now! So much has happened in this mere minute, and this battle is riskier than I thought.*

I'm in Panic Sister Mode, blindly running through the insanity, searching for my brother. I break through a section of the crowd, met by the loud clashing of blades. I stop, looking for a way around the two fighting, regaining my grip on my knife. I gasp as a person, clearly one of the Hunters, shoves their opponent to the ground, and in another second he lies lifeless. I recognize the man from the tunnels, but other than that I don't know anything about him. I quickly turn away from the morbid scene, feeling unwelcome tears threatening to break free for the second time today. *I just saw someone die. One of us.*

I stand there too long, and the Hunter turns toward me and approaches. A dark, mortal fear grows up inside me. I know I won't win against this guard, and there's no one here to save me now. Glancing around desperately, I dive into the crowd, hoping to lose him, battling a barrage of vindictive thoughts.

The sound of metal against metal rings through the air, mingled with screams and sickening sounds of death. Seeing an opening, I crouch and crawl through the battle army-style.

I nearly get stepped on several times, but it's more effective than almost getting killed again. Mud seeps through my jeans and tangles in my hair as I make my way through the battlefield. The ground is merely dirt, mud, and gravel, with sparse tufts of trampled grass growing sadly among the rubble. Suddenly, a boot lands in the dirt right in front of me, pinning down the sleeve of my button-down. I stare at the red cursive "M" in front of me.

Impulsively, I unsheathe my dagger, hesitate for an instant, then drive it into the ankle. I close my eyes as the guard screams and reels. I want to throw up from the cracking sound and the blood that drips way too close to my face as I remove the blade, and I crawl away as fast as possible.

The ground trembles and vibrates with the nearing thunder of footsteps. I quickly examine my surroundings, struggling to get an adequate grip on my knife while still lying on my stomach. It alerts me in time to see a Hunter barreling toward me, a blade ready to crash down on my head. I scream and cover my head, burying my face in the metallic-scented, blood-soaked ground as time slows.

People shout, and over the clamor of metal clacks I hear someone gasp, saying, "What am I doing?! This is so dangerous!"

Shakily, I lift my head, trying to recover from panic's after-effects. I stumble to my feet, shock intensifying inside me. "Reece?"

Reece stands there, rocking back and forth, holding out a dagger at arm's length toward the guard laying on the ground writhing. He yelps as the guard pushes herself up on her arms with a groan.

"What do I do?!" Reece asks frantically. "I can't kill her!" He had somehow rammed into her back with the hilt of his dagger and stunned her before she reached me.

I've got to do something now. I quickly take off my belt and start working at my bootlaces.

"Stay there, Reece!" I order. I kick the Hunter's sword out of the way and tighten my belt around her ankles. The woman is injured from Reece's attempt to save me and previous battle wounds, so I kick her arms out from under her and frantically force them behind her back. She curses, howls in pain, then weakly crumples as I start tying the laces tightly around her wrists. Reece gapes and stares through his hands as I secure the knot. Together, we drag the guard behind two buildings where we can have a second to breathe and so no one will find and release her.

"I thought you were going to die," he whimpers. "I really did." To my complete surprise, Reece runs over and hugs me tight. "I thought you were going to die," he repeats, hyperventilating, then scrambles away like he suddenly realizes he's touching another human being.

"It's okay, Reece. I'm fine," I say, shaken but touched. "Thank you. I wasn't paying enough attention. Are you okay?"

"Yeah, sort of," Reece says breathlessly. "I'm so scared."

"So am I," I admit, leaning against the hard brick wall to my back.

"We'll be okay," Reece states, peering out at the battle behind the edge of the white siding of the building across from me. "Right?"

"Of course," I reply.

"God will take care of us. Even if we die. It's all for His glory," he recites. "And we'll go to heaven if we believe it. Isaiah told me that, and I…it's true."

"Yes," I say, though it's something I'm having a hard time with myself. It's odd for Reece to be the one encouraging me, whether it's intentional or not.

Reece claims his dagger from the ground, puts it away, then crosses his arms nervously. "Are *you* okay?"

"Yes," I say as he clutches his arm and grimaces. "Is your shoulder hurting?"

"Yeah," he responds. "I'll be alright."

"Okay," I say. "Have you seen Isaiah?"

He shakes his head, anxiety subtly creeping into his pale eyes. "I'll look for him. Let me know if you find Marie and the others. I've got to go help Dad." He gives me an encouraging smile then steps out from the small alley and disappears into the fray.

Reece has changed a lot from the boy I met in the Infirmary closet. He's saved my life more than once, and I even consider him my brother at times. *Maybe I'll mention it if we get out of this alive.*

I stay alert as I crawl the rest of the way to the barrier. Rising to my feet under the gate's great shadow, I run a hand across the smooth metal wall. It's cold against my sweaty palm like the door to a refrigerator. Neither Marie nor Graydon has returned to the top of the wall; clearly something isn't going right, and the gate remains just as steady as it was this morning. Spinning around, I'm accosted by a blur of violence, blood, and death. Repressing my calculations of the current fatalities, I force myself to focus and ignore the ringing in my ears.

We're trapped, everyone's fighting, and I don't have any contact with our friends on the Ellismark side. Someone has to get this gate open, or we're all going to die. I step back into an alley made by the wall and one of the buildings to find some respite where I can formulate a plan.

"Excuse me!"

Quickly, I spin around, drawing my knife from its sheath and holding it out at arm's length. A few yards away, hidden behind the stone wall of the building, stands a man. He's old and stooped, and only a few strands of white hair fall from behind his cloak's hood. He has a terrible face, but a smile spreads across his wrinkled complexion as he beckons me closer. Apprehensive, I step a little nearer, running my thumb across the swirling quillion and steadying my arm. He isn't dressed like the Mordolus, but I don't recognize him.

"Sorry, I'm trying to get this gate open!" I say. *If he's not from the Infirmary, chances are he's with the Mordolus. I presume no one else is left.*

"I know!" he yells over the noise. "The mechanism is broken. It can't open!"

"How do you know?" I ask, straightening.

"Because I've seen it! The only way is to break it," he calls out mystically, adjusting his cracked glasses as if I should know what that means.

"Sorry, what?" I scream, raising my voice over the clamber of the battle.

"The blades! Look for dark metal. It's the only way!" the man cries, gesturing to the crowd before disappearing behind the building.

I run back to the gate and peer through the fight, examining the weapons the Mordolus are using. A few of the Mordolus do have blades made of shadowy, dark metal.

Must be what he was talking about. Don't know if I should trust a stranger, but it might be my only chance. Taking a deep breath, I dive into the crowd again. Frantic, I look around until I find a guard nearby with one of the dark swords. An older girl, probably seventeen, with long brown hair and a sallow complexion fights against him. She blocks a strike with her sword, but fumbles and isn't prepared for the guard's next move. Clearing my mind, I barrel toward them with purpose. Planting my combat boots in the mud, I jump, blade in hand.

I scramble away as the cold metal sinks into his spine, he screams, and the body falls to the ground. I can't stop to think about what I just did and sheath my knife.

"Thanks," the brunette says wearily. I nod and stoop to the ground to pry the dark blade from the guard's icy two-handed grip. "What's your name?"

"Ele," I say absentmindedly; making friends is the last thing I'm thinking about. The hilt of the blade is decorated with intricate swirls surrounding small, glistening, ruby-red jewels. The obsidian-colored metal glints in the sunlight that beats down on my neck. The metal is so pure looking, unlike anything I've seen before, and the variegated Damascus pattern is beautiful.

"I'm Lilliana," the girl says with a smile. "You saved my life. Be safe."

I grin and nod, watching her disappear into the crowd. Surprised by its weight, I drag the sword with haste to the gate. I freeze in front of the towering wall, hoisting the blade up with both hands. *I have no idea what to do. No possible way he meant for me to break the door that's ten feet tall with this, but there's nothing else; not even a handle or lock. Either the man lied, or this is what I'm supposed to do. If this doesn't work, I'm going to look ridiculous trying to break the gate down with a single sword. But I'm willing to try anything if it will save my family and the people of Senneforte.* Raising the blade over my head, I approach the gate. *The gate is made of the same material as this sword. Has to be some sign.* With all my force, I bring the sword down at the center of the gate.

A screeching sound rings through the air as the blade glides down the gate and slides into the soft ground. As the sword tremors in my grip, a cracking sound breaks out. A sizable fracture splinters across the two doors, growing across the smooth metal like glass. There's a second of soft clinking, the same sound as when you step onto weak ice, then the gate shatters.

Heavy pieces of metal rain down, and I hurry out of the way before I get hit. Dumbfounded, I drop the sword and stare through the gap, right into Ellismark. *The gate is gone.* Gasps erupt from the mortal melee, and momentarily the fighting subsides as everyone stares at what just happened. Several cheers erupt from behind me, and I feel one of my own rising within. However, as quickly as it stopped, the fighting commences again. *Not only do I need to find my brother, but also I need to make sure Marie and the others are okay and don't need help.*

"Go!" I urge a woman leading a child not old enough to fight, but not young enough to travel in the car, forward. "Just get through the gate!"

She stands frozen, watching the fight, a panic-stricken expression blanketing her face. I grab her free hand, dragging her through the entrance and helping the two of them through the mess of shattered metal.

Overwhelming joy and hope erupt as I head into the new province. Tall, regal buildings surround me, and in the distance, it only seems more modern.

"Maybe you can hide behind those buildings," I suggest, gesturing to my left. As I stare at the woman, I begin to recognize her. *The woman I saw the first day at the Infirmary while I was waiting to be tested. I was able to help her after all.*

Too scared to speak, she clutches the child closer, nods, and disappears behind the smooth, gray-sided store.

Noise comes from the structures around me on all sides, so I quietly attempt to avoid them. Nearly instantly, I locate the gatehouse to the right of the archway. Hidden between a group of evergreen trees, I peer through the branches. *The door's obviously locked, and those guards must be trying to open it.*

"Ele?" someone asks from the branches behind me, touching my shoulder.

I jump and almost stab whoever it is. "What are you doing?" I ask, suppressing a yelp.

"Jeez, you don't need to go slicey-dice on me!" Marie says, watching dubiously as I put my blade away.

"I'm so sorry," I say, brushing pine needles from my stained shirt. "What's going on?"

"I don't know!" Marie says excitedly, dirt streaked across her bronze cheeks. "We gotta get everyone over here. Like, this side of the wall. What happened to the gate by the way? It just sort of…" She makes a shattering motion with her hand.

"I'll explain later," I say. "Did something happen to Jess?"

Marie tilts her head. "Yeah, but I thought she still made it to—to bring you guys?"

I shake my head. "No, she didn't. Jess never came. Something strange happened, and we all just knew. We just knew to come."

"What?" Marie says. "That's so weird."

I nod in agreement. "I know. I'm trying not to ask questions about it right now. So, Jess…?"

"She gave herself up as a distraction. I don't know what they did with her. They called her a traitor," Marie says with a frown. *Could Jess be…gone?*

I clear my throat. "Where are the others?"

"Hallston's in there. That's the gatehouse," Marie says, pointing to the little door, which I'd already assumed to be such. "The open-y thing got broken, and she got trapped."

Not good. I hope that door lasts a while longer and it takes them time to retrieve another key.

"I haven't seen the second group yet, but I saw the car go down that way. Graydon said that Ms. Kassy will probably drop off the children with your mom outside the city and then go find a place to stay. Graydon's over here." Marie leads me out of the evergreen grove, past the buildings, to an alley right across from the trees.

"Ele! How's everyone else?" Graydon says.

"I don't know," I say honestly. "Are you alright?"

"Yeah," he replies, but he won't keep eye contact. Graydon wipes some remnants of his mud disguise away. "What's happening?"

"With the gate gone, the Mordolus have free passage to both provinces. That's going to make things so much harder," I say, thinking. "Has someone found a place to go?"

I've lived most of my life in Senneforte, but we rarely come to Ellismark. It's always super busy and regulated because of Solstice Keep, and it's changed significantly over the past year with Morzanna as Queen, such that it's almost unrecognizable.

"Yeah, it has to be secret," Marie says.

Graydon's been silent pretty much the whole conversation, and he begins to walk down the alley. "I'll be back. That was my mom's job," he says quickly, turning. "I'll find her and see if she's found a destination for us."

Marie nods, and I glance down the alley.

"We better go help," I say, and we both run off toward the others.

I've only been gone five minutes, but when I return the situation has entirely changed. The street within the wall, the

Senneforte side, is painted with blood, but empty aside from the carnage. The sun rises, brightening the land, and bringing to light the truth of the destruction. *They've all made it into Ellismark.* But the fight still goes on, and every second more of the Mordolus come from the surrounding areas. Any pride I felt for destroying the gate disappears when I realize how much I've enabled the Mordolus.

"Luna!"

"Shirla?" Marie says nervously as we turn around. An older girl wearing Hunter apparel approaches looking furious, armed with a silver bow, staring at the two of us with wide eyes.

"What are you doing? I thought you…?" Shirla asks, standing right in front of me, pointing at Marie. Her eyes flicker from me to Marie, her lips pressed into a firm line. Marie smiles uneasily and glances at my feet.

"Why do you know her?" I whisper. *Maybe Marie betrayed us…maybe she joined the Mordolus and this is her Hunter buddy. She has abandoned me before. This would get her out of here safely.* But she's my friend. *Marie would never, right?*

"Listen, it was accidental. I'll deal with it," Marie whispers back, walking toward Shirla, but internally, I'm panicking. Shirla is several years older than Marie as well as much taller, and she has a bow and multiple knives.

"Hey, yeah, sorry," Marie says, with a wave of her hand, leaving her blade in its sheath. "I'm not Luna. Also, I kinda hate Morzanna. A lot."

Marie shrugs with odd casualness, and Shirla looks disgusted. "What? How? You—Ugh!"

Before she finishes, Marie punches her right in the stomach. I gape as Shirla falls back several paces, clutching her middle. Marie giggles then reaches and picks something up from the ground as Shirla gasps while holding her stomach. It's the silver bow.

"We got to go now," Marie says, grabbing my hand and running away from where we left Shirla stunned and missing her favorite weapon.

"What was that, Marie?" I ask. "She could have killed you, and you hit her?"

"She wasn't expecting it!" Marie says, laughing. "And it was fun! Not quite as awesome as giving Morzanna her what-for, but close!"

Marie and I both stop dead as shouting suddenly grows from behind us. Marie stares at me and drops the bow. "It's coming from the gatehouse."

I run as fast as I can to the field, pushing through the crowd, seeing that the gatehouse door has been destroyed as one thought repeatedly crashes around my head like a mad drunkard: *Hallston.*

I stand there breathless and quickly look around, realizing that everyone else has also come to see what's happening.

A shriek shatters my thoughts like a rock hurled through a window. Two Mordolus guards drag Hallston out of the gatehouse by her arms. Suddenly, everything goes eerily quiet and still. Hallston stands surrounded by guards, her hands shackled behind her back. Some of her braids flick in the wind around her tense jaw.

Any of Marie's triumph over Shirla vanishes as her eyes grow serious, and she seizes my hand tightly. Atticus, Hadley, and Ledger stand beside me, and the only comfort is in knowing these four made it through.

"There is no escape!" one of the guards yells, walking up to the middle of the yard. She wears an embellished jacket, rigid with authority, and I assume she's highly ranked. Her voice echoes through the silent emptiness, "Morzanna was protecting you, and you betrayed her! You are all traitors! Escape and assisting escape will end in death! Soon, without redemption, you will all die for your betrayal!"

Hallston clenches her fists, and two of the guards hold her arms to keep her from moving. I recognize the one on the right; deep russet brown-skin, buzzed black hair, and tall frame.

Ash.

The main guard steps closer to Hallston, a look of anticipation plain across her face. Hallston stares back at her with such intensity that I shift, waiting to see what unfolds.

"You are all felons and betrayers, and this is punishable by death! This is your last chance to surrender to Morzanna's mercy," the guard says. "Or die."

"Never!" Hallston screams. "We will *never* surrender. All she's done is destroy us! Her job was to serve our country, and she's done nothing! Morzanna is a murderer! The Queen hid the antidote! She's killed thousands! She's a tyrant! Morzanna is the traitor to Willowmire!"

"You'd rather rebel and die than submit and live?" the guard hisses, gesturing with her gloved hand to our helpless, surrounded group.

"The goal of my life is, and the goal of a ruler should be, to serve others, abide by Willowmire's laws, and glorify God. Morzanna has fallen short on all accounts. I'm not going to give up on us now. Senneforte, Ellismark, all of Willowmire; do not give up fighting for what is right. What can separate us from the love of Christ? Shall tribulation, or distress, or persecution, or famine, or nakedness, or danger, or sword? No, in all things we are more than conquerors through him who loved us—Christ. That's from Romans eight. It also says that we're treated like sheep to be slaughtered, and if that's what God has planned, go ahead. I'll gladly die if that's what it takes to prove my defiance to Morzanna and bring glory to my Lord. For to live is Christ, and to die is gain," Hallston says confidently. Her brown eyes sparkle with new light, and she doesn't falter for an instant as she gazes at the crowd gathered in the field.

The guard nods, rage congesting her every move, and takes something from another guard. She holds the gun to Hallston's head.

In that final instant, the condemned girl looks up at us one last time. "Auxillia: I love you all. Remember Erethen! Remember Tannellith!"

Then the guard pulls the trigger. The immediate realization sends a shock of pain through my body and soul like someone's shot *me*.

"Hallston!"

Atticus blocks Hadley from running to her sister and likely receiving a similar punishment. Hadley collapses in listless sobs at his feet, screaming for her sister.

"I'm so sorry, Hadley," Ledger says, holding Hadley as she breaks down, tears in his eyes.

"Hallston!" Hadley cries, burying her face in her hands while Ledger tries to comfort her.

A jolting rush of shock and pain stabs my heart like an icy sword. *Hallston can't be—she can't be dead!*

Suddenly, a murmur breaks out across the field. The guard who killed Hallston stops and stands paralyzed beside her. A grimace spreads across her silent countenance as blood blossoms on her shirt. As confused as we are, the two other Mordolus members drop Hallston and step away.

Hallston and the guard fall, hitting the ground at the same moment, and I stifle a gasp. There's an arrow shot right through the guard's back, leaving her lifeless.

Bexley runs from the woods behind them, throwing Shirla's silver bow down and falling at her sister's side. Hadley breaks away and joins her, and the three Kamryn sisters spend a final moment together. Atticus tensely watches the scene, remaining aware in case the Mordolus try to interfere or take advantage of this vulnerable moment.

Hallston's dead, Graydon's still gone, Bexley just killed that guard, and we're surrounded. How are we going to get out of this?

I wait for either of the girls to confirm or deny our fears. Bexley weeps and pulls a fine metal bracelet from Hallston's wrist, slipping it onto her own. My chest aches with sorrow, anger, and guilt like something is physically awry with me. I slam a fist against the hilt of my knife, and one of the women cries. *Must protect them. . . must get to safety before we lose someone else.*

"Ele!" Graydon runs over to me, glancing at Hallston, and a dark expression falls over his face. "We have somewhere to hide. We've gotta go now," he tells me, panting.

I scan the field, confirming we're surrounded, and it sets my heart burning in a violet fire of adrenaline. There's going to be a slaughter. I freeze when one of the guards draws a blade again.

"No!" I cry. It was someone from the Infirmary; the brunette girl from the first room has been murdered. *We need to go now or the Mordolus are going to kill us all.*

"STOP!" a shocking female voice demands from behind us. "Stop right now! You will not do this to my people! I'm the leader, and you WILL NOT kill anyone else! I'm responsible for all of this!"

The crowd parts and people gasp as the young woman walks toward us, stepping into the glow of the wall's lights, her long, dark ponytail swaying as she flicks her head around with rage. A man and woman clothed in simple, white outfits accompany her. Even the guards stop, surprised at her appearance and brazen claims.

"Is that—?" Graydon starts.

Ledger's expression turns a bit brighter. "That's Auxillia's leader. The one we've kept a secret. Now you know why we couldn't tell."

The woman walks closer, the secret leader of Auxillia, and no one can believe it. She stops only feet away from me, and the silence is so intense I barely get the words out.

"Delegate Hettler?"

49
ELEANORA: FREE?

"This needs to stop right now! I am the delegate, and I will not allow you to kill these people!" Devyn Hettler orders, marching into the center of the field and rhythmically tossing her ponytail. As her gaze settles over Hallston's body, no one speaks. Taut silence hangs in the air as everyone watches, shocked by the sudden appearance of Senneforte's delegate, who's been gone for months due to undisclosed circumstances. I just suspected Morzanna had captured or silenced her.

"Hettler is the leader of Auxillia?" Atticus asks Ledger.

Ledger nods excitedly as if he's surprised Atticus actually spoke to him. "She started the Haven. She stayed away to keep us safe and continue speaking out against Morzanna."

"I thought Jess started the Haven," I say, puzzle pieces finding their places in my mind.

"Jess is Delegate Hettler's cousin," Ledger explains. "They started it together."

"Put your weapons down right now!" Hettler screams, surveying the crowd, her perfect black eyebrows intensely knitted together. No one obeys. *I'm not acting first and leaving myself vulnerable.*

One of the guards looks at the delegate. "This isn't Senneforte, Hettler."

"If you're with these people then you're a traitor too," another says, regripping a sword.

Hettler looks furious and stands up taller. "Go ahead then. Do it. But I will not stop fighting until either Morzanna is dead, or I am! Kill me and see what happens. Kill them and see what happens! This evil will not go on forever! Injustice will not endure!"

Delegate Hettler's two bodyguards stand strong, postures volatile.

Marie watches to my right as Bexley walks toward us, away from the horrible scene. I can't focus on anything Delegate Hettler says as the broken, redheaded girl approaches. I'm surprised Bexley can still walk after what just happened and that she can be that strong. It leaves me conflicted.

"She's gone," Bexley says, silent tears glistening on her rose-red cheeks as she grasps the silver bow and a handful of glinting arrows.

"Bexley, I'm so sorry," Graydon says.

She rigidly nods but doesn't reply. A fresh cascade of tears glides down Bexley's face as Marie embraces her. Graydon gently lays a hand on her shoulder until Marie steps away, and he holds her tightly. I can't articulate a condolence, nor do I know how to console someone after a loss that substantial, especially since *it is* Bexley, though that bravery gives her major points. My chest is heavy with grief, and I give Bexley a sympathetic nod, trying to suppress the guilt growing rapidly inside me. *How could I be so horrible to Bexley? What's wrong with me?*

"We should get out of here," Bexley whispers after clearing her throat.

She glances around then crouches and crawls under the Mordolus truck blocking our way. Harnessing all my courage, I follow Marie and Graydon under before anyone notices us. Nearly thirty Mordolus members stand surrounding our friends, unaware that we are sneaking away.

Jess, Hallston, all of them. And what about my family? I haven't seen them in an hour. This isn't fair. They could be lying among the dead or injured too. *Why is this all happening?* I ask silently into the universe, fear rising within me like a tidal wave, ready to crash against the weak defenses of my depravity. *Please. Please give me peace. I don't want to be like this anymore. You said 'come to me and find rest'. Give me rest, God. Give me rest from this crazy world.*

Hot twinges of anger and impatience play at the edges of my mind as we sneak out of the field and into the street outside the gate.

It's over. There's no getting out of here. There is no hope. We're all going to be slaughtered. I turn and run. I just can't face anything anymore.

"Ele?" Graydon calls after me, but I don't reply; I keep running.

I run through the distorted street until I collapse against the cold, concrete of a building. I take deep breaths, a dark, strong feeling mounting and threatening to consume me. I draw my knees to my chest, not intending to ever leave this spot. *This must stop.*

Footsteps approach and I tense, hiding further in the dark corner. "Eleanora?"

I glance up, and Graydon's dad, Mr. Madison, comes over and kneels beside me.

"What are you doing?" I ask numbly. "How'd you get away?"

"I stayed behind on the other side of the gate to see if anyone was still alive and to wait out the last few minutes with those I found," he says grimly, a weariness blanketing his composure. "There was a guard I found tied up. She was dying, and I couldn't just leave her alone like that. There were a couple of others, too. I stayed with them. Are you okay?"

I shake my head, and suddenly tears of pure anger and hate for this world pour down my face. "I hate this. I hate everything. I'm done with it all. I've done what's right; I've prayed, gone to church, and tried to be nice to Bexley. Why isn't it enough? Why doesn't God just stop Morzanna? How could He let Hallston get killed like that? I've tried so hard, and I'm finally giving up. I can't take this anymore. I just can't," I divulge between furious sobs.

Mr. Madison lays a hand on my shoulder and stares at me before slowly responding. "'As for me, I would seek God, and to God would I commit my cause, who does great things and unsearchable, marvelous things without number: He gives rain on the earth and sends waters in the fields; He sets on high those who are lowly, and those who mourn are lifted to safety.' (Job 5:9-11). The Lord is good,

Eleanora. Without Him, everything would be far worse than it already is because of the curse of sin. We can never escape sin. We can never escape our punishment. But there is hope. 'For the wages of sin is death, but the gift of God is eternal life in Christ Jesus our Lord' (Romans 6:23). What you do is not enough. Nothing *you* do will *ever* be enough. It's not about us. It's Christ working inside us for His glory. And no matter what, everything that happens is for His exaltation. If He's allowing this evil to continue, then it must be what He has planned because nothing happens outside His will. We have to trust that. We can have hope in the promises of God, renewal in the Holy Spirit, and peace in the work of Jesus."

I bury my face in my arms. I've heard that all before, and I know it's true, but I'm just struggling with it now. "I know God is real. I believe it. I want to trust him."

"Ele, if God changes your heart, the Holy Spirit is in you, and you believe that you can be made clean from your sin by the blood of Christ, and only through Him, you will."

I take a deep breath and try to sort through my feelings. Fragments of peace and an upwelling of hope begin to chase the night in my soul. Hallston's dying words claim the forefront of my mind, feeding the hunger inside me. *God, please help me. Please help me to believe in you and trust You. Lord, I want to follow You. Maybe the fact that I'm praying shows that You already are changing something. I know how holy You are and how sinful I am. This darkness inside me isn't from You, and only You can fix it. I know You can change it. Change my heart.*

The two of us just stay there in silence, and the darkness inside me continues to stir and dissipate, and a rush of gratitude floods into the empty place that it vacates. A feeling, not only a feeling but a knowing, builds up inside me, unlike anything I've experienced before. The verse posted on the wall of our room at the Haven pops into my memory, and I begin to truly understand and find meaning in it.

I have said these things to you, that in me you may have peace. In the world you will have tribulation. But take heart; I have overcome the world (John 16:33).

I'm so sorry. I'm sorry for everything, God. Thank you. Give me faith, I pray.

"Hettler's right; evil can't go on forever. We've got to keep fighting," I whisper to myself, dragging a sleeve across my eyes. I jump to my feet.

"Thank you, Mr. Madison," I say. "I'm beginning to understand now." I give him a quick hug.

"I'm glad, Ele," he says, smiling. "Trust Christ."

"I'm going to try. Well, I suppose I've got to go," I say, turning to leave.

"Ele?" he asks before I disappear. "Have you seen Graydon? He's okay, right?" I nod. "Good. I have to find my wife."

Mr. Madison runs off down the street, and I head off in the other direction, back to where I left the others. Something inside me burns and sends a lifelike flame spreading through my whole being. When I return to the shattered gate, I find them in the same place, having a discussion. *I can't do a thing about my family if they're gone, but I can still fight for everyone else and make a difference.*

"Where'd you go, Ele?" Graydon asks, but I don't have time to explain it all now.

"Your dad's okay," I blurt out, and he gives me a slow nod.

"Come on, we've got to get everyone to safety," Bexley orders the three of us, Marie by her side. Drying her face, she looks empowered.

"We will not stop fighting! At least explain to me why, why you are killing the people of Senneforte, the people of Willowmire!" Hettler demands from the crowd on the other side of a line of buildings.

She's buying time for us. We've got to get out of here.

I glance down at my dagger then quickly throw it down and run back to the ruined gate. Sifting through the shards of metal, I find the sword I used to secure our passage into Ellismark. I draw a deep breath, clenching the red jeweled hilt in my sweaty grasp.

I turn around and see that Graydon, Bexley, and Marie have followed me into the empty part of the street, while everyone else is still distracted by Hettler's bold speech.

"Ready?" I ask. Bexley gives me a certain look, and the other two nod.

Peering past the cold gray siding of one of the structures, I watch as Marie makes it to her position across from me. I can only find her glossy black boots peeking out beneath the evergreen boughs to locate her, and I follow them up until I meet her sparkling brown eyes. Right now, the Mordolus have everyone trapped, excluding the four of us. *They're trapped for now, but if we don't do something, the Mordolus will follow through with their threats.*

Marie looks in the distance to her right, then nods, meaning Graydon and Bexley are prepared as well. The adrenaline rush is real. One of the guards stands just in front of the building I'm hiding behind, unaware of our revolt and the sword I find myself raising. *I have to do this to save my family. There's no other option.*

"Eleanora," someone says behind me. Ms. Kassy jogs up, eyeing my weapon.

"We've got to rescue them," I whisper.

She puts a hand on mine, the one holding my blade, and I lower it. "I have a better idea."

We run back to the street where the empty stolen car waits. "I've got it, you go tell the others we have a different plan."

Ms. Kassy climbs into the car and starts it; I obey and sprint off to find Marie first. Just as I creep into the bush where she's waiting, Marie notices me.

"What are you doing?!" Marie asks.

I take a deep breath. "Ms. Kassy's got a new scheme, and she said to tell you that this one's off—"

I'm interrupted by a long revving noise. I quickly peer out of the branches. Suddenly, the Mordolus car, driven by Ms. Kassy, comes racing across the grass, straight towards the crowd. A loud crash echoes across the glade, followed by screaming as a section of Mordolus guards fall beneath the tires. A few gunshots shatter the glass windows and plink into and metal body of the car.

Marie watches, wide-eyed. "Dang. That's some plan."

The guards quickly draw weapons, galvanized by the realization that we slipped out on them earlier. Atticus is the first to notice what's going on and signals for everyone to flee. Hadley looks as lifeless as her sister as Atticus coaxes the distraught girl to leave her sister's body and come with us to safety. Hadley's beautiful appearance is blemished by torrential grief over the sudden, horrible loss of Hallston. I still wrestle with reality and try to rationalize the shock of what happened.

I couldn't tell Bexley of the change of plans, so she is still stationed atop the gate, shooting her bow at the guards below.

Delegate Hettler stands beside her on the wall between Senneforte and Ellismark. "Fight for freedom!"

I take up my sword and run out of the bushes toward the road, while Marie heads the other direction. Lost in the chaos, I freeze when I reach the street, twirling a strand of hair. *I need to get out of here, now. But I have no idea where we're going!*

"Ele!" Graydon says, appearing behind me. He reaches for my hand and seizes a sword from the dewy ground. "Come on, it's this way. We're going to the mountain."

Graydon leads me into the paved streets, and I set my gaze on the rising sun and refuse to look behind me, the morning's light and night's darkness blending into radiant colors on the horizon. Bexley sprints down the wall's stairs, bow in hand and out of arrows, half of which are embedded in the ground, far from their targets. A few

Senneforte refugees are picked off by the onslaught of gunshots as we dash through Ellismark's streets toward Neremos mountain.

A blade falls beside me, so close I'm shocked it didn't slice through my shirt sleeve. Graydon quickly parries the attack, and I jump forward, sword in hand. My heart lurches with guilt as the injured Hunter collides with the ground. Soon, Marie is by my side, dragging Reece with her. Enough of the guards are indisposed to allow us to escape, and the realization is exhilarating. Right outside the city, Ms. Kassy ushers all the children and elderly into the dented and deformed car.

"Get to Neremos Mountain!" Hettler says from behind us. "The Southeast side!"

A peak of rock grows above the treetops, giving way to the mountain's summit. In the opposite direction, the city grows thicker, but here the land is clear and beautiful.

"Graydon, is this place on the mountain?" I ask breathlessly.

"You could say that," he replies, urging me to go faster.

As we run through a mile of open land toward the mountain, I realize there were twice as many of us this morning. A blueish expanse grows in the north: the cool, lapping waters of Lake Superior, but soon it disappears behind the jagged rocks of the mountain.

In the distance, Solstice Keep peeks over a swathe of buildings as daunting as midnight. Surrounded by thick hardwood trees, the dark walls contain ragged castle towers. Solstice isn't a palace, more like a fortress with a medieval look. Dark, sharp, and spooky like the evil witch's castle from a fairy tale. An icy shiver tickles my spine. *That's where the Queen is right now, safe within the sturdy walls.* The Queen is the foundation of all our adventures and disasters so far. I wonder what secrets lie within Solstice Keep and what dark plots have been whispered within Willowmire.

The last few moments blur as we run into the rocky forest. Each of the children is helped out of the vehicle and most are carried after we escape into the trees where driving would be impossible. We managed to fight our way out of the field, and Graydon is certain he has a place for us to hide. A sense of wonder pricks my head. *Surely the Mordolus have followed us, and how will we hide? Shouldn't they have caught up with us by now?*

Solstice Keep confirms that we are now within the forests of Ellismark, and the ground becomes steep and rocky. After we enter the forest, everything becomes calmer, leaving me to question why. I glance behind me. *Why aren't we being followed? There's no way we fought off all of the Mordolus members in Ellismark; that'd be insane. Something's keeping them from following us.*

The forest is composed mainly of evergreen and oak trees, and the ground is so densely covered with pine needles and leaves that little else is growing besides thorny vines. Some areas are swampy, and it's still warm enough that each puddle of water breeds mosquitoes, which I can feel landing on and biting my skin.

The sky ominously darkens like the stars, moon, and sun have been eclipsed by some unknown evil's shadow, and the forest awakens with noises.

When the trees finally break, the sheer rocky mountain stands in front of us. I stop and follow the stone up until all I see is the clear dawn sky. I stay behind Graydon and Marie, and we heed the natural path made by the mountain range and thick trees to our right. As we continue on, the path becomes thinner and thinner and soon it becomes so severe that I can't see anything in front of me other than a small space of ground and then Marie. The trees grow denser on one side, and the rocky mountainside soon begins to create a roof above us as if we're inside a passage, growing cold and dark.

"Graydon, where on earth are we going?" I ask.

"Just trust me. It's hard to explain. You'll see in a minute," he says.

When I'm about to inquire again for more details, Marie stops in front of me, and it's so dark in this rocky walkway that I nearly slam into her.

"Wow, this is so cool!" Marie says and disappears into the darkness ahead. As I step forward behind her, I hesitate, wondering if I'm going to run into a rock wall or fall into an eternal pit. I reach out my hand and feel along the wall until my fingers graze a gap between the rock. I take a breath before stepping into the dark cave entrance. Inside, there's a short corridor, like an endless closet doorway, and if I was any taller, I'd have to duck. I pass through a secure doorway carved into the stone walls.

First, a light glows ahead, then, without much warning, the passage opens up. The space inside is enormous, and the ceiling reaches high, studded with glistening stalactites. The cave room is wider than my house and just as tall, lit by an unknown source as if each wall glows from the inside. The huge roof is domed like the mountain peak has been hollowed out. Of course, it hasn't—it's far too small to be an *entire* mountain—but it is vast and brilliant.

The other escapees step in and marvel at the hidden mountain hideout with me. I take a moment to enjoy the final and lasting safety as adrenaline springs from joy.

"What is this place?" I ask, twirling around and examining the beautiful ceiling.

"Fathomane. It's sort of my dad's lab. Well, it was. My dad and his coworkers were fixing it up and expanding it at the beginning of the Virus to be a shelter. We got locked in by the walls before they could hide anyone here," Graydon tells me excitedly. He's talking very fast and smiling. It's been a long time since I've looked at Graydon and known exactly what he's thinking: everything will be okay. "My mom sent me earlier to see if it was still safe. Delegate Hettler said to come to the mountain because she actually funded it and helped plan it. My dad was sort of paranoid for years, so he came up with the idea of Fathomane in case of an event like this. It started off as a work project. Then, the Virus and everything happened. There's plenty of room, and there should be enough provisions here for everyone for a while, at least." He points across the enormous room to where several hallways lead further into the mountain.

I chuckle. "Graydon, you're so dumb! This is so awesome! Why didn't you tell us about this place before? Like at the Haven or something?!"

He shrugs. "I don't know. Dad told me it was a secret. I didn't know if it would be helpful, anyway. Honestly, I sort of forgot about it for a while."

I want to ask him so many more questions, but suddenly someone calls my name.

"Eleanora!"

I spin around, a mixture of relief and worry creating a frenzied cloud in my mind as my mother calls me to the other side of the room. Graydon leaves to locate his parents, and I run over to my mother, disturbed by her tone. A second later, I'm in her embrace, so thankful she made it.

"Isaiah!" my mother cries suddenly, a grave alarm in her tone.

Atticus carries my brother through the passage and into Fathomane. He gently lays Isaiah on the ground as a moment of fear and guilt sets in. When Isaiah sits up and thanks Atticus, my initial concern is washed away now that I know he's alive.

"Are you okay?" I ask frantically, kneeling next to my brother. Holding his breath, Isaiah rips off his boot, and from the bruising, I can tell his ankle is broken. There's blood everywhere, mixing with a blackish silver fluid that oozes out from the cut—or more likely, stab wound. The same color spiders out under his skin, suffusing.

"I'm alive," Isaiah responds, raggedly.

"What happened?" our mother asks, yanking a strand of blond hair with one hand and touching Isaiah's dirt and blood-streaked cheek with the other.

"Don't really know. We were in a battle. A lot of things happened," Isaiah says weakly. "It was when we were leaving. Thankfully, Atticus was there, or I'd be dead."

"I'm going to get Reece's dad," I announce at once.

"No. I'll be okay for a while," Isaiah says, cringing. "Other people are worse off right now." I want to disagree but gazing at the others in our midst who appear to be less than alive, I decide Isaiah's not just trying to act tough. I nod but still remove my thin overshirt so my mother and I can temporarily dress the injury. Isaiah glances down at his leg and blanches.

"Don't look at it," I say. Isaiah has an intense fear of blood, especially his own, and I think if he was more lucid right now, he'd freak out.

My brother nods and glances up at the ceiling. The last of our group files into the hideout, making what I surmise less than fifty survivors. "Ele, we finally made it," Isaiah says, and gestures to the whole room, wincing as Mom pulls the knot tighter around his ankle.

"I'm free, Isaiah," I say. "I'm truly free."

"Really?" he asks.

"I'm free from myself," I say. "Free in Christ." Isaiah gives me the first sincere smile I've seen all day.

My mother sits down beside Isaiah on one side, me on the other, frailly drawing both of us closer.

"Everyone okay?" Isaiah asks, sitting up straighter but careful not to jostle his leg.

I nod, weariness setting in as aches and minor battle injuries surface. "Yeah. Graydon, Marie, Bexley, and Reece I've seen."

Isaiah sighs, exhaustion pervading his behavior. "And there are Zia, Hadley, and Ledger."

I smile, but my heart feels cold. *Jess, Hallston, Gabby—all from Auxillia, and all gone.* I don't dare look at Ledger; I just know, someone's told him about Gabby, and I can't bear it.

I believe Isaiah notices because he looks at me strangely and breathes deeply. "For this to happen, so did everything else. For anything to get better, there has to be sacrifice. All things happen for the good of those who love God. That's what Hadley kept saying over and over to herself on the way here. I mean, I didn't want to get this injury. But I guess it'll be for good, right? We can get through it. If we have hope," he murmurs.

Everything I've put my hope in: my parents, my friends, sulfavirdoton, myself—they weren't enough. All those hopes were disappointed because I trusted in something dead. The only hope that is steadfast is hope in God that I've gained through this, and that hope, I've come to realize, I cannot achieve on my own. That hope was given through grace, and it's the only hope that will prevail through death— the same hope Hallston had. My only living Hope.

I reach into my jean pocket and pull out the ragged, crumpled piece of cardstock paper.

Peace I leave you; my peace I give you. Not as the world gives do I give to you. Do not let your hearts be troubled, neither let them be afraid. (John 14:27).

I smile, finally rejoicing in the verse's meaning and finding comfort in its truth. There is authentic lasting peace found in Christ, and it's been revealed to me at last.

When my father safely joins us, I can hardly contain my joy. *Oh Lord, thank you!* I hug Isaiah, savoring the serenity of the moment, knowing that my family is alive and together. I hold my mother's sickly hand in mine, knowing soon she and everyone else will be healthy. We discovered the cure, made it to safety, and I'm surrounded by my whole family and so many friends. Free from Senneforte, I'm confident our despairing story is changing to one full of bright opportunity. Finally, new hope emerges.

Once everyone has settled, there's an involuntary moment of reflection and silence for Jess, Hallston, Gabby, and all the others, only interrupted by the cries of those who knew them. I'll never forget what happened and those we lost. Now we are finally, truly safe.

"BUT IF WE WALK IN THE LIGHT, AS HE IS
IN THE LIGHT, WE HAVE FELLOWSHIP WITH
ONE ANOTHER, AND THE BLOOD OF JESUS HIS
SON CLEANSES US FROM ALL SIN."

1 JOHN 1:7

EPILOGUE

I suddenly jar awake and sit up so quickly that half of my blankets slide to the ground. A cursory memory of today's battle flashes through my mind. With a surge of relief, I realize where I am, safe inside the new mountainous hideout Fathomane, but nothing can calm my pounding heart. Adrenaline surges through me, and an unnatural chill racks my sore muscles.

I remember.

The dream I had nearly a month ago while we were hiding out at our house. The strange man that stopped me in the tunnel desperately told me to remember someone. The old man in my dream, that face he showed me—I shiver, but not from the cold.

Given that these dreams are not random, questions course through me. I've met both of them and now recognize it. *That man, he's the same one who helped me find the sword at the gate. He saved us today, yet he'd been in my dreams weeks before I ever met him. How can that be?*

But that isn't the most horrifying part. That person, the one he told me so desperately to remember, is someone I know all too well. Unscarred and younger, but the resemblance is clearly there.

It was Merris.

-TO ALL THOSE WHO EVER FELT HOPELESS:

THE ONLY TRUE HOPE IS FOUND IN CHRIST.

LOOK TO HIM TO FIND THE REASON TO LIVE-

ABOUT THE AUTHOR

R. G. Brown is a teen writer who published her debut novel in 2023 at sixteen. She has always had a passion for writing and has written stories her whole life. Publishing a book was a natural goal for her. She hopes her Christian faith is reflected in her writing and that her books encourage readers, specifically teens like herself. While writing Positive, she graduated home school a year early to make time for future novels and to hopefully grow her writing career.